MW01132800

# A Question of Sanity

## Katherine Black

# Contents

# Acknowledgements

S pecial thanks to Peter J. Merrigan, a best friend. And for Mark, more than a best friend—he gets me.

# Prologue

Sometimes, things are just too big and too sad to hold in a memory. Sometimes they have to be written down, and trapping them in written words is the only damned way to contain them.

She had been witness to love and hatred, murder and evil, and with the seeing, she had learned how to care for the first time in her life. Evelyn knew little about the nuts and bolts of writing. This was her first attempt. The day held all the promise that only a young day can, and the unpalatable, cooling coffee was her reason for being rooted at the dining room table watching that promise unfold.

Jake padded in from the garden and sat in front of her chair, demanding attention. He looked ridiculously feminine, his great big head adorned with lavender blooms and cocked to the right, with a question. Eve laughed, despite her mood.

'You've had your nosy snout in that lavender bush again, haven't you? You daft dog. Those bees will have you, and then you'll be sorry.'

Jake grinned and chuffed at Eve. He was a clever German shepherd, and he knew the bee word.

Bees: fat things that don't make sense. They shouldn't be able to fly with that round, furry body and tiny, thin wings. It's not right that they should be able to fly, and Jake can't.

Jake sometimes forgets that he only has one human now. He used to have two. Jake mustn't forget that he only has one because Eve gets sad when he looks around the house for her—the other one. Jake thinks she's in that hole where they saw a mouse last year. The mouse went into the skirting boards and never came out again. It's all very confusing, though, when the whole house smells of her. Eve doesn't sense her everywhere like Jake does. Eve would whine all night, too, if she could smell her all the time and had an itch behind her ear. Bees shouldn't oughta fly like that; it's not right.

Eve put her hand down and stroked the dog's head. The strawberries were almost ripe. The first ones would be ready for picking next week. This grieving game was a miserable process, and somebody should invent an app to make it easier, or faster, or not happen at all.

'Oh well, Jakey boy, we can't sit here all day, can we? I've made a momentous decision while you've been having fun without a care in the world. I'm going to start writing today.'

Jake cocked his head, deciphering the unfamiliar words from the familiar. There was no dinner or out in them, but sometimes humans disguised words, so they sounded like something else.

Eve got up from the table, and before she was upright, Jake bounced around like a puppy.

Oh yes, he decided, this is the out. Do the round and round thing. Make Eve smile. No, Eve, that's the study, that's not out.

The door's this way. C'mon, Eve, I'll teach you how to catch bees without them getting the ouch thing in you. Eve. Out. Oh, sometimes humans are no fun.

Eve hadn't been in the study much since that day. From today, it was her room, and she had to get used to that. Things were different now. As an act of defiance and stamping of her ownership, Eve picked up a jewelled elephant from the windowsill and put it on the occasional table. It had looked better in the window with the light shining behind it. Eve glared at the elephant as though it was the ornament's fault.

Lowering herself into the swivel chair, she took a calming breath, and Jake flopped down beside her. He sighed like an old man and seemed older than his six years. He rolled his eyes to show that he was sulking. Five seconds later, his heavy lids gave up the struggle to stay open, and he fell asleep.

The computer sensors monitored Eve's approach, and as she sat down, it fired up. Eve envied the computer's ability to come alive within seconds of waking. She only aspired to what the computer could achieve in a second after a shower and three cups of strong coffee.

'Good morning,' said the computer-simulated voice.

'Good morning, George,' replied Eve.

'It is eight forty-five a.m. on the tenth of June, two thousand and fifty-one. What can I do for you this morning?' asked the deep tone of the butler in the box.

Eve slumped into the chair. The hairs on her arms rose, and she was transported to another place, another time and another world, where every morning, an impersonal voice chanted the date and time at her. It was a place where she had been kept, contained and controlled, unable even to think for herself. She wanted to run, but her legs were leaden. She couldn't do this. She was mad to think she could continue where things had been left. There had been so much sacrifice to bring her to this point. People far better than her had been killed. She raised her head. Jake, alerted to the change in Eve's mood, sat up, whined and cocked his head at his new mistress in alarm.

She had to do this. She owed it, not only to herself but to the only person in the world she had ever loved. She would do this. She took another inhalation, just to check that she was calm, and spoke to the computer in as level a voice as she could manage.

'George, my darling, I will be coming in here at roughly this time every morning from now on. I only intend to say this once, so I hope your receptors focus on exactly what I say. I like your chirpy good morning, George, really I do. Sometimes yours will be the only voice I hear during the day. But, listen up, my technological friend. If you ever tell me the date and time when I walk into a room again, I will pull every wire from your circuitry and stuff them so far down your memory hole that you'll choke on techno-spaghetti for a month. Do I make myself succinctly and unconditionally understood?'

The computerised voice bristled with indignation when it replied. 'Well, there's no need to take that attitude, I'm sure. I was only trying to be helpful.' Then it lowered its voice to a mumble. 'Succinctly and unconditionally understood. Anyone would think she's a writer.'

Having done with whingeing, it raised its voice back to the default volume level. 'Will that be all for now, Miss?'

'Oh, George, drop the insulted affront, or I'll pinch your emotion chip and use it for a solar token. And George, remind me to take a large submachine gun and shoot whoever decided to give computers an emotion chip in the first place. It can be damned irritating. Right, then, to business. I want a squeaky clean new document, please. Today is the day I begin the new book.' The computer spluttered and laughed in a sarcastic monotone.

Eve smiled despite herself. Sometimes it was hard to believe that blood and organs formed no part of the make-up of George. 'New document, please, George, then that will be all, thank you.'

'Very good, Miss,' said George, in his most acceptable simulation of the dutiful servant. 'I'll just fade into the background until the next time you feel the urgent desire to abuse me.'

As requested, George brought up a new word processing document and altered his status. The *Voice Activation on Standby* icon appeared in the top right of the monitor screen.

'And George?' Eve said, bringing him back online.

'Yes?' he answered in a perfect long-suffering voice.

'I love you. Save every five minutes, please, George.'

'You asked me to remind you to take a large submachine gun and shoot whoever it was that gave computers emotion chips.' The screen went black then flashed with a huge red lips icon. The lips puckered, and a smacking sound crackled from the speakers. They were replaced, after two seconds, with the document waiting to be written.

This time she laughed out loud. 'Bugger off, George, and let me work.' The hardware that produced the computer's voice seemed to know when she needed cheering up. She contemplated the white screen, still smiling.

Eve took a lungful of air and began by writing the title, *A Question of Sanity*, in the header, followed by her pen name *Eleanor Erikson*, in the document's body. She wrote the first sentence of the novel that had to be written, even though she didn't know what she was doing. It was a story of evil and courage and truth. People had died, and it had to be documented.

She began with the following:

Sometimes, things are too big and too sad to hold in a memory. Sometimes they have to be written down, and trapping them in written words is the only damned way to contain them.

# Chapter One

Ellie was tired. Her head swam, and her feet ached. No, she decided, to swim was far too energetic a verb. Her brain floundered against a tide of incoming exhaustion, and she was just plain knackered.

It had been one of those long, hard days that everybody moans about on a Wednesday evening. Not close enough to the beginning of the week to be enlivened from the weekend, yet too far away from Friday to feel a lie-in looming. In her line of work, it didn't matter much what day it was. Being her own boss was both a blessing and a curse. Today was different. She hadn't been working on her latest book. Today she had been going five rounds with hospital bureaucracy. She locked the car and wondered who had called. The gate was open, and it was always her habit to close it on leaving.

She was still pondering the caller's identity as she opened the front door. A small white envelope lay on the mat. She winced as she bent to pick it up but forgot her pain as her attention focused on the unexpected letter and who it might be from. The first thing she noticed was the small neat handwriting in a delicate cursive hand much like her own. The other thing was the fact that the letter had no stamps. It had been hand-delivered.

Inside was a single sheet of simple white notepaper, folded once widthways. In the same handwriting as the envelope, centralised on it, was a single sentence.

*Better the devil, you know.*

Jake whined from behind the kitchen door. He had been locked up since nine-thirty that morning, and his plaintive whimper told her he was distressed.

'All right, big fella, Mum's home. I'm coming to let you out.'

It served to make Jake's plea more urgent. She opened the door to be greeted by a six-stone fur-ball in the shape of her one-year-old German shepherd. As she struggled to get to the back door with the dog leaping around her body and jumping up, despite being told it wasn't a polite thing to do, Ellie crooned and spoke to him. If the dog noticed that she seemed to have aged ten years since leaving the house that morning, he was too well-mannered, in that respect at least, to let on. He jumped and wagged and chuffed and preened, happy to know that he was a good boy who hadn't peed by the back door. Ellie managed to turn the key with stiff fingers. The excited dog shot to freedom. He made for the lavender bush to shoot a few of those pesky late-summer bees with a mighty fine blast of his own special fertiliser.

As she watched the dog, her phone rang. She went to the study, where the nearest phone extension was located. The day had taken its toll, and her footsteps were slow and laboured. She realised for the first time that she would need telephone access in every room in the house over the coming months. So far, she had avoided the voice reactor telephones that worked through

2

any building via the computer. She was a creative type and appreciated the solitude and not being disturbed. For that reason, she'd managed to avoid owning a mobile phone for the last ten years. Matt, her boyfriend, said it was one of her eccentricities, and it drove him insane—but she wouldn't be swayed. Now, she would have no choice but to move with technology. She picked up the phone on the eleventh ring, and the receiver died in her hand. Three steps towards the kitchen, and it demanded her attention again with its persistent command. This time she caught it on the second ring.

'Hello?'

After a pause, she could hear slow, rhythmic breathing.

'Hello?'

The connection was aborted.

'Bloody hell,' she swore aloud. You'd think they'd have the manners to explain if it was a wrong number.

While Ellie made a coffee, fed the dog and fixed a sandwich, Jake came in from the garden and dropped his rubber ring at her feet. He looked up, wagging his tail, convinced that she was going to stop everything for an instant game of fetch. He smelled his food, and all thoughts of the ring game went out of his mind in an instant. The abandoned toy lay at Ellie's feet, positioned to trip her up had she not seen it—something else she would have to be more aware of. Jake gave two barks, asking for his meal to be delivered to his feeding mat right this second. Ellie grinned at the mutt and complied. She patted him on his head as his nose dropped into the dish.

So often these days, she couldn't be bothered to fix a proper meal in the evenings. Tonight, she was so fatigued and mind-weary that she could barely be bothered to eat at all. Even though her growling stomach had been reminding her, for the last three hours, that it hadn't been fed since breakfast, ten and a half hours earlier. *Coronation Street* would be on after the evening news. Ellie's routine meant that her day's work and household chores were finished for the evening by now, and she and Jake would curl up on the sofa while Ellie watched some television to unwind. Tonight, the artificial lives of the soap stars held no interest for her. All she could concentrate on were the same three words, in the same order, which kept circling around her mind in the same direction.

Tay-Sachs disease.

TSD has been around for a long time and was traced to East European Jewish fur traders in seventy AD. It wasn't a new condition. She concluded that she deserved ten out of ten for originality, a typical writer, always going for the dramatic angle. I couldn't have any old common-or-garden bout of terminal cancer. No, I have to go for Tay-bloody-Sachs disease, which is not only bloody rare but virtually bloody unheard of in adults. Although TSD in children was a rare disorder, it was well documented, and there were guidelines and procedures to follow. Adult-onset TSD was obscure and challenging to diagnose and treat.

Nice one Eleanor, girl. What do you do for a sodding encore? If her thoughts were audible, the bitterness and anger would have singed the atmosphere, leaving the acrid smell of burning fury in its wake. Today, the test results were only to make an official appointment for death to come calling. The consultants—she had many, were already sure about the diagnosis. Ellie had done her crying in the three weeks leading up to today. She had said, 'Why me?' and had pouted at the unfairness of it. But although she bitterly grieved the loss of her right to the menopause, stress-incontinence, senility and toothless old-age dotage, she had not come to terms with her condition. And she had not accepted that she was going to die prematurely. She had not run out of fucking swear words to fit her mood, and she was not going to roll over and play dead without making a lot of noise about it.

As Ellie pondered, her mind took her past the loved ones she would leave behind. It went beyond that she had between six months and ten years left to enjoy. It skimmed over the painful treatments and changes that she would have to accept and endure. It took her to a place that she scurried to in an obsessive need to make sense of it. Whenever she thought about her illness, she focused on her writing. The formation of her recurring thoughts was so irrational that she laughed at herself as she analysed them. She felt tears stinging the back of her eyes as she thought of all the words that she wouldn't have time to write. To date, she had six novels in rough synopsis in her mind, scraps of jotted notes outlining the stories that wanted to be written. There were characters and plots, twists and one-liners. Six complete beginnings, middles, and endings may never be written and may never be read. She worried about her final novel, the one that would be left incomplete. The only way to avoid that part-written book would be to finish the current one while she was fit enough and not begin another. How could she not write? Not writing was akin to not breathing.

As the thought that she might be too sick to write crept in among her other thoughts, she shot it through the heart with an arrow and left it dying on the attic floor of her mind. She would always be able to write, and if she couldn't, she hoped the end would come soon.

Ellie concentrated on her writing because thinking about the bigger picture hurt too much. She couldn't worry about the day she would leave Jake, her long-time boyfriend, Matthew High, or indeed her mother. Those were things that stung too much to think about. So, for now, until her personal demons forced her to think those thoughts, she'd concentrate on how much the loss of her writing meant. That was good. It was safe and very nearly bearable.

So impossible was the thought of her mother's anguish that Ellie hadn't told her about being ill. Her mother lived in blissful ignorance of the situation. The most significant blight in Esther Erikson's life was the fact that her clematis was smothering the honeysuckle and that smoky-bacon was up five pence at Booths. Esther was a law unto herself. She lived in a world Ellie didn't like to intrude on very often.

Although Matty knew about the illness, she hadn't been candid with him about the result date. She didn't lie to him, but when he thought she was at the hospital the day after the date of her appointment, she didn't correct him. The guilt she felt was an extra weight to bear. Matt's anguish was smothering, and today was going to be difficult enough to get through without having his pain on top of her own.

The phone rang. Sitting next to the lounge extension, she picked it up before it finished the first ring. Her thoughts must have been guilty of tweaking Matt's concern because it was him.

'Hello, gorgeous. How are you?'

His voice was deep and soft, like a warm snuggle blanket. She ached anew with the thought of losing him. The joint in her right big toe was throbbing, but it diminished in intensity compared to hearing Matt's voice and knowing she was about to destroy his world. Matthew was the eternal optimist. He believed that although the results were a foregone conclusion, something would come up at the eleventh hour to prove that Ellie just had wind.

'Hey, darling, I'm fine. A little tired, but okay. So stop fussing. How about you? What are you up to?'

'Ellie, don't bullshit me. I can tell by your voice how tired you are. Do you want me to come over? I did as I promised and left you to work in peace today. And look what it's done to you. You sound exhausted. I can be there in half an hour; I'll bring a pizza.'

'No, not tonight, Matt. Remember what we agreed? Tuesdays and Thursdays, we do our own thing. So tell me why you're talking to me when you could be on your third pint with the lads?'

'Because you've got fantastic breasts, and they don't kiss me the way you do.'

'So how do they kiss you, then?'

'Too much tongue and bristle. Not enough lipstick. Why? Are you jealous?'

'Madly.'

They enjoyed the lightweight moment before Matt's voice was serious again.

'I love you, Eleanor Erikson.'

'I love you, too, sweetheart, more than you can possibly know.'

'Ellie? There's something wrong. What is it?'

Damn him and his bloody intuition. She wanted to delay the moment of destruction for a few minutes more until she felt braver. She knew well enough that she was a miserable coward for telling him over the phone rather than face-to-face. Still, she couldn't bear having to see his brick walls of conviction tumble down like paper streamers in a Christmas breeze.

'Matty, you're right. I do have something to tell you. No fooling you, eh?' She laughed. It was hollow.  She didn't know how to go on and wanted to run away, leaving the phone dangling on its flex. The urge to flee to the safety of her bed and bury herself in Jake's fur until the madness of her world righted itself overwhelmed her. She wanted to sleep until a doctor said there'd been a terrible mistake. That her records had been mistaken for another lady with a similar name. But here was now, and now was here. She had to tell Matt the truth.

'I went to the hospital today.'

'What is it? What's the matter? God, I knew you'd overdo it with that bloody book. I shouldn't have listened to you. If I'd been there, I'd have looked after you.'

'Matt, shut up and let me finish. God, you always do that. You cut me off when I've got something to say. Have you any idea how bloody annoying that is?' Matt was silent. She could hear him breathing hard. She knew he was gripping the receiver too tight, that his knuckles were white with the pressure. She knew he was biting down on his bottom lip the way he always did when he was perplexed. She knew that the pressure point in his left temple was pulsing and that if she could kiss it, he would let the tension go and relax with a great sigh of release. She wanted to spare him the next sentence, but she couldn't.

'Matty, love, I had the test results today.'

'But, that's not until tomorrow. I'm coming with you to the hospital. It's all going to be a big mistake. Everything's going to be just fine. I'm booking a table at Clancy's to celebrate.' His breath broke into a heartbreaking sob on the final word. 'Ellie, if you'd just waited until tomorrow, everything would have been all right. I know it would.' The last sentence rose in pitch and held a note of hysteria to it.

'They came back positive. I'm dying, Matty.'

Ellie's voice was a whisper, as though by speaking the hateful sentence quietly, it would lessen its power. Somehow, the string of events put into motion by the words would not be triggered.

'No, no, no.' Each repetition of the word was drawn out longer than the last. It had to be stretched long enough to hold the pain coming across the phone connection at her. He was sobbing and struggled to speak.

'I'm on my way.'

'No. Matt, no, I'm sorry. I know how much you're hurting, darling. And I wish I could hold you and take the pain away, but tonight, I need to think about myself. I'm so tired. I need to sleep. I'll see you tomorrow, I promise. And we'll talk. I want to go out. You can buy me the most expensive meal on the menu—Steak Dianne with the works. Book that table at Clancy's anyway. I love you, baby.'

Ellie knew her words had cut Matt. She didn't mean to imply that he was selfish or put his needs before hers. He wanted to help and didn't know how, and she had no energy to be more tactful. She just wanted the conversation to end so that she could fall into bed. Despite the devastating news, she thought she would sleep without any problems that night. Matt took a moment to recover. She heard his sobs quietening.

'Gold digger,' he managed with a false laugh. 'You only want me for my money. I know your type. All diamond necklace and deep pockets.'

'Tell you what. Take out some life insurance and, then, if you die before me, I'll inherit. You'll have to be fast, though.'

'Not funny, Ellie. That's so not funny.' There were no tears in his voice. Just a heavy sadness that knocked the breath out of his lungs.

'It's the only way I know how. I don't know what else to do but laugh at the bastard. The disease isn't so scary if you laugh at it. I need to sleep, love. I can't cope with it anymore tonight. I'll see you tomorrow, and don't stay up all night fretting. It won't do any good.'

'I won't,' he lied. 'You get to bed. Sleep tight. I love you, Ellie.'

'I love you, too.'

Something pinged in her head, or her heart, or her right big toe. She couldn't bear the thought of him hanging up. She didn't want to be alone. Every second they had together was precious. Was this the start of the mood swings that the doctor had told her to expect? She didn't want to give in to the bone-numbing tiredness and fall into a deep sleep, in case she never woke up from it. She wouldn't give in to the evil disease robbing her of life. All she wanted at that moment was to feel the strength of Matt's arms around her. She didn't want to go to sleep anymore. She had to make love—no, she didn't even want that. She wanted to fuck like a teenager. She wanted to suck Matty's life into her broken body and fuck him hard until she was too exhausted to feel anything. She was still alive, so far, dammit.

'Matty?'

'Yes, Ellie? What?'

'Will you come over, Matty? I can't bear it on my own. Will you come? Now.'

He forgot to say goodbye in his haste to get out of the house. Ellie couldn't help smiling through her tears. Without another word, the line buzzed its disconnection in her ear.

All thoughts of sleep were banished as she went upstairs as fast as her aching body could carry her. While the bath filled, she shaved her legs. She didn't have much time before Matt arrived, and she wanted to be clean and fresh to seduce him. Only ten minutes earlier, she had been enervated, and the thought of doing anything was a thought too tiring. Now she was filled with desperate energy that was borne of fear. 'Move or die, move or die, move or die,' she repeated to herself as she rushed around.

His timing was perfect. Ellie had just stepped out of the bath and was wrapping a large, white towel around her breasts when she heard the door security system scanning him for entry. She squirted a light mist of perfume to her neck and wrists, and, feeling much better after her bath, she ran downstairs to meet him.

Before he could speak, she wrapped her arms around his neck and kissed him. Lust welled up from nowhere and took him by surprise. What started as a sweet, 'Hello' kiss turned into a wanton need.

Ellie pushed him against the front door. Her hands roamed his body, her mouth ground on his, and her tongue flicked over his top lip and into his warm, minty mouth. His arms tightened around her waist and pulled her into him. He stiffened as he pushed against her thighs. She moaned into his mouth, not giving in to the need but drawing it savagely from her body and pushing it onto his. The heat from his hands made her spine

11

tingle. She squirmed into a better position so that his hardness pushed into her.

He moaned in her ear in a voice heavy with passion and disappointment. 'Ellie, we can't. You're not well enough. You're tired. What about your illness?'

'Sod my illness,' she said, her mouth covering his to still the words that she didn't want. 'Fuck the illness. I'm alive, Matt. I want you. Make love to me now, right now.'

His hands pressed into her back, circling until he cupped her buttocks. She felt the pressure of his short nails indenting her flesh as their bodies ground into each other. Without hurting her, he bit on her lip, his teeth grazing the fullness of her mouth as her tongue sought entry. He dropped his head to take the flesh of her neck into his mouth. Sucking hard, he stopped just short of bruising her before nuzzling into the cleft between her breasts. He was tormented, centimetres from reaching her erect nipple, from being able to feel it between his lips without losing the pressure of his cock between her legs.

She could barely hear his words for the rasp of his breath coming in gasps between each thrust of him against her. 'Jesus, Ellie, I need to be inside you. Let's go to bed.'

'I can't wait that long.' She backed her pelvis away from him, and the towel dropped. He groaned at the loss of her. The sensual attack of his senses was so unexpected that he'd come to arousal fast. After two minutes of holding her against him and sensing a need in her at least as great as his own, he was already feeling the sensation of being close to coming. He knew Ellie's body and her orgasm wasn't far from fulfilment either. Another minute and they would both have come, and Matt was still fully clothed and dry-humping her like a teenager. He was like a horny schoolboy, and this was something that hadn't happened since the early days of their courtship when they'd tortured each other with long sessions of heavy petting weeks before they made love. Her hands clutched his belt, her fingers clumsy, getting it undone in her need to release his erection. His pants were around his ankles within seconds, and his cock sprang free. A blast of heat caused by the friction they'd generated rose from between his legs, and the smell of him, mixed with his soap, made her salivate with the need to taste him.

She dropped to her knees, and without the usual nuzzling and foreplay, she took the length of him into her mouth. He groaned, pushing his head against the support of the door and jerking his pelvis forward. The pleasure coursed from his groin to his brain, and a feeling of dizziness made his head spin. His balls contracted, and he pulled himself from her before she'd finished her third voyage down his stiffness.

'No, Ellie, I want to be inside you. I want to make love to you.'

She tried to take him back into her mouth, but he put his arms under hers and lifted her from the floor. He kissed her once before she grabbed his hand and headed with him for the stairs. It took all of his concentration not to trip over his jeans and pants that were still bunched around his ankles. It was easy for Ellie to swivel him around and push him onto the stairs before he was aware of what was happening to him.

He was winded, the treads of the stairs dug into his back, but Ellie was standing above him with lust in her eyes and a scent that told Matt what she wanted. Her lower lips glistened. His cock jerked as they rived his clothes from him. He never grew tired of the sight of Ellie's naked body. She lowered one hand to guide him into her and dropped onto him with a hard thrust.

She drove him into her quickly but with a force that made him gasp as his foreskin took a second to catch up with the rest of him. Her juices had been flowing since the first kiss.

Ellie tensed her pelvic muscles, and he felt squeezed by the rippled walls of her pussy. She arched her back and rode him with more aggression and force than ever before. His back pounded onto the stairs. He made a bridge of his body, thrusting his pubic bone onto Ellie's and feeling the extra half-inch of penetration that made her scream in pleasure. Her juices squelched with the forward motion, an indication that Matt was stimulating her G-spot. She'd always been embarrassed when this had happened before. Twice since they'd been together, she'd been on the point of having a G-spot orgasm, but as soon as the fluid was produced and some of it was released, she'd stopped him. Both times he'd been drenched and knew that another couple of thrusts, and he'd have had the full blast of female ejaculate as she'd squirted. Both times Ellie held back and wouldn't allow it, scared of the animal instincts of her body. She'd altered their position, calmed it down, and they'd gone on to finish making love—but he said he felt cheated of something more. He'd told her that what would happen if she hadn't stopped him was the fodder of his fantasies when he was alone.

This time she didn't stop. She ground on him hard.

She was moving with every ounce of her mustered energy. 'Fuck me, Matt, fuck me. I'm going to squirt all over you.'

Matt felt his passion waning as the unfamiliar words came from Ellie's mouth. 'Fuck me, you horny bastard. Harder, harder, come on; make me scream your name.' Sweat was pouring from her body, and her breathing was ragged and rasping. 'I'm alive, and I'm well, Matt, and I'm going to be the best sex you've ever had. Make me squirt for you.'

He felt the last of his erection dwindling inside her, 'Ellie, stop a minute.' She looked at him, her eyes clouded with confusion.

'What's the matter, Matt? Don't you want me anymore?'

'Ellie, I want you more than I've ever wanted you. The way you just proved you still need me drove me crazy. You're the best lover I've ever had, you know you are, but that's not because of your sexual prowess, not because of how hard and fast you can ride me or how dirty you can talk. It's because of the way we feel about each other. It's because I love you. I don't want to fuck you. I want to make love to you the way we always have. Sometimes I like it rougher than normal, that's fun, that's keeping sex alive. But darling, you don't have to prove to me that you're still the best even though you're ill because, even when lovemaking is difficult for us, you'll still be the best, more than that, you'll be the only.'

He wiped tears from her cheeks and carried her upstairs. Kicking the door closed with his foot, he laid her on the top of the bed. As she watched him, he took off the last of his clothes and lay beside her. Keeping eye contact for as long as possible, he stroked her, trying to restore the mood and bring her back to arousal. Her tiny, naked body was lost on the quilt. He dropped his eyes to her neat triangle of soft downy hair. Matt kissed her inner thighs at the top of her legs, and she parted them for him. He kissed her slowly, teasing her back to the excitement that'd been broken. He didn't stay there. It was so sweet that soon he wouldn't be able to stop himself from losing his restraint and devouring between her legs until she writhed in ecstasy. He needed to regain a feeling of sensual lovemaking rather than rampant sex.

He came back to the head of the bed and saw that tears were still rolling down Ellie's cheeks, though her mouth was open and her breathing was hard and excited. He kissed each of the tears away, tasting this second of Ellie's fluids on his tongue. He took her parted mouth. She was immobile, the breath escaping through her lips. He enjoyed the feel of his mouth on hers until he couldn't hold back. She responded, raising her hand to stroke his face and moulding her lips to him. Her skin was soft and her mouth so pliable that Matt felt a new, protective love for her. A murmur of want escaped her lips, the sound amplifying in his mouth. His hand brushed across her small breast. The nipple was hard and budded as it scraped over his palm. She gasped, and he cupped it, kneading. It was more than he could stand. His kiss was demanding, and this time Ellie took her lead from him. They kissed for a long time.

Matt's erection rubbed against Ellie's outer leg, and he ached with the need to feel himself expanding inside her. She tried to resist when he pulled her on top of him. She was embarrassed about earlier and wanted him to take the lead.

'You, please, Ellie. I want to look at you, and that's the best view.' He smiled at her, and she smiled back. Her eyes were still wet and shining, but the tears, now stationary on her cheeks, didn't brim over her lids.

This time they made love with long, languid movements, easing each other back when one of them got close. Ellie waited for Matt to be ready. Normally she took her orgasms as they came, multiple explosions to each of his, but this time, one was all she needed. She leaned forward and brushed her nipple across his lip until he took it into his mouth. Her movements were shorter, tiny intense motions, relying on internal muscle contraction. When they came, the force of their love and mutual timing gave them an orgasm that neither one would ever forget.

Ellie sat up, and the last tear fell from her eye to mingle with the perspiration on Matt's chest. She smiled at him, and her grey eyes shimmered with tears that moistened and made them glisten. Matt saw a beauty that was something new, more than the natural beauty that nature had blessed her with. He loved her. Ellie was five foot six, with soft, natural blonde hair cut into a short bob. She was slender, with small breasts. His girlfriend was the most beautiful woman that he'd ever seen.

Afterwards, she lay in the crook of his arm, and when she fell asleep within seconds, he didn't have the heart to disturb her. He watched her sleeping for a long time. What was a cramped arm compared to what Ellie was going through?

She never saw him crying in the night.

# Chapter Two

George interrupted Ellie's writing as a vital clue was being uncovered.

'Somebody's at the door, Ellie.'

Ellie tutted, annoyed with being disturbed at a crucial point in the plot. I bet that's Matt offering rich-tea and sympathy, she thought, and then felt contrite.

'Okay, George, show me,' she said, her voice heavy with resignation. The computer monitor went black for a moment before the security screen focussed, showing a view of the front door with a fresh-faced lad standing on the doorstep.

'Intercom, please, George.' The intercom system crackled.

'Hello. Can I help you?'

'Parcel for Miss Erikson.'

'Okay, love, just a sec, please.' Ellie got up from the swivel chair, easing her aching muscles. She'd been sitting in the same position for five hours, and her lower back was killing her. It's time I took a break anyway, she thought, wincing. Jake was excited by his mistress' movements. Perhaps this activity meant that, at last, he might be in line for a walk.

She signed for the parcel, thanked the delivery boy and brought it to the study. She wasn't expecting anything except for some manuscript edits from her publisher. This wasn't the delivery of scripts. They would be in a brown envelope displaying the company frank. She tore off the outer brown paper packaging. Inside was a long, flat box. It had to be something from Matt. She smiled, lifting the lid from the box to be confronted with yards of bright red satin. Not my colour, she mused as she lifted what she thought was a tarty negligee out of the box.

It wasn't sexy bedroom wear; it was a red satin cape, a rubber black cat-suit, red tail, headdress complete with horns, and a trident style three-pronged fork associated with the devil. What the hell, she thought, and then the penny dropped. Matt must have arranged a fancy dress party that night instead of dinner. She pulled the invoice from the box. The costume was on hire from Fancy Pants party shop. It was due to be returned by four o'clock the following afternoon. Ellie was put out by his arrangements. Matt was always dropping surprises on her; he had a knack for knowing what would please her. Six months ago, she would've been delighted at the prospect of a party and his costume choice. The black rubber cat-suit was clingy and sexy. It could lead to some post-party fun, and her black stiletto boots with the five-inch heel would set the costume off. Ellie was disappointed at his lack of perception of her mood. It was thoughtless of him to arrange a party when she was told she was dying. She thought back to their lovemaking the night before. He must realise that she needed to relax and take things easier than normal. She understood his need to cheer her up and that he might be thinking that a return to normality would be the best way to do it. How often had Ellie said she wanted to live whatever time she had left to the full? Tonight, she didn't want to party. She wanted a quiet evening with her boyfriend, for them to come home to talk and maybe have sex. She expected him to understand.

She didn't feel up to a party and rang to cancel.

Matt said that he was as baffled as she was. There was no fancy-dress party, and he had not ordered the costume. In fact, the table at Clancy's was booked for eight o'clock.

'You can keep the costume for when we get home if you like, though, I don't mind being taken in hand by a naughty devil.' There was a chuckle in his voice, and she smiled.

Better the devil, you know. Five words fluttered into Ellie's consciousness.

She remembered the letter from the night before and told Matt about it.

'Someone's having a joke with you, Ellie. It'll probably be Rob.'

Rob Price was Ellie's close friend and agent. It wouldn't be unheard of for Rob to play a practical joke on her. He'd caught her out with some good ones in the past. After she said goodbye to Matt, Ellie rang him.

'Okay, wise guy, what's going on?' she demanded, without any formal greeting, after Shirley, Rob's personal assistant, had put her through.

'Now then,' began Rob, 'which of my literary starlets might this be? Maisy Dog, author of How to Shag Around and Not Become Green and Drippy? Or Reginald Bott, writer of The Student's Guide to Recipes Made with Three-Week-Old Milk? Or then again, maybe it's Ellie Erikson, pain in the arse, thorn in my side, and general tormentor when I'm trying to work.'

Ellie laughed. 'So, getting back to the original question, what's with all the devil-worshipping stuff?'

'Oh, this is getting more interesting by the second. Tell me more. Do we get to cover ourselves with goat's blood and dance naked around an altar?'

Ellie explained about the letter and parcel.

Rob said that he hadn't a clue what she was talking about and passed the buck back to Matt. She told him it wasn't Matt. And if it wasn't Matt and it wasn't Rob, then who the hell did send them?

'Woohoo. That's it now, girl, you've made it bigger than big. Forget topping the bestseller list, the true accolade to literary genius is having your very own, really truly, no shit, psycho-stalker.'

Ellie laughed and told Rob not to be ridiculous, but a shiver travelled from one end of her spinal motorway to the other. She made arrangements to meet him for lunch in a couple of days, but Rob tried to dodge the meeting. He had a hectic week, and Ellie agreed that it could wait if it had to, but Rob said he was alerted to something in her voice that made him want to cancel previous engagements to see her. Ellie wished that Rob had stuck to being too busy as she hung up. She'd jump at the chance of putting off telling him about her illness. But as her agent and her friend, she knew that it had to be done, and soon.

Talking to Matt and Rob had put her in a good mood, but she felt her balloon popping at the thought of telling her closest friends and relatives about her condition. Telling Matt had taken its toll physically and mentally. One symptom of her condition was non-regenerative fatigue, a core-sapping weariness that went way beyond tiredness, one that a few hours of decent sleep could neither help nor cure. Everything took a toll on her health and her compromised immune system.

The bell jangled as she opened the Fancy Pants costume shop door. The lady behind the counter looked up from the catalogue she was browsing and smiled in recognition. Ellie noticed that she was chewing gum; it struck her as odd for a woman of middle age. It was a habit that annoyed Ellie when she was served by young girls, but the churning mouth of this lady was amusing.

'Hello again, lovey. I didn't expect to see you back so soon. Is there a problem?'

Ellie looked around to ensure that the lady was talking to her. She was the only person in the shop.

'I'm sorry, I think you've got me mixed up with somebody else. I've never been in here before. I've just come to return this. It must have come to my address by mistake this morning.' Ellie put the box on the counter.

The shopkeeper looked at her. Her eyes narrowed though her voice remained pleasant. 'But you ordered the costume this morning. I remember you. It was the red devil outfit. I must point out that any damages have to be paid for in full.'

Ellie didn't mind a joke. She was happy to play along and be a good sport, but the previous day's news must have had a bearing on her reaction. It was so out of character, or perhaps, she thought later when she was trying to make sense of it, it was a symptom of the disease itself. It could have been a culmination of tiredness and draining emotion. Whatever the reason for her tantrum, Ellie felt that she was being made a fool of and lost control of her temper.

'Look, you old bitch, I don't know who has put you up to this or why, but I had to leave my work to return this stupid thing to you. I don't think that's funny. Do you? It's taken me half an hour to get here. And no doubt, it'll take the same to get back. Maybe I should bill you for my lost earnings. I never ordered the bloody costume. I don't want it. It's tawdry. And, may I suggest that you might have a more prolific clientele if you didn't presume to make a fool of people when they walk through the door. You can take your tacky costume and shove it up that gorilla's arse for all I care. I don't fucking want it, you frosty faced, cud-chewing old cow?'

Ellie flung the box at an empty gorilla suit and flounced out of the shop, leaving the dazed assistant staring after her in bewilderment. The lady's mouth hung open in suspended animation, and the chewing gum stuck to her tongue and defied gravity, like a ping-pong ball to a paddle.

Adrenaline carried Ellie along the street and around the corner into the quiet of a narrow back alley. A prowling tomcat eyed her with distrust. Perhaps he thought he'd have some competition for the ripest pickings of the alley bins.

Ellie leaned against the dirty wall. She felt ill, and she was frightened by her reaction. She'd never spoken to anybody like that in her life. Her lungs expanded with air that beat her with vicious punches all the way from the inside out. Her eyes watered with temper and unshed tears of anger and humiliated self-pity. The blood pumped through veins in her temple, and she felt her heartbeat pounding like a military drummer against her optic nerves, clouding her vision and making her head throb. She'd have said that she didn't have a temper if asked. She was conscious about how she behaved in public. It wasn't her style to scream like a harpie. Her outburst was out of proportion to the inconvenience that she'd had. Calmer, her cheeks burned with shame as she relived resorting to personal name-calling to the shopkeeper. She felt that she ought to go back and apologise, but sweat clung to her forehead and her upper lip. She felt sick. There was no way she could face the lady and would write her a letter later. Ellie was fighting two strong impulses; one was to pass out, the other the urge to vomit like a syphon. Neither option appealed to her, especially in this dingy back alley with the sinister eyes of a suspicious ginger tom watching her every move. She battled control of her rolling stomach with supreme effort and forced herself to regain composure.

She heard Jake barking as soon as she opened the car door, but that was the least of the noise. There was something very wrong. She put her eye to the sensor at her front door for the security device to give her clearance, but the door swung open without the check being made. Locking the door was a habit, like brushing her teeth or washing the pots after tea. It had been put on the snick, and the locking mechanism didn't connect with the frame. Ellie was sure she'd locked the door when she'd left. The noise was deafening. Leaving the front door ajar, she rushed through her rooms. Two of the three downstairs plasma screens were on full blast, each tuned to a different channel. Only the one in the kitchen was silent. Heavy rock music screeched from the lounge, and loud classical rose in combat from the speaker in the study. Every light blazed except those in the kitchen. The heating was on full, and the house could have baked bread. The vacuum cleaner was burning its motor out and was switched on in the hall. Her hairdryer screamed on the highest setting, and her three electric heaters, one in each bedroom, blasted more heat into the stifling house. As she went towards the kitchen to soothe Jake and turn appliances off as she moved, she was aware of hammering at the front door.

'Coming,' she yelled as she instructed George to shut down all the entertainment systems. The silence was instant except for the noise that Jake made. He was happy to be let out and jumped around yelping in greeting and vying for Ellie's attention as she went to answer the door. As she opened it, the smile died on her lips. Mr Jackson, her next-door neighbour, was standing on the step and going redder in the face by the second. Ellie had engaged in several altercations with Mr Jackson, usually caused by Jake. Mr Jackson didn't like dogs. In fact, he didn't like anything much, apart from complaining. He was happy in his loneliness and misery, and God help anybody who tried to deprive him of them. She'd tried to get on the good side of the cantankerous pensioner but to no avail. Ellie cringed.

'I'm so sorry, Mr Jackson.'

'Two hours. Two bloody hours I've had to put up with that. I knew you'd show your true colours eventually, missy. Swearing at an old man like that. I fought in the battle of Tora Bora, you know, and I've got rights. Well, I'll tell you, lady. I'm not standing for it. The police are on their way. Let's see you talk your way out of this one. And another thing, that dog of yours has been at my Pauline again, God bless her. Can't you just leave the poor woman in peace?'

Ellie had to admit that the Pauline situation was a problem. Mr Jackson had buried his late wife's ashes beneath her

25

favourite honeysuckle bush. When the neighbour wasn't complaining about the dog, he was complaining about the height of the garden fence and the fact that it blocked the light from his kitchen window. No matter how high Ellie extended the fence, Jake cleared it.

Mr Jackson was the perfect toy. Jake loved getting into his garden, and his favourite place to dig was at the root of Pauline's honeysuckle. He once managed to uncover her urn and yapped to show the world his treasure. Jake delighted in inciting Mr Jackson to go red and jump up and down, shaking his fist. It was Jake's favourite game, even better than annoying the bees in the lavender bush.

The irate neighbour was pointing at Jake, who was grinning, like only a dog in trouble can. He had the good grace to drop his ears in shame and was wagging his tail. Ellie put a hand to his collar. She knew it was only a matter of time before Jake wanted to take the game up a notch by jumping all over the angry man.

'You want to keep that bloody dog under control. If he comes onto my property again, I'll take a garden spade to the back of his head. You foul-mouthed wench, the police will bring you down a peg or two, you see if they don't.'

It seemed the rant would go on forever before Ellie could get a word in. Mr Jackson filled his lungs to continue, and she took advantage of it and jumped into the space left by the temporary pause in his torrent of words.

'I'm sorry about Jake, Mr Jackson, and I'll try, as always, to make sure that it doesn't happen again.' She raised her hand with authority to halt her visitor's next outburst.

'As to this morning's disturbance, I can only apologise for that as well. But someone has broken into my house and turned everything on while I've been out. I haven't even had a chance to see if anything's missing yet. If you saw something, please can you tell me because I've no idea what's happening?'

'I've heard it all now, you bloody liar. That's the line you'll take with the police, eh? So you deny gesturing to me with your finger and swearing at me on your garden path this morning? I came out to see what all the noise was about, and there you were, coming out of your house with all that blaring music behind you. I know you only did it to terrorise me. Gives you pleasure, does it? Yelling at an old man, you with your goody-goody image. Miss high and mighty author. I'll tell the police the truth. You won't get away with it this time. Harassment of an old man, that's what it is, harassment. And me, a veteran of the Tora Boras in Afghanistan, too. You ought to be ashamed. You think you've got the monopoly on being rebellious, don't you? You young people know nothing. I was a Butlin's redcoat. I did Ecstasy. I had my nipple pierced and had Newcastle United tattooed on my backside. If I still had my Black Sabbath on vinyl, I'd show you a thing or two about making a racket and terrorising your neighbours. The police are coming, I'm telling you. You've had it now.'

True to his word, as he yelled at her, a police car rolled up outside her gate. Two police officers got out of the car and approached Mr Jackson, still shouting at Ellie on her doorstep. Everything was taking on a nightmarish quality that didn't make any sense.

And things only deteriorated. Her involvement with the angry neighbour and the two police officers was a fiasco. Ellie repeated her version of events several times. Each re-telling caused Mr Jackson to go a deeper shade of purple. Harry Jackson was a pain in the backside, but Ellie had to admit to the police that she'd never known him to tell lies. Because he was insistent that he'd seen Ellie after all the appliances had been turned on and had spoken to her, the policeman said he had no option but to believe him.

The male police officer said that he recognised Ellie from the sleeve of one of her books. However, if she thought this would curry her any favour, she was mistaken. He knew that Eleanor Erikson wrote psychological-horror mysteries and had a following in some subversive cultures. The officer seemed to think that this made her a raving lunatic who may be prone to psychotic episodes. When he realised who she was, he retreated a step. His tone adopted the attitude he might take with an escaped convict guilty of hacking up old ladies in a supermarket. It would have been hilarious if the stupid experience wasn't so humiliating. The ordeal was closing, and Ellie was lucky to get away with a caution to keep the peace and was told not to irritate her long-suffering neighbour. He requested she keep her dog under control as a side note.

Jake was bored with the humans but realised that the attention was focused on him. That was odd. He hadn't heard the Jake word.

Hmm, lots of humans looking at Jake. How many? Two eyes. And yes, four. Um, four eyes. What's next, whine—oh, Jake Good Boy, whine—but Jake can't think numbers too good. Lots of eyes, that's it, lots of eyes watching Jake. It must be playtime. Jake likes playtime.

He took a flying leap at the policeman, bumped into the lady officer, and almost knocked her flying. She stumbled backwards onto the lawn and trod in the deposit that Jake had left behind the police officer's backs. He grabbed the policeman's sleeve and ragged it while growling and wagging his tail at ninety miles an hour. He liked his new friend.

'See?' Mr Jackson was delighted at the new turn of events. 'That bloody dog's vicious. It's a killer, a devil dog, I tell you. How can I set foot out of my door when she could set that crazy animal on me at any time? I live in fear of my life and me, a Tora Bora veteran. That animal should be taken away and destroyed.'

Ellie had taken the debacle on the chin and wore it well. But the suggestion of somebody destroying her dog was too much. For the second time that day, she let go with both barrels. She stopped trying to drag Jake off the policeman and turned to rag-out her neighbour. Ellie's face was centimetres from his, her features distorted in a decal of rage.

'You nasty, spiteful, venomous, withered old bastard.' She took a breath and re-stocked on adjective missiles. Jackson took a step backwards, and Ellie took up the space with one forward. Her finger came up between them to stab her point across, and Jackson flinched as though she would hit him.

'That's right, you feeble, twisted, pathetic little pariah of a man. You've pushed me too far this time. You'd better be scared.'

While the barrage of words took place, both police officers fought with Jake. WPC Sally Woods was wiping the side of her shoe on the edge of the grass as she hauled backwards on Jake's collar. As she bent over his neck, her cap dislodged and fell to the path in front of the excited dog. Quickly as an eagle on a mouse, Jake dropped the policeman's arm, picked up the cap, and flew across the lawn. He dragged WPC Woods through the already trodden-in dog turd as she clung to his collar.

'You think you're such a hero, don't you? You're not. You're a bloody joke in the village. I bet the only fighting you saw was in the NAAFI queue. Do you know something, Mr-Sanctimonious-Bloody-Jackson? Even your precious wife couldn't stand the sight of you. She told me what a pain in the arse you are.'

She watched as tears formed in Harry Jackson's eyes. She'd gone too far. It was true, Pauline used to chat to her about her husband's annoying ways and maddening habits, but she followed by saying that it just made her love him more and want to look after him. Ellie knew of few couples who were more devoted. It was only after Pauline died that Harry shut himself away and turned his anger on the world that had taken his wife. Ellie remembered when she'd first moved into Cherry Tree Cottage. Even though she had her own strawberry patch, Harry gave her freshly picked strawberries. She felt ashamed and contrite.

At the same time as her outburst spent itself and fizzled in the wake of its gasses, Ellie felt the firm grip of PC Ferguson on her upper arm. He threatened arrest if she didn't calm down, and she was led inside the house.

Jake stopped his game to watch his mistress going in, and he followed. Maybe there'd be food, biscuits perhaps, or sausage. Jake liked sausages best of all.

Ellie listened to the lecture and stern warnings of the police while Mr Jackson, who had taken it upon himself to step into the house uninvited, watched. Jake was worried. All thoughts of food and play were chased away as he wrangled with new input that needed sorting. Jake didn't like being ignored, especially when he smelled a not-Ellie smell in the kitchen. He put his nose to the floor and followed a scent around the room. He

30

traced it to the back door and whined. The smell was a not-Ellie smell. It confused him, and he complained. Nobody took any notice of him, so he snuffled for a few more seconds at the back door and then went to his bed to flop down in a sulk.

After the police and her hero-of-the-moment neighbour left, Ellie collapsed in a chair at the dining room table. She sobbed and asked the question. Am I going mad?

She didn't feel insane, but nothing in her world made sense. Her consultant, Doctor Fielding, assured her that there shouldn't be any mental retardation—however, it couldn't be guaranteed because the disease wasn't typical. As far as she was aware, there were no periods in her day unaccounted for, yet two people had seen her when she hadn't been there.

Here she was, twenty-four hours post-diagnosis, going crazy. She took some medication to calm her and to help her sleep.

Lying her head in her arms, she broke her heart, and exhaustion took her to a shadowed realm of tormented dreams.

She dreamed that she was still sitting at the kitchen table. She looked up and saw Matt coming towards her. He was smiling. Jake was barking somewhere. It was a warning. Matt had a bouquet of roses in his arms. As she looked at them, the flowers withered and desiccated. The delicate pink blooms turned tea-coloured and fell in brittle shards to the carpet. Matt wasn't smiling anymore. The roses turned into a pistol. He was coming at her. She tried to run, but she couldn't move from the chair. He raised the gun to eye level, and Ellie woke up, terrified.

Somebody was in the room with her. A shadow passed across the door, moving fast and silent. She got up. The chair clattered behind her as she called. 'Matt? Who is it? Who's there?' Nobody answered. She ran to the front door as it clicked shut.

She heard George's cheery voice saying, 'Sizzling. See ya later, hot lips.' Ellie was dopey from the medication. She felt as though she was still dreaming. Her legs didn't want to carry her. By the time she got to the gate, nobody was in sight. It must have been Matt. But why had he left without waking her? The street was deserted, and Jake was barking. He'd been barking all the time, but she hadn't registered it until now. She ran into the house. He wasn't in the kitchen, but his insistent scratching at the back door, coupled with the angry barking, told her he was in the garden. The back door was locked. Somebody had shut him out. Why would Matt do that? Ellie was confused and frightened. She let Jake in and re-locked the door. She checked all the doors and windows were secure. Making a coffee, she left it untouched, fighting against the medication-induced sleep fogging her brain and bringing shadows to lull her into her nightmares.

That's how Matthew found her, four hours later. She roused, disturbed by Jake's excited greeting.

Matt usually made a fuss of Jake when he came. Sometimes he had doggie-chocs in his pocket or those little round biscuits to stop Jake farting.

Jake was ashamed of farting.

He would fart, look at his rear-end in shame and run away from the smell. It made Ellie laugh, which made him more embarrassed.

Jake has not farted now.

He smelled his backside to make sure.

No, no fart. Matt was making the 'Down Jake' noise. He didn't like Jake today, but Jake's a Good Boy. He hadn't played chase with Matt's hat. Matty hasn't got a hat, so they can't tell Jake off for playing chase with it. Jake's going back to bed.

'Down Jake,' Matt said, firmer this time, pushing Jake out of the way. The dog padded to his basket. He was confused and upset and thought he must have done something bad because Matty was shouting at him. Matt rushed to Ellie's side.

'Ellie? What's wrong? Are you all right?'

Since the onset of her illness, it took her longer to wake up. She raised her head from her arms, and her eyes were puffy from crying. She squinted at Matt, with the fugue of sleep leaving her. She smiled before the day's memories seeped back into her mind, but they did come back, starting with a trickle and developing into a flood. Her eyes closed, and she groaned.

'Hello, love. I'm fine. I've had a shitter of a day, but I'm okay, honest.' She didn't tell him about the intruder. Something held her back. She remembered the pistol in her dream, the look in Matt's eye. But that was just a dream. She frowned, reasoning that dreams don't usually lock doors. For the first time ever, she felt the trust in her boyfriend jolt.

'Are you sure you're all right? You aren't bathed and ready to go out.'

There was no accusation in his words, just concern. She remembered the dinner date and groaned again. Going out was the last thing she wanted to do. She'd rather face another three rounds with grumpy-arsed Jackson.

'I'm sorry. I must have fallen asleep. Give me half an hour, and I'll be ready.'

'You look shattered. I know you're looking forward to it, but we can cancel tonight. We can go out anytime. Let's get a takeaway and relax here. What do you fancy?'

His words were a sweet salve to her tattered nerves. God, she loved this man. She pushed the next thought away—but what about the pistol, Ellie?

'I'd like that, but only on one condition. For putting you out, tonight is my treat.'

'No, Ellie, I was going to take you out, and now I'll treat you to dinner in. No arguments, okay?'

The stranger, who was becoming a frequent visitor, crept onto her shoulder, and for the third time, Ellie felt something snap. It came from nowhere and without any warning.

'I am not a God-damned invalid. Don't treat me like a crippled degenerate just because I'm dying. If I want to buy a meal, I will, all right? You come in here with your eyes spewing pity. You can take your fucking pity and shove it as far up your good intentions as your moralistic finger will reach. If you can't treat me normally, you can fuck off. Go and save a whipped puppy.'

Ellie's voice broke into a sob, and tears poured down her face.

'I'm not going mad. I'm not going fucking mad. And I will not be treated like a broken doll. Do you hear me?' She ran out of words when the snot at the back of her throat threatened to choke her. She was sobbing so hard that it took all the oxygen from her lungs, leaving no air to fuel any more angry words.

Matt stepped back in shock. Ellie was always placid. In the two years they'd known each other, she had never lost her temper. She rarely even raised her voice. Apart from the night before during sex, he'd never heard her say a word stronger than shit. He looked shocked and upset.

'Matty, I'm going insane. Hold me, please.'

He took her in his arms. He said he didn't know where the notion came from that she was losing her mind. He'd never insinuated it as her accusation suggested, and Ellie knew she acted out of character.

She moulded her body to his and cried herself out. He made placating noises in her ear and whispered to her as the anger melted away. He joked about a wet patch on the front of his best shirt and wondered if she'd left snot stains on it. He said he didn't give a damn if she had. As she wilted, he led her to the lounge. Between the residual sobs, she told him about the horrible day. At least her irrational behaviour made sense, but he looked shocked by the vehemence of her anger. An hour later, Ellie said she was starving. Matt said he didn't dare offer to buy the meal. That was what set her off, so he sat quietly, his brow knitting into a jumper of worry lines as she went to get her purse. It was a matter of seconds before the next drama unfolded.

The back door was unlocked, and Ellie's purse had been stolen.

# Chapter Three

'Good morning, Ellie. It is nine fifteen AM, and the date is the twenty-first of October, two thousand and forty-six.'

'Thank you, George. I won't be writing this morning, I have to go to the bank. My purse was stolen from my handbag last night.'

'Oh, that's wonderful news, Ellie. Congratulations, I'm very pleased for you.'

She grinned and made a mental note to download the latest update for her Personal Humanicon Organiser. Sometimes George was so spot on with his responses that it was hard to believe he didn't have feelings, emotions and a wicked sense of humour. But, sometimes, he made the wrong choice from his six hundred and fifty thousand phrase response database, and the results were hilarious.

'Thank you, George. That's very sweet of you.'

Ellie was on her second cup of coffee and working through a morning cocktail of drugs when she heard Matt.

'Come in if you're good looking and sexy.'

'Hiya, gorgeous. Mmm, breakfast. They smell good,' he said, eyeing the handful of coloured pills and capsules. 'Have you calmed down yet? Or are you still gunning for the whole national police force and anyone else who gets in your way? Do I need my boxing gloves, or will ball protection be enough?'

When Ellie rang the police to report her stolen purse, she was convinced that the police officer on the desk had a tone to his voice. Matt hoped so. And although she was so tired that she'd run out of the ammunition necessary to give him a performance of her newfound temper, to say that she had been frosty would be like saying that Antarctica was a bit chilly. She assured Matt she was fine, and the tantrums were a knee-jerk reaction to her bad news. Neither of them liked the new side to Ellie.

The trip to the bank was uneventful, though Matt kept glancing at her with concern. She looked tired, drawn, and the skin on her cheekbones was taking on the appearance of being stretched to fit.

'Miss Erikson.' Philip Hughes, the bank manager, took her hand and shook it. His palm was damp with sweat. He flashed his fake smile that didn't reach his eyes, and she was transfixed by his teeth. Surely he had too many in that insincere grin for one mouth. He ushered them into his office.

'I'm so glad you've come back. I hope you've had time to reconsider your decision. And we, of course, are more than happy to welcome you back. Now, if you step this way, there will be a bit of paperwork to sort everything out, but we'll soon have it done. Mr High, good to see you again, too. So what's it like being linked with Cumbria's most eligible lady?' The manager laughed. It was a grating sound, high and shrill, that contained all the sincerity of a fox in a hen hut but without Reynard's wisdom.

It took Ellie thirty seconds to process the words prattling out of the stupid man's mouth. Once she'd made sense of them—they still didn't compute. She had a rudimentary handle on the phonics, but what the fuck was he on about? Her first thought was, Oh God, no, not again. She didn't know what was happening, but she knew it wasn't good. She interrupted Hughes as he launched further into his camaraderie spiel, and Matt was glad to be rescued from the sickly man with sweaty palms.

'Excuse me, Mr Hughes, I have no idea what you're talking about. I have come to verify the report I made over the phone last night that my purse—containing all my credit cards—has been stolen.'

Hughes moved from one foot to the other. 'I don't mean to speak out of turn, but is this a joke? Miss Erikson, forgive me. I live in a tidy world, and I know you're one of those arty types and that maybe you have a lot of things on your plate with writing and books—and more writing. However, you've already caused considerable confusion this week, and to come back and do it a second time is, well, it's a bit inconsiderate, if you don't mind me saying. I don't mean to be confrontational, but you understand this is highly irregular.'

'What on earth are you talking about?'

'Oh, dear. You say your purse has been stolen?'

'Yes, Mr Hughes. My purse, containing a lot of my personal details, has been stolen. Bank books, credit cards, driving licence, the lot.'

Philip Hughes looked more uncomfortable by the second. 'You left your bank books and credit cards here yesterday when you closed all of your accounts.' Despite his obvious discomfort, he had plenty to say when he started.

'And the thing is, Miss Erikson, as we explained to you, it was most uncharacteristic of you to maximise the expenditure on your Goldcard like that yesterday lunchtime. And then to come in straight after and close the accounts. Well, as you know, we were reluctant to acquiesce to this and give you clearance. It was only the fact that you've been with us for so long, and you being who you are, that we acceded to your request, but we really do need to have those cards cleared within the month.'

'I have no idea what you're talking about. I haven't been near the bank for weeks.'

'We at Northwest National have always been impressed with the way you manage your accounts, Miss Erikson and, frankly, we were sorry to see you leave us. You have been one of our most valued customers.'

'Not for much longer if you don't stop prattling on in riddles and tell me exactly what I'm being accused of.'

Hughes cleared his throat. 'If you are in any financial difficulty, I'm sure we can sort something out to help you. Our terms are very competitive.'

The impact of his words made their way through his simpering bumph—cleared the accounts. Ellie had always been frugal. She lived a simple life in a modest house. Almost all her money was tied up in investments. She gave silent thanks to her accountant. Due to his management, she only kept a hundred thousand Euros with this bank. Had she lost the lot? The rest of her assets consisted of stocks and shares and a few private company deals mainly aimed at helping the local community.

Hughes sat behind his vast mahogany desk that contained three acres of the Brazilian rain forest. He pen-twiddled, scribbled on his blotter, wobbled his head and looked uncomfortable. Far from giving him stature and authority, it only served to diminish his slight frame and make him look lost. He fidgeted, unable to meet their eyes or sit still.

Ellie made the usual protestations of innocence. After the last couple of days, she had no temper left and sounded defeated. She knew the outcome, and anything she said would be useless. She told Hughes she had an alibi for the previous afternoon in the form of the local constabulary. However, it didn't aid her cause.

'You've had dealings with the police?'

After ten minutes of verbal tennis, the evidence was presented. They were taken to the security office and shown the CCTV footage. At two thirty-three in the afternoon—about the same time Ellie had fallen asleep alone at her kitchen table—the footage showed her walking into the bank and demanding to see the manager. She wore her green Adonis jacket that Matt had bought her the previous Christmas. She had on jeans and her Nova trainers. The video showed her shaking hands with Philip Hughes and being led into his office with a slimy hand to the small of her back. Thirty-one minutes later, the tape showed them coming out of the office with Hughes looking harassed and unhappy. Ellie left the bank with her hair swaying and her poise jaunty.

There was nothing left to say. The camera doesn't lie. Matt looked embarrassed, and Ellie was ashamed. They made an appointment to re-open the accounts when Ellie felt a little less distraught and left the bank with their heads low. Ellie was relieved to be in the bite of a chilly, late October breeze.

She wanted to walk for a few minutes. She couldn't face sitting in the cramped interior of Matt's car. He had one of those awful vanilla air fresheners. It was cloying and overpowering. She was sure she'd puke all over his beige upholstery in Technicolour if she got in the car. She wanted to clear her head and think. They wandered to the Windsor Café for a coffee.

They talked—or at least Matt did. He told her that he saw how serious her condition was. It was the first time he'd seen it for what it was, and it blinded him. All he'd considered to this point was her imminent death and how that would affect him. He hadn't thought about the ramifications of her condition pre-death. He said he'd do anything to keep her safe and would work from home to look after her.'

Then he lowered his head and muttered quietly, 'But, Ellie, I don't know if my love is going to be enough. I feel inadequate, and your illness seems so big.'

Ellie was numb. She wanted to think, but unless thought begets logic, sometimes it's easier not to bother. Her world had a hole in the bottom, and all the sense had trickled out, leaving a wake of the shattered reason behind her. She'd seen the evidence for herself. She wasn't going crazy at all. She was already there—one hundred per cent, spectacularly bloody fruit cake. And now, the only thing on her mind was whether to have a strong and sensible cup of coffee or a hot chocolate with lashings of whipped cream and chocolate sprinkles. By the time a waitress came, she'd made up her mind. She went for the chocolate and a slice of raspberry pavlova with more cream. Sod it. There was no point in being a crazy dying woman if you didn't take advantage of it.

Matt wanted to nip into the newsagents for a paper. Ellie said she'd walk on until he caught her up. In retrospect, the Pavlova was a mistake. It lay heavy in her stomach, and she felt sick.

She wasn't paying attention to where she was going and collided with a woman coming out of the fruit and veg shop.

'I'm so sorry.' Ellie never finished her apology. She looked at the woman and met her own eyes—her own face—her own Adonis jacket.

'Boo!' the woman said.

Ellie grabbed the wall for support and wheezed in shock. After a couple of breaths to ease her dizziness, she looked up, but the woman had vanished.

'Are you all right, dear? You look peaky.' A lady took her by the elbow and looked into her eyes. This woman bore no resemblance to Ellie. She was middle-aged and overweight with a fleshy face and brown eyes that seemed to care. Ellie couldn't trust what her senses showed her.

'You're not me, are you? But you were a minute ago. Yes, thank you, I'm all right, but I've seen myself in the strangest places, and now I'm other people, too.' It was the most ridiculous thing she'd ever said. But before she could stop herself from talking more rubbish, and as she was about to apologise to the lovely lady for being nuts, the world went black. She never felt the pavement coming to meet her as she wilted towards it.

Matt came out of the newsagents and saw a crowd further down the street. 'Ellie.' he yelled. He knew whatever had drawn them, it had something to do with his girlfriend. He set off at a run.

'Excuse me. Please, get out of my way. Bloody move.' He pushed through the tight wad of people and saw Ellie lying on the ground. Blood pooled on the pavement by her right temple, and a lady had put her in the recovery position and was trying to bring her round. Realising that Matt wasn't another onlooker, the Good Samaritan explained that an ambulance was on its way.

Ellie regained consciousness to an abstract collage of writhing faces that came in—'It's that author, isn't it? Her what writes?'—and went out of focus every few seconds. —'Yeah, I've seen her with an Alsatian by the river.' Only one face stayed clear and steady in the throng of fuzzy people.

It was her own.

'It's her,' she tried to sit up and point. Matt pushed her back down, leaning forward to kiss her forehead, obscuring her vision. She jerked away from him, and the woman had vanished.

'It's okay, sweetheart. An ambulance is on its way. It's Matt. I'm here, and everything's going to be all right.'

'I'm not bloody blind. I know who you are. I don't want a fucking ambulance.' She tried to get up and regretted the sudden movement. She felt her stomach rebelling and vomited over the kind lady's knees. Ellie couldn't apologise enough, but she was so very tired. She heard the ambulance siren rounding the corner and summoned enough energy for a final protest.

'I told you, I don't want to go to the hospital, you stupid bloody idiot,' she yelled at Matt. He didn't call the ambulance but was singled out to bear the brunt of her anger. 'On second thoughts, yes, I bloody well do. I'm going to get that bastard Fielding and rip his head off his shoulders. He said there was no damage to my mind.' It took the last of her strength. She closed her eyes and embraced unconsciousness with relish.

The paramedics refused to let her walk into the ambulance as she'd passed out again when she tried to stand up. She felt such a fool being loaded onto a stretcher and wheeled in. Most of the onlookers were bored by this time—nobody had died, and although there was some blood, it wasn't that dramatic. They'd dispersed, but the older woman had stuck tight to Ellie's side, despite Matt telling her they were okay now.

Matt talked to one paramedic while the other left her for a second to open the ambulance doors. The lady leaned in.

'Keep your mouth shut in future, or you and that pretty boyfriend of yours will die.'

Ellie's mind was fuzzy. She was shocked into silence and must have misheard. 'Excuse me? What did you say?'

'Ah, nothing of importance, dear. I was just saying you'll be in the best place, safe there. They'll look after you, dear.'

Ellie tried to grab the woman's arm, she called for Matt. Alerted to the terror in her voice, he came over.

'That lady. She threatened me, Matty. She said she was going to kill us.' The woman was gone.

'Sush, now Ellie. Nothing's going to happen to anyone. It's just the shock, love. You banged your head, but you're going to be fine now.'

She woke up once in the ambulance. She vomited, told the paramedic he had, come to bed eyes, vomited again, asked for second helpings of morphine and went back to sleep. Despite not being seen by the triage team, the paramedics gave Ellie a sedative and pain relief. Her pulse was erratic, and her respiration was poor. In sleep, she calmed, and her breathing and heart rate returned to an acceptable output.

Matt explained everything to Jeremy Fielding, who'd made himself available to see Ellie. Words were muttered about lumbar punctures and other tests that sounded horrific. She was given an MRI and a CT scan. Seven vials of blood were taken from her for analysis.

After the tests were done and the immediate results analysed, Fielding sat on the stretcher bed Ellie had been allocated. He took her hand in his. The man had hands the size of baseball mitts. Yet, they were soft and smelled of antiseptic soap and somehow, when he stroked the back of her hand, he made her calm. He was in control and would make everything all right. She still wanted to kill the bastard for lying to her, though.

Fielding explained that they didn't find any sign of brain damage or mental retardation.

'So what's happening to me?'

'I'd put it down to the stress you've been under. There's nothing wrong with your brain, but your mind is tired and overworked.'

'That's okay, let's have a party then. You're the bloody doctor, the Great I am, and from the gumph, you've just given me, you haven't got the faintest bloody idea what's sodding well going on. I might as well ask the lady who cleans the toilets what's wrong with me. She'd have a better idea than you, and she might just have the guts to tell me straight that I've lost the fucking plot and fallen into a slimy hole of insanity. And that's a damned sight more than you're telling me, you useless bloody tosser.'

Fielding had to turn his face away to hide the smile that threatened to crack his face and his professional demeanour. Nurses, doctors and the general public bowed and scraped to him, fawning and cowing to his every whim. He was the demigod of St. Joseph's, and nobody ever contradicted what he said. To have this feisty little woman call him a tosser was like a stab of blinding sunshine breaking through the clouds on a dismal day. It stung, but the pleasure of a new experience came with the initial sting.

'Ellie, you have to understand, this is all new ground to us. There have been so few recorded cases that there's no such thing as a textbook case because there've never been enough cases to write a textbook. I said there probably wouldn't be any mental retardation because we had no reason to suspect any. In previous cases, the effects of adult sufferers have been isolated physical symptoms rather than mental impairment. Only in many classic TSD sufferers—that is, the juvenile case scenario—are there histories of violent mood swings and dementia. From what we've read, the adult form is a different fish-dish.' Fielding finished his lecture as he saw Ellie's eyes glazing over with exhaustion. She'd heard enough for one day.

'For Christ's sake, just stick me in a cage and call me Gus the Guinea pig.' Ellie was exhausted, and her good humour was low.

'What I suggest is this.' Fielding's voice had taken on an air of knowledgeable authority. He knew what would happen next, and he was on familiar ground. Or at least he thought he knew what was going to happen next.

'You will stay in here for a couple of days to get your strength back, and we'll use that time to run a few more tests' He got no further, and his familiar ground was trodden underfoot by Ellie's steel toe-capped boots with soles of stubborn defiance.

'Oh no, you don't, I'm not staying here. There'll be plenty of time for that later when I've progressed to seeing flying

46

elephants and hearing voices telling me to kill my consultant because he's the Anti-Christ. I'm going home.'

'Eleanor, you need to rest. Oh, sod it.' For the first time in his life, he spoke to a patient like an irritating but loveable teenage daughter. 'I'm wasting my breath. Go on, go home. Try not to worry, and I'll get back to you if I find anything to report. I'll let you know when I get the blood test results, and I'll ring to see you at my clinic next week. The only other thing I can say, and I can't stress this strongly enough, is—rest.'

Matt helped Ellie from the car to the front door as she leaned on him, grateful for his support and strength, and she wasn't just thinking of the physical arm holding her up. On the way, they'd talked about everything that had happened over the last fourteen hours and since leaving the house that morning, so long ago.

'I swear, matt, I did see myself in that crowd. And that woman did threaten to kill us.'

'Honey, you've been through a tremendous shock in such a short time. It's too much to take in. Is it so big a stretch to put it down to your brain playing games with you?

'No. Fuck you. I know what I saw.

Matt dropped the subject.

It was almost midnight. Jake had been alone all day. He was whining as they tumbled from the chill of the night into the hall's warmth. Ellie's green Adonis jacket hung on its usual hook behind the door. It mocked her as she thought about the footage showing her coming out of the bank wearing it. She shivered, and Matt led her to the lounge before he sorted Jake out and made them a hot drink.

The lost purse was in plain sight on the table beside the settee. She must have left it there before taking the costume back. It explained why it hadn't been in her handbag. She felt stupid and humiliated. This was the last straw. She hung her head onto her arms and used the last of her energy in an excellent self-pitying bawl.

# Chapter Four

Ellie counted to ten for the third time that morning. Matt was driving her crazier than she already felt. She wanted to write, she needed to write, and goddammit, if she didn't get to write, somebody was going to suffer.

'Would you like another cup of tea? Are you sure you're all right? Why don't you stop now? You look worn out. Let me take you out for lunch.' Each of these statements was preceded by a timid knock on the office door and his concerned voice saying, 'I'm sorry to disturb you again but.'

'George, so help me, I'm going to train you to shoot on sight, and Jake, look at you, lying there snoozing. Shame on you, dog. Can't you bite his ankles or something?'

She'd changed the Humanicon's database and updated it to the smooth Irish voice of the morning radio DJ. George's new processing chip couldn't come up with a suitable response to this one. Pre-update, the old George would have said, 'I believe there may be some suitable software available for guidelines on shooting people. Shall I search the 'net for downloads, Ellie?' New George just came off standby and said, 'Awaiting instruction, Ellie.' He did say it ever so well, but it didn't have the same giggle value as old George. It was like losing a friend and gaining an acquaintance.

On the other hand, Jake heard his name and knew exactly how to respond. He jumped up, prancing and whining for attention. He didn't make much noise, but it was enough to bring Matt to the door, the same knock, the same irritation.

'Is everything all right in there? Only, I heard Jake. Are you okay?'

'No, I'm bloody-well not okay,' she muttered under her breath. 'I can't get my filleting knife sharpened quickly enough.' In a normal voice, she answered, 'Yes, I'm fine, thanks, love. I'm as well as five minutes ago when you asked the same question. I'm still trying to get the last bit of this chapter boxed off before I adopt boyfriendicide as my new career venture.'

'Excuse me for being concerned. If you're going to be like that, I won't bother next time.' Please, God let that be true, Ellie thought. She was lucky to have a man as caring as Matt. But his feelings were hurt, and she felt guilty for being a bitch.

'Tell you what. Why don't you take Jake for a run on the green, and on the way back, you can pick up a couple of éclairs from the bakery? I'll stop work then, and we'll have them with a brew. I have to meet Rob at one, and I need to finish this chapter before I go.'

He agreed, mainly because Jake had heard the words run and green. These two words were exciting by themselves but put them together, and they were almost as good as ice cream. There was no way Jake was going to settle until he'd been taken out. Matt protested that he didn't want to leave her alone, but finally, dog and boyfriend's retreat was heralded by the soft click of the front door, and Ellie felt sanity, at least for the moment, being restored.

The previous evening they'd enjoyed a quiet meal together. Matt wanted to wash up after the meal, but Ellie had pulled rank and said the dishes could wait until this morning. As well as getting fat by eating éclairs, another luxury of dying was giving yourself permission to be slovenly. A month earlier, dirty dishes left overnight would have been unacceptable, but now she didn't care. It was only washing up. They'd sat in the lounge with Jake taking up more than his share of the sofa. Matt didn't approve of dogs being allowed on the furniture, but it was a fair trade-off because Jake disapproved of the humans having steak while he was given dog food. It was a good night with nothing out of the ordinary happening. Ellie and Matt had watched a film with a glass of wine, and the topic of illness was banned from all discussion.

After finishing the chapter, Ellie shut down her work and walked into the lounge, wrinkling her nose in disgust. The wine glasses were on the coffee table, along with an unfinished bottle of red. The curtains were unopened, and the room had the tinge of a vinegary red wine smell. Matt had offered to wash up again that morning, but Ellie, still irritated about losing work time, said it was his fault that things hadn't been done. 'Damn him. He could have taken these through to the kitchen.' She snatched up the glasses and set about waking the room.

Satisfied with the living room, she moved into the kitchen, filled the sink with hot sudsy water, and washed up when the phone rang. The audio connection was distorted in the kitchen, so she went to the study to answer it. She dried her hands on a tea towel as she muttered to herself.

After talking to Rob about the artwork for her book cover, she went back to the washing up. Matt would be back any minute. Feeling contrite for being horrible to him, she wanted to have everything cleaned up and the coffee made. She was in a better frame of mind and hummed as she plunged her hands into the hot water.

The hum died in her throat and escalated into a scream as the water turned crimson.

Despite the severity of her injuries, she didn't feel much pain until she took her hands out of the water. Her eyes widened as her wrists emerged, and a fountain of deep red arterial blood gushed from her forearm. Pulling her hands out of the sink caused the plug to come out of its mooring. As the bowl emptied of blood and water, Ellie saw the cruel jagged spikes of their two broken glasses sticking up from the dishes like crystal icebergs. The bleeding was severe, and she needed hospital treatment. It was really hurting, but the more significant worry was the velocity that her artery sprayed blood in an arc across the kitchen. She grabbed teatowels and swaddled her hands and arms. There were cuts on the fingertips of both hands and a gash across her left palm. But what frightened her most was the jagged laceration from the base of her palm that travelled four inches up the inside of her forearm. It was deep and happened when she'd pulled her hands out of the water during the shock of the first cuts.

Matt came home as she was talking to the hospital on the phone. He assessed the situation. Blood was soaking through the wad of teatowels binding Ellie's arm. She was pale and shaking. He took control, bundled her into his car, and quickly got to A&E.

The cuts to her fingers and hands were superficial and only needed cleaning and dressing. The registrar on duty assured her that her typing wouldn't be affected after a couple of days. However, he was concerned about the cut to her inner wrist. He said that she'd been lucky, that no vital nerves or tendons had been severed and that she should retain full use of her left hand. He told her that she'd got off lightly by only needing seven stitches.

But the wound wasn't what concerned him.

While a nurse cleaned Ellie's wounds, Matt took the doctor to one side. They muttered in whispers outside the cubicle. She couldn't hear what Matt was saying, but he kept motioning towards her and frowning. Dr Fielding was called to see her. As her consultant, the registrar felt it was best to have him take a look. Another doctor arrived on the scene at the same time as Dr Fielding. He introduced himself as Dr Adam Merryweather, the hospital's medical psychologist.

Dr Fielding spoke to Ellie, asking her how she'd been before the accident and how she'd been feeling after everything she'd had to cope with. She told him everything that had happened to her, and the three doctors looked at each other above her head.

'What's the matter? What's wrong? Have you found something else wrong with me? What is it?' Her voice rose to a pitch of hysteria.

'We're concerned about how you're coping with things, that's all,' Dr Fielding said, patting her hand.

Dr Merryweather said, 'Ellie—may I call you Ellie? We know you've had a lot to take on board. We were wondering if perhaps everything has become a bit much for you. We understand, of course.'

Matt cut in before the doctor finished speaking. 'Ellie, if this was a cry for help, we're here, love, and we're listening. We'll help you, but this isn't right. I can understand why you'd think this is a better way. I know how hard it is.'

'What?' Ellie screeched at him as the implication of what they were saying hit her. 'You sanctimonious prick. The only help I need is to get these bloody bandages off so I can wring your bloody neck. You think I did this,'—on purpose? Do you think I was trying to kill myself? And you,' she accused, glaring at Fielding, 'you've listened to this bullshit and taken it seriously? You're all bloody mad. Help me up. I'm getting out of here before I really lose my shit and tell you all what I think. Matt, how can you think that of me for Christ's sake? I've gone mad, but I'm not bloody suicidal.'

'Ellie,' Fielding crooned, 'Matt thinks—well, we all think it would be a good idea if you had a rest. We think you're working too hard. We have a facility here in town. It's a nice place.'

Ellie had an answer for him. She had several, none of them very pretty. She left the hospital fifteen minutes later with a furious Matthew trailing in her wake.

'You made a complete fool of yourself in there, Ellie. You made a fool of me. Can't you see that we're trying to help you? Why did you do it, Ellie? Why?'

'I didn't, you idiot. It was an accident. It was just a stupid bloody accident.' They argued all the way home. Later, while Matt slept, Ellie lay awake, troubled and confused. The same few moments of mental cinefilm ran through her mind.

She'd walked into the kitchen carrying the two dirty wine glasses. She'd put them on the island as she filled the sink with water. The phone rang. She went to answer it. The glasses were still on the island when she went to the phone. She came back from talking to Rob and went straight to the sink to wash the dishes. She didn't think about the glasses. She didn't know if they were still on the island or not. But, she was sure that she hadn't moved them from there to the sink—she was almost certain.

The following day the news channels and daily papers were full of the alleged attempted suicide of Eleanor Erikson, the bestselling novelist. But word of her illness hadn't leaked to the press yet, and for that, she was grateful. Rob had done his best with damage limitation and dulling the press sensationalism, and Matt had threatened GBH to more than one pushy journalist when they'd rung the house for information. The accident was reported as an alleged suicide attempt. She tried to put the horrors of the previous week out of her mind. She had to settle down to a normal day, doing normal work and had replaced the hospital dressings with light gauze on her fingertips to type. She could have dictated her work to George, but Ellie was Old School and needed to feel the keys beneath her fingers to get the best from her brain, and if ever her old grey matter needed a leg-up, it was now. She instructed George to divert any calls to the answering machine, opened her word processor and shut out the world.

When the doorbell rang, Ellie groaned.

'Show, George, please,' she waited for the security cam program to click open. There was the usual three seconds of the black screen and then nothing.

'Show, please, George,' she said again, the irritation back in her voice.

'Security program open, Ellie.'

'Well, it's not working,' she grumbled, as though it was feasible to argue with a computer. 'Are you sure you set it?' She got up went into the hall.

When she opened the door, there was nobody there. Her feet knocked against something on the doorstep, and she looked down. A circular wreath was lying on the ground, dressed with green ivy and white lilies. Alerted to a feeling of danger and being watched, she saw the piece of black material thrown over the surveillance monitors. She wondered why George hadn't told her that somebody was messing with the camera. The new programme needed some tweaking and additional security downloads. She made a mental note to attend to it. Whoever had left this didn't want to be seen. Ellie was trembling as she bent to pick up the wreath. Rob's joke about a stalker seemed too close to home, but, whoever it was, they scored no points for originality. What would be next? Unordered pizza deliveries and tonnes of horse manure emptied onto the drive?

Matt rushed into the living room, alerted by his girlfriend crying. Ellie was on the settee, with the wreath on her knee, staring at the card she turned over between her fingers. Questions filled her brimming eyes as she looked at Matt for the answers he couldn't give.

'Why would anybody do this to me? I've never hurt anyone. I'm a good person, and I always put money in Barnardo's en-

56

velopes. Why would somebody want to persecute me like this? I mean, if they want me dead, it's not as though they're going to have to wait long, is it?'

Matt didn't know what to say, so he sat beside her and pulled her to him. Taking the card from her, he read the words, trying to understand what was happening, but nothing gelled. Their world had not only turned upside down but was spiralling towards a distant galaxy of which they had no understanding.

'It's some sicko that's read the papers today, love. That's all. Don't worry, we'll sort it out. And when I find the twisted bastard who did this, I'll knock his bloody head off his shoulders.'

He read the card for a second time, biting down hard on his bottom lip.

RIP: Eleanor Erikson.

Further to the hand-written inscription were the printed words, *In deepest sympathy* and the Send Some Flowers company logo and telephone number.

'I don't know what's happening, Ellie, but I'm going to find out. This is sick.' Matt's words were clipped and terse with seething anger.

Ellie now had the voice-activated telephone system installed, but it could be over-ridden and the handset and used normally if privacy was preferred. Matt didn't need to make the call in private, but he was blazing mad, and Ellie could see that it gave him a feeling of control. She knew he felt more able to channel his anger into a telephone handset rather than talking into the air. He had to feel the comforting hardness of the plastic receiver in his hand. He stabbed out the number, his right temple throbbing, his blond fringe fell over his left eye, and Ellie knew he was furious.

After a couple of seconds, the connection was made.

'Ah, yes, I wonder if you could help me, please.' He spoke calmly, but the tension was audible in his voice. 'We've just had a delivery from your shop, and I wonder if you could check your records and tell me where it's come from, please? Yes, it was a wreath with white lilies. What do you mean; you have no record of such a delivery? Yes, of course, I'm sure that it was ordered through your shop. I have the card in front of me. I don't know who delivered it, do I? They just left it on the doorstep. That is something to take up with your delivery person then. Well, I'm afraid he did just leave the delivery on the doorstep, and my partner is, rightly, very upset. I'm sorry, but you had better recheck your records. My girlfriend has just taken delivery of a funeral wreath announcing her death. I can assure you, she's very much alive and is ready to take this further if it isn't resolved.' He stumbled over the next statement because he was clearly trying to combat the urge to take his feelings out on the lady on the other end of the telephone. 'And, well, it's somebody's idea of a sick joke, and I'd like to know who that someone is, please. Yes, I'll hold. Yes, that's right, Cherry Tree Cottage. Oh, right. Personally, collected? Her uncle George? Cancer? Yes, that's okay, so sorry to trouble you. Yes. I do apologise. Thank you very much. Yes, I'll be sure to do that. I will. Yes, I agree. Grief is a funny thing. Thank you. Goodbye.'

He slammed the receiver onto its carriage with enough force to send the phone crashing to the floor. Ellie winced.

'Let's play twenty questions to guess who our sicko-freak is, shall we?'

She knew what was coming and shrank into the settee's cushions to get as far away from the vehemence of his words as she could. She had never seen him so angry.

'You've just made a fool of me again, Ellie. Getting to be a habit with you, isn't it? Funny, is it, playing these games, getting everybody jumping through hoops, mad with worry, only to find out that it's you every time? That florist described you to a T. You Ellie, you. You. You. Did you think I wouldn't recognise your handwriting? Well, of course, I damned well did, but I didn't want to believe it of you. What's happening to us, Ellie? What's happening to you? What's going on?'

He lunged towards her. With each 'You,' his finger became a foil of accusation, and she backed away from him. Matt was the most gentle man she'd ever known. She'd never had any reason to fear him, and yet, he was so angry that she hardly recognised him. The last few days had brought changes in both of them. Ellie didn't know what to say.

'I don't know what the hell's happening to you, Ellie, but I know I can't take much more.'

With these words, he deflated. The fury was compartmentalised and taken away. A box of misery with the same proportions was put in its place. And where the fury had stung, the misery throbbed. Matthew looked wretched.

He went to stand by the bookcase and saw a Demons Nightclub matchbook. He didn't shout or yell, just picked it up and looked at it back and front. He opened the flap and looked inside.

'What's that?' Ellie asked, curiosity overcoming her newfound wariness of Matt.

'Oh, it's just a matchbook from some Demons nightclub you've been frequenting. Nothing that your boyfriend should feel in any way threatened about; after all, I am only the man that you sleep with when you can stand to have me over.'

He said it in a voice so matter-of-fact that it was more frightening than his yelling. Matt's temple was throbbing, and she could see the blood rushing through the blue vein to his brain. His heart was working too hard.

'I've never heard of a nightclub called Demons.' Still a small voice, but this one was almost out of short pants as the indignation hit her.

'Of course, you haven't. That goes without saying, doesn't it? I've heard of Demons, Ellie. It's the new club on Greengate Street in Barrow. I thought we might try it sometime when you feel up to it, but you already have, haven't you?'

'Honey, I swear, I've never been to the rotten club, and I've never seen those matches before.'

'Don't you honey me.' He put the matchbook to his nose, 'If you've never seen them before, why do they smell of your perfume? Answer that one. Or, just sit mute and let me answer for you. Because they've been sitting in your handbag, that's why?'

She buried her face in a cushion and sobbed bitter tears.

'I don't know you anymore, Ellie. Where have all these lies come from? I want to help you, but I don't know how. This illness has changed you, and it's bigger than both of us. I don't know what to do.'

He threw the matchbook at her. It landed open on her knee. She saw what was written inside the cover.

Better the devil, you know.

They argued again later that morning. Matt wanted her to cancel the meeting with Rob Price, but Ellie wouldn't hear of it and explained that Rob had cancelled other engagements to meet her. She realised they had fought more in the last three days than the rest of their relationship put together. If she insisted on going ahead with the meeting, Matt said, he wanted to be with her. He'd only worry himself sick if he couldn't be there to keep an eye on her in her present condition. At this point, he was lost for words and stopped talking. Ellie finished it for him.

'While I'm as nutty as a fruitcake, you mean.' She couldn't help grinning at his guilty look.

She was ready to go. And she was going alone. Dressed in tailored black trousers and a simple pale lemon blouse in the new Stymex material that rippled with a soft sheen when she moved, she felt almost good. The summer was fast becoming a memory, and she hoped that the yellow top would cheer her flagging spirits. She brushed serum into her blonde hair until it shone a healthy, natural flaxen. Her elegant bob rested just below her ears. 'I might as well make the most of it before it all falls out.' An unpleasant symptom of her condition was that she would suffer abnormal hair loss. Matt had commented that bald people were sexy. Funny, she thought now, as she looked in the mirror, I've only heard of that when referring to men. Maybe I'll go the whole hog and develop a beer gut as well.

Matt was still unhappy about her going out alone when she came downstairs. She promised not to dance naked on the restaurant table. She said she would at least wait until they were out in the street to indulge in any naked cavorting in case they wanted to use that restaurant again. Matt managed a weak smile.

'Watch out for frostbite if you do dance naked. It's nippier than it looks out there today. I'd hate for your nipples to go black and drop off.'

'You never know that could be another of the mystery symptoms of TSD that I have lurking in my future. Enjoy them while you can, babe.'

She wrapped her arms around him, and they kissed. She half expected him to push her away after their fighting, but he didn't. He needed the comfort that their kiss gave as much as she did. He said he felt impotent and small. That rationale told him Ellie didn't mean to do any of the crazy stuff that she'd done and that, if he loved her, he had to help her through this weirdness and not be accusatory. His anger was a heat of the moment reaction. He told her he found her behaviour embarrassing, then followed it by adding that he could only imagine how embarrassed and ashamed she was. He reassured her that he'd get over himself and be stronger—he was in for the long haul, and Ellie was grateful. She told him to go home and get some rest. Neither of them had slept much in the last three nights.

Matt decided to stay, clean the house and make a light evening meal as a surprise for Ellie, an apology for his temper and lack of understanding. The place would be warm, welcoming and smelling of good cooking when she came home. Matt knew how her meetings with Rob could extend from one hour to four.

In the beginning, he was jealous of Ellie and Rob's relationship, even though he knew that Rob was happily married to Gail.

Ellie and Rob had something that he and Ellie didn't. At first, he saw it as a threat, but as he became friends with Rob in his own right, and they double-dated as a foursome, he realised that Rob was an asset to their relationship—never a threat. Any jealousy that he felt had long ago been replaced by a deep trust in his girlfriend and his friend.

'I love you, Ellie Erikson,' he said as she disentangled herself and headed for the door.

She turned and smiled, and for the first time in days, it was his familiar Ellie looking at him, the old Ellie. 'I love you, too, Matt, you big dope. And don't you ever forget it.'

The restaurant was crowded and bustled with lunchtime life as she was escorted to their table by the maître d'.

Rob was already seated, and he stood to greet her when she arrived. Both Matt and Rob had good manners; she appreciated that in a man. Ellie remarked, more than once, that she wasn't one of those hard-edged, one-legged lesbians dressed in camouflaged Stymex who wouldn't let a man open a door for her. However, she still considered herself to be every inch the feminist woman of the forties, the new millennia woman.

Rob helped her out of her coat and handed it to the waiter, who eased her chair into the table, and she thanked him, grateful to have something soft to sink into.

'Enjoy your meal,' he said, handing them a menu each. Ellie ordered an orange juice while the waiter eyed the giant mushroom standing on the table next to Rob's place setting. Ellie remarked that he looked as though he was chewing on a dog turd as he walked away.

'I took the liberty of ordering you a vodka and coke,' Rob said, after leaning over and kissing her on the cheek.

'Bad move Rob. I'm driving, but thank you. I guess one won't hurt.'

Ellie could have guzzled down a bucket full of vodka. She didn't mention that she'd been advised against alcohol with her medication.

'Now, I'm really worried. You always come to our meetings in a taxi. I'm sure a meeting with me is only an excuse for you to get totally bladdered in the middle of the day.' Rob paused, then he screeched, alarming everybody sitting at the nearest five tables, 'Oh, my God,' he yelled at the top of his voice. 'You aren't preggers, are you?' Ellie blushed, smiling her apologies at the other diners who waited for her answer too, and she wasted no time in assuring him that she was not.

As they ordered food and talked, several waiters, walked by, eyeing the enormous mushroom as they passed. Rob and Ellie made small talk for five minutes. Rob hadn't mentioned the mushroom, and so, playing the game, neither had she. Ellie felt the vodka warming her stomach. It felt good, but she had no intention of drinking more than a sip. They talked families and Matt, touched on how the latest book was going, neither one brought up the reason for the meeting, and still, neither Rob nor Ellie had so far mentioned the upstanding mushroom that was leaking compost on the delicate pink tablecloth. Ellie could stand it no longer. She had resisted, truly she had, but now she was bursting with curiosity.

'Okay, wise guy, what's with your friend the mushroom?'

'What this? This one sitting here? Oh, I'm sorry Ellie, I completely forgot about him, do forgive my terrible manners. Ellie, Fred. Fred, Ellie.' He motioned between the mushroom and Ellie as the introductions were made.

'Hello, Fred. I am very pleased to meet you.' She whispered from behind her hand. 'Not a great conversationalist, is he?'

'Well, it's like this, you see, I knew this meeting would be heavy, so I brought Fred the mushroom along because he's such a fungi to be with.'

Ellie groaned and stared at Rob in disbelief. It was an appalling joke. Then she giggled. It was just like Rob, to go to so much trouble to set up a pathetic punchline. The joke was never worth the effort involved in executing it. Her giggle bubbled from the lowest point in her belly and turned into a chuckle. The chuckle was too big to contain, and before she knew it, she was laughing harder than she had laughed in weeks. She laughed hard and couldn't stop. Everybody in the restaurant turned to stare, but there was no holding back. Every time the hilarity subsided, and she thought she had control of herself, she'd look at the mushroom or at Rob, who was laughing at her laughing, and off she'd go again for another bout. Her sides ached, and her ribs were tortured. Tears streamed from her eyes, and her jaw was tired with laughing, but she couldn't stop. The waiter brought their meals and eyed them and the silent Fred with distaste—and off she went again. Her bladder was full, and she had to jiggle in her seat to prevent a flood, but she couldn't get a grip. She was aware that she was making a spectacle of herself—and it felt wonderful. It was normal-crazy not, I-haven't-a-clue-what's-going-on-crazy. She shut up, but only because her body couldn't take any more.

Rob was still laughing at her and looked delighted by her response. 'Well, it wasn't that funny.' And because it really wasn't funny, off she went again.

'Robin Price, you have no idea the good you have just done me. Thank you.' With that, she burst into tears and had to go to the ladies to relieve the pressure on her bladder, tidy herself up, and regain control of her emotions. Rob patted her hand as she left. His eyes were concerned. He had no idea what was happening, but he knew his suspicion that it was serious had been confirmed. He was frightened of what Ellie was going to tell him.

'Well, I've never been so humiliated in my entire life. How could you embarrass me like that in public?' Rob said as she came back. Ellie might have taken him seriously but for the twinkle in his eye and the fact that he had one of the restaurant's substantial pink linen napkins tied under his chin. It looked like an old lady's headscarf from the last century. He looked ridiculous, but Ellie's brief respite from her troubles was over, and she knew that she was about to bring the forced merriment to a close.

They were skirting around the reason for the meeting. For Ellie, it was cowardice, but for Rob, it was as though he knew that nothing would ever be the same again once the words were spoken. Their feelings for each other ran deep. Ellie was aware that Rob loved her. He loved her differently from the love he had for his wife. It was a platonic love that was not harmful or wrong. She was like his younger sister, best friend, colleague and drinking partner. Hell, he was a modern man. He was even big enough to admit that he loved Matt, and if he was going the whole hog, he'd have to say that he even loved that great big stupid mutt of hers that dug his roses and crapped on his lawns. Rob was big enough to admit that he was scared.

Ellie didn't do the lobster royale and salad much justice. She picked at it for ten minutes as they tried to make small talk, but the elephant between them had grown too big. For the first time ever, Rob left food uneaten. As though on cue, they laid their cutlery down and pushed the plates to one side.

'God, I need a cig,' said Rob, who hadn't had a cigarette since they became illegal in the twenties. 'Just goes to show you, gal, once an addict, always an addict.' He twiddled with his napkin as a waiter cleared the table. Then the waiter was gone and with him their excuse for not talking.

'So, come on, darlin', give. What is it?'

'Oh God, Rob, this is hard. And there's no way to say it that isn't going to hurt.' She took a nervous sip of her second orange juice.

'I'm dying, Rob.'

'Well, I know that. You kill me with your demands every time I see you. You want this deal. You want that cover design. You're so demanding.'

'Shut up, Rob.'

Rob laughed a hollow, empty laugh. As soon as she'd said the words, he knew it was true, she wasn't joking, but it had to be a gag. They joked with each other all the time. It had to be a prank.

Ellie talked in a strange storytelling voice, distancing herself from the words she was saying. They were words, just words. That's what she was good at; they were the tools of her trade. Only words and words can't kill you, can they? Ellie knew that it took only three letters to kill you. Not even a proper word. TSD was all it took.

'I have this disease, you see. Funny, really, I have this disease that doesn't affect adults, it only affects children. Well, usually—I'm the exception to the rule. It only appears in children, but it usually just affects Jewish children. Again, I'm the exception to the rule. I think my guardian angel stamped Ashkenazi Jew on my heaven records instead of Church of England. You can see how the two sound similar. He'll have been at the cheap cider again. He's already had two official written warnings about drinking on the job. You just can't get decent guardian angels these days. Hey, it's not all bad news, though. I get to go bald. Just think, no bad hair days. And I get to go blind, so I won't have to see myself with no hair, and the added bonus is I won't see all the dust piling up. But you know the best bit of all? I only get to die once. Not bad, eh? Well, as nasty life-taking, killer-bastard diseases go.'

'Shut up, Ellie. Just shut up.' Rob didn't shout at her, but his words stung nonetheless. A tear that seemed way too fat to be ordinary hung on the tip of his nose, and Ellie reached up to wipe it away.

'How long?'

There was no attempt at sarcastic wit this time as Ellie spoke.

'I don't know. It could be tomorrow, could be ten years. They reckon that, with a good headwind, I've got between one and ten years.'

'What is it?'

'It's called Tay-Sachs disease. Very rare, apparently. Designer, exclusive. Models would pay a fortune for it.'

'And there's no hope whatsoever?'

68

'Officially, no. But, darling, I'm hoping as long as I'm breathing.'

Rob stood up. Tears were streaming down his face. He threw notes to the value of a hundred and fifty Euros on the table and grabbed her arm.

'Come on, let's get out of here. There's a park over the road. I need some air.' His voice was gruff with concern as the enormity of what she told him sunk in.

'Are you okay to walk? Will it be too cold for you?'

'Hey, I'm not dead yet, you know. 'Of course, I can, but I'm not sure I'll survive this death hold you've got on my wrist.'

Rob looked down at Ellie's arm to see a red mark forming under his fingers.

'Oh, my God, Ellie, I'm so sorry. I had no idea I'd hurt you. I'm so sorry.' He put his arm around her shoulders, asked the waiter for her coat and led her out of the restaurant.

She shook his arm off.

'Hey, Rob, don't. Don't do that to yourself, and don't do it to me. I'm still me, you know? Still Ellie, still here. I get a bit stiff, and I'm dropping things a lot, but I'm going to be a long time crippled. I'll be in a wheelchair at the end. You can have the job of chief-gimp-pusher.' Rob winced and smiled an apology at the seated diners who were staring again. 'I'll even buy you a chauffeur's uniform if you like, but don't bring on my dependence sooner than need be, eh?'

They walked out of the dining room, and the maître d' called them back.

'Excuse me, sir, you've left your, um—fungus.'

'Fungi! Fungi, you pompous fuck. You know, fun guy to be with.'

69

Rob couldn't believe his ears and was rooted to the spot with his mouth open. He had never heard Ellie talk like that. She grabbed him, and together they ran out of the restaurant, giggling like a pair of kids.

'Aw, you said fuck. I'm gonna tell Matt that you said the naughty word.'

For the next hour, they walked in the park, ate ice cream from a vending van, and Ellie spilt her heart to him about the other stuff—the worst part of the disease to date. She explained to Rob how she was going mad.

# Chapter Five

J ake whined.

His nose was against the bottom of the kitchen door, and he snuffled along the length of the gap between that and the floor. Jake was worried. He'd lift his head and sniff the air, but he'd drop back to scent the base again when he'd tasted it. He couldn't get very close to the smell, but this is where it was closest to him.

It was the not-Ellie smell. Jake has the not-Ellie smell in his nose a lot now. It doesn't go away for a long time even when he shakes his head; sometimes, it makes Jake sneeze. He smells it in the garden, under bushes, and even when he pees on the smell, it doesn't go. The not-Ellie smell is just like the Ellie smell. The same as the Ellie smell, but not Ellie. The Ellie smell is good, and the not-Ellie smell is bad. It isn't bad like white coat and needle man, but the bad that makes Jake's hackles rise. Jake isn't bad. Jake is a good boy.

Matt was enjoying himself. He'd vacuumed right through downstairs and polished the lounge. He'd cleaned the kitchen until it gleamed and prepared a lasagne for the evening meal.

On his way upstairs, he put the palms of his hands together and bowed his head low to Aphrodite. She was a solid bronze statue of the Greek goddess Ellie had fallen in love with in an exclusive gift shop on Corfu. The celestial lady lived on the table in the hall. Matt paid homage to her on his way upstairs.

He had his head in the bath and his bum in the air as he gave the bathroom a good freshen up. It baffled him why women made so much fuss about housework. It was satisfying. Then he remembered the festering pile of washing, throwing tentacles out in the nether regions of his own bedroom. He amended his thought to the fact that other people's housework was a bit satisfying. Sometimes.

As he laboured, he sang an old song from the turn of the century, 'I like my men like I like my coffee, hot, strong and sweet like toffee.' After several self-elected encores, he realised that the window was open, and he gave it up with a sheepish grin in the mirror. He opted for singing 'A Man's Gotta Do What a Man's Gotta Do.' It didn't have much in the way of melody, but it was a good manly song for a house-working bloke to be singing.

The bathroom finished, he gave it a squirt of peach air freshener with a flourish and admired his handiwork. In reality, the house looked much the same as when he started. Ellie kept it spotless, but it was a masterpiece on virgin canvas to him. Matt wasn't driven to have a go at things domestic, and he was proud of himself.

He was coming downstairs, still singing, when he heard the security filter on the front door scanning. It could only be Ellie home. Anybody else would have knocked. That's odd, he thought. She's only been gone an hour.

He stopped on the third step from the bottom, lint duster flung across his shoulder, and feather duster held out in front of him like a fencing foil. His other hand struggled with two spent toilet roll inners and a can of Mr Sheen. His surprise at Ellie being home stopped him from calling out to her. Ellie home at this time could only spell one thing. Trouble.

The door opened, and Ellie walked into the hall. She was the first to close her mouth, looking back towards the closed door and then at the kitchen, she met his eyes and stood her ground. She mimicked Matt's stance when she saw him on the stairs with his mouth open in surprise.

The first thing Matt was aware of was that Ellie was wearing different clothes from those she'd gone out in. The other thing that hit him was that she gave every impression of not wanting to be seen. She didn't expect him to be there, and the fact that he was displeased her. But more than that, she seemed almost—it was ridiculous, but Ellie looked scared of him. So many things flew through his brain, and one was how he'd yelled at her that morning. It was out of character for him to lose his temper. The tension and anguish had got to both of them.

'Just call me Mr Muscle,' he said, in an attempt to break the tension, brandishing his feather duster so that particles of dust twinkled in the weak sunlight of the hall. 'You're home early, love. Is everything all right?'

Ellie looked like a startled rabbit desperate for escape, but she recovered her composure and pulled her face into what was a forced smile. This was no Ellie smile, it was a weak imitation. Matt had been with her long enough to know the real thing. When Ellie smiled, the temperature rose with the warmth she shared, and the sun surrendered behind a cloud of defeat.

'Ellie, what's the matter? Talk to me. What's happened?' He stopped himself before adding, 'now.'

Still looking unsure, she smiled again and moved a couple of steps towards him. He opened his arms to her, and as she moved into his embrace, he noticed that she wasn't wearing the eternity ring that he bought for her after they had been together a year.

He'd been going to surprise her with an engagement ring, but Ellie said she wasn't ready when he'd hinted at them getting engaged soon. The diamond and sapphire eternity ring was a good compromise when he gave her it the previous year. Ellie was delighted and said that the ring, and its symbolism, was all she could ask for. Maybe she'd taken it off because she realised that eternity was a small measure of time, and what had seemed so very far away for them was approaching at a gallop. Matt was shocked to see that her ring wasn't on her finger. He thought about the moments just before she left. He was sure she was wearing it when she left the house to meet Rob. Where was it? Had she lost it? Sold it? Pawned it for crack cocaine? Something else wasn't right. She felt different in his arms, unyielding. It was as though she didn't fit him, yet she'd neither grown nor shrunk in the last hour and a half. Why wasn't she saying anything?

'Ellie, where's your ring?'

He felt movement and stood back to look at her. His mind registered two things. The first was the look of sheer hatred on her face, and the other thing he saw was the bronze Aphrodite statue inches from his head.

Matt swerved, and the bronze plummeted in an almighty swing. In swaying out of the way, he knocked Ellie off balance, and the impact of the blow was deflected and lost its power when it hit him. If he hadn't moved, he would have been killed.

As it was, Ellie's hatred of him was the last thing he was aware of as the lights flickered, dimmed, then went out altogether, taking with them the tremendous pain from the side of his head.

Matt opened his eyes and tried to raise his head. He was on the floor at the foot of the stairs. A fan of crimson speckling spread from the deeper ruby stain on the cream hall carpet. Ellie would be pissed about that. The carpet was ruined. Although Matt knew where he was, he had no idea how he got there. Ellie's statue lay beside him. He must have knocked it over when he—what? Fell? It was difficult to think with the pain in his head and his consciousness threatening to pack its bags and leave him again. Every time he tried to move, a wave of nausea slithered over him and left him feeling weak. He mustn't throw up on Ellie's carpet; she was already going to go mad about the blood. He tried to call out to her, but his mouth was dry. Blood had trickled from the wound in his head onto his lips. Some had already caked, and it tasted like the back of a tarnished spoon. He remembered Ellie went to meet Rob. Something had bothered him about a ring. Her eternity ring, where was it? He fingered the side of his head. The feeling of finger to raw nerve turned his digit into an electric cattle prod.

He licked his caked lips and grimaced as the disturbed blood came off in a congealing lump onto his tongue. He spat onto the carpet.

His voice was small, the sound not recognisable as his own. 'Phone, George,' he managed, the effort of speech making him dizzy. There were no sensors in the hall, and the phone connection wasn't made. He crawled to the study door and pushed it open. This time his voice was louder, but the sound from his mouth was alien to him. 'Phone, George. Number 999.'

He was weaker when the computer made the connection.

'Emergency services. Which service do you require?'

'I've had an accident. Need an ambulance.'

The darkness was more aggressive; it wanted to take him back to the world of sleep. Must stay conscious. He wouldn't give in to the dark. He was fighting it well until his memory came back with sticks and stones to beat him. He remembered Ellie's face full of hatred. He saw the bronze flying down to take his life, and he called the darkness back from its retreat and begged it to take him away.

'Sir? Are you there?'

Ellie tripped over the can of *Mr Sheen* lying behind the front door. The hall table had been knocked over, and Aphrodite lay on her side at the foot of the stairs. She stared at the red stain; her eyes followed its progress to the study. Three bloody fingerprints stained the door. There was no mistaking them for what they were. A groan began inside her and held the same note for a long time. She wasn't aware of the noise, only of the blood drawing her to the study. She pushed the door open, not knowing what she'd find on the other side. Everything was as it should be and in order. She felt no relief, only a wild, crazy panic. Her calm rationale was a herd of stampeding horses disturbed by an eagle's cry. The blood had no right to be in her home. She didn't invite it in. Think. What to do? Think, damn you. Ring Matt. Yes, that's what she should do. No, that's not right, I need to find out if the phone's been used.

Instead of asking for Matt's number, she instructed the computer to give her the last number called.

'Emergency services. Which service do you require?'

'Oh, no. No.' Ellie broke down and told the operator that she thought there'd been an accident. The cool, efficient voice on the other end of the phone tried to calm her but to no avail. The operator checked the log and confirmed that a man had been taken to St. Joseph's hospital from her address that afternoon. She told Ellie she had no further information, and Ellie ended the call without remembering to thank her. She was halfway out of the house before the operator finished speaking. 'Call end,' she screamed at the computer.

Ellie went into room three-sixteen, her face etched with worry and concern. Matt was propped up in bed, the left side of his head covered in a white dressing, blood seeping through the gauze. A nurse offered him water to wash down the pills that were his licence for a pain-free four hours.

'Oh Matty, love, what happened to you?' She rushed to the side of his bed and flung her arms around his neck, careful to avoid the bandage. Matt flinched away from her touch.

'Hello, darling,' he said with a tight smile. 'You came then?'

It was an odd thing for him to say, but she couldn't address it because the nurse spoke to her.

'He's had a nasty knock on the head, love. He needs to rest. No more than five minutes, please.' She left the room in a bustle of starchy efficiency.

The smile left Matt's face, and he pulled away from her, throwing her from him. His eyes were wide, and he didn't try to hide the look of revulsion on his face.

'Come to finish what you started, have you?' His lip curled in contempt as he spat the words at her. 'What the hell's wrong with you? You could have killed me. No, let's be honest, you tried to kill me. Didn't you?'

His voice rose, and although he was whispering so they wouldn't be overheard, he couldn't have instilled more bitterness or venom into his voice if he screamed the accusations at her.

Ellie recoiled. The anger fuelling the words pelted her with force enough, but the meaning behind them hit her with a second blow.

'Matt, love, they said you have a concussion. What are you saying? Do you think I did this to you? Don't be bloody stupid. You know that's not true. I love you. I'd never hurt you.'

Matt clapped his hands three times in a slow, exaggerated manner and winced as a new pain shot through his head with the movement.

'Clever, Ellie, very clever. An excellent performance from the dutiful girlfriend. What's the matter? Scared I've told them something? Don't worry, your secret's safe with me. I don't know what I've done to make you hate me. All I've ever done is love you, but don't worry, I get the message. Obviously, something was wrong with you, but this proves that you're a psycho, you bloody lunatic. As long as I live, I will never forget the look on your face when you brought that statue down on my head.' His voice lost its power as he whispered the last words she thought he'd ever want to say to her. 'Now fuck off out of my life. I never want to see you again.'

'But Matt, you're wrong.'

He turned his face, as white as the pillow he rested on, away from her and closed his eyes.

Ellie ran from the hospital, crying.

Rob and Gail dropped what they were doing to go to Ellie when she called them. Gail gathered her into her arms, and both women sobbed.

'I'm so sorry, I'm so sorry, sweetheart,' Gail kept repeating it. 'I can't take it all in. It's too much.'

Ellie comforted the other woman. After all, she'd had weeks to deal with her illness. Gail and Rob had it thrust on them that afternoon.

'How's Matt?' Rob asked.

'Not good, fractured skull and thirteen stitches. They're keeping him in overnight for observation. They don't think there's any danger of brain damage. It's just a precaution, they said. But Rob, he thinks I did it to him. How could he think that? I tried to tell him I was with you all afternoon, but he didn't give me a chance.'

'Shush now, don't cry. It'll be all right. I'll talk some sense into the big moron.' Rob had an arm around both women. 'It'll be fine. We'll explain everything to him, and when he's had a chance to sleep and get over any concussion and the shock, he'll be in more of a mind to listen. Don't worry, we'll sort it out.'

Matt rang Rob and asked to be picked up from the hospital the following morning. They had to wait an age in the waiting room until the consultant gave Matt the all clear and discharged him. Rob and Gail were the first ones to walk into the room. Rob shook Matt's hand. Matt's face broke into a relieved grin when he saw his friend.

'Hey, how's it going, mate?'

'Thanks for coming, Rob, Gail. I can't wait to get out of here.' His face set into a tight expression of determination as he saw Ellie crossing the room towards him. She had what she hoped was a warm smile on her face.

'Get that crazy bitch away from me. She's a bloody lunatic,' he ranted.

'Matt, love,' Ellie's voice was a lot calmer than she felt. 'We've come to take you home. Don't worry, we can explain everything. It'll be all right now.'

Matt refused to look at her. 'Rob, I am not going anywhere with her. I don't want to see her. Get her away from me.'

'Matt, mate, the bump to the old noggin's addled your brain; Ellie didn't do this to you. I know she didn't because she was with me all afternoon. Come on, let's get out of here, and we can sort this over a coffee at home.'

'I've told you, I'm not going anywhere with her.'

Ellie tried to get through to him. She was crying, and the patients in the other beds watched the scene with interest.

'Matty, I love you. Come home and talk to me. I've got everything ready for you.'

'What? You honestly think I'm going to sleep with you after everything that's happened?'

'I'll make the guest room up for you, then.' Ellie spoke softer, trying to grip her emotions and end the embarrassing scene.

Two nurses came onto the ward to see what the noise was about. Rob smoothed things over enough to get Matt out of the hospital and into the car by agreeing to take Matt back to their house instead of Ellie's. The nurses glared at Ellie, having gleaned enough of what was going on to put two and two together. Matt was a favourite patient. He was the best looking man on the ward, and the young nurses had fought over whose turn it was to attend him.

Although Matt agreed to stay with Rob and Gail, he wasn't happy about Ellie being invited and didn't want to be in the same car. The four-mile drive was endured in terse silence. Gail tried to make small talk, but the atmosphere swallowed her words before they'd left her mouth. She cut her losses and gave up. Ellie sobbed and felt that the few inches of space between her and Matt on the car's rear seat were an ocean that could never be crossed. Matt accused her of terrible things that she was incapable of doing, even if she'd had the opportunity or the desire. Apart from what he'd been through, he seemed to have forgotten her illness. How could he be so insensitive?

Gail made coffee and sat beside Ellie on the sofa, taking her hand and comforting her friend. Matt sat in an armchair as far away from Ellie as he could get and refused to look in her direction. He was the first to speak.

'That's it, you just sit there crying and gunning for the sympathy vote. Never mind that you tried to murder me. You know something, Ellie? You scare the pants off me. Can you imagine that? I'm scared shitless of my girlfriend because I don't know when you'll go off your head and do something crazy. You're a liability. I don't know you anymore.'

'Matt,' Gail said, 'how could you? You know Ellie's dying.'

'Ha, dying my arse. Who says she's dying? After all, we only have her word for that, don't we? Did she tell you she lied to me about the result date so I couldn't go? Bet she never told you about that, did she? How do we know she's not making that up as well?'

Ellie couldn't believe what she was hearing. This was the man she loved and wanted to share the rest of her life with. He'd seen Fielding with her twice in the past week; he knew she wasn't making her illness up but was so messed up that he was as nuts as she was supposed to be. Ellie felt she might be the sane one, and everybody else was ready for the dribbling house.

'Listen, mate,' Rob cut in. 'I don't know what the hell happened with you yesterday, but whatever it was, you've made a mistake. It had nothing to do with Ellie. She was with me the whole time that she was supposed to be at home caving your head in. What time did it happen?'

'I don't know. Sometime between half one and two, I suppose.'

'Well, there you go then. At that time, we were tucking into an excellent dinner while a snotty waiter with a fancy title looked down his nose at us.'

'Maybe she went to the loo.'

Ellie had tried to be reasonable, but she'd had enough.

'Oh right, so I left the table, drove the eight miles home, tried to kill you—for no apparent reason, though I could come up with one or two corkers right now—and then drove back to the restaurant. And I did all this in the time it takes to have a pee. That must be one helluva bladder I'm packing. I wouldn't get downhill of me if I need a leak. You'll be washed away in the current.'

'Right, but you forgot the bit about changing your clothes and taking off the ring I bought you, which I see you've put back on, by the way. I don't know how the bloody hell you did it, do I? Or why, for that matter. Especially why. I just know you did.' Matt looked at Ellie for the first time and saw her glance at her ring.

Rob spoke as though he was talking to a small child. He enunciated each word and tried hard to be calm and keep the irritation out of his voice.

'Listen, Pal, I'm telling you, Ellie was with me all afternoon. She wasn't at home. There was no time she was away from the table for more than a few minutes, and she didn't hurt you, Matt. You must have fallen down the stairs, and you're confused about what really happened, mate.'

Matt's eyes opened wide. 'Finally, I can see what can be the only other explanation. Of course, I'm such a bloody fool not to have seen it sooner. You're right, Rob, I was confused, but I'm not now. It makes perfect sense. Bravo for pointing it out to me, mate.'

'Eureka, we have a breakthrough,' Rob said, 'Glad you're seeing sense mate, now we can sort this out.'

'You're in it together. I know Ellie hit me because I was there and I saw her. You say she was with you in the restaurant all afternoon. And that's impossible for her to be in two places at once. You must be covering for her. You drove her home. You are, aren't you? You're in it together to get rid of me.'

Rob gave a mirthless laugh. He shook his head in disbelief. 'Oh, now you're being bloody ridiculous.'

'You're having an affair.'

'Bullshit.'

'Listen. It's the only thing that makes any logical sense. I hear what you're saying to me, but it's only words. What proof is there in a bunch of words? I know what I saw. I saw my girlfriend knocking me out and trying to kill me with a Greek goddess. So she wasn't with you the whole afternoon. Therefore, you must be lying to cover up for her. Why else would you do that other than because you're having an affair? I'm sorry, Gail.'

'Matt. I love Ellie. There you go, I've said it.' Rob gave a rueful smile across the coffee table to Gail. 'I'm probably a little bit in love with her too. Let's face it, what man wouldn't be? Everything about her is gorgeous. But I've been with Gail for seventeen happy years. I've invested my life in that woman sitting over there.' He pointed towards Gail and gave her a comforting wink. 'I've loved my wife through all the good and bad times we've had— and probably despite some of them, and I'm telling you, mate, she's the only woman for me. I love her. Do you know we were apart for three years while I was away on tours in the army? She sat by the telly, waiting for news from the frontline. We had trust, and her only worry was that I'd be killed out there. We've never once doubted each other. You're bang out of order, my friend and I can't believe that you'd even think that. We've been friends, Matt, and I'm insulted and want you to apologise to my wife when you come to your fucking senses.'

Rob and Gail looked at each other, and their trust was like a renewed wedding vow. Rob had spoken with the openness that can only be between two secure people in love.

Ellie raised her head. Her face was swollen with the tears she'd shed, but she was done crying. Now she was just plain red hot mad. Her grey eyes glinted like steel. She'd tried to be reasonable. Through whatever misguided reasoning, Matt believed that she'd hurt him. The trust between Rob and Gail touched her and brought home the fact that she and Matt didn't have that level of trust to rely on. If they had, she'd have been able to convince him of the truth, no matter what he thought he saw. She felt the familiar knot of temper rising. She tried to swallow it down, but it was too strong to be eaten whole.

'Okay, you're right, of course. Because you're always right, aren't you, Matthew? Couldn't possibly be mistaken. So, yes, all right, Rob and I are having an affair, and rather than just finish with you to be with him, it makes much more sense to kill you and leave you bleeding on my hall floor for the police to find lots of forensic evidence? But it doesn't matter because Rob and I have a flight booked for Hono-bloody-lulu at three o'clock.' She glanced at Gail, too angry to hold back. 'He's got his bags packed in the car's boot, ready for us to leave, Gail. But hey, you won't have time to be upset about it because he'll do you in before we go. I mean, that's the logical thing to do, isn't it? We'd do that if we're having an affair behind your back.' She looked back at Matt. 'Well, if that's what you want to believe, you go right ahead

Dickhead. I hope you and your bloody conspiracy theories and accusations will be very happy together. I'd just like to know which one of us is fucking crazy because this makes bugger all sense to me. So why don't you go and fuck yourself?'

Ellie was livid that Matt had put their friends in an awkward situation. He'd been jealous of her relationship with Rob in the past, but she thought that idea had been flushed down the pan a long time ago. All the love they shared was dissolving into a simmering pool of bitterness and distrust, and there was no way back or anything to stop what was happening to them. She felt more alone than she had ever felt in her life. There were no tears left to cry. She was exhausted and ashamed.

'This is getting out of hand,' Rob tried to calm the situation. 'Okay, you only have our word for it that nothing's going on between us. But Matt, everything else can be proven. You can go with Ellie to speak to her consultant about the illness if previous visits to him haven't convinced you. And we weren't the only people at that restaurant. Waiters will remember us. All you have to do is talk to them. We went for a walk in the park after making a pretence of eating. Neither of us was very hungry under the circumstances. We sat on a park bench in front of the snack kiosk. We drank several cups of horrendously strong coffee. The lady is bound to remember us. Don't just take our word for it, Matt. Ask. We can account for almost every minute of yesterday afternoon. We bought two ice creams with raspberry topping and sprinkles; that one will remember us too because she recognised Ellie and talked about her books. The woman insisted that we have two flakes each. Go and check it out. Everything I'm telling you is the truth.'

Matt dropped his head into his hands. Ellie sat in abject misery at the other side of the room. Rob was right, everything they said could be proven. If they had wanted an alibi, that was a crap one because Ellie couldn't have left for long enough without her absence being noticed. She had no reason to want him dead. They'd always been happy, and surely her illness couldn't account for becoming a psychotic madwoman overnight. Everything was muddled. Her thoughts wouldn't clear because she kept coming back to the same thing. Rob actually saw her hit him with the statue. It wasn't somebody who looked like Ellie and wore the same perfume. It was Ellie. But it couldn't be because Ellie was with Rob in a restaurant full of people somewhere else at the same time. But he said he saw her, the national bank saw her, her next-door neighbour saw her, the woman in the costume shop saw her, and all of them saw her in places and at times when she wasn't there. She looked over at him. She was so tired, miserable, and vulnerable.

'Ellie, no matter what, I can't stand to see you so upset. I'm sorry. I still love you. We have to find a way to sort out the craziness.'

The colour had drained from Ellie's face. It was too much for her. She said she felt unwell and could she be taken home, please.

Rob and Gail wouldn't hear of it. Gail helped her to the spare room to lie down.

It was dark when she woke up. She'd slept for hours. The day was gone, and the night was well in. She'd been partially undressed and covered with the quilt. The biggest surprise was the lean, naked body lying beside her. Matt stirred and came fully awake within a couple of seconds. He looked smiled, tightening his grip and pulling her body into him. He put his finger to her lips to shush her, then kissed her with all the love and gentleness he felt.

'Matt, I'm so sorry about everything. I didn't hit you. Please say you understand that.'

'Shush, baby, let's not talk about it anymore. I don't know what's happening. I know that I think I saw you. Maybe the concussion has mixed everything up in my mind, and I really did fall down the stairs and only imagined it. Maybe they sent an alien down to take your place. I don't know, but I know that I love you, and somehow, we'll sort this out, and I'll be there for you for as long as you need me.'

She cried, and they hugged and then later, sometime later, they made love.

# Chapter Six

The next couple of days passed without incident. On Thursday, Ellie insisted that Matt go back to his flat and back to work; he'd taken too much time off. She felt stifled, and they'd talked around the happenings of the last week until they were dizzy. When rational suggestion didn't explain things, their theories stretched to the more outlandish and bizarre. Although they laughed about it, Ellie was convinced she'd been taken over by a crazed psychotic alien, an evil spirit bent on destruction. She even believed she was having out of body experiences and turning into a twisted, homicidal maniac during the episodes.

After Matt left, Ellie went for a long walk with Jake, first up Hoad Hill and then around Ulverston market. She had her eyes peeled for trouble all the time. She felt she was being watched but told herself it was paranoia. She hadn't been able to settle to writing. Her hands were stiff and uncooperative, and her mind was restless and unwilling to concentrate. After writing a couple of hundred words in half an hour, she gave up in disgust and felt the need for a cleansing wind to blow her anxiety away. She wanted to walk in the countryside as often as she could—while she could. One day, she'd be restricted to a wheelchair in the garden. Jake was delighted at the prospect of the unscheduled walk and sniffed lots of doggie backsides that afternoon. Brief friendships were forged and forgotten as a new hedgerow came into view. There were so many good sniffs to be had.

The paranoia of walking through town unsettled her, and Ellie felt more uptight than when she left. As she opened her garden gate, she nearly turned away again. She couldn't face whatever horrors might wait for her on the other side of her front door, the same door that had always been safe and protective.

Everything was just as she'd left it.

On Thursday night, the shadows in the lounge were long. Ellie and Jake snuggled on the sofa together, but she was on edge. The room didn't feel cosy and warm. It was claustrophobic and in her face. The walls seemed to move in an inch every time she looked at them. Taking Jake out, the darkness closed around her as the walls had done at home. The moon was hiding behind black night-time clouds, the shadows longer. They looked more oppressive outside than indoors. Twice she heard footsteps in the night behind her. Within seconds her heart was thumping, and she was in a state of panic. Jake was nervous, picking up on her mood and growling low and deep in his throat. Both times it was only people going about their business. Ellie felt that there was no escape from her paranoia. It clung tight and followed her, even into sleep.

On the Thursday and Friday nights, she slept with her bedroom light on. She hadn't done that since she was a child. Her sleep was fitful and troubled. She woke feeling worn and irritable.

Saturday morning broke vivid and beautiful. It was one of those late October mornings reminiscent of the faded summer. One last rebellious splendour of autumn before it was bullied into retreat by winter's stronger, aggressive grip. The sun shone bravely to melt the morning frost, and the world was clean.

She felt an awakening of hope. Nothing had happened for two days and three nights. Maybe the nightmare that had stolen her life was passing. She couldn't do anything about the illness other than keep fighting, but the awful, ever-present feeling of danger and malice seemed to have passed. Ellie felt hope for a short but content future returning.

Matt was coming by. Although they'd kept in phone contact the last two days, she'd asked that he give her some space. Their relationship, though still intact, was fragile. They'd been tested, and both felt bruised and delicate. She missed him, and the realisation made her smile.

That evening, they decided they would meet providence with defiance. The night was to be part pleasure, part something else. It was decided by Ellie and against Matt's better judgment to go to Demons nightclub. They'd see if there were any clues to explain how one of their matchbooks had turned up in Ellie's lounge. It was an excuse to live a normal Saturday night, a night of forgetting and forgiving. Ellie was looking forward to it. It was so long since she'd felt strong enough to go out clubbing, but she wanted to conquer the world this morning. They'd take Jake to Matt's house on their way out and stay in Barrow. Ellie was excited to see him and felt happy in her new confidence.

Matt didn't scan his identity when he arrived. He rang the doorbell. Ellie felt sad at this glaring sign that things weren't right between them. Never mind, tonight, they would have time to work on that. Jake got to the door before her and whined, wagging his tail. Ellie had told him Matt was coming, and the dog had been watching the door for him and waiting.

Instead of using George to open the door, she answered it. Her irritation at him not using his entry access had passed, and it felt nice to open the door to her man in welcome. It felt like being taken back to the early days of their courtship when everything was new and exciting.

Jake's greeting almost battered the huge bouquet he held in his hand. Ellie stood back, smiling. She had no chance of getting a look in until Jake had been petted and calmed. A blurring of anxiety clouded her sense of peace as she remembered the last floral delivery to her home, but she suppressed the feeling before it insinuated its ugly self too far into her mind. She pushed away memories of her nightmare and refused to think about roses desiccating and a pistol. Nothing was going to spoil today, nothing.

'Hello, sexy,' she murmured, managing to separate man and dog, 'Are they for me?'

'Nah, I bought them for Greasy Gertie down the fish shop, but she said they make her sneeze, so you might as well have them.'

'Oh, that Gertie has no class. They'll be far more appreciated by Jake and me.'

Matt left after a lunch that Ellie prepared while he showered. Their intense lovemaking had heightened the good mood Ellie had woken in. She sat in her dressing gown for a long time. For the first time in weeks, she indulged in peaceful reflection. She would never be complacent about her illness or the death sentence hanging over her, but she accepted it. And whatever the kneejerk reactions were that'd plagued her since she was given the results, they were in the past. She had a future to look forward to. And Ellie's future was all the sweeter because it had a shorter lease than most.

She was sitting at the table when the doorbell rang. Damn, she thought. It was Saturday afternoon, and she'd forgotten that Jamie Matthews was due to arrive at one-thirty. Jamie was a young lad from the town who came to help around the garden every Saturday for two hours. With some embarrassment at her state of undress, Ellie used the computer to let him in.

'In here, Jamie,' she shouted when she heard him taking his boots off in the hall. She usually made him a drink, and they discussed what she wanted him to do before he made a start. The only difference this week was that Ellie was sitting in a short satin dressing gown and was aware that she was unwashed since she'd made love to Matt.

Jamie Matthews' seventeen-year-old eyes almost jumped out of his head when he walked into the dining room and saw Ellie. In his youthful ineptitude, he couldn't disguise the body scan he took of her or that his gaze rested a split second too long on her exposed thighs. She pulled the dressing gown around her as firmly as she could and was furious with herself when she felt her cheeks burning. Jamie couldn't meet her eyes and shuffled from foot to foot as he examined his socks. He was fixated with the small hole that his right big toe played peek-a-boo through. His face was crimson, right into his hairline. Ellie couldn't imagine what he was thinking and prayed to the god of purity that he didn't think she was sitting like that for his benefit.

'Right, Jamie,' she adopted as normal a voice as possible under the humiliating circumstances. 'You're going to have to sort yourself out with a drink this afternoon. I've had a headache all morning and stayed in bed.' She forgave herself for the outright lie. 'I'm going for a shower; help yourself to something to drink and a biscuit. Maybe you could begin by going over the lawns, please. I know they were only done a fortnight ago, but we've had a lot of rain, and they could use a tidy up.' And they aren't the only thing, she thought, as she ran a hand through her tousled hair. It caused her dressing gown to open, revealing to Jamie, who had felt it safe to look up, the crescent of her left breast. Ellie beat a hasty retreat, knowing that the dressing gown only just covered her bottom and the very tops of her legs. Oh my God, she thought, the poor lad must be terrified.

In truth, terror wasn't the uppermost thought in Jamie Matthews' mind at that moment. His thoughts were wholly to do with concealing the movement in the front of his trackies.

Ellie felt her cheeks returning to their normal hue as the needles of warm water pounded into her naked body, her mind wandered to the young gardener as she soaped and stimulated the blood cells with vigorous lathering. They didn't make lads in the Jamie Matthews mould when she was seventeen. Her male peers had been pimply cretins, with buckteeth and halitosis. Jamie was a young hunk. He was well past the six-foot average height. Lads were wearing their hair longer these days, and Jamie's dark brown eyes always peered self-consciously from beneath a shaggy fringe that framed his sun-browned face. Jamie probably had the wrong impression of her completely.

She just hoped that he didn't say anything to his mother. Or worse, the lads he hung about with.

Jamie tried to concentrate on mowing the lawns. Ellie was a good boss, and he was grateful for the extra Bitcoins that his Saturday job gave him. The new Government paid for his tuition and living expenses at college, but he still had to pay for his course materials. It was more than just job satisfaction, though. The truth was that it was an excuse to be near Ellie Erikson. They all fancied her. Pete Harvey even thought she fancied him because she had asked him the time at the bus stop one day.

Jamie knew Ellie was way out of his league, being a famous writer and older and what with her fancy solicitor boyfriend, but he still had the hots for her in a big way. All the lads did. Jamie was a virgin. Despite his good looks and confident manner in most things, he was shy and unsure around girls. They were a species he couldn't fathom, and Jamie was, by nature, wary of anything he didn't understand. He had a good body, he knew that and he had the rough, unkempt looks that girls go for, but none of that was an automatic license to self-confidence. He liked sport and computers and gaming, he understood those things. The offside rule was easy to understand, girls weren't. Jamie was clumsy around them, but he'd always been able to talk to Ellie. She was different.

The smaller front lawn was almost done. His balls were heavy, and his cock throbbed, despite forcing himself to think about his coursework as a distraction. He turned his thoughts to the national failings of the government and its totalitarian regimes for social reform. He couldn't settle to work after being taunted by Ellie's naked tit almost flopping out in front of his face, and trying to force himself to think about politics wasn't working. He carried the mower to the back of the house.

He eyed the garden shed. It wouldn't be the first time he'd nipped in for a quick wank. Risky, though, he'd almost got caught last time. Well, the alternative wasn't looking good, either. She'd be out of the shower soon and coming to talk to him. He knew that, unless he did something to ease his discomfort before then, the second he saw her, his friendly mate would be swelling up to say hello. He moved the lawnmower out of sight of what he assumed was Ellie's bedroom window and unbolted the shed. He checked that she wasn't coming out and went inside.

Opening one of the folded garden seats, he sat down. His cock was really throbbing now. He could feel a small wet patch making his boxers sticky. He freed his penis from the front of his sports pants and gripped it in his hand. His hand went straight into speed wank, not bothering to ease up the tempo. Another minute and he would've been shooting the low shed ceiling, but his eyes came to rest on the set of ladders running the length of one wall of the shed. He looked through the shed window and into what he thought was Ellie's bedroom, imagining what it would be like to look inside.

His voyeuristic fantasy took on a realism slant. He could have the ladder up against the ivy next to the window within a couple of minutes. But what if she was already out of the shower and looking towards him when he set the ladder up? Was that a chance he was willing to take? Damned right it was. It had gone from teenage masturbation fantasy to the decision to actually do it in a matter of seconds, yet he wasn't aware of making the transition. He was so engrossed in his plan that the sexual urges that had driven him to action were, for the moment, forgotten. His cock lay neglected in his hand, still turgid but no longer on the point of release.

On his way around the path with the ladder, he wondered what he should do if he got caught. What would he say? What would she say? Maybe she'd like to think of him spying in her window at her and wanking for her. Maybe she'd get off on it. His penis twitched as he drew level with the rhododendron bush, and his breathing accelerated again. Checking that the ladder was anchored in the flowerbed, he climbed. This was the moment if any, when he'd be caught. Once he was safely up the ladder and in position, he could wait for her to come out of the bathroom. Everything rested on the fact that she hadn't come out yet, if she had, then the slightest noise might alert her to activity outside her window.

He was sweating as he reached the top and peered into the bedroom. He had one pang of, 'What if I've got the wrong room', before his hope and faith in the god of south-facing sunlight was confirmed. It was her bedroom, all right. He almost choked on the knot of excitement that rose from the pit of his groin to lodge somewhere in the region of his throat. Although his breath was leaving his body in loud rasps, he wasn't getting enough oxygen to his lungs. He'd never done anything so wrong. He felt daring and perverted, and that only added to the excitement. He wanted her to catch him and would like to expose himself to her.

While he waited, he peered into her bedroom. The back garden was enclosed so there was no danger of him being seen by interested neighbours or anybody else. The not-Jake-proof fencing saw to that.

Christ, that room was girlie, but it was raunchy, too. A white duvet with delicate purple flowers dominated the bed. A black wrought iron headboard and loads of matching candlesticks made the room feminine but with a kinky gothic theme. It was a sexy bedroom. He imagined being tied to the headboard with his belt as Ellie gave him oral sex. His cock reacted so violently that he almost came in his boxers without even having to stroke himself. There was a dress laid out on the bed. A simple, silver cotton dress with thin straps, it looked short, and Jamie tried to imagine what Ellie would look like in it, but all his mind could see was her taking off the dress and letting it drop to her feet to expose her creamy-brown nakedness.

The door was opening. Oh shit. This was it. Jamie pulled back to ensure that he was concealed behind the overgrown ivy. His view of the far side of the room was impaired, but he could see the rest of the bedroom perfectly. Dear God, please don't let her close the curtains. Ellie walked into the room with a short towel covering her from above the nipple to well above the knee. She had another towel on her head.

She went to the bed and leaned over, taking the towel from her head to rub her hair dry. She was in profile to Jamie, and he could see all of her leg and just the merest hint of paler buttock beneath the other towel. His left hand slid down his trousers, and his right tightened his grip on the ladder for support. He stroked his cock slowly, he wanted to savour every moment of this and hoped it wouldn't be all over for him—and indeed all over him, too quickly.

Ellie straightened up and threw the damp towel on the bed where it wouldn't land on her dress. She ran her hands through her hair, and then came the moment Jamie had been longing for. He'd fantasised about this so many times, and it was being played out for him. He felt his balls boiling and had to take his hand off his cock and grab the ladder with both hands otherwise, he would have come within another few seconds. He enjoyed that he'd left his dick hanging out of the front of his pants, and he pressed it against one of the ladder's rungs, loving the feel of the wood pressing into his erection. He was holding his climax back but couldn't resist rocking his pelvis so he rode the wood.

Ellie took the towel from around her body. She was magnificent. Jamie had never seen a naked woman before. His fourteen-year-old sister didn't count, and he'd only seen bits of her when he peered through the crack in her door. Ellie was stark naked, in front of her mirror and in full view.

She rubbed her body with the towel, and her tits jiggled in time to the movement. Jamie moaned, he couldn't take much more of this. The head of his dick couldn't throb any harder if it had been hit by a hammer. It took an almost super-human effort not to grab hold of it and wank himself silly for the last three seconds that he could hold out. He may never see this again, and he wanted it to last. It would have been nice if her tits had been bigger, but apart from the size, they were perfect. She was perfect. His eyes travelled down her body to her partially shaven pussy. He imagined her spread-eagled on the bed with his cock hammering into her, all the way up to his balls. This was the best moment of his life to date. Better even than seeing Jane Prescott piss her knickers when he put a spider down her back in biology class. Better even than seeing Black Cyber in concert.

Ellie was dry, and Jamie was disappointed to see her reach for the silver dress. Wouldn't it be amazing if she'd frigged herself off in front of the mirror? He imagined the moment when they'd come in unison. He'd had to get a move on, if she was getting dressed, she might be downstairs in a minute, he thought, grabbing his cock again and stroking faster.

Ellie went to a drawer and took out a white thing that looked like a pair of panties. It was a little triangle of white silky material with a couple of bits of elastic at the back. Jamie wished he could feel it against his cock. He wondered how hard it would be to steal one. She slipped her legs into the thong, and Jamie upped the speed of his wanking a notch. Her arse hung out of the fucking thing. It was the most awesome sight, like a fucking moon, split in the middle. God, her arse looked tight and smooth. He imagined sinking his teeth into the softness of her bum-cheek and groaned. When she turned around, he could see the impression of the little bit of golden hair that showed through the white material. It was as sexy as hell. Jamie was close. He couldn't hold out much longer.

She slipped the dress over her head and studied herself in the mirror. Jamie looked at her, too. She didn't put a fucking bra on, Jeeezus fucking Christ. Her nipples stuck out through the thin material of the dress. They were upturned, and there wasn't even a hint of sagging. She kept in good shape. Jamie worked out and liked to see it in a woman, especially a good-looking woman like Ellie.

She seemed pleased with her dress and grabbed it from the bottom. In a fluid movement, she dragged it from mid-thigh to right over the top of her head. There was no stopping it this time. He pulled on his cock, panting and felt the spunk rising up his shaft, ready to lubricate his blurring hand and a good portion of the dark green ivy. He bit his lip to stop himself from crying out as it jerked out of his cock in a six-spurt fountain. 'I'm coming, Ellie, I'm fucking coming,' he whispered, imagining her watching him, though he was well covered by the plants. 'Fucking awesome,' he whispered when he felt his penis diminishing in his sodden hand.

He realised he had better get away. He was taking a chance guessing that she'd dry her hair properly before coming downstairs, which would give him time to get rid of the ladder and clean himself up. Jamie reckoned he knew women pretty well, his mother and sister wouldn't dream of coming downstairs after bathing without drying their hair first. He was banking on Ellie being the same.

As he wiped his hands on his pants, he watched as she took the pantie thing off and turned to her drawers. She took out another thong and slipped it on. Downstairs, Jake barked. Oh shit. Somebody was coming. What if it was the boyfriend? He'd pretend to be cutting the ivy. Would he buy that? Oh shit.

Ellie heard Jake and stopped halfway through, slipping into a pair of cut off jeans. She listened but heard nothing and put on the shorts. Jake stopped barking, and Jamie breathed a sigh of relief. It didn't look as though there were any visitors, just that stupid dog freaking out over nothing.

Ellie was facing the window when she straightened to do up her zip. Jamie had to wait until she turned around to move. He needed her to be a hairdryer freak. He would be out of luck and out of work if she let it dry naturally. But hell, it would be worth all the shit he'd get off his mother. Ellie was finished zipping up, and Jamie looked for an escape when the wind was forced out of his lungs by what he saw next. He couldn't believe his eyes. And there was nothing comedic in the fact that he nearly fell off the ladder in shock.

His eyes had widened into huge saucers, and his mouth hung open, unable to scream. He didn't know what to do.

Ellie had walked into the bedroom. Her hand was raised above her head. The blade of a six-inch kitchen knife glinted in the streaming afternoon sunlight. But that couldn't be. Ellie was standing by the bed, pulling on an orange halter-neck top with a bright yellow sunflower on the front.

Jamie's mind was processing what was unfolding in the room he was peeping into. It was a direct result of being a seventeen-year-old boy with the body of a man and the mental capacity of a trained chimp. As most lads of that age were, his first thought was for his own predicament. Here he was stuck up a freaking ladder with his dick out while his boss was about to be—murdered?

As that last word seeped into his brain, he realised that he had to do something. Jamie rationalised that a slap on his tired wrist for being a sick pervert, which was perfectly acceptable in teenage lads, was not in the same league as being hacked to death by your evil twin. Ellie had never mentioned that she had an identical twin, especially one that might pop up out of nowhere with a fucking big knife to kill her when a lad indulges in innocent masturbation. Information was flashing through Jamie's mind in a manner that was making him feel sick. Less than two seconds had elapsed since the woman had come into the room. While Jamie had to think harder than pleased him, Ellie II had only taken three stealthy footsteps towards his Ellie. What if it was the other way round, though? What if the woman by the bed was not his boss, and his boss was a fucking mad, murdering maniac?

Two more steps, and the woman with the knife would be within reach of Ellie. Oh shit, do something.

Galvanised into action, Jamie pulled the elasticised waistband of his pants up over his diminished boyhood.

He leaned out as far as he could on the ladder and hammered on Ellie's bedroom window gesturing for her to look behind her and screaming a warning.

'Ellie, turn around. She's going to get you!'

The moment was freeze-framed. For that solitary, de-fined-from-all-the-rest, moments in time, everything stopped. Perhaps it was a mere blip of a second, or maybe they all petrified for three weeks. It made no odds. Time stopped.

Ellie looked up from dressing. She had her arms in the top to pull it over her head, her tits jiggled without constraint. Jamie didn't even notice. She saw him and dropped her hands to cover herself. Her eyes widened to ape Jamie's, and her mouth made an O, making her look like a blow-up doll.

The other Ellie saw Jamie at the same time. She was level with Ellie, and her arm raised with the knife glinting in the sunlight. Her expression differed from Ellie's, whereas Ellie's mouth made an O, the other one's face closed down. Only the eyes of all three players had the same startled look. The eyes were the giveaway of fear.

The second Ellie was the first to break the petrifying spell. She dropped the knife and turned to flee. The Ellie Jamie assumed was his boss, heard the commotion and turned. She locked eyes with her twin in the second of stillness before the woman ran. The dropped knife was the only movement in the tableaux. Ellie drew air into her lungs to scream.

The knife was falling through the air, and Ellie II turned.

The blade thudded louder than expected as it hit the carpet. It bounced once before lying at Ellie's feet, a steel-tongued serpent to hew her body into tattered layers. Ellie screamed.

Jamie stared.

Ellie II ran to the door. Jamie heard her clattering down the stairs, and she knocked a Lloyd Loom chair over to hamper Ellie's pursuit as she left.

Jake barked and threw his body against the kitchen door, desperate to get out. The not-Ellie smell was bad.

It was pandemonium, barking dogs, screaming women, nosy neighbours coming in the front gate to see what the noise was about.

Jamie scrambled down the ladder, and Ellie scrambled into her top as fast as she could wrestle with material and neck fastenings.

And the other Ellie was flying out of the door and down the path, knocking Mr Harry Jackson on his geriatric backside, in the process.

Jamie was almost down the ladder when he missed the sixth rung from the bottom and landed in a heap on the floor. He jumped to a standing position, but a bolt of white-hot pain shot through him when he put weight on his right foot. He'd twisted his ankle when he fell, but ignoring the pain, he gave chase across the garden and into the street, limping on his injured leg.

Ellie was last to leave the house. She caught up with Jamie halfway down the road. There was nobody in sight and a choice of several roads the woman could have taken.

Ellie yelled. 'Let Jake out.'

Although she yelled at nobody in particular, Harry Jackson was closest to the house and in Ellie's eye-line when she shouted.

'Eh?' said Harry, rubbing his back and checking himself for injuries, seeing as nobody had bothered to stop and help him up. Two of them, two of the bloody blonde tarts from next door. No wonder I can't keep up with it all, he thought.

'Hey, she knocked me over. I fought in the Tora....'

Jamie was in trouble, the swelling already ballooning his ankle to twice its normal size, and the daft old bastard from next door was no help. Ellie ran back to the house.

Jake had never been an obedient dog or a dog with a great deal of understanding. You said, 'Sit,' and he jumped, 'Lie down,' and he licked while still following the former command of sit. But the moment Ellie flung open the kitchen door and shouted, 'Jake find,' he was off. He understood danger as well as humans. In fact, he understood it better because he could smell it. He tore off down the street in the direction the woman had taken.

Jake was gone ten minutes while Ellie tried to follow, but she lost him. Jake liked nothing better than to escape. He'd run for miles until Ellie got the car out to track him down. Sometimes he was out for hours with no road sense and a personality too friendly for his own stupid good.

This time, however, he came home quickly. Jake was miserable. He slunk in the front door and rolled his soft, brown eyes towards her.

Jake was a bad dog. He had lost the one that was Not Ellie. He ran fast, but the big, red thing with lots of people and wheels ran faster. Jake was tired and went back home to tell Ellie he was a bad dog.

Ellie was just putting coffee on the table for Jamie and Harry when Jake came back. She'd called Matt and the police and waited for them to arrive while she made a huge fuss of Jake and told him what a big, brave boy he was.

The critical fact was that the world was crazy, not Ellie. This time, three of them had seen the other woman who looked just like her. She felt terror at what happened but also an overriding feeling of relief that she was as sane, at least, as the miserable Mr Jackson. Knife-wielding lookalikes could be fought— but madness had no form to battle with. Ellie was scared to death but felt strong, knowing that her mind hadn't deserted her.

# Chapter Seven

S he stood in front of the cracked dressing table mirror, brushing out her blonde hair. The brush swiped aggressively, and her hair lacked lustre and was dull and motionless as the air swept through it. Her grey eyes stared back with a hard coldness that made them look steely and brutal.

'I'll get you, you bitch.'

She yelled it aloud, and it echoed in the under-furnished bedroom that only had small squares of unmatched carpeting on the floorboards for warmth.

'You might have escaped this time, but I'll get you, and your pathetic dog, and your snotty bastard of a boyfriend, too. I'll get you all and make you suffer. I'm going to make you die slowly for what you did to me. That was my life. My life.'

Her voice rose to a crescendo on the last four words, then dropped to a sibilant whisper as she added, 'And I'm going to take it back from you, just like you stole it from me. I hate you, and I hate your face. Before you die, I'm going to take your face away. You should never have taken it. I'm going to cut you, Ellie Erikson. Cut you and slice you and disfigure you. I'll hurt you, hurt you, hurt you. You are not me. You are not me, Ellie Erikson.'

She stepped backwards and flung the hairbrush at the mirror with all the force her hatred could summon. The already cracked and aged glass shattered and fell in a glittering shower at her bare feet. She was oblivious to the shards coating the bare piece of floorboard and moved from one foot to the other, ranting and swearing at her kaleidoscope reflection in what was left of the shattered mirror.

'Twenty-seven years you stole from me. Twenty-seven long years I watched you live your happy life, the life that was mine, and I was imprisoned, denied everything but what I was fed of your life, the life that was stolen from me. You sit in your fancy house, with your fancy life and your posh boyfriend. How many times have you felt guilt over what you took from me? I've read your books, Ellie Erikson. They forced me to read them. They made me. That'd surprise you, wouldn't it? Me, reading your books, the words you wrote after you stole my life. Did you ever once think I might read your pathetic stinking books? Did you? Well, they're a pile of shit. So there. I read your books, and I watched your life from a screen in the whitewashed room. And what did you ever do to get me out of there? Nothing.'

With her fury spent, she looked at the ruined mirror, and her eyes dropped to the dressing table. She had bought a vanity set for one Euro at a second-hand shop. In a pathetic attempt to make the hovel more homely, she had laid out the items with care on the top of the dressing table, a brush with somebody else's hair mingling with hers between the bristles, a hand mirror and comb and a matching powder puff. The items were old fashioned, somebody else's junk, but they were doing her a turn, for now, until she took back everything that was rightfully hers.

She looked at her most treasured possession. It took up all of the space on the vanity unit. It was ugly and wrong and yet perversely fitting, sitting, proudly, amongst the squalor. It was an unbelievably lucky find. It was risky stealing it. It was there, waiting for her, a gift from God, hers for the taking. Providence led her to waste a couple of hours in the heritage museum, and fate had taken the curator away to answer the phone. There were two on display, one open, gaping for the visitors to be horrified. The other one had been at rest, lying beside the first, its great mouth, full of brutal teeth, closed, at rest, sleeping. She took it and did her best to hide it underneath her jacket, but the end had stuck out and banged against her knees, bruising them as she ran. The man in his office never even saw her leave. But she took flight anyway and didn't stop running until she was back in the safety of her squalid hole. She couldn't wait to show the poacher's snare to the bastards.

'I hate you, Eleanor Erikson—and I hate your fucking dog.'

She looked around the tawdry bedsit, aware of her surroundings for the first time. The dirty cups left to go sour in the sink, the junk-room furniture slung in haphazardly by an uncaring landlord. She could have afforded better with the money that she'd stolen from Eleanor, but this enabled her to melt into the lower-class, bedsit-land culture of the town. The only place where people didn't ask questions, and neighbours weren't neighbourly. The beauty of it was that it was only four miles from the home of her nemesis.

She slumped on the bed with the stained mattress and dirty grey sheets used by countless others and said in the small voice of a hurt little girl, 'I hate you, Ellie Erikson.'

She sat for a long time on the tattered and cigarette-burned bedspread. When her fury left her, she rocked. She crossed her legs as she swayed and sang a nursery rhyme.

*Miss Polly had a dolly that was sick, sick, sick.*
*She called for the doctor to come quick, quick, quick.*
*The doctor came around with his bag and his hat*
*And he knocked at the door with a rat-a-tat-tat.*
*He looked at the dolly, and he shook his head*
*And he said to Miss Polly, 'Put her straight to bed.'*
*He held her down and gave her a pill, pill, pill*
*And forced her to follow his will, will, will.*

She repeated the rhyme in a sing-song voice until the moon shone through the window, and the shadows grew long in the room's corners.

# Chapter Eight

The Scenes of Crime team did their job well. Every surface was dusted for prints, every fluff-ball, fibre, and follicle bagged and labelled as possible evidence. Everything in the bedroom had been photographed from every possible angle, and Ellie's world was covered in a film of dirty black grime.

She was gripping Matt's hand and window gazing at the dining room table. Chief Inspector Morgan fired the same question at her, in a different form, for the umpteenth time.

Her mind drifted in an unconscious effort to block out the attack. She focused on the thoughts of Jamie and Harry Jackson. They'd been filtered into the lounge and sat on her settee, drinking her tea and eating her chocolate biscuits.

Huh, one's a juvenile peeping tom and the other a cantankerous old bastard whose only pleasure in life is making himself, and anybody else in a three-mile radius, miserable.

Today, however, these two people were akin to glowing demigods in her eyes. She could forgive them anything because they had seen her.

Punch and Judy, as Ellie thought of police constables Woods and Ferguson, were interrogating them. Jackson had plenty to say, and Ellie could hear his droning monotone drifting through as she watched a magpie pulling up worms from the lawn. Jamie Matthews was terrified. His first thought when he heard the police, and even worse, Matt, were on their way, was one of flight. Sitting there, his cheeks rosy with shame, was the last place he wanted to be. Various threats were used to make him stay put for initial questioning. The relevant two being the old, 'We can do this here, or formerly at the station. Which do you prefer?' And, 'If you don't help us, sir, we can, and will, place you under arrest on a public indecency charge.'

Jamie had little choice but to sit, disgraced and sullen. He answered the less humiliating of their questions with honesty and a good eye for detail and squirmed at the intimate ones. As he spoke, he watched Harry Jackson munch through twelve biscuits until the plate on the coffee table was empty apart from a few scattered crumbs.

'Bloody disgusting,' the old man said. He sprayed half-chewed chocolate digestive over the three other people in the room.

'In my day, you'd have been packed off to war, laddie, no choice in the matter. You'd have had little time for playing with yourself then. Had to go to war, we did.'

This was not strictly true. National conscription ended nearly thirty years before Jackson's day. However, it was the lead-in Harry had been waiting for to boast about his service in Tora Bora.

Ellie heard it all while she shut off her own police attack in the form of questions. She rubbed her fingertips together, trying to remove the ugly staining from her hands. She and

112

Matt were fingerprinted so they could be eliminated from the investigation. The magpie flew away, and her fingers gave her something to focus on so she didn't have to concentrate on the probing eyes of the Chief Inspector. The words he repeated like a mantra floated away on the magpie's tail. She wasn't thinking about the answers she gave to his questions. He had asked, and she had answered the same ones twenty times. She'd told them everything she knew, and her mind was shutting down. She didn't want to think, so she answered without interest. Morgan may have been trying to trip her up, to contradict herself on previous replies. Or maybe he just wanted to squeeze every memory from her while it was still fresh. Whatever his reasoning, Ellie answered quietly and truthfully, never wavering from her first answer.

No, she didn't know her attacker. Yes, it would seem that she might be an unknown twin sister. No, she hadn't touched the knife. No, her mother had never spoken about another daughter. She was an only child and always had been as far as she was aware. No, of course, she didn't have a sibling vendetta with her sister. How could she? She didn't know about her existence until all this started. Yes, she was aware that this was a serious accusation. No, she didn't know where her attacker might be. Yes, she was sure she never touched the knife. Yes, no, yes, no, no, no, yes.

Morgan scanned the used pages of his notebook and made a show of looking puzzled. There was no point in Ellie thinking about his tactic or procedure. She had nothing to hide and hardly flickered when he told her he was trying to catch her out in a lie.

'I'm about to give you a hard time, Miss Erikson, and I have no idea why.'

'Okay.'

'Okay? You don't care about what happened to you, love? Is there something you want to tell me?'

'Inspector, my girlfriend's been to hell and back. I think she needs to lie down.'

'I'm sorry, Mister High, I won't keep you much longer. Miss Erikson, apart from the obvious, that a murderous twin is floating in the ether, my instinct tells me something is off about this scenario. What are you withholding? I know there's something?' Chief Inspector Morgan had learned to trust his gut feelings over the years. They didn't tend to be wrong.

'I've told you everything a dozen times.'

'Okay, Miss Erikson, can we go back to an incident reported on Monday, the twentieth of October, please? Officers Woods and Ferguson attended a disturbance at this address. A Mr Harold Jackson claimed that after complaining about loud music coming from your home, you abused him and made threats against his wellbeing. Would that be correct?'

'It is, but I can explain.'

'And that's the same Mr Jackson whose sitting in the other room, is it?'

'Yes, but you see, it wasn't me.'

Morgan held up a hand to silence her, and she bit down on her lip, feeling like a little girl standing before an irate headmaster.

He rubbed the tip of his pen across the side of his temple and pondered his notes.

'It says here, Miss Erikson, and I quote, "I don't know what's happening to me. Nothing makes sense anymore. I'm accused of doing things I don't remember doing." Do you remember saying this, Miss Erikson?'

'No. Yes, I'm not suffering amnesia. Look, you've twisted it out of context. You see, I received some bad news, I have an illness, and I put my odd behaviour down to that. I added that while I was supposed to be raising hell at home, I was talking to a shop assistant in the middle of town. So I couldn't have been here, could I? But now it all makes sense. It wasn't me doing those things at all—it was her.'

Ellie felt detached from her body. She listened to her rambling and sounded confused, even to her own ears as the jumbled words poured from her mouth.

'"And I put my odd behaviour down to that,"' Morgan repeated.

He let the silence run on too long, and without him having to, it said he wasn't buying her story.

'This is the way I see it, Miss Erikson.'

'Bloody hell. I've told you three times. Eleanor, my name is Eleanor.'

'I put it to you, Miss Erikson, that you seem a little bored. I mean, stuck in this house all day, with not much to do but write your novels. Maybe you crave a little attention, want something to spice your life up a bit, something to remind you that you're an important person. Perhaps, if news of you being stalked by a crazed twin sister hit the papers, you'd sell more copies of your books, eh? Boost the dwindling sales a bit? Now, I wonder if that thought's occurred to you, too?'

Morgan glanced from Ellie to Matt and as he goaded her and watched Matt's temper rising.

'How dare you,' Ellie, had two points of furious colour rising to her cheeks. Matt cut her off and yelled at the Chief Inspector.

'Right, Inspector, you've gone far enough. My—Miss Erikson has been through too much. She's a sick woman and isn't strong enough to take this bullying. Can't you see how tired she is? Some psychopath has just tried to kill her. Instead of hounding Ellie, get out and catch this woman.' He glared at the other man. 'And when you do, Inspector, you can charge her with a serious attack on me. No, in fact, you can charge her with trying to fucking murder me.' He scowled at Morgan, who met his gaze with cool reserve as he looked at the healing wound on Matt's head.

'I was coming to the attack on you, Mr high, but as you've brought it up. Let me understand you correctly, Mr High. You are saying, are you not, that the same woman assaulted you?'

'It was more than that. She hit me over the head with a bronze statue and almost killed me. If I hadn't deflected the blow with my arm, I wouldn't be sitting here now. Now, do you see how serious this is?'

'Oh, I never doubted the seriousness of the accusation, Sir. I merely want to ascertain the facts and ensure that I have everything down correctly. Now then, this blow to the head that almost killed you did you report it to us?'

'No.'

'I see. A woman tries to kill you with a brass ornament, and you don't bother to report it. Isn't that a little—odd?'

'Bronze, Inspector, the ornament was bronze, a limited edition.'

Morgan coughed, but Ellie saw the smirk. 'Oh, do forgive me, Mr High, my mistake. You didn't report being hit with a limited edition bronze statue to the police? Why?'

Matt realised the trap, and his voice dropped to a low mumble.

'Well, at the time, I thought it was Ellie.'

Ellie lowered her head into her hands and groaned.

Morgan feigned shock as he looked from Matt to Ellie and back again.

'Pardon? I didn't quite catch that, Mr High. Did you say it was Miss Erikson that tried to kill you? Why was that, sir?'

'I know it wasn't Ellie, now. It was this lookalike person.'

'Miss Erikson's long lost twin sister?'

'Well, whoever the woman is, yes.'

'I see,' said Morgan.

'Look, Inspector. Two witnesses in the lounge have seen this woman. Why don't you talk to them if you don't believe us?'

'Oh, I will, Mr High, rest assured of that. I think I have everything that I'm going to get for now. I've been in the force twenty-five years, and something doesn't smell right. My policeman's instinct tells me there's more going on. It doesn't add up, and all this crazy twin stuff's too convenient, too made to fit. I don't like it.'

'We're not doing cartwheels about it ourselves.' Ellie's tone was vacant, but it showed she was taking some of it in.

'I admire your guts. I see sincerity when you meet my eyes, and I'm impressed by your defiance. I've interviewed hundreds of liars over the years. They say I have a nose for them like a scent hound with blood. But you look as though you believe everything you say. I'd lay money on you sailing through a

117

polygraph. No, don't worry, we're not going to ask you to take one. We don't have the resources. I do, however, want to ask you about your suicide attempt last week—but that can keep until you're rested. Just one last thing, Miss Erikson, would you object to us contacting your mother? Perhaps if you could give me her address as a follow-up to our inquiries.'

'Oh, for goodness sake, is there really any need for that? I've told you everything you need to know.' Morgan sat with pen poised, waiting to write down Esther Erikson's address, and Ellie had no choice but to give it.

After Morgan went into the lounge to speak to Jamie and Mr Jackson, Matt helped her into her bedroom to lie down. Any thoughts she had of being the pleasant hostess in adversity had long been driven out by sheer exhaustion. The throng downstairs could see to themselves.

'Matt,' she said as he lay on top of the bed beside her. 'Ring mum, please. I want to go and see her.'

'Okay, love, we will tomorrow. But you need to sleep now. I'll get rid of the circus downstairs and bring you something to eat. You aren't leaving that bed until tomorrow morning at the earliest.'

'But what about our night out?'

'I don't think so, do you?'

Ellie was asleep.

She needed answers. It seemed she had an identical twin sister. Perhaps her mother had packed off one half of the pair to an adoption agency, with Ellie being the lucky bunny that got to stay in the happy homestead. Was she the adopted half of the picture? That made more sense when you considered her parents—her mother. Ellie was scared of the imminent confrontation with Esther. She pleaded with Matt to take the long route to Morecambe. Esther might not be her mother. Her head swam with unaccustomed thoughts.

Driving from Ulverston along the Lakes road gave her time to clear her head and work out how she'd approach her mother. She thought about what she'd say and how she'd play it. For the first half-hour of the journey, she sat in silence. Matt turned the radio on, and Ellie asked him to leave it off. She wanted to think clearly. Matt said he could feel the tension effusing from her like the heat from a lover on a scorching summer night. She knew he was trying to ease her anxiety, but he didn't get a smile for being cheesy. He gave her the silence she needed and went back to the twisting road.

Ellie played the scene, as it would unfold, the way she ran book synopsis in her head. The lightest conversation ended in a full-scale war when the women got together. Mrs Erikson had become disturbed since her husband died. A mixture of offspring guilt for not doing more for her mother and genuine irritation made things difficult when they came within yelling distance. Esther Erikson lived in a world not inhabited by many people. It was a relived time of the past. Esther replayed her life as a showgirl, a time belonging only to her. In her version, the entire world was in front of her, and she made the supreme sacrifice to give it up for marriage and Eleanor. In reality, she was a lap dancer in a seedy club on the seafront. And although Ellie's father had kept Esther grounded since his death, she dreamed of greasepaint and sequins. She had even taken up tap dancing.

Backbarrow gave way to Newby Bridge, and they left the serenity of the Lake District behind as Cumbria morphed into Lancashire, just south of Milnthorpe.

'Matt?'

'Yes, love?'

'I'm not going to tell her about my illness.'

Matt's voice was soothing as he spoke to her. He said he didn't want to interfere with her thoughts or force his opinion on her decisions. He only wanted to be a sounding board to help her bring her thinking into tidy order.

'She needs to know, doll, and the longer you leave it, the harder it'll be. You know what she's like. Your accident has already been reported in the papers. It's only a matter of time before they get hold of your illness. Somebody will tell her, and I think it should come from you.'

'I know that, but it's too much to cope with for her and us all at once. We need to find out who this woman is, and that's enough. I know what Mum's like. She'll bring up the subject of coming to live with me again. The way she's been losing it lately, there's no way she can stay there much longer. The neighbours are up in arms about her. She's more of a nuisance every day. Mrs Caldwell rang to say Mother was tap dancing on the balcony in her underwear. It gave Mr Caldwell a turn.'

Matt smothered a smile, but it wasn't lost on Ellie.

'The mental image of my future mother-in-law cavorting around half-naked terrifies me. Hell, she scares the shit out of me with her clothes on. But whatever's right for you, love is right for me.' He grabbed her hand and squeezed it. 'Don't worry. I'll take my lead from you.'

Matt turned right at the traffic lights at Bolton-le-Sands, and they had a glimpse of Morecambe Bay. Ellie grew up there, and although the town had undergone many changes over the years, the sea was unaltered. The tide was in, and she wound down her window and inhaled a lungful of the salty air. The water was calm, a dark slate grey with a dangerous malevolence that had taken many people unfamiliar with its anger over the years. But this wild sea was her friend. It knew her youthful secrets and had never told. It listened to her loneliness as she stood on the cliffs at Heysham, yearning for love. No matter how much she liked Ulverston and the Lakes' calm, this was her home, and the sea would always welcome her back.

She wanted to ask Matt to stop the car. They could walk along the prom; feel the stiff breeze take their hair, sculpting it into a frenzy of medusa tendrils. She wanted to stroke dogs and pass small talk with their proud owners. She tried to lean over the guardrail with Matt pressing his body into hers, to smell the familiarity of him, and feel his maleness. She wanted the sea to protect her from what she would find out. Ellie felt cowardice rise in her, and she swallowed it with brave resolve that she had to grab by the bollocks and hold on to.

Esther Erikson had lived alone since her husband died five years ago. Her house was a beautiful, detached limestone building on Sandylands at the south end of the Morecambe promenade. All the front-facing windows opened onto the sea, and the large back garden was secluded and surrounded on all sides by rambling rose bushes and fruit trees swollen with their autumnal bounty. Ellie spent hours sitting on the second-floor balcony as a child, watching the trawlers casting their nets to the horizon. Sometimes she'd wave at the fishermen in their tiny boats—just dots on the horizon, but they were too far out to see her. She liked the feeling of being small. It was easy in those days to be overlooked and go unnoticed. Sometimes that was a good thing.

Ellie cringed as they pulled up outside the house. Thankfully muted by the morning sun, rings of neon fairy lights flashed on and off as though in time to a beat from long ago. She could only imagine how gaudy they looked at night. Two bushes, one on either side of the door, were draped with pink feather boas. A four-foot plastic moulding of Robbie Williams in his black leathered heyday stood, with a cheesy grin, to the left of the entrance. There was no mistaking that this was Esther Erikson's house. Ellie's expression was part shame, part pity, for the houses skirting Esther's. Ellie remembered when her father sat in the big front window looking over the sea. It seemed her dad would always be there, damping down her mother's exotic spirit. But now he was gone.

She didn't have long to contemplate her youth. As they got out of the car, the front door was flung wide, and Esther Erikson made her exit.

'Darlings,' she screeched like an upper-class parrot. 'It's so lovely to see you. It's been too long. I've cancelled my bridge club this afternoon so that we can have a lovely time catching up. How lovely. Oh Matthew darling, you look lovely. Eleanor, you look peaky. Have you been eating five servings of fruit and vegetables a day? I've got a lovely casserole in the oven.'

Ellie kissed the proffered leathery cheek and resisted the urge to spit the clog of loose powder sticking to her lips. The word lovely was already grating on her nerves.

'Hello, Mother, yes, I'm eating properly. Really, there was no need to give up your bridge club; we could have done this another time.' To Ellie's shame, the last was said with a tinge of petulance. Damn, she was that never-quite-perfect-enough little girl. *To hell with my lovely mother for having the ability to make me feel like shit.*

Esther waited while they took off their shoes in the hall and put on slippers from the rack by the coat stand. Ellie glared at Esther's back. She saw the way her mother's lips held a second too long as they brushed across Matt's cheek. Her fingers sought the back of his neck, where she ran her scarlet talons across his skin. Esther talked nonstop as she ushered them to the lounge.

'Mrs Greystone thought your book was simply marvellous, dear. I told her it was lovely that she thought so. I said that the ending was weak. She said she didn't find it so, but she was just being polite. Have you got rid of that awful animal yet? Dogs should be kept in a zoo, dear. That's where they belong and where they feel happiest.'

'So should mothers,' Matt whispered.

'What was that, Matthew?'

'Oh, I was just remarking to Ell—Eleanor how lovely you look—so young and vibrant.'

'Oh, you lovely, silly boy, I'll turn fifty-three next month. But I love that you've noticed how flawless my skin is and that my breasts are pert. You'll have to watch this one, Elenor. He's got a roving eye, and he takes far too much interest in your poor mother.'

Ellie and Matt struggled not to laugh and didn't dare look at each other. They knew she was about to celebrate her sixty-third birthday. Ellie spent half the time cringing in her mother's company and the other feeling wholly inadequate. This was so typically Mother that she felt the tension lifting. She was determined it wouldn't turn into a fight. She just needed answers. She had to know the truth.

Esther was a perfect mismatch of taste and tasteless, a contradiction of the upper-middle-class widow and the seedy one-time stripper. The décor in the elegant lounge hadn't been touched since her father died, Ellie fell into her usual routine. She walked across the room with her head tilted to the picturesque sea-view window and away from the ornate fireplace. She stopped in front of the chair by the fire and turned it until it faced the room. Then she dropped into it, sinking into a cream hole of feather-soft, under-sprung upholstery. Matt took the end seat on the sofa opposite, and Ellie glared at him, lest his eyes dared to glance at the fireplace wall.

Esther, a stripper at the turn of the century, met and very quickly married Eleanor's father. She was a bar dancer in a lowlife promenade nightclub. Jerry Erikson hated mentioning his wife's former profession, allowing only minor details that Esther used to dance a bit. Since his death, Esther had been liberated. At last, she was free to brag about her time in the clubs. Her prized possession hung proudly above the fireplace. A small photograph had been digitally remastered and transposed into an oil painting of huge and glorious proportion. The picture would have been inappropriate in any lounge, but here, amongst the restful cream décor, it seemed an insult to the hard work Ellie's father had put into buying this beautiful home. Ellie hated the picture and begged her mother to at least move it into her bedroom, if not to the tip, but Esther wouldn't hear of it.

The gilt-framed portrait measured five feet by four. A young Esther pouted sex through a glut of heavy stage makeup. Her slim body, naked bar a tiny glittered G-string, was posed without shame. Her breasts were perter and jutting than they had ever been in real life, depicted by one of the top artists in the country. Esther loved this reminder of her colourful youth. Ellie hated it with a vengeance and couldn't bear to look. Its vulgarity clashed with the prim perfection of the cream and eggshell room, but more than that, the aberration was an unpleasant reminder of Ellie's childhood. Esther may not have been a stripper by the time she was born, but she was always the diva in bitter competition with her daughter for her husband's attention.

Esther finished making the tea and brought in an arrangement of silver and fine china on a golden hostess trolley. Ellie and Matt were more comfortable with big chunky mugs. Ellie loved her Dyllis Bear mug with a chip on the rim that was too precious to throw away. Her mother would be as unlikely to use common mugs as to lose her ugly wig in favour of her ageing hair.

Esther sat down after making a huge performance of pouring the tea. The tension in the room rose, and Ellie sat as stiff as the chair would allow, twisting her eternity ring around her finger. It was time to speak, and she didn't know how to begin.

'Some things have been happening to me—to us, Mother.'

'Oh yes, dear? What kind of things?' Esther sounded disinterested, her focus commanded by the stray dog hair that had fallen from Ellie's sleeve onto the coffee table as she reached over for her cup and saucer.

'Somebody's trying to kill me, Mum.'

The little girl desperate for her mother's love showed through her mask for a moment. Esther bristled at the use of her maternal title. She preferred mother or mummy to mum,

'Really, dear, you do have the most extraordinary imagination. I'm not in the least bit surprised you became a two-bit writer. Who could possibly want to kill you?'

'My sister.'

Ellie watched her mother as she made the blunt statement. No Royal Doulton crashed to the floor, there were no tremoring hands or sharp intakes of breath. Esther took a delicate sip of her Indian tea and stared at her daughter with amusement.

'Darling, is this the plot for your latest book? You know I don't understand your ghastly stories. What on earth are you talking about?'

If Esther was acting, it was a performance worthy of an accolade. She seemed genuinely confused and had the look of somebody on the receiving end of a joke, knowing that a punch-line was coming.

'Darling, what on earth are you wittering on about?' she repeated, after a five-second silence in which she hadn't heard her voice. 'You quite simply aren't making any sense. Did you put that silly policeman up to coming around this morning? All those boring questions, and him undressing me with his eyes the whole time—I've a good mind to lodge a complaint. I told him it was nonsense and that you've had the most ridiculous imagination since you were a small child. I told him you were always jealous of having a famous mother and felt you had to make up little fairytales to feel important. Don't worry, though, dear, you aren't to be arrested. You have some competition for my affection, Matthew dear. Oh, we did laugh over some of your elaborate tales. He was quite dashing and had a twinkle in his eye for me. Her laugh could have shattered glass, and Ellie winced.

'Tell me about my twin sister, Mother. You know—the one you never bothered to tell me about.' despite her self-promised calm, Ellie felt her temper rising, and the word Mother was spat across the room.

Esther's mouth fell elegantly open. Her eyes widened until she looked like a startled doe. Her surprise was caused more by the venom behind her daughter's words than the words themselves.

'Eleanor, you are talking in riddles, girl, and I'll thank you not to take that tone with me, young lady.'

'I am twenty-seven years old, for Christ's sake. Yet you insist on treating me like a teenager. Why didn't you tell me I had an identical twin? I want answers, Mother, and I want them now.'

'My darling, misinformed daughter, you are very obviously distraught. Now I don't know who has been feeding you these ridiculous stories, but I can assure you, I have had one child and one child only, and that child is you. Now can I freshen up your tea for you, dear?'

'Esther?'

'Yes, Matthew sweetie, more lovely tea?'

She raised the teapot and gave Matt her simpering, sex kitten look, the one she claimed numerous times that 'No man could possibly resist.' Ellie thought the odds of her throwing up over her mother's cream carpet were increasing by the second.

'Esther,' Matt tried again but with more temerity. 'Ellie and I are terrified. We're in fear for our lives. We've been attacked by a woman that's identical to Eleanor in every minute detail.

The only conclusion that it's possible to draw is that she's a sister, possibly given up for adoption. Or alternatively, that Ellie is adopted.'

Esther lowered the teapot and seemed to take in what they said for the first time. Her face crumbled. The façade left, and she folded in on herself. The cast of its greasepaint remained, and the husk of her face was a lonely and frightened, ageing woman trying to keep hold of the shadow of her youth the best way she knew how.

'But I only ever had you. I swear I did. Only you, Eleanor. You were the prism in my otherwise colourless life.'

In other circumstances, Ellie would have laughed out loud at this remark. Esther Erikson's life had been many things, but colourless was never one of them.

'Did she have that little strawberry birthmark just below her waist?'

'Oh, for goodness sake, mother. Do you think she came lunging at me with a great bloody knife, stark pissing naked? How the hell do I know?'

'Right, that's it, missy, I'm not having that. Don't you dare come in here, using foul gutter-talk and flinging your promiscuous accusations around? I tell you, if your dear Daddy was around, he'd be horrified.'

She sat forward in her chair with her legs crossed at the ankles. Esther was slight and still had a reasonable figure, despite her years. With modification, she might be described as an attractive woman, but her hideous pink wig dislodged, and flopped at the side of her head as she emphasised each word with a nod.

Her eyes, hooded with creased lids, had enough bright green eye shadow to cover an ocean liner. Pursed lips loomed out of her face in a barrage of crimson grease, even though her upper lip had disappeared as age took the fullness from it. She'd applied a thick layer of red lipstick to the point where her lip used to be, only adding to the effect of a three-year-old playing with Mummy's makeup. Her under-padded bottom perched on the edge of her chair, she had forgotten what Daddy would have said to Ellie, but as soon as she remembered, Ellie was sure she'd be ready to let fly.

'Mother, Matt and I are in danger, and you're terrified the hallowed walls will crumble around your head because I said piss. We believe you gave up a baby. With a lifetime of bitterness and revenge in mind, this woman is here to find the family that abandoned her. At the moment, she's targeting me, but has it occurred to you, Mummy dearest, that the next name on her hit list might be yours, the mother who didn't want her?'

'She's here? Now? Oh, Matthew, she said a woman's here to hurt me. Make her go away.'

They didn't know if she meant Ellie or her twin, but Esther looked genuinely scared. For once, she wasn't flirting with Matt as she said in a tiny voice, 'Don't let anyone hurt me, will you, Matthew? You know I'm not good without Eleanor's father here. I just can't do it on my own. Please, don't let anybody hurt me.'

Black mascara tracks left a ruined trench in the clotted make-up on her face. Tears coursed down her cheeks, genuine tears, borne from the loss of the man who looked after her, acted for her, and even thought for her for thirty years. Ellie forgave her for considering her own plight in all this.

She put an arm around Esther's bony shoulder. Physical contact was uncomfortable between them—it always had been, and she felt Esther stiffen.

'Mother, we'll do everything we can to protect you, but you have to tell the truth for us to do that.'

'I have told you the truth. I swear I have. There was you, Ellie, only you. "Jerry, Dear," I said after I had you. "If you want another one of those baby things, you can hire yourself a broodmare. I'm not putting on another two kilos for anyone." It was awful, dear. I strongly advise against having children, they're a millstone around your neck.'

Ellie winced at her mother's thoughtlessness.

'Thank you for that, Mother. I'll bear it in mind should the need arise.'

'Esther, are you quite sure you only gave birth to one daughter?'

'Matthew, darling, you are a man, and if I might say so without my daughter throwing a jealous tantrum, a very lovely one at that. I can assure you that I am agonisingly aware of how many offspring I produced that day. You couldn't possibly have the slightest inkling of the pain, the mess, and the humiliation Elenor put me through.

They discussed the ramifications of the problem for the next half hour amidst more cups of insipid, weak tea, but it wasn't long before Ellie and her mother were fighting again.

'But why won't you buy the house next door, dear? It would be so lovely. We could knock a door through the properties, and then we could do lots of lovely things together.'

Ellie didn't attempt to hide the look of revulsion that crossed her face.

'Mother, I can't think of anything worse than being at your beck and call all day. I already have a cantankerous elderly neighbour and, as far as I'm aware, his house isn't for sale. How would I write a word with you screeching for attention every minute?'

Ellie was sorry for her hard words as the hurt registered on her mother's face. 'I'm sorry, Mum, it wouldn't work. You know it wouldn't.'

'But, Eleanor, we could have a lovely time. I could take Jock out for lovely walks while you got lots of lovely writing done.'

'Jake, Mother, his name's Jake, and anyway, you hate dogs, you'd have him sold off to the first tourist who stopped to stroke him.'

Matt looked at his watch and settled into his chair with a rueful shake of his head until another mother-daughter war reached its usual conclusion. Ellie would storm off in a huff, with Esther slamming the door behind them.

'You've never loved me.'

Esther trotted out her old favourite. It was never long before this one appeared.

'I gave up everything for you. I had a career that would have made me a star, but I gave it away to look after you and your father. I gave my life up for you. And now that I'm not as young as I used to be, is it too much to expect a little of the love I lavished on you to be returned? I weep, Eleanor, I weep salted tears into my silken pillow at night when I think of your ingratitude.'

'Oh, here we go, Mother.'

They were under starters orders—and off. There was no stopping them until it ran its course.

'As usual, the "I could have been a star" speech. Mother, you were a nude dancer in a seedy club. Your life was a sordid disgrace until dad found you contemplating suicide on the cliffs and pulled you from the gutter. The only stardom you came close to were the stars floating around the drunk's heads as you rubbed your crotch into their faces. I never loved you? What about the love I deserved as a child? What about the love I craved and yearned for and needed? There was none of that, was there, Mum? No, because the world revolved around you. From the time I was six, you always had to act as the delicate child who needed looking after and needed attention. You were the one who dressed up in the evenings and gave performances of your talent, singing and dancing in front of my father and his friends, always you, Mother. Whatever happened to my childhood?'

'Oh, Eleanor, really, you always were jealous, weren't you? Such a jealous little girl. "Look at me, daddy. Look at me," you used to say. You wanted to be just like me, but you never had the poise, dear—chunky legs. You always tried to take your father away from me. But it didn't work, did it? You had solid ankles, you see. It was me he loved, always me. He used to watch me dance the ballet for him at our evening soirees, and he was entranced.'

'Ladies, please,' Matt tried to stem the inevitable before it got out of hand.

'Do be quiet, Matthew,' Esther snapped.

'Yes, shut up, Matt, this is between us and needs sorting out once and for all.' Ellie agreed with her mother for the first time in years.

'No, Mother. He watched you lumbering around with a bellyful of whisky in a ridiculous tutu and felt disgusted. You embarrassed him in front of his friends and brought him deep disgusting shame, Mother. Have you any idea of the misery you caused us, Daddy and I? Our whole lives were taken up with looking after you. Is it any wonder I broke away as soon as I could? Well, never mind, Mother, you have a new daughter now. And if she doesn't murder you in your sleep, you and she can live happily ever after, just as you would like. She can do your fetching and carrying and bow to your every whim. Just don't leave any knives lying around the house, Mother, or you'll be wearing one sticking out of your head as a fashion accessory.'

'Eleanor, how can you say those horrible things to me? Your father and I were devoted. Devoted—everybody says so.'

'No, Mother, Daddy was devoted to you. And you sucked him dry. He was tired, so very, very tired of it all, but you whined your pathetic demands on him, day after miserable day. And in the end, Mother, I think his heart attack was a blessed means of escape.'

'You wicked, evil girl. Get out. Get out of my house and don't ever come back.'

'Ellie, that's too much.' Matt tried to have his say but was ignored.

'Gladly, Mother, I can't think of anything that'd please me more. But before I go, I have another little piece of news for you. Oh, nothing as interesting as Yorkshire Street opening a new dress shop or anything like that, just the fact that I have a disease, it's terminal, and I'm dying. I'll leave you to my evil twin as her inheritance when I'm dead. I'm sure you'll live in domestic bliss for many psychotic years together.'

Esther wasted no time in her retort, not stopping for a second to digest what her daughter had said. 'Lies, lies, lies. You are full of cheap attention stunts today, aren't you, dear? People wanting to kill you, incurable diseases. Matthew, darling, I think she needs to see a doctor.'

'She's been to several doctors, Esther, and I'm sorry, but it's true. Your daughter is very sick.' Matt's voice was drowned out against the screaming females.

'I've seen my fill of them, Mother. They all say the same thing, I have Tay-Sachs disease, and it's killing me.'

'Well, before you die, close the door on your way out will you dear?'

As Matt followed, still trying to make the women see reason, Ellie gave it a good resounding slam.

# Chapter Nine

E llie fumed most of the way home. She ranted and cursed. Esther always brought out the worst in her.

'Oh well,' she was calming down, either through loss of steam or lack of sufficient profanities in the English language. 'Fuck her. We have enough to worry about without my mother's histrionics. I have another theory, though. What if I was conceived through IVF? It was very popular back then. Couldn't someone have stolen one of my mother's embryos? They harvest more than they need, don't they? Damn, I wish we'd thought to ask her about IVF. That could explain it, couldn't it, Matt? I'll ring to ask her when we get back.'

In her temper, she hadn't noticed Matt's silence. His answers were noncommittal monosyllabic grunts. He didn't look as though he'd heard a word. He was submerged in his own thoughts, and when he surfaced, he said that he'd shut out the fury of Ellie's storm and the passage of miles. 'I've been thinking, and I don't like the reasoning I've come up with.'

'Never mind that IVF solves the mystery, Matt. Someone must have stolen one of the embryos and sold it. Maybe Daddy was impotent, so they had to go down the IVF route.'

Matt's tone was sinister when he answered her, and she was shocked into silence. It was full of foreboding, and it scared her. Her forearm hair rose to dance to the tune of forthcoming danger.

'No, Ellie.'

'What do you mean, "No, Ellie?" Don't you believe Mother's story?'

'I do, and that's the problem. Far from the mystery being solved, it's only deepened and twisted further from all bloody logic and reason.'

'I don't understand.'

'We went to your mother's with an egg-box. We took the pieces of information as they came and slotted them into position until the box was full and everything explained. But Ellie, now the egg-box lid won't shut. The information doesn't fit into its holes all neat and tidy.'

'What are you talking about? Stop prattling on about bloody chickens and explain.'

'I'm trying to. I need to think. Let me get the words out.'

She nodded, his tone still scaring her. Matt hadn't said any words to frighten her, but there was something in the numbness of his voice.

'Last night, while you were asleep, I spent hours on the internet researching twins. To produce an identical twin, just having half DNA is not enough. To get identical babies, they would need the necessary ingredients of the same mother and father.

They need the ovum from your mother and the sperm from your father.'

'Well, maybe they stole some of that, too.'

'Okay, it's possible, but we're are getting into the realms of making things fit again. Sperm has a short life once it's been cannoned into this big old world.'

'Yes, but they had the eggs in one Petri dish, or whatever they use, and the sperm in a test tube. They could have squirted some into an egg that was given back to my mother and some into another woman with a fat wallet?'

'Now we get to the biggest mystery of all, then. I'm not a geneticist, a paediatrician, or, thank God, a midwife, but I think I'm right that what you've said is impossible. If I read it right, I'm not sure if this is correct, but I think it's near enough until I check the facts. The moment of conception produces a single embryonic cell, as a sperm embeds into the woman's ovum. That cell—it's called a stem cell—replicates. As the fission occurs, at the first replication, that's when an identical twin is produced. Then, and only then, you understand?'

Ellie didn't really, but she nodded anyway.

'Instead of the two new cells dividing to become four, each replicates independently, producing two babies of the same cell. At that point of the first division, sometimes the cells don't divide properly, and that's when you produce a con-joined pair of twins. So you see, Ellie, using your theory, even with your father's sperm and your mother's ovum, one of the other embryos could never be an identical twin to you. A twin, yes, but not an identical match.'

'Couldn't they separate the embryos at the point of fission when they separated into two babies instead of one?'

'No, well, I don't think so—not in the last century, anyway. Don't forget, back then, IVF was less evolved. I don't know, but why would they go to all that trouble when they had a bowl full of ripe and ready embryos that wouldn't involve an even more dangerous procedure? It wouldn't make sense for them to split a forming twin-sac when they had other eggs that would just be destroyed if the procedure was successful. Surely they'd take those.'

'True, but maybe the other woman isn't my identical twin. Maybe she is from one of those other embryos and just looks like me. Look at my cousins, Lesley and Patricia, they have two years separating them and still get mistaken for each other. That can happen, can't it?'

'Oh, for god's sake, Ellie.' Matt's voice had risen in frustration. 'You've seen the woman. To all intents and purposes, she is you. She looks like you, walks like you, sounds like you, smells like you. Hell, her shadow even matches yours. This is no lookalike, she's the perfect double of you. Do you think somebody who bore a passing resemblance could get close enough to bash my brains in? Bloody hell, girl, have you forgotten how convinced I was it was you? Everything about her was the same, her manner, her essence, even the way she displaced the air. I was convinced she was you. I would have made love to that woman, Ellie, believing she was you.'

Ellie screwed up her nose, but this was too serious to come back at him with flippancy.

'We come full circle to the original conclusion then. My mother's lying?'

'No. I don't think she is. I watched her, and your mother's not that good an actress. I'm sorry, love, but she's not that clever.

Listen, when we get in, I'll hit the Net and dig around to see what I can find in parish records and such. I'll get all the information I found on twinning too. And then we'll check out local fertility clinics and see what we can dig up there. Let's arm ourselves with as much knowledge as we can.'

'Okay, but I'd still prefer to think of my mother as a scheming, conniving, two-faced, lying bitch.'

This time she managed a smile.

Ellie walked Jake, played teas maid, tidied up and intermittently sat by Matt's side, adding her input. He obtained birth certificates and parish record documentation concerning all children born to Esther and Jerry Erikson. No legal documentation indicated a second child was born to the couple. He checked adoption records of the time. He drew a blank. Closed files were abandoned ten years earlier, and all adoption records were available in the public domain.

He had to call Ellie in from the kitchen several times to identify herself before documents could be released. This was done via Retinal Vein Pattern Recognition. She sat in front of the computer screen, and a picture of her eyes was taken. It was matched up to her retinal print in the National Hall of Records. With RVPR, everybody could voyage the net feeling secure that they couldn't be impersonated.

The most important information came from a news report dated March 2019.

The Greendale Fertility Clinic in Keswick was burned to the ground. Five people were killed in the fire, and several others, including two firemen, were injured and needed hospital treatment. Further investigation told Matt that all files and records were destroyed when the clinic burned, along with the Petrie dishes and turkey basters. Initial investigation indicated that arson was to blame. However, this had yet to be confirmed. The report suggested there might have been some dodgy dealings surrounding the clinic's running. Several ex-employees had been detained for questioning. The first thing occurring to Matt was the coincidental fact that the burning of the downtown clinic happened within weeks of Esther's pregnancy.

Matt voiced his thought aloud. It was the first time he'd spoken since Ellie left the room earlier.

'It all seems like too much of a coincidence.'

He jumped when George broke the silence. When she was writing, Ellie always turned the *Random Chatterbox* option off. George only responded when spoken to by name. Matt had forgotten to do it. George had a database of several million words, phrases, and one-liners to suit any occasion. While writing, if Ellie came up with anything she was pleased with, she would often program it into the database.

When George spoke, a typical Ellie gem came from the computer speakers.

'If it looks like a duck, waddles like a duck, and quacks like a duck, it ain't going to be wearing an elephant's tutu, is it?'

'Eh?'

'Matt, dear.' This was not just Ellie-speak but parroted in perfect mimicry of Ellie's voice. 'If it appears to be too much of a coincidence, it probably is.'

'Sometimes you are too damned smart for a big hunk of plastic. Chatterbox off, please, George,' Matt said.

'I'm a hunk, a hunk a burning love,' the software flashed the screen twice, just to be annoying, before turning himself on *Standby*. The makers advertised Humanicons as the nearest thing to a human being. The brand had an irritating jingle.

*It'll get under your skin and into your hair. It'll drive you insane, but you won't even care.*

Ain't that the truth, thought Matt, grinning. Thanks to these computer programs, Victor Khazanza, the inventor, was one of the world's richest men.

The next few days passed without incident. Matt and Ellie were on their guard. Ellie felt that she was being spied on but didn't mention it to Matt because she attributed it to her paranoia playing hide-and-seek with her. Matt thought he was being watched, too and didn't say anything for the same reason.

Despite his heavy caseload, Matt continued his investigations between clients. He spoke to adoption agencies and fertility clinics; he met with council officials and doctors. He tried every avenue he could think of to gain information. It seemed everywhere he turned, he drew a blank. Their only option was being on their guard and vigilant and waiting for the next outburst of violence or mischief against them. They knew it was coming, and they were ready. Surely the psycho would slip up and give them a lead otherwise—Matt preferred not to think about otherwise.

Esther rang four times on Sunday. And again at three-thirty on Monday morning. There was somebody in the house. They stayed on the line while Esther rang the police on her mobile. They weren't taking any chances. Sometime later, when the sun was rising, and birds sang their morning songs, Matt and Ellie crawled back into bed. The police had searched Esther's house and garden and found nothing out of the ordinary. Esther was on the phone again at twenty past eight. There was a strange noise coming from the kitchen. On investigation, it turned out to be the kettle switching itself off.

When Ellie asked Esther if she had been born due to IVF treatment, a silence lasted a half breath too long before her mother assured her that it wasn't the case.

'Don't be silly, darling. I didn't even want to have a baby that much, and I can assure you, your father had perfectly healthy sperm.' Something in her mother's voice didn't ring true, and Ellie wasn't convinced, but when she tried to question her further, it invited the usual arguments, and she got nowhere.

The highlight of Monday was *Let Sleeping Dogs Lie*, Ellie's latest book, had made it onto the bestseller list. Rob phoned them early with the news. It was going to be a busy time for Rob and Ellie. A frenzy of publicity and PR rolled out when a book hit The List. Rob rang magazines and talk shows to keep the momentum high. The book had gone straight in at number five; it was his job to see it made the top slot. Unfortunately, four agents ahead of him and ninety-five behind had the same idea. It was a competitive game. Ellie would have a range of book signings and cocktail parties to attend. It was exciting but tiring. After the congratulatory phone call ended, Rob went to splash Ellie's name around the people in high places.

Matt was leaving for work on Wednesday morning when DCI Morgan called with the results of the forensic evidence. Matt invited him in and explained that he was about to leave. Morgan said he would like Matt to hear what he had to say and promised he would only keep him a few minutes.

Morgan refused a cup of coffee and said he preferred to stand. His attitude was stiff and polite but unfriendly.

'It took you long enough to get the results, Inspector,' Ellie wanted to show that she wasn't intimidated by his high-handed attitude.

'We've had them a couple of days, Miss Erikson, but we took the opportunity to keep an eye on things for a while before we got in touch. And it seems to have been quiet around here.'

'By things, Inspector, I presume you mean that you wanted to keep an eye on us. Well yes, I'm thankful to report that, apart from feeling as though we were being watched, things have been quiet.' Her voice was heavy with sarcasm, her chin upturned, and her expression a challenge.

Unabashed, Morgan got to the point. Matt looked at his watch every few seconds, and Morgan said he had a busy day lined up too and wanted to move things along and close the case.

'Before we go any further, I'd just like to clarify one point from your earlier statement.' He did the familiar notebook-flipping.

'Ah yes, here we are. Are you quite sure that you never touched the knife at any time?'

'Quite sure, Inspector.'

'Okay. And can you remember if your assailant was wearing gloves or had any other form of covering over her hands?'

'No, she was not wearing gloves. Her hands were free.'

'It says here, quote, "Everything happened so quickly, I turned around, and she was standing behind me with a knife raised above my head. I panicked." In those circumstances, do you think it's possible that you wouldn't notice if she wore gloves?'

'Inspector, I'm sorry if this sounds pompous, but I'm a writer. It's my job to observe. I notice things. I notice people. For instance, I see that you've changed your cologne since the last time we met and this time you're wearing matching socks. And, Inspector, I notice if knife-wielding murderers are wearing gloves. My attacker was not.'

Morgan clearly swallowed the urge to grin at her retort. He seemed simultaneously flattered that she noticed his cologne and embarrassed about his previously odd socks.

'And just so I have this straight in my head, you did not touch the knife.'

This dickhead was pushing his luck.

'Damn it, Inspector, I've told you time and again. I did not touch the bloody knife.'

He spoke candidly. Ellie had that effect on people. They said things to her that they would tend to keep to themselves. It was one of her attributes. 'I know you aren't telling the truth, you're lying to me, but I've built grudging respect for you despite myself. I'm a misogynistic old bastard, I know that. But I want you to be the good guy. I'm really trying to give you a break. You're a little woman with a big attitude, and I respect that.' She

144

met his stare for unwavering stare, and her grey eyes never gave an inch under his questioning.

'I presume this is leading somewhere, Inspector. '

'Indeed it is Miss Erikson. I'm closing the case, but loose ends are sticking out all over this situation. If there's one thing I detest, it's a messy ending. Why would two independent witnesses—who have nothing to gain by it— lie for you? And before you interrupt and shout at me, we know they did. Why are you so bloody resolute and sure of your story? What's your game?'

'I have no game. I don't know what you're getting at.'

'What if I told you I have evidence that blows your story out of the water?'

'I would say that you are the one who's lying, Inspector.'

A shadow of doubt crossed her face. For the first time, she wavered, but her chin rose to a defiant angle. He annoyed her with his accusations and suspicious looks. She demoted him to the lower rank of Inspector at every opportunity to irritate him. It was a deliberate attempt to rattle his cage. She'd been waiting for him to retaliate, but Morgan didn't bite. She was quick and bright, and despite being under the line of fire, she was holding her own well.

'Miss Erikson, you're a feisty woman, and you remind me of my daughter. I like you. For possibly the first time in my career, I'll try and give someone an out.' His tone altered, inflected with warmth. 'I don't want to show Eleanor Erikson as a liar. It's important to me, for some God-only-known reason, that your reputation remains intact. Listen, Ellie,' it was the first time he had used her Christian name. 'By your own admission, everything happened fast. Things were blurred around the edges, and you were in a state of fight or flight panic. Sometimes we

145

forget things that seem unimportant at the time. Maybe, when she dropped the knife, you picked it up to give chase and then thought better of it and let it drop. That could be possible, couldn't it?'

Ellie's tone was haughty as she replied without hesitation. 'I'm sure it could, Inspector, but that wasn't the case. I'm telling you that I never touched the knife once and for all.'

Morgan sighed. 'I feel like a magician destroying the magic of a remarkable new illusion, but I derive no pleasure from what I have to do.' He took a piece of paper from the back of his notebook and unfolded it.

'I have the results of the forensic tests that we carried out. The knife showed several clearly defined fingerprints.'

Ellie and Matt both knew what was coming.

'All of them belong to you.'

'I never touched the knife.'

Morgan told them not to hesitate if anything untoward happened, and they needed him. He warned them to be on their guard and said that the matching statements from two independent witnesses niggled at him like a toothache. The evidence was clear, and he had to close the case, but he didn't have to like it. And then he bid them a good day.

Rob phoned the next morning to say arrangements had been made. Ellie had a list of engagements pencilled in, awaiting approval. The first was a party at Killbriney Grange, in Buckinghamshire, for the following Monday evening. Lady Kilburn, who was hosting the grand affair with her husband, was purportedly a massive fan of Ellie's. Several high-ranking press and national media members were attending, and she would be shoulder-to-shoulder with celebrities. It was a push-the-boat-out charade, full of glitz and pretension. During the publicity for her first novel, Ellie had loved all the pomp and glamour involved in occasions like this. The food, the champagne, everything was of the highest quality. Hobnobbing with celebrities made her dizzy with excitement. Now, several books on, the insincerity and deceit were wearing, and the food and wine too rich. The brash bashes were one more element of her work. It was still exciting to know her book was doing well, but the crystal chandeliers were tarnished in Ellie's eyes.

She would be in London for a week, and her time would be spent in a blur of interviews and functions, interspersed with daily signings at the larger bookstores.

Although he was expecting it, Matt wasn't happy about Ellie's absence.

'Let me take the week off work and come with you. Expenses can run to an escort.'

'Darling, you've taken too much time off lately, you're needed here.'

'What if you're ill or that maniac shows up?'

'If I have a funny turn, there are hospitals in London, too, you know. And as for her, I'm damned if I'm going to put my life and career on hold on the off chance that she might show up in a blaze of mayhem and madness. And anyway, Rob knows the score; he'll keep an eye on me. Just think of the publicity if she makes an appearance, like that pompous git Morgan said, it wouldn't hurt my book sales, would it?'

Ellie was being flippant and putting a brave face on things. In reality, she was uneasy about leaving and worried about Matt. But this was her choice when she first put her finger to the keyboard, and it was her duty to go. She was expected to attend these engagements, being incessantly pleasant and shaking a lot of hands while smiling endlessly. Writing books was the easy part of her job.

Saturday dawned, and it was an anniversary of sorts. One whole week had sailed past without any sinister happenings. Although Ellie would have a busy week ahead, she insisted they have a good night out together before she left. They had all the following day to be lazy and recover. Matt didn't want to go to Demons. He said it evoked bad memories of the recent trouble, but Ellie was insistent. She was often fatigued and listless, and they hadn't been to a club for months. The times when she felt well and could summon energy were fewer, and she had to grasp those days and make them count. She was curious about the new club, but more than that, she felt her double wanted her to go. She was playing along and being led.

As a writer, she had a heightened sense of inquisitiveness ingrained in her psychological makeup. She was born to be curious and enquire into things. Matt said she was just plain nosey. Although things had been quiet for the last week, they were far from over.

She didn't know a damned thing about the other woman, who she was, where she lived, why she was doing this, but she felt that she knew something about her character. There was no way her doppelganger was going to give up. Some attackers may have backed off, been scared into defeat by such a near miss, seen it as a failure and dropped the idea, but not this one. She wouldn't stop at anything. Ellie felt it. She may be lying low to refuel, but that's all she was doing.

That matchbook was left in her lounge for two reasons. The first was the woman leaving a spoor, a mark that she'd been there and had staked her territory. She'd shown her prey that she could enter at will, anytime she felt like it and piss wherever she wanted. But it was more than that, it was a taunt, an enticement, a blatant, 'Come and get me if you're hard enough.' Ellie had no idea if anything would come of it, but she had to go to Demons because she'd been summoned and to ignore it would be admitting cowardice. She didn't know when she was meant to be there, perhaps it was an open invitation, or maybe she was expected to go the night after the book had been left, but again, instinct told her the date didn't matter, only that she rose to the bait. Ellie was all for rising. She wasn't dead yet.

Going through her wardrobe, she tried on several things. She nearly decided on a pair of black trousers and glittery top, but in the end, opted for the silver dress that she would have worn the week before if she hadn't almost been hacked to death in her bedroom.

Matt wolf-whistled, she looked good. He said he had a bad feeling about the evening, some instinct, just as strong as Ellie's, told him going to Demons was a mistake.

'But I can't deny that I'm looking forward to holding you close and dancing with you and getting deep inside you when we get home.' Ellie was right, a clubbing night was overdue and would do them good.

'I know this mood of yours, Ellie, and you're wearing that defiant look with your silver dress. Without you having to, it tells me that you would go with or without me.'

Their life together had become far too serious, and they needed to let off steam. Ellie loved dancing, and the look of sorrow in her eyes when she said she would miss it as she deteriorated into disability visibly broke his heart. 'Tonight, I just want to see my girl smile.'

After settling Jake in Matt's house at Barrow, where they'd spend the night, they walked into town and wandered around the pubs. They were in high spirits and hadn't had such a good time for ages. Fielding had told Ellie that if she wanted to drink more than a couple of glasses of wine, she could leave out two aggressive tablets from her medication regime—as long as it was a one-off. For the first time, she was giving it a go. After several vodkas, she was tipsy. They laughed and enjoyed holding hands and feeling all the love that used to be there but was strained. Matt saw several men looking at her, and he was overcome with love. Let them look. He didn't mind and knew who was taking his girl home. He was glad she'd persuaded him to come; they had a fantastic time.

They arrived at Demons a little after ten. The doormen glanced over Matt as they walked in, but they all smiled at Ellie.

'Hey,' said a gorilla of a man with a laugh as he grabbed Ellie by the arm. 'No trouble from you tonight.'

He let her go, and they were pushed forward from behind by the queue, waiting to pay their entry fee. Ellie smiled at him, and Matt stared, but the opportunity to ask what he meant by the remark passed. Ellie wanted to go back and confront him, but they were carried on a sea of people towards the stairs that led into the basement club. The moment was lost, and they had to make do with an exchanged look of confusion for now. They'd come back and speak to him when the opening rush had died down.

Demons was big on atmosphere. After leaving the brightly-lit foyer, it felt as though you were walking into a demon's lair. The club was at basement level, adding to the impression of descending into a subterranean den. The décor was simple but garishly effective. Everything was painted in red and black, the theme was sinister and exciting. A steady bass thumped up to them and created the illusion that the music was pulling them further down into whatever lay beyond. Matt squeezed Ellie's hand, and she smiled at him, loving every minute.

'Vodka and coke?' he asked

'Yes, please. Isn't this great?'

'The look in your eyes is greatness enough for me. The club and all its glam fade into insignificance next to that.' This was the first time Ellie had seemed relaxed and happy for weeks.

It was the first time either of them had.

Matt ordered drinks and turned back to her as a man, dressed head-to-toe in black leather, walked past and grabbed Ellie's bottom. He took the whole of her left buttock into the palm of his large hand and squeezed. Ellie let out a shriek and turned, hand outstretched, palm upwards to hit the man, but he was gone, lost in the sea of ever moving people.

'Hey,' Matt shouted, his expression was dark, and his eyes aggressive. He moved in the direction the other bloke had taken, but it was useless trying to give chase, he had melted into the people on the dance floor, and it was a mass of swaying torsos and flailing arms. He turned back to Ellie.

'Are you all right, love? Let me find him. I'll kill the bastard.'

She managed a laugh, 'Let it go, Matt, I'm fine, cheeky bugger. Maybe he does that to all the girls.' Ellie grinned at him.

'Huh, well, if he tries it on with you again, he's history.'

'Shush, he's not worth getting wound up about. Come on, let's dance.'

The music playing was a fast dance track, heavy on bass and easy on synthesis. This was the new skull beat, and Ellie laughed as Matt had trouble coordinating his feet and his body, but she didn't care. She was in love. She looked at her man and felt protected. Matt was tall, over six feet. He towered above her, and Ellie was accustomed to having intimate conversations with his left nipple. He looked after himself and worked out. He looked as good in a suit and tie as he did in jeans, something that only a self-assured man could carry off. His blonde fringe hung foppishly over his face, but his swarthy looks and sculptured chin detracted from any hint of a geek about him. The thing that had attracted Ellie was his smile. He had a great big open smile that disarmed and put a person at ease. His eyes crinkled at the corners more than you would expect for his thirty-six years, and he always looked happy. He had an honest face, a long generous body and a penis that drove her to dizzying heights of pleasure. At first glance, he appeared slimmer than he was. When you noticed the defined chest muscles rippling beneath his white shirt, you realised that he was a well-made man and far from skinny.

Ellie picked up the moves. She was grinning like a loon and flinging herself about all over the place. Matt yelled in her ear that he was worried she'd overdo it, he knew she'd suffer for it over the next few days, and with the London trip looming, she'd be exhausted.

Ellie told him to shut up.

While they danced, she made eye contact with several people. They seemed to know her and nodded or raised their hands in acknowledgement. When Matt nodded a greeting, it seemed they were weighing him up. One girl waved back with a look of uncertainty on her face, but most of them just ignored him. The exchange with the bouncer was odd, but it was clear that people in this club thought they knew Ellie.

It was prooved as they moved off the dance floor to find a seat.

Another man came towards them. He was grinning.

'Evie, honey. You look damned good.'

Before she had a chance to stop him and as Matt looked on in horror, he grabbed Ellie and kissed her full on the mouth. Ellie pushed him off, and the ape saw the look on Matt's face hardening.

'Hey dude, check it. It's all good. Eve and I are mates. So Evie, are you going to introduce me to your angry friend? Not your usual type. You going upmarket on me, girl? Hey man, I'm only joking, chill man, any friend of Eve's and all that, man.'

Ellie was recovering from the stranger's full-on kiss. Matt was the first to get a handle on the situation. He grabbed the guy by the front of his shirt.

'Hey, you know her? You know the woman that looks like this?' He gestured towards Ellie.

Ellie jumped in on the conversation, her words coming fast, her breath harsh. This was the break they'd been waiting for.

'I'm not who you think I am. I'm not the woman you called—Eve? Is that her name? Eve? Please, listen. This is important. You have to tell us everything you know about her. Who is she? Where does she live? Do you know where she lives?'

Ellie's voice rose, partly to be heard over the loud music but mainly through the exhilaration of finding a man who knew Eve. Matt still had his hands on the man's shirt, and Ellie gripped his forearm. The stranger took two steps back, releasing their hold on him.

'Hey, back off, man. Get your fucking hands off me.' He raised his hands in a defensive attitude.

'Eve, you want to slow down on those drugs, my lady, they ain't doin' you no good man.' He backed away and then turned around, shaking his head.

'Fucking weirdos.'

'Please don't go,' Ellie screamed at his retreating back.

'Wait,' Matt yelled, but the man was disappearing into the crowd.

Sensing the tension in the air, a few people stopped dancing to watch the awkward exchange. They'd attracted some curiosity. Matt used it as an opportunity.

Meeting the stares of the people nearest to him, he shouted, 'Does anyone here know this woman?' Ellie blushed but smiled at the blank faces in front of her.

The people turned away. Matt said he felt like a freak. He was impotent to do anything and was frustrated by the lack of response.

'Come on,' Ellie said, 'let's mooch around a bit and see if anyone else says anything to us. But if they do, for Christ's sake, let's play it cool and not frighten them off.' She laughed hard.

'You sounded like a right dick. Like one of those old street corner evangelists.' She put on a deep voice and flung her arm out as she mocked Matt.

'Does anyone know this woman? Speak now, or the fires of hell will burn around your soul for all eternity.'

He put his arm around her and kissed her to shut her up, but it wasn't the most romantic kiss ever as they couldn't stop laughing. So close, but all they had that they didn't before was a name.

Eve.

Ellie tried it out in her head. Their attacker had an identity. It was a pretty name, not the sort you would associate with a crazed killer. It was sweet and earthy. Ellie wondered who had given it to her.

For the next half hour, they danced and mingled. However, they felt eyes on their backs often, but nobody spoke to them, and after scaring the last man off, they were wary of making an approach themselves.

'I'm going to go to the ladies, love. I need a wee anyway, but you would not believe the conversations that unfold in ladies' toilets. When I come out, we'll try the bar people and doormen. See if they can tell us anything.'

'Okay, but don't be long, or I'm coming in to get you and then I'll be labelled a pervert as well as an average common or garden weirdo.' She smiled and moved towards the toilets through the throng of packed people.

155

Matt bought more drinks and sat down when she appeared beside the table.

'Well?'

She looked confused, 'Well, what?'

'Did you enjoy urinating? Did you find anything out about Eve, of course?'

'Oh, no, tell you what I did find out, though.'

'What's that then?'

'That I'm with the most fanciable bloke in the place.'

'Oh really, and how did you deduce that, Miss Holmes?'

'You should have heard what those horny women in there were saying about you. Made me want to take you home and show you how a real woman can handle you.'

She leaned forward and kissed him. She wound her arms around his neck, and when he tried to break the kiss, she opened her mouth and ground her lips onto his. He pushed her off him.

'Hey, Miss, Not-in-public, what's all this then? I think the vodka's gone to your head. Come on, woman, show me some more of that fancy dancing of yours.' Matt looked as if he couldn't believe his luck. After the kneejerk reaction of the night she'd had her test results, and just a few times since, their sex life had dwindled. He was a man. She knew he tried to be understanding, but the look she was giving him and the words coming out of her mouth turned him on faster than a ring full of female mud wrestlers in Amsterdam.

He dragged her to her feet. Her body moulded into his side, and he felt the warmth of her skin through the sheer material of the silver dress. 'Damn, if you don't behave yourself, I'll be walking onto the dance floor with a hard-on.'

'Hey, I've got a better idea, one I think you might like, mister.'

'What's that then?'

'I've had enough of this place. I've got some brand new moves to show you.' how's about we go home and do some dancing of our own.

'What about having a word with the staff to see if they know anything about a certain crazy lady who wants to kill us?'

'Listen, you, either we go home now, or I'm going to rip your clothes off where we stand. Bugger the staff and everything else. I want to make love with you.'

'Lead on, Lolita, a man can only resist for so long.'

As they left, there was only one man on the door. 'Excuse me,' Matt began, but Ellie grabbed him and dragged him into the stiff breeze of the late-night street.

'Hey,' laughed the bouncer after them. 'Be gentle with him, Eve, don't eat him all at once.'

Matt turned back, 'Ellie, come on, let's go and talk to him. He knows Eve. did you hear that?'

She'd missed what the doorman said and was already climbing into one of the taxis lined up outside the club.

'Too late, hun, we're in the taxi now. It's been a long night, and all I want to do is get home. Don't worry; we'll grab him next time.'

Matt wanted to stay and question him, but the taxi had pulled into traffic. He figured the alcohol had hit Ellie. She didn't appear very drunk. Maybe she was so sick of it all that she wanted one night where she could go back to being normal. He understood that. When Ellie got something between her teeth, she didn't let go until she'd got to the bottom of it. Like she said, there was always another time. It seemed Eve was a regular customer of Demons nightclub. It was a good lead they could work with.

In the taxi on the way back to Matt's house, Ellie was at her most beguiling. He tried to tell her to behave herself until they got in and that the driver might hear or see something, but she was having none of it. She teased him, kissed him and purred down his ear. He was hard by the third kiss and ready for her within seconds. He remembered how she'd seduced him behind the front door, and although it alarmed him then, now he was excited by the memory. He wanted to take her hard tonight. It was his turn to put thoughts of her illness to one side and love his woman the way a man should.

'Saved by the bell.' Matt whispered, half-relived and half-devastated when his mobile phone rang. 'Who the bloody hell's ringing at this time of night?'

He reached into his jacket pocket for the phone, but Ellie pre-empted him and took it out of his hand. She smiled her sexiest smile, her eyes never leaving his for a second, and she turned the phone off, dropping it back into Matt's pocket.

Ellie put her hand on his cock and undid his flies, right there on the backseat of the taxi. 'Leave it,' she demanded as he reached for it if only to see who had rung. 'Whoever it is, they'll ring back if it's important. Now, sir, I believe you were kissing me round about—here,' she whispered so softly in his ear that every hair along his forearms rose.

She moved her hand to his knee, teasing him, then stoked up his inner thigh. She tickled him, kissing the side of his neck, while poor Matt tried to keep up his end of the weather conversation with the driver. Her fingers drove him crazy, and when she ran her hand over the front of his pants, he almost moaned. Her fingers were inside his fly, touching him and squeezing until he was wet with pre-cum. Thank God they were nearly at the house. He couldn't wait to be with her. When she tried to pull his cock out of his open flies, he pulled her hand out and put it back on her own knee, searching in his pocket for money. He grabbed a handful of coins and almost dropped them on the cab floor when Ellie let her hand slide up her own thigh, and he saw the tantalising triangle of her white thong. He watched her slide one finger inside it, teasing him with a naughty smile.

Matt looked up and saw the driver watching in his rear-view mirror and craning his neck to see. He couldn't see anything more than Ellie's bare thigh, but the driver knew what was going on in the back seat. Matt blocked Ellie's body with his while he leaned forward to pay the man.

The thought of another man looking at Ellie made him jealous, but it turned him on beyond reason, and his cock was straining against his open fly. Ellie straightened her clothing and patted her hair. Matt could smell her sex on her fingers. He paid the driver and gave him a generous tip.

'Thanks, mate, you have a good night now,' the driver said with an exaggerated wink. Ellie whispered that they hadn't fooled him for a second.

He was already moving away as he called out of his window. 'See you, mate. See you, Eve, be gentle with him.'

159

Matt ran into the middle of the road, waving his arms and shouting for the driver to stop, but like most taxi drivers, once the fare was paid, he was off to pick up the next punter.

'He knew her. He knew her too, Ellie.'

'Bugger, he might know where she lives if she's a regular fare. He's gone now, but I'll ring the taxi office in the morning and talk to them.'

Ellie slipped her arms around his neck and kissed him hard. He could taste the vodka. 'We've had a gutful of that woman, and tonight I just want to enjoy being with you. Lots of people know her. The net's closing in, and we know how to locate her now. She'll keep. I'd say that was a good night's work, wouldn't you?' She took his cock out of his pants on the garden path, and Matt was in no position to answer.

He pushed the taxi driver to the back of his mind. His erection had done nothing to diminish as he waited for the retinal prints to be cleared on the door pad, and Ellie masturbated him on the doorstep. He remembered the last time they had fooled around with his back against a front door, and he wanted her so much.

'Easy,' she said as he kissed her hard on her mouth and neck. 'Hey, slow down. I want this to be good. You fix us something nice to drink and put some good, soulful music on, and I'll go and have a quick freshen up, okay?'

Matt didn't want her to wash. She'd never come in and cleaned herself before. He wanted to make love to her with the smell of fresh perspiration and her oozing sex juices on her body. He wanted to smell the club on her and taste the vodka she'd drunk. He wanted her just the way she was. Tonight he needed a wild woman, but Ellie was already halfway up the stairs. He controlled himself. If that's how she wanted it, he could wait a few minutes.

He went into the kitchen for a bottle of wine and a couple of glasses singing the old Billy Joel song. But he was worried about the amount Ellie had already drunk—it wasn't a great deal, but with her illness, he didn't want her to overdo it and make herself ill. He was deliberating over wine or coffee when he heard the bathroom door close and the bedroom door open. He grabbed two wine glasses and a bottle of cola and tried to get past Jake to go upstairs.

Ellie came out of the ladies' toilet. Nobody had shown any interest in her while she was in there, despite her hanging around the mirror. She was disappointed, but maybe the bar staff knew something.

When she got back to the table, Matt wasn't there. She waited a few minutes. Maybe he'd gone to the loo and would be back soon. When he didn't return, Ellie panicked. She searched the club, looking for him. A deep sense of wrongness was pounding in her head, and it had nothing to do with an overabundance of vodka. Everything was tightening in on her. The people were tighter, closer, the music deafening. No amount of excusing herself got her anywhere fast. The world slowed down, and while she was walking in double four-time, Matty could be in rapid-danger-time.

She fought through to the exit stairs and into the foyer. A fight had broken out between some drunks, and the doormen were in a huddle trying to keep them from killing each other. It looked bad, and she heard a police siren coming towards them. The neon lights of the shops and bars were shimmering. Her breathing was harsh, and she had a panic attack. The lack of oxygen in her heightened state gave every streetlight and neon sign a tracer and made them blur into each other. Everything was distorted. Ellie skirted past the fight. Matt wasn't waiting for her outside. She didn't know what was wrong, but she knew he would never leave her.

She searched for her phone and rang Matt's number. Thank God, it's ringing. Three, four, five, Ellie counted the rings.

'Come on, come on.'

The phone cut off in mid-ring. A mechanised voice informed her *The person you are trying to contact is temporarily unavailable*, but she could leave a message if she wished. Ellie knew Matty would never switch his phone off. The feeling of danger raised a couple of notches on the meter in her mind. Jumping in the nearest taxi, she gave him Matt's address and begged the driver to hurry.

Jake was in a strange mood. Matt had shut him in the kitchen, and he was snuffling at the interconnecting door and growling deep in his throat. A soft, low grumble, he wouldn't leave the door, and he whined to be let out.

'Hey, fella, come on, you can't have her to yourself all the time, you know. Come on, give a guy a break. Don't cock-block me, Jake. We have some unfinished business to attend to, and then you can come up and slobber all over my best bedding all night, if you like, huh matey, is that okay?'

He put his hand down and stroked the dog's raised hackles. 'I'm on a promise here, son. Come on, we're both men of the world. You must understand that, huh?'

Jake lifted his head and licked the back of Matt's hand before dropping his nose to the bottom of the door.

'Jake, move boy. Get out of the way now. You can come up soon, I promise. Hey honey, you all right up there? Coming up, ready or not.'

Matt balanced two of his best champagne flutes and a bottle of cheap cola in his arms as he pushed Jake away from the door with his leg.

As Matt got to the bottom of the stairs, he heard the front door click open. How the hell could anyone get in? His mind did a double-take, but only he and Ellie had access to the door security.

Ellie walked through the door and almost sobbed with relief when she saw Matt standing whole and healthy by the stairs.

Matt had been here before. The only difference was that Ellie was in the bedroom upstairs and needed protection this time. He looked at the stairs in a blind panic.

Ellie took in the scene, the two glasses, the bottle of pop, Matt in his stocking feet preparing to go upstairs.

'Oh my God.'

Matt threw the first glass. In his panic, his aim was high, and it sailed above Ellie's head, hitting the wall behind her with a tinkling crash. She moved to the side as the second glass hit her on the arm. It didn't break but fell to the floor to shatter in a thousand crystal shards.

'Matt, stop. It's me.'

'Get away from me, you crazy bitch. Haven't you done enough damage? What do you want?'

He was indecisive now, unsure what to do next. If it was a man, he'd plough in with his fists, but he couldn't hit a woman. Ellie took advantage of his pause.

She pushed past him and took the stairs two at a time. 'It's me, Matt. It's Ellie, love.'

What convinced him was the change in Jake's manner. He was scratching furiously at the door to get out, and the aggressive barking changed into excited yaps. By the time Ellie reached the last step, Matt was two stairs behind her.

The bathroom door was closed. Ellie flung it open as Matt ran to the bedroom door that stood wide. 'Be careful, Ellie,' he screamed as he burst through the bedroom door.

The bathroom was empty. The faint smell of Ellie's perfume permeated the air, and the bathroom cabinet stood ajar. Red lipstick was used on the full-length mirror to scrawl the words, *Better the devil, you know.*

Everything stopped.

Silence.

'Oh God,' she murmured as she left the bathroom and ran into the bedroom. Matt was standing inside the door, and Ellie rammed into his back, almost knocking him over in her rush to save him.

The window was open, the curtains blowing in the autumn breeze. Eve had left through the window onto the garage roof and into the garden. Two tall, black candles had been lit on either side of the bed, their flames flickered in the breeze, but the window was far enough away to not extinguish the flames. A black silk rose and a stuffed toy had been left behind on the pillow. The toy was similar to the snatch-and-grab cuddlies in the machines at fairgrounds. It was a red devil with horns and a fork.

Matt's voice was quiet. 'She had none of this stuff on her. She must have broken in earlier and laid them out. When we came in, all she had to do was light the candles.'

'How did she get in, Matt. Did you leave the door unlocked when you put Jake in?'

'Which time?' He laughed, but it was mirthless. 'No, I checked it to make sure it was secure. The only people that can get in are you and me. Nobody else is eye-printed for my house, and there's no way Jake would have let her in the back. You should have heard him growling, Ellie. I should have listened to him. I should have known. Fucking hell, Ellie, why didn't I know?'

Matt dropped onto the bed and put his head in his hands as he remembered that woman's body all over his. His aching cock was in her hand. He remembered her touch, her kiss, her fingers all over his body, for Christ's sake.

'Oh God, Ellie,' he rocked in distress. 'She was all over me, and I responded. I kissed her. I'm so sorry.'

'It's okay.'

'It isn't okay. I let her touch me.

'You didn't know.'

'But, I was going to make love to her.'

# Chapter Ten

Things were progressing as expected. The face searching the bathroom mirror for approval wasn't disappointed. Green eyes spliced with a core of psychotic intelligence, and alive with excited joy, stared back. The overall expression was smugness, pleased with the day's work. Yes, it looked as though things were moving up a notch. It was time to sit back and watch the display of fire and ice explode in a volcano of flame and crystal spray.

What a spectacular and poetic image to conjure, the cool of mercury to temper the heat of magma. One could feel the tension building, the emotions were boiling. The pawns were on the run, scared and scrambling for safety, yet with defiance admirable and demanded of a player in this game.

If she wasn't a worthy opponent of the black rook, the white pawn would have been taken out at opening gambit. Desperate pieces were bound to take desperate measures, and the events were exciting.

The white pawn was running scared, checking dark corners, jumping at shadows. But the black rook, although performing as predicted, was playing a challenging game.

She was cool on the surface but had a gutful of bitterness and venom. A passionate one that, of course, it was always apparent. The white pawn would die soon; it was coming to a head.

The green eyes flashed, and the cruel expression widened to a hard smile. Yes, things were progressing nicely.

The eyes closed while The Creator enjoyed the mental images of pain and destruction. The death of Eleanor Erikson wouldn't come easily. That would be tragic—she had to fight and be worthy of the game. It was a delight to be a part of her suffering.

Now all that was needed was to choose the perfect wine to accompany the grande finale.

# Chapter Eleven

T he goodbyes had been said, the luggage packed up to the roof of Rob's car, and Jake instructed to be a good boy and look after Matt. Jake liked the good boy words, but Ellie was leaving him and going away, so he only managed a slight tail wag.

Sleep was a long time coming on Saturday night, and Ellie and Matt had been nervous and jumpy since. Rob was driving to London so that Ellie could rest.

She slept solidly from the moment they left Ulverston until getting to Charnock Richards services on the M6. Rob intended to stop for breakfast at Forton, but as Ellie snored like a snuffling hedgehog, he left it and carried on to the next services. By then, Ellie had slept a good couple of hours, and Rob's stomach was growling in harmony with his passenger's snores. He ordered food while Ellie went to the ladies to freshen up. She wasn't hungry until she saw the works—full cooked breakfast, orange juice, a mountain of toast and fresh black coffee. She did justice to the overpriced service station meal and felt ready for anything.

When they arrived, the hotel was a five-star dream. A bed that could accommodate a football team was a minor feature of the suite. Everything was in football-team proportions. Every care was taken to ensure that she enjoyed celebrity luxury. Expensive bathroom products overflowed a wicker basket by the circular bath, champagne and fruit left on the dining table, chocolates by the bed and fresh, exotic flowers in every corner. Ellie would feel decadent and wasteful filling the enormous sunken bath for herself. And yet the only luxury she yearned for was to feel Matt's arms around her and Jake's wet nose begging attention. She missed them both already.

Rob had their itinerary mapped out in detail. After a couple of hours of rest, they had a long night ahead made worse by an early start in the morning. They ate early with a sandwich that they took in her suite. Rob's room was basic. It would leave Ellie a couple of hours for a long bath and time to pamper herself in preparation for the party. A car was picking them up at nineteen hundred hours sharp. Oh, the pretension, thought Ellie. What happened to good old seven o'clock?

She took her time getting ready and was pleased with her efforts. If there's one thing Ellie detested, it was evening dress. Every woman the world around has part of herself that she would like to improve, and for Ellie, it was her height. She had a model's features and figure but only a petite frame. She felt ridiculous in a full-length dress. She thought it looked as though somebody had stolen her legs. But these occasions bore no respect for her stature and demanded full evening dress be worn. Ellie's grumbles about her size were born in her imagination. She looked good in anything, and in some ways, her height made her seem all the more elegant.

The dress she chose for the evening should have been made with her in mind. It was simple yet accentuated her figure. The colour failed to stop at bronze but hadn't quite made it to gold. The style was a shift that clung where it touched and floated where it didn't. A hint of naughtiness lay in the cutaway back that plunged almost to her bottom and showed off her tanned torso. She gave thanks that nature had been kind to her advancing years in the gravity department. Her underwear was a minimal thong, and due to the clever and elegant design of the dress, it wasn't apparent that she was without a bra. The garment was classy without the merest hint of slut about it. Ellie felt good. Her legs were bare, her sun-kissed colour the only coverage they needed. Her shoes were expensively-cut stiletto heels, adding four precious inches to her height. Her almost shoulder-length bob had grown enough to be put up. Ellie swept it off her face and neck and crafted it into a creation of random sophistication. Apart from one detail, she was ready. All she had to do was wait for Rob and bang on cue, there was a knock on the door.

'Come in if you're gorgeous,' she called.

Rob walked in and gave a wolf whistle as he shut the door behind him. Ellie twirled to show him the full effect.

'Wow, you look fantastic. Poor Matt, if only he could see you now. But you know something? There's a vital element of that outfit missing.'

'And what might that be?' she asked, eyeing the black velvet box in his hand, knowing what was in it, because she and Gail had agonised at length when they chose it online.

Rob opened the box and held it out to her. Inside was a neck-lace encrusted with diamonds and amethysts. Rob motioned her to turn around with his finger. He fastened the chain at the back of her neck, and it fell onto the front of her dress. The amethysts brought out the soft grey of her eyes, and the diamonds sparkled in the light. The piece's highlight was the large teardrop pendant falling to sit below her shoulder blades and dressing her back. Rob kissed the tip of her nose.

'There, as your agent and speaking purely on a professional level, of course, you will be the loveliest thing in that room tonight. So wonderful that if I wasn't very happily married to my devastatingly beautiful wife, I'd give you one myself.'

The tux did beautiful things for his physique. Used to Rob's banter and playing along, she made a show of eyeing him up and down, lingering too long on his crotch before raising her little finger and twitching it.

'Poor Gail.'

'Oh, sod off you. I give you a barrage of compliments, and you attack my manhood. It will never stand proud in society again.'

'Well, thank God for that. You get a stiffy for Mrs Smithey-What's-Her-Britches, and I'm telling Gail.'

'Hussy,' he retorted. 'My wife warned me about girls like you. Now just remember that little trinket is on hire. For God's sake, don't lose it or we're both fucked.'

Rob had been nagging her since her first book did well to buy some decent jewellery, but diamonds and jewels weren't Ellie's style, so they hired her finery when the need arose.

'Come on, Cinderella, we've got a party to go to.' Rob offered his elbow and escorted her out of the suite.

The white limousine took them through the City of London and into the open countryside of Buckinghamshire. It was a scenic drive, and they enjoyed it. Ellie called home, using the impressive facilities built into the flash car. She was assured that everything was fine and that Matt and Jake were missing her something terrible. Matt said they were likely to wither from broken hearts and starvation if she didn't hurry home.

Rob butted in and said he'd spoken to Matt, and they were coping just fine. Matt joked that he'd mastered the can opener and the microwave to produce a tin of soup. Ellie felt a pang of guilt as she thought of the fare laid on for them that night. Matt laughed, knowing he'd tickled her guilt button and admitted that he and Jake had eaten Cordon Bleu pizza from the local takeaway and had thoroughly enjoyed it. They were settled in for the football. As an Arsenal fan, Matt said that Jake had no taste, and they might get to fisticuffs and football hooliganism before the game finished.

Rob phoned Gail and, after failing to describe his client's dress in enough detail and being called useless,  he passed the phone to Ellie. As the rolling fields sped past, the two women giggled like teenagers. Ellie was happy. Perhaps this working time-away was what she needed.

They joked with Geoff, the chauffeur from Skipton in North Yorkshire. Far from being snooty, he was fun and had a sense of humour. Ellie wormed the truth out of him about his clipped accent. After much coaxing, Geoff admitted he'd practised for six weeks with a tape recorder to perfect the upper-class accent and get the job.

They drove through an enormous pair of gates. The driveway seemed to go on for miles. According to Geoff's philosophy, the richer you are, the longer your drive is. Even the way the gravel crunched beneath the tyres sounded posh. They rounded the final bend, and the house came into view.

'Reet lass,' Geoff lapsed into his Yorkshire accent to please Ellie. 'That theer is Killbriney Grange. Now, tha'll have to watch thee pees n cues in theer, or't ald lass'll have thee on tha hands and knees cleaning the kahzies aart.'

Ellie giggled.

'Well divn't thee be worryin', lad. I'm telling thee now, I pee the same colour as that lot in there, and I can talk just the same amount of bullshite.'

Geoff straightened his face as they drew up outside the big house. A man in starched uniform rushed forward to open the door for Ellie, and she stepped out. In her most refined accent, she gathered her dress and said, 'Just pull around the back driver. I'll have a man call you when I'm ready to leave. And please, do try not to steal any garden ornaments this time.'

The marble steps leading to the grand entrance of Killbriney Grange were littered with strutting peacocks not yet gone to roost.

They expected it to be quiet when they arrived, but the party was in full swing. The low hum of genteel conversation rose from small groups of people around the vast ballroom. The evening was warm for the time of year, so they had no coats to give to the attendant who stepped forward to assist them. Another man in coat tails coughed politely beside them.

'If you would care to give me your names, Sir, Madam, I'll announce your arrival.'

The master of ceremonies stepped up to a dais and hammered twice to get people's attention. The conversation continued, the guests paying only the most remote attention in case it was a name that they should make a bee-line for.

'Ladies and Gentlemen, bestselling novelist Miss Eleanor Erikson, accompanied by Mister Robert Price.'

There were polite smiles all round, and a couple of people standing closest nodded their heads in acknowledgement.

A large lady in a black dress with a plunging neckline walked towards them with arms outstretched. She took both of Ellie's hands in hers.

'Miss Erikson, how lovely it is to meet you. I've been so looking forward to it. I'm Cynthia Kilburn, dear. My husband is over there somewhere talking dull old finance to anybody who will listen. We'll butt in, in a minute and make him play host.'

Ellie liked the lady. Despite the accent, she didn't seem too up herself. Her smile reached all the way up to her eyes, and she was interested in meeting Ellie. After Cynthia Kilburn said a polite hello to Rob and shook his hand, he was dismissed. Ellie's arm was linked with her hostess, and she was whisked away and introduced to an endless throng of people. Rob was left in the wake of swishing dresses and clipping heels. He was used to being ignored at these functions. It was the way they worked. In the early days, Ellie was sweet, trying to have him brought into any conversation she was a part of. Rob had to take her to one side and explain it didn't work like that. She looked crestfallen when he explained that she was the peacock, her role was to sell herself to the people. She had to be bright and vivacious and get noticed to be remembered. It was about splashing her name around the people that mattered.

Rob knew his role. He recognised others in his position. He was friends with some of the agents and managers. He'd had dealings with them, and they passed business between each other if a particular client wouldn't be suitable for one but slotted in well with another. Mainly they just had a look. Rob would soon be in conversation with them, playing his part of the game and selling his product. Ellie was there to impress the wallets and contracts, but if any of them wanted to sign her for anything, it was Rob they'd speak to. It drove Ellie insane at first. 'Don't I have a brain? Am I not capable of knowing if I'm available to open a bloody charity gala on the fifteenth of next month? What the hell am I, a bloody Barbie doll with plastic for tonsils?'

As much as she didn't like it, Ellie learned the rules. She did her job and left Rob to do his. Although they may only meet for a few minutes throughout the evening, Rob kept an eye on her. He watched for signs that she needed rescuing from amorous, drunken letches or the party bore. That was his job, but this week, Rob kept a close eye on her because of the trouble she'd had and her illness. She was relaxed and happy so far and was enjoying herself. When she moaned at him for being an overprotective arse, he said it didn't stop him worrying about her, and he'd promised Matt that he would look after her.

'Ladies and Gentlemen,' the master of ceremonies an-nounced. 'May I give you Mr,'—the MC coughed in disap-proval—'Smartassed Jack, and Miss Clarissa Croft.'

Ellie looked towards the entrance. Smartassed Jack was a pop star who had almost had his day. He was with the latest in a line of models, which he serially married and then dragged through the divorce courts a couple of years later in an attempt to keep as much of his vast wealth as possible. He looked ridiculous in what could best be described as a black lace tuxedo. The garment was see-through, and his private secrets were only protected by a black garment similar to the underclothing Ellie wore.

Clarissa, who could never be classed as a shrinking violet, paled into insignificance in her flesh-revealing white toga-style evening dress. They made an entrance. Smartassed made a show of turning his head to listen to the classical music playing as a backdrop to conversation and then did the monkey across the floor. The monkey was last year's craze in the clubs. The youth culture was centred around the jungle, clubbers talking jungle, dancing jungle. Clothes reflected jungle, and a new range of tropical drinks was launched to jump on the back of the trend. Nothing that hadn't been done before, but like most fads, it was worthy of another trot around the floor, thirty years later.

'Ladies and Gentlemen, Mr Victor Khazanza.' He needed no other introduction, but he seemed wary of any publicity or attention typical of the shy man. He gave a curt nod to the room and drifted away as a hand shot out towards him with a cry of, 'Victor, dahling, come and tell me all your delicious news.' Their hostess broke off from greeting the previous guests and welcomed Mr Khazanza.

Ellie was always happy to see Victor. The son of a computer programmer came from modest means and built his empire on hard graft. He had been Ellie's first financial investor and was such a kind gentleman.

Khazanza was a household name for the last fifteen years. His early career had been in medicine. Born in Poland, before the turn of the century, he went into general medicine.

Poland was still a depressed country, having never recovered from the Second World War, and later suffered economic decline in the aftermath of the 2038 invasion by the Middle

East. He had specialised in genetics, and through hard work and determination, he became one of the most respected men in his field worldwide. In 2008, while still a young man, his research—and the endless nights of working until dawn—paid off. He invented a drug that the world had been waiting for. The drug sailed through the trials, though certain corners were cut to get it into the public domain as quickly as possible. Victor was assured that it was standard industry procedure and done all the time.

The day it went on sale, women were queuing at health clinics across Poland, hoping to be eligible for the treatment. But, it all went very wrong for Victor and his patients. The scandal was kept quiet. The drug wasn't released for sale outside Eastern Europe, so it was small news for the rest of the world. Some guy had invented another bad drug. It was like the Thalidomide disaster, but somebody else got it this time. So what?

Victor Khazanza, shamed in his own country, moved to California and worked in computers as his father had done. Only Victor was not a designer like his dad. He had a lowly job working the conveyer belt on chip production in a factory.

It was a story, and Ellie admired his tenacity. Many men, guilt-ridden and shamed, would have taken their lot and lived with it, but Victor had a dream of making life better for the people of his own country, those he had hurt. Like his father, he worked his way up into programming. He couldn't go into anything controversial. Medicine was a closed door for him professionally, but he had a keen interest in psychology. As a young man, it was one of his majors. He thought about the next big thing the world wanted and came up with a revolutionary game. One that everybody would like to play at least once in their lives. At night, after working a twelve-hour shift at the factory, he'd settle in his dingy apartment miles from the famed Californian sea-views, and he worked into the night on his idea. The game Psyche was born in the early hours of one winter's morning.

Victor patented his idea, quit his job, and went out to sell his product. At first, he was laughed at. It was ridiculous, preposterous; board games had long had their day. He followed toy fairs and exhibitions, and everybody ridiculed his idea. It was six months before he could persuade somebody to at least sit and play the game, then they would see that it was so much more than just a board game. He was hungry, thin. His landlord had been a patient man, but he was money hungry. Victor would be put onto the street if his rent arrears weren't paid.

At last, somebody took his idea seriously. One year later and he had a mansion and six cars. After five years, he'd boosted the economy of his native Poland by several billion Euros. And Khazanza was made.

He worked on small computer programs, psychology-based games and teaching aids. Some years later, he had an idea, just a little idea, to build an integrated program that would fit any computer. He had in mind the notion of inventing a radical computer butler. A program that sat in the background until needed and proved invaluable. The Humanicon was born—a program that, five years later, no computer could function without. He became one of the richest men in the world.

Ellie liked Victor, but more than that, she owed her career to him and was grateful. As an entrepreneur, he was constantly asked to sponsor business ventures. He never forgot his time in the factory or the months when nobody would take him seriously. If somebody needed money to go into business, as long as they were hungry to succeed, Victor would sponsor them. He was a businessman. He wanted his money to grow. So he took an interest in the business, and if it needed his name, he would lend it to the owner until they could stand on their own. When the venture was solvent, he would take his money, plus his cut and let the business fly free.

He had taken a small but personal interest in Ellie's work. He saw somebody like himself, who wanted to succeed, and they had become friends. That was how he'd come to be part of Steppingstone Journey Publications, the publishing house that gave Ellie her big break.

'Eleanor, my darling, how are you?' Victor held her hands in his and kissed her on both cheeks.

'Victor, it's so good to see you. I'm fine, thanks. How are you?'

'Oh, I'm the same as always, but a little bit worse. Congratulations on yet another success, my dear. I am very proud of you, you know?'

Ellie laughed. She admired and liked this big gentleman.

'Victor, I wonder if you can help me. I'm doing some research. Do you know anything about Tay-Sachs Disease?'

'Shoptalk at this delightful soirée? Darling, don't you ever come off duty?'

'Oh, Victor, I'm so sorry. Have I offended you?' Ellie was ashamed for asking. Of course, the last thing Victor wanted to do was talk business. For Ellie, the point of evenings like this was to conduct business, but Victor could talk about whatever he damn well chose.

He laughed heartily, 'Sweetie, I was teasing you. Anyone else wanting to pick my brains at this time of night would bore me rigid, but you, my love, could talk about horse manure, and I'd hang on your every word. Now then, Tay-Sachs, yes, I know a little about it, not a lot you understand. It was never my field. What do you want to know?'

'Anything you can tell me about it, really. Could we get together, perhaps sometime soon?' Not tonight, obviously. As you so rightly point out, tonight is for laughter, merriment and getting sloshed. Work and other boring stuff can be done when the stars aren't shining so brightly.

'Eleanor, I can think of no treat sweeter, but unfortunately, the rest of this month's out. I've got seminars and business stuff to attend for the next few weeks, and then I'm flying to The States for a conference that can't be delayed. I could email whatever I can find to you in the meantime, and then we'll get together for lunch when I get back. Are you in any hurry?'

Ellie almost didn't catch the arrangements. It was only when Victor repeated her name that she came back to the present and agreed to his suggestion. She was still trying not to laugh at the words, 'Are you in a hurry?' The sweet irony.

'Khazanza, old man. Here, you can settle this argument. You don't mind, do you, my dear?' A man with a tuxedo screaming for mercy around his colossal frame dragged Victor away to argue about whatever it was that men of a certain age argue about. And before Ellie knew it, another cheek was proffered for the obligatory air-kiss, and a woman with too much make-up and an insincere smile had cornered her.

Ellie was starving by the time the food was served. It was an elegant buffet that would feed a deprived country for six months. The fare was rich—freshly caught, killed or sliced that morning, everything of the highest standard. After eating, there

181

were plenty of opportunities to work the calories off when the dancing started. Ellie danced with many men, not least Smartassed Jack, much to his girlfriend's displeasure. Despite being larger than life, he was a good dancer, and Ellie enjoyed herself.

She was ready for home when Rob tapped her on the shoulder.

'Excuse me, Miss, don't I know you from somewhere?'

Ellie laughed and gave him a hug.

'Oh, I don't think you missed me too much. I saw you dancing with that Lady No-drawers over there.'

Rob grinned. 'Come on, you. Finish your goodbyes, and let's get outta here.' Geoff's brought the car around and is waiting outside.

Ellie pouted.

'Oh, you're just a rotten old party pooper.'

'Yes, madam, and you just remember that when I'm banging on your door at six in the morning. Sleeping beauty will not want to get up after a bellyful of champagne, very little sleep, and a case of alcohol-induced vertigo.'

'Damn, I hate it when you talk sense.'

As much as Ellie's mind wanted to play, her body had had enough. When she got back to the hotel, she sank into bed and was asleep within minutes.

# Chapter Twelve

E llie didn't realise just how bitterly cold it was in a television studio at seven o'clock on a chilly and frosty morning. She had to pat her arms to keep warm. Later, when the lights-camera-action brigade got to work, the place would be like a sauna with huge overhead fans cutting in to stop the makeup from turning into rivers on the show host's face-of-many-valleys. Ellie could see her breath in the air, and her fingers were stiff and uncooperative.

She was up and at 'em with incredible energy. She rose at six as Rob knocked on her door—not ten-past or half-past when Geoff would be waiting outside, with Rob flinging a minor nervous breakdown. Since getting away from her problems at home or, as she honed the thought down further, since putting distance between herself and Eve, she had a new feeling of joie de vivre.

When the rolling hills of Cumbria had dissolved into the autumnal mist, and the M6 was a heralding highway taking her a long way from Eve, she was more at peace. As each hour passed in London, more of her eased up and let go of the tension. Mr

Tay-Knacker-Sachs was still chewing at her relentlessly, but the anxiety eating into her core was lifted. She still worried about Matt, but he was on his guard. He'd been so upset by how much Eve had fooled him the previous Saturday, and they had devised a password to identify Ellie from Eve.

Ellie spent an hour in makeup and came out with the same result she'd have achieved on her own in ten minutes—but that was show business. The expected hangover had not kicked in. Rob had insisted on a nightcap of fresh orange juice before bed. She looked good and felt confident. She wore a pair of camel coloured trousers, they were simple with a timeless cut and comfortable style. She had black leather boots with an elegant heel, and a black roll-neck tunic with a thin gold chain belt finished her outfit. They wanted to do something extravagant with her hair, but Ellie insisted that she'd be more comfortable with it down and just brushed through well. The stylist came at her with serums and gels and various deposits of gunge in funky colours. Ellie declined, and the poor man moaned about his reputation being at stake. 'Oh, the shame of letting her go on like that.' In the end, Ellie got her own way, and the pouting man brushed her hair without any product other than simple shampoo and conditioner. He brushed it hard until it shone like golden filigree under the harsh lights.

Talk shows had died out years earlier. They had their day and were tired and done, after several untimely contestant suicides. But recently, a new husband and wife team had forced their way to the limelight, and they had resurrected morning television talk shows. The *Jules & Jerri Show* followed the old format but was new and alive. This was Ellie's second appearance. The last time had been a riot, and she'd enjoyed their banter.

A flutter of butterflies danced in her stomach ten minutes before she was due to go on. Rob looked over the interview questions and crossed out the third question on the agenda about the accident with the broken glass. He talked about slander, and that's an ugly word only used in the serious, getting your point across, discussions. He was clear that any mention of the incident would be dealt with in court.

Rob handed her a cup of coffee, but her fingers had left home. All sensation finished at the end of Ellie's wrists. Every nerve-end of feeling left her, and she had no control or grip. The cup of coffee slipped through her hand, splashing to the floor. Luckily—or not for Rob—the coffee missed Ellie. Rob said he was thankful that he'd been standing like a tit with two disposable coffee cups in his hands for ten minutes while the sound engineer faffed around Ellie. He wasn't hurt, but if the coffee was any hotter, he might have been. He was wet, and Ellie said he smelled moist and exotically Brazilian.

The incident knocked her confidence, and instead of doing a walk-on, Rob decided the interview would begin from a sitting position. He would never have mentioned it to Ellie, but the coffee incident, and the fact that she'd been seen staggering into a wall by one of the runners, sent a whisper round the studio that she was drunk. She told Rob, her medication was slow kicking in. She didn't usually start the day with so much activity, and her tablets could take their time, put their feet up for a while, read the morning paper and slip into the day's work gently.

This morning her medication was overworked and was complaining. Rob wanted to call the interview off, but Ellie wouldn't hear of it.

'And now, dear viewers, we are very excited, aren't we, Jerri? Very excited indeed.'

'Well, you are, darling. But don't worry, just keep it covered with your hand, and there'll be no litigation.'

The crew tittered obligingly on the mic.

'As I was saying before, my lovely fishwife butted in, we are thrilled to welcome back the bestselling novelist, Miss Eleanor Erikson.'

Jerri rose first and leaned over to kiss Ellie on the cheek, Jules followed suit, and they were off.

'It's good to see you again, Ellie and congratulations are in order. We hear you've done it again—made the bestseller list, that is. What's this, the third time? Fourth?'

'Seventh actually, but hey, who's counting? And yes, I'm very pleased, thank you.'

'So, how's life all the way up in the beautiful Lake District? What's been happening since the last time you paid us a visit?'

The interview rambled along, following the time-worn tram-lines. Ellie smiled politely and said she would rather not comment on her love life, and no, she would neither confirm nor deny that she was getting plenty.

'But you are still with the same man as last time?' persisted Jerri.

Ellie laughed, knowing Matt would download the show to watch when he finished work. 'Yes, I am with the same man, and yes, we are very happy. But that's all I'm saying on the subject.'

Jerri looked at the sound booth. She was used to trouble. It was what made the show successful. The producers wrote the rules and the show hosts broke them. Her wrinkles smiled, but her face was hard.

'But Ellie, darling, not everything is rosy in your rose covered haven, is it? We read those awful newspaper reports about an attempted suicide. Please, honey child, tell us it's not true.'

Ellie stiffened. This wasn't part of the schedule. She was furious but smiled with the same empty sincerity that Jerri inflicted on her. She laughed, but it was mirthless. 'Jerri, I'm surprised at you, fancy subscribing to the gutter tabloids. Of course, it's not true. I had a little accident with a broken wine glass, that's all.' She glared at the show host, warning her to let the subject drop. Camera three caught the look and zoomed in for a close-up. Jerri relaxed in her seat, letting Ellie think she was surrendering.

Jules' turn, his face took on a sombre expression.

'Ellie, I know this may be difficult for you to talk about, but you've had a nasty shock lately, haven't you?'

Ellie stiffened. Oh, God, what did he know?

'Some health issues?'

Ellie glared at Rob, who was watching the interview offset. He spread his hands and shrugged, miming that he had no idea how this had got out. He turned to the research manager to find out where he got his information, and Ellie saw him snarling at the producer to cut to an ad break.

Ellie's eyes were hard as she faced her interviewers. These people, who two minutes before had felt like friends, had turned into prying scavengers, determined to prize out everything personal and intimate. Ellie was reminded that she belonged to the public and was owned by the readers who paid for her books. They felt entitled to what was private and belonged to her.

'Now then, who's been filling your head full of rubbish?' She smiled for the camera, but her eyes were like steel. They bored into her interviewer's face as though challenging him to continue with the line of questioning. 'And anyway, Jules, where did you get that tie? I hope you're going to sue.'

Jerri smiled a sickening smile intended to ooze feminine empathy. It was a smile that said, 'Wherever you are today, I have been, and I understand what you are going through because I'm a woman, too.'

Bullshit, Ellie thought.

'Sweetie,' Jerri spoke, in a voice dripping syrupy, insincere words like puss from an abscess. 'One of our researchers was passing your dressing room and heard you and your agent talking about an illness you have. It sounded pretty serious. It might help if you talk about it, you know. We are good listeners.'

Ellie felt the familiar temper rising. 'Good listeners? Help to talk? What, to all three million and fifty-seven of you?' God, how could she have liked this woman? 'Darling, you wear imitation sincerity like a sable mink.' Ellie swallowed hard to send her temper down.

'Yes, I have some health issues, as you put it. Some days are good, some are bad. Sometimes I drop things, and I tire easily, but I'm recovering and expect to be back to full health very soon. That's all there is to say about it, really. Thank you for your concern.' Ellie couldn't resist trying a sickly smile to put one of Jerri's to shame. Her voice was so heavy with sarcasm that she could barely lift it to say, 'You're right, it did help to talk. I feel so much better now. In fact, I think I'm cured, halleluiah.'

The effort was not wasted on a fuming Jerri. These two were renowned for making fools of their guests if they could get away with it. But, in typical celebrity fashion, they weren't so keen if the tables were turned on them. Jerri bristled, and her face hardened into a tight knot that gave away the secret of every one of her fifty-two and a half years.

Jules muttered, 'Touché.'

Whether the sensitive microphone was meant to pick it up was known only to him, but the muttering and the smug grin he flashed his wife went to several million viewers. Jerri glared at her husband. This was what made them so successful. Sometimes they bickered between themselves and their guests. Still, on a good day, a genuine, full-scale war broke out between the volatile couple, and that was the stuff television was made of.

'Wanker,' retorted Jerri, and the studio went into a frenzy.

The producer yelled obscenities at Jerri down her earpiece. The camera crew cut to film a blue-glassed vase of flowers, denying the viewers coverage of the warring couple and the guest smirking in amusement despite her best efforts.

'Well, I think it's time to go to the phone-in,' Jerri said in a tight voice as she read the prompt.

'But, before we do, I would like to apologise to the listeners for my unforgivable behaviour,' she paused and then added. 'Again, it seems I'm not allowed to call my husband a wanker on set—even though he is.'

Jules wasn't about to let Jerri steal the limelight. With a grin, he asked, 'Sweetness, what about me? Do I get an apology, too, oh light of my life?'

Jerri wouldn't forgive him for siding with Ellie over her. She was every inch the prima donna and an insanely jealous wife.

'Well, you know what you can do, don't you? You can just f—'

The producer yelled so hard in her ear that her head jerked to the side, and she caught herself just in time.

'You,' she spat the word at him. 'Can just forgive me too, dear,' she finished sweetly before launching into the phone-in.

'And on line one, we have Michelle from Oxford. Good morning, Michelle. What's your question for Eleanor?'

Ellie noticed that the informal, 'Ellie,' had been dropped in favour of her Sunday name. She smiled, warm in the sensation of her victory. 'Hello, Michelle,' she said brightly.

'Hello, Miss Erikson, I'm a big fan.'

'Thank you. Please call me Ellie. What do you want to know?' Ellie had made a good recovery and was back in control. She led the interview and was ready for any trick thrown her way. They'd caught her off guard once, but they wouldn't get her a second time. She hoped she'd played her illness down enough for the press not to jump all over it. Ellie was enjoying herself again. This is what she liked about the PR game, talking to people who read her work. She liked talking to genuine, ordinary readers.

'I do a little bit of writing. I've started my first novel and wondered if you could give me any tips about getting published. You understand, I'm only just starting, so I'm not very good.'

Ellie heard the hunger in the young girl's voice and remembered the feeling. It was being so convinced of your own talent, knowing you can do it, but needing that first small break to get you on the ladder. Ellie had no idea if this girl was any good. Still, beneath the nerves of being on television, she heard the determination in her voice.

'Well, the first thing you do is get your manuscript as good as it can be. Go over it until you can't stand the sight of it, and then do it again. When you think it's perfect, give it another read through because no matter how good it is, it can always be better. A publisher or agent will not waste time on shoddy work. The next step is determination. If you believe in yourself, don't for one second let anybody tell you you can't make it. Send your script out as many times as it takes to get it accepted. If you're going to roll over and die with the first rejection slip, you'll never be a writer. I tell you, Michelle, I have a box full of rejection slips big enough to wallpaper Buckingham Palace. Just believe in yourself, and don't give up. That's the best advice I can give.'

'It's excellent advice, thank you. I'll remember it when things get tough. Thank you, Ellie.'

'Tell you what, Michelle,' Ellie flashed a look at Rob. She knew he wasn't going to like this. 'Have you got a synopsis and the first three chapters done?'

Rob knew what was coming. He stood off-camera, shaking his head and making cut motions by dragging his hand across his throat.

'Er, I haven't got a synopsis yet, but I have fifteen chapters.' Michelle's voice had risen with excitement. Ellie ignored Rob.

'Right, put together a synopsis and send it to me with the first three chapters. If you stay on the phone, the researchers will give you an address. Mark the envelope Jules and Jerri's Michelle, and I'll know it's you. I'll have a look at it for you, and I'll get my agent to read it, too. There are no promises that you'll get anything more than a three-chapter edit and some advice that you may or may not want to hear. But if it helps, we'd be happy to read it.'

Rob would be furious, but Ellie was shrewd and saw it as good publicity, and if it helped the kid along the way, that was a bonus.

'Oh, Ellie, would you? I can't believe this.' Her voice had risen to a screech, and Ellie grinned, pleased to have made her happy. 'That's so good of you, thank you.'

Jules cut in, 'There you go, Michelle, what do you think of that, eh?' Without waiting for an answer, he pushed on. 'Well, we have got Jennifer on line two. Good morning, Jennifer, and what would you like to ask Ellie?'

'Hello, Ellie. I'd like to know where you get your inspiration from?' There was no preamble with this one. She sounded cool and got straight to the point.

'Hello, Jennifer. Oh, that's easy. I get inspiration from every-where. There's drama in every situation, and I get my characters from all walks of life. Sometimes I'll be sitting in a café having a cuppa. I'll see somebody, or maybe even just a small part of somebody, the way they screw up their nose or a certain speech pattern that strikes me as interesting. So I take the person home with me. Not literally, you understand, that would get me arrested, but as soon as I get home, I scribble down whatever it is that struck me about them.'

'That's a good answer, thank you, but what about your story-lines? How do you come up with the twists? How do you channel your imagination?'

Ray Jefferies, the chief engineer in the sound booth, stared at the recording monitor. Computers did everything these days, and his only function was to make sure that the levels on the huge graphic equaliser were balanced. Every few seconds, he gave a cursory glance at the screen to make sure the sound was delivered to the subscription-paying public. What he saw while Jennifer and Ellie were talking made his head turn. He dropped his chocolate bar onto the side of the control desk and stared hard for a few seconds to make sure his eyes weren't deceiving him.

'Hey, Bill, come and look at this,' he said to the second sound tech.

As each person spoke, the sounds they made were transposed to a graph on the monitor. Ellie's line was green, and the caller's line was red. Ray listened to the caller's voice. He'd been in the job a long time, and sound was his business.

'She's disguising her voice. Listen. See there, how deep it is? You can tell from the timbre that it's not her natural pitch. She's dropped it by an octave. See how she struggled on the word from?'

'Yeah, but why would she do that?'

'Anybody's guess, mate, anybody's guess. But look at this. Have you ever seen that happen before?'

He pointed to the sound graphs. The red line aped the speech patterns of the green one. Both voices made identical waves on the screen. It was impossible.

'That woman's pitch, tone, inflexion, everything, is exactly the same as the writer's. Even though she's trying to disguise the sound of her voice, the pattern stays the same. You know, Bill, if I hadn't seen it with my own eyes, I wouldn't have believed it was possible. I think we'd better give Bernie a yell and tell him to look at this, I don't know what it means, and maybe it's a coincidence, but I don't like it.'

Bill left the sound booth to look for the programme director.

'Thanks for the advice, Ellie,' Jennifer was saying, 'it's been nice talking to you. Oh, just before I go, I read in Spiral magazine that you have a German shepherd?'

'Yes, that's right. Jake. He's my baby. I love him to bits. He's as daft as a clown in a joke shop, and he eats me out of house and home.'

'That's lovely. I've got a shepherd, too. A word of warning, though,' the caller's voice remained light and never altered in its chatty friendliness. 'You've got to watch those German shepherds. Little devils, they are. You have to keep an eye on them, or they can get hurt. You need to watch them and see they don't get into trouble. Mine's a right demon, better the devil you know and all that. You must miss yours when you're away from home. I hope he's okay. I'd hate to hear about him getting hurt. I bet he's a right little devil.'

Jules and Jerri looked at each other. 'What is this? Bloody Crufts,' Jules said. 'Where's all this dog talk suddenly come from? He listened on his earpiece to see if they were lined up for the next caller.

Ellie sat for a few seconds, letting each word, every disjointed piece of information, infiltrate her brain. In those seconds, her natural colour beneath the stage make-up left her face like the last wave of the evening tide leaving the beach.

And then she was moving.

She jumped out of her seat and ripped the microphone planted down her bra. She flung it onto the sofa. A sob escaped her and was picked up by every viewer nationwide before white noise was all that transmitted from her discarded mic.

She set off across the studio at a run.

'Ellie,' Jules shouted after her. 'Ellie, are you all right?'

'Oh dear,' Jerri oozed, 'I don't think she's very well. Puke bucket! I don't think she's very well at all. One too many complimentary drinks last night, you know what they say about

194

Northern women and their secret drinking habits. The crew were just telling us how they saw her staggering around this morning. Poor thing, another one for The Priory.'

The producer cringed at the thought of another lawsuit falling on his desk over the next few days.

Ellie drew level with Rob.

'Ellie, what is it? What the hell's happening? Are you all right? Do you need a doctor?'

'Phone,' screamed Ellie at the top of her voice. 'Where's my phone?'

She ran in the direction of her dressing room to find her bag. Rob caught her arm.

'Here,' he said, fishing his phone out of his breast pocket, 'use mine.'

Ellie dialled, not taking the time to thank Rob or look up her home number in his listings. He wouldn't be there anyway.

'Come on, come on. For fuck's sake, come on.'

'Ellie, calm down. Jesus, will you just tell me what's going on?'

No signal.

'Shit.'

She was running again, this time down the warren of corridors that would take her to the outside world and a phone signal.

Partly due to her illness, but mainly because of the height of her heels, she stumbled twice as she pushed her way through cameras and crew members. Without slowing her charge, she lifted her leg, then the other and pulled the elasticated boots from her feet, dropping them as she ran.

She ran at full speed and then a little bit faster, using every ounce of energy. Unhampered by the high-heeled boots, she could lift her legs high. She pumped her arms to aid momentum and sprinted like she hadn't done since her school day athletics. Her bare feet slapped hard on the cold, tiled floor with each step. She remembered a snippet from an advert for hi-tech running shoes. With each step, the advertisement said, something like the equivalent of half a ton of pressure was forced through the tarsal joints. That was a hell of a lot of pressure, and Ellie would pay for this tomorrow, but she didn't care. She had to get a phone signal, fast.

She burst through the swing door, releasing her into the blustery day outside. She didn't wait to hold it open for Rob, who was behind her trying to keep up. It hit him in the chest, knocking the air out of him. He managed to push through after Ellie and stood at the top of the steps, doubled over with his hands on his knees, waiting to see if his lungs were going to burst. They didn't. Maybe, just maybe, he'd survive this.

Ellie stabbed the screen.

It rang three times.

'Good morning, Goldman, Graham and Smith Solicitors. How may I help you.'

'I need to speak to Mr High. Don't give me any bullshit about him being in a meeting. I need to speak to him now. It's urgent.'

Brenda recognised Ellie's voice. She'd been instructed that Matt would be found immediately if Ellie rang. 'I'm sorry, Miss Erikson, but Mr High isn't in the office today. I believe he's working at home.'

Ellie disconnected without courtesy or goodbye.

Damn, he was at home after all.

The phone rang, and Matt answered on the fourth ring.

'Where's Jake,' Ellie screamed at him without any greeting.

'Ellie, what's the matter? I thought you were doing a show. I've got it taping to watch later.' The hysteria in her voice sunk in, and he answered her question. 'Jake, he's in the garden. Why? What's the matter?'

Matt had the back door open. He was fixing himself an early lunch before getting back to the reams of paperwork he had to get through for his court appearance the following day. He'd opened the back door to let Jake into the garden to clean himself.

Quiet, midday suburbia was shattered by a sickening howl. The peace of sleepy Beech Hill was broken. The howl turned from surprise and shocked pain into a scream of terrifying agony.

Matt dropped the tomato he was slicing as he spoke to Ellie and ran for the garden.

Ellie heard her dog screaming in agony, and she sobbed hysterically into Rob's shoulder.

# Chapter Thirteen

Maria was motionless, her eyes glued to the television set long after the morning-show guest had run off the set. She heard what the caller said. The show host said she was ill, but what did they know?

She knew.

On her battered settee, Maria sat in her rented flat in a dressing gown with one button missing and a cheap red wine stain on the left breast from weeks earlier. She scrutinised what she had turned into. What would people think if they saw her like this? There were at least two cigarette burns on the dressing gown, but she wasn't going to worry about burning herself to death in this festering hell. She had more important things to think about than that.

She curled her stout legs underneath her. The necessary weight gain to hide her identity was something else she couldn't wait to shed, along with the nasty dressing gown. She let the thoughts in that were knocking on the door of her mind. They begged to be brought in from the cold.

It was cold. She'd been trembling for the last ten minutes. It had taken that long for the goose pimples to tell the nerve endings, and the nerve endings to tell her brain stem, and for her brain stem to tell her fat arse to get up and put the fire on. Her routine rarely altered. She'd come down, flick the remote to activate the TV, ignite the fire and make a cup of coffee—on a good day. A lousy day had her hitting the red wine before the sun rose. She hated those mornings, but she had to be convincing. On those rare good days, she'd go back up after an hour to wash. On the bad days, she reasoned that no one was there to smell her, so what was the point? This was the life she had to live for now. The horrible flat was her hideout until she could emerge into the light. This wasn't the way she wanted it, but it had to be like this for now, and at least the wine was numbing while she needed the sedation. The police were still poking around. Three employees had been killed in the fire and they were looking for her. She had to lie low. She would emerge from this dingy flat when she could drop the cover of anonymity. This way of living was only an interim disguise, a just for now measure until she could take control.

Today, her routine was broken. She came down, flicked the remote control to activate the television—she still used phrases like activating the television. The cheap 'n nasties hadn't turned all her brain cells to piccalilli yet. But then, after taking two steps towards the fire, she saw her. Well, not her, the other one.

The writer.

'Is it too early for a drinkiepoo?' she asked herself aloud. She had taken to talking to herself more often as the days alone had lengthened into weeks. In reality, it wasn't so many weeks, since the institute burned, but to her, it felt like a lifetime. It was their fault for bringing her to this, but it wouldn't be forever. In fact, she'd be leaving here and resuming real life very soon if things went according to plan.

'Well, my dear,' she answered herself. 'The jolly old cock is over the yardarm, so why not?' She giggled as her thoughts refused to align themselves. She was sure the saying had more to do with suns than cocks, and that the old cock-a-doodle belonged to a different idiom altogether. Cocks were related to mornings and may or may not have had something to do with worms. It was suns and yardarms that went together, silly girl. That inevitably set her mind off on a different train of thought. It was a long time since she'd had a nice bit of cock in the morning—or at any time of day, come to that.

'Now then, about that drink.'

She was about to heave herself up off the sofa when the voice of reason put its oar in. Damn, she hated the voice of reason. She didn't really have a drinking problem, she told herself. She would stop it short the day she could leave this awful place.

'You can't have a drink. What are you going to do about the girl?'

Why is it, she thought, that voices of reason can never mind their own bloody business?

She wasn't old, only one generation older than Ellie Erikson. Everybody knew that each generation spawned faster than the last. Hardly geriatric yet, old girl. But she always thought of them, both of them, as girls rather than women.

She knew this moment of responsibility would come. Hadn't she been waiting for it all these weeks? She was waiting for a sign like this to show that the girls needed her in their lives. The fireworks had begun. Oh, but that was funny. Life? Life? This wasn't living. It was cornering. No, she determined, to be exact, this was being cornered and having nowhere to run. Not yet, at least. But soon, it would be different.

She wondered, not for the first time, not even for the hundredth time, what had happened to her bungalow on The Heights. By now, somebody must have discovered its lack of occupancy. Was anybody looking for her? There was nobody to care about her disappearance, but police or Social Services? Perhaps not, eh? Packing a single rucksack—she had not dared be seen with a suitcase—she simply walked away from her home. She left her car, her possessions and everything she'd worked for all those years. It was the hardest thing she'd ever had to contemplate, never mind put into operation.

Was it divine retribution? God knew, all right, God probably did know. He knew how wicked she'd been. She would tell the girls. She'd say to them with tears in her voice that she'd wanted to stop it. She knew it was wrong, but they—he—was too strong. That's what she'd say when she came together with them. All those years and now she was as trapped as the girl—but Maria was trapped in a prison of her own making. She was incarcerated in a cell of waiting. How much of it was his doing, and how much her own? This was a thought that sent a shiver down her spine when she mulled it over. It was exciting, and she was a woman driven by need and excitement.

'So,' said the bastard voice of reason. 'What are you going to do about it?'

Her voice was weak and pathetic, whiney like a reprimanded child.

'I could ring her.'

201

'Oh, bravo. Yes, you ring her. Good idea. That's a sure way of flushing you out, isn't it? How long after ringing her do you think it would be?'

'What?' she whimpered.

'Before the shit hits the fan.'

Her voice came back a little stronger, thinking, thinking.

'Okay, so it's too dangerous to ring her, but I could ring him. Yes, that's it, if I'm very careful, I can ring the boyfriend. I can't risk giving too much away.'

She got up from the settee with fresh determination. This was something positive, something concrete that she could do. It wouldn't atone. Nothing could ever atone for what she'd done. This thought made her smile.

Why would she want to do that?

Maria shuffled into her bedroom and re-drew the curtains that she'd drawn half an hour earlier. Anybody entering the room might be surprised to see a crucifix standing on the dressing table. It was an ordinary crucifix, nothing there to cause surprise. There were thousands of practising Catholics in the country, even after Jesus had been proved an urban legend. What would make people uncomfortable was the fact that Jesus had been dressed like one of the scarecrows they used to use to protect crops. Little tufts of straw stuck out of his neck and his floppy hat, and tattered and torn farmhand clothes had been attached with glue to his naked body.

Maria grunted with exertion as she pulled her bed across the room and lifted the carpet. Glancing around her to ensure she was still alone, she pulled up the two loose floorboards and thrust her hand into the cavity. These journals contained every foul deed that Maria Kiltcher had ever done in her entire life.

One hundred and eighty volumes laid out in stacks of ten—her life's work. Twenty-seven years of human suffering and torment were contained within those benign ledgers. These were hers. She'd earned them.

She felt the piles, gauging which stack of ten would have the information she sought. Pretty lilac boxes bought from an expensive department store, boxes that belied the horrors contained in them. Each collection was in its own storage box.

She was edgy as long as the books were out. Unsafe, open, a primed sitting duck waiting for exposure. She found Eleanor Erikson's phone number and checked Matthew's name.

Her hands trembled as the telephone rang, shaking so much that she expected the ring tone to warble. Four rings, five.

'Hello, you're through to Ellie and Jake the Wonder Dog. Leave a message, please, and we'll be sure to get back to you soon.'

She hung up quickly.

'Damn.'

She rang half an hour later, and then half an hour after that. On the fourth attempt, she got an answer.

# Chapter Fourteen

One minute Matt was reassuring Ellie that everything was fine. The next, the most God-awful scream of agony came from the garden. The dog's cry carried through the backdoor and into the kitchen on a wave of rising hysteria.

Matt dropped the knife he was using and ran as the first sound of Elle's matching cry of anguish shot through the telephone exchange and into the kitchen to mix with Jake's howling.

He left the room at a sprint, following the howling to the rhododendron at the end of the garden. He skidded to a halt.

In a split second, he took in the scene, Jake writhing and biting savagely at his hind leg without letting up on the maniacal scream for a second. Matt didn't know, until that moment, that dogs were able to scream. He couldn't believe the cruelty. How could anybody be so bloody savage? His priority was to keep Jake still and try to stop him from doing any more damage. He told Ellie what was happening and promised he wouldn't let Jake die. Hanging up on Ellie while she was so upset was hard, but he knew Rob would care for her.

He flung his body at Jake's head and pinned him to the ground. Putting his knee into the resisting flesh at the side of the big dog's neck, he struggled to hold him in position. Jake whirled on Matt, trying to bite him, strong white teeth gnashed uselessly on empty space, fear at for all mankind in his eyes. Jake was terrified and in such pain that he was beyond reason. Matt murmured soothing words to calm him with a soft voice.

The merciless teeth of the poachers' snare had cut into Jake's left hind leg, tearing at the flesh and exposing the smooth white bone. Matt was swearing in anger, frustration and pity for the dog as he tore open the relentless jaws of the snare. This had to be the work of Eve. Where the hell had she got hold of the snare? These things were antiques. And how could she even consider using the brutal and illegal death trap on a defenceless animal? His thinking told him that the crazy bitch would stop at nothing to bring destruction to their family—him, Ellie and Jake and, goddammit, even Esther.

Once the snare was released from his leg, Jake wilted. He was exhausted, and shock was seeping through his body like the chill from a snowdrift. His gums were white, the blood retreating to feed his numbed brain.

Jake realised that Matt was holding him and trying to help him. Jake loved Matt. He was sorry for trying to bite him. Jake didn't need to be punished. Jake was a good boy. Jake had looked after the house, just like Ellie told him. It was the not-Ellie that punished Jake. He could smell it all around the bush. Jake wants to tell not-Ellie that he's a good boy, then not-Ellie will go away and won't hurt them anymore.

Matt carried the bleeding dog into the house and laid him on the sofa. He talked to him all the time. Jake had fallen silent. His eyes were heavy, and he made no attempt to move as Matt laid him down. His head lolled, and he was listless, as though he'd been sedated.

'Phone, George,' Matt yelled. He instructed George to dial the vet's number. He tried to stay calm as he spoke to the veterinary assistant, but his voice cracked several times. He told the vet that he was on his way with the hurt dog and for them to be ready when he got there. The vet said to apply a cold compress to the dog's leg and keep him as warm and calm as possible.

Matt wrapped Jake in a travel blanket they kept in the car and carried him out. He was worried about him damaging himself further by jumping around as he drove, but he needn't have worried. Jake lay still and silent on the backseat, not even bothering to lick his wounded leg.

They worked on Jake for a long time. The nursing assistant suggested that Matt go home and they'd ring him, but he couldn't forget the look of confusion in the dog's eyes. He knew he was a sentimental fool and that he should go home in case Ellie rang, but he couldn't leave Jake. The lads down the pub would rib him forever and a day if they saw him almost crying over a dumb dog. He didn't care. He felt the dog would sense he was alone if Matt left. There would be time enough to go home when he knew Jake was all right. He drank a cup of strong, bitter coffee that the receptionist pressed into his hands, and he barely tasted it.

He was ready for them when they asked what had happened to Jake. He said that he'd shot through his legs as he opened the front door that morning. He told the vet that Jake ran off and refused to be called back. It happened sometimes, Matt told them, but he always came back after he'd had a nosy around.

He made sure he mentioned all the wood and farmland around the cottage in case later connections were made to the type of injury Jake had sustained. He told them that Jake had limped home in that state and that he had no idea what had happened to him.

The vet reappeared from treatment room two with a reassuring smile on his face.

'Is he going to be all right?' Matt jumped to his feet, his voice heavy with concern.

'Yes. He'll be fine, Mr High. It's a nasty wound, mind; he's been lucky. Another inch, and we'd have had to take his leg off. There are no bones broken, and I expect him to make a full recovery. Now then, he's had a shock and still isn't feeling himself, so we want to keep him in overnight, just to keep an eye on him. He's had some heavy sedation, so he's going to sleep. That's what his body needs now to reduce the shock to his system. He'll be as right as rain in the morning, and you can pick him up. I'll want him back in seven days to have another look and to see that the stitches are dissolving properly.'

Matt drove back to Ellie's in a daze. Every time he tried to think, his mind hit a roadblock of fury that he couldn't get past. He tried for the umpteenth time to get through to Ellie, but there was no reply. There was no way she'd turn her phone off at a time like this or go on to her next engagement. That meant that wherever she was, there was no signal. Matt knew Ellie as well as he knew his own mother. Sure as eggs were brown and came out of a hen's arse, Ellie was on a plane right this minute on her way home. Matt knew she wouldn't wait for the car to get her back. Poor Rob thought Matt, he'd be tearing his hair out. Matt decided to call in the supermarket on his way home to get something nice for their evening meal. He knew she was on her way. She may not feel like eating a lot, but after she heard that Jake would be okay, she'd want something. It wasn't doing much, but at least it was doing. Matt felt guilty that it happened while he was looking after Jake. He just hoped Ellie didn't blame him for it. Her moods were so erratic that he couldn't be sure of anything.

He let himself into the house to a strange, eerie silence. This wasn't Cherry Tree Cottage. Where was the bouncing dog, yelping with excitement, or the warm, soft kiss from Ellie? He went through to the kitchen with his shopping bags and stopped in disbelief.

Their photo albums had been savaged. Each photograph of Jake had been cut into quarters. The pieces had been mixed up, and every surface, cupboard doors, worktops, the window—all of them were covered in glued mosaic pieces of Ellie's vast array of Jake photographs. Every one of them was ruined. The snare had been re-set and left triggered and ready on the floor.

Matt considered it a stage set up for Eve's entertainment, not a serious attempt to hurt Ellie or himself. It was a mockery, a bragging of Eve's envisaged superior intelligence. How the hell was she getting in? Matt had locked the door behind him. Nobody could access the eye scanner but himself and Ellie. He shook his head in disgust as he looked at the floor. A bottle of tomato ketchup was abandoned on the worktop, and scrawled across the floor, in six-inch-high letters, was an epitaph written in the sauce. RIP Jake. The viscous fluid had congealed and stiffened. Matt wasn't surprised by Eve's lack of subtlety. This childishness seemed to be the level at which she remained. What did shock him, though, was that she knew the dog's name.

Miss Psychotic Knickers wasn't as clever as she thought. It showed that Eve assumed Jake was dead. Tough shit, lady. Jake lives to tear your miserable throat out another day.

Matt was cleaning the kitchen when Ellie rang to say she was on her way in a hire car from the airport and would be home within the hour. Matt reassured her that Jake was going to be okay.

He'd no sooner finished talking to Ellie when the phone rang again.

'Answer, please, George.'

'Hello.' For three seconds, all Matt could hear was harsh, rapid breathing. Then the woman's voice cut in. She sounded anxious, scared, and she was rambling, not making sense.

'Is that Mr High? Matthew High?' Matt was about to confirm he was, but she didn't give him a chance to speak.

'Please listen to what I'm going to tell you. Just listen, if you say one word, I'll hang up, and you'll never hear from me again. You have to listen to me, and God knows you have to trust what I'm saying, even though it sounds ridiculous.'

She took a deep audible breath. Her voice was shaky, her words tumbling over each other in a frantic attempt to get out and be understood. The lady sounded on the verge of hysteria.

'I know about Eve.'

She heard him gasp and almost laughed. She knew that this was the single link that could get her back where she needed to be. She'd given up everything because she had to lay low and be swallowed into anonymity. And here she was running the risk of bringing the whole asylum of lunatics crashing down on her. Delicious lunacy kept the blood pumping. Her act sounded convincing on the phone, she put on a good show of being anxious, but the lady was smiling at her end.

'I know what she's up to, and I know that Eleanor is in serious danger. But listen to me. It's far more than that. Someone is playing with all of you. He's tried to kill me. He thinks I'm dead, and if he finds out I'm alive, he'll hunt me down and finish the job. He's pure evil, sick. Oh God, there's so much more you should know, but I've already said too much. I had to warn you. That's the least I owe the girls. But this is the most important part. You mustn't tell Ellie about me. You can't mention this conversation at all. I have to tell you, you have to know. Everything that Eleanor sees, hears, or says goes straight back. Please don't say anything to her. He'll know. He'll know.' That was enough for now, a few hooks to bait them. She ran her dry tongue over cracked lips. Not long now.

Matt had to speak. This was the break they had been waiting for, and he answered the woman.

'Listen to me, lady. You know Eve? You know about her? You have to tell me. Where is she? Who the hell is she? How is she connected to Ellie? Is she her twin sister? Why the fuck is she doing all this to us? Please tell me what's going on.'

The woman gave a loud sob, and the phone clicked as the connection was broken.

In the dingy bedsit, Maria picked up a large glass of red wine and laughed. She'd left Matt reeling. The garbled message wouldn't make sense, and he'd be asking, 'Who the hell was that? Eve's mother?'

The woman on the end of the broken connection smiled. She looked around the hovel, picked up the Valencia suitcase filled with journals and walked out of there for the last time. No trace, no trail, next roll of the dice.

'Last call search, George,' Matt said.

'The number of the last caller was withheld, Matt.'

'Okay, standby.'

It was as he'd expected, but it was worth a try. Matt went over the mysterious phone call after cleaning the kitchen and preparing a meal. Was the woman suggesting that Ellie was relaying information back to this crazy somebody? None of it made sense. Just three weeks ago, he'd have written the woman off as insane, but nothing was as it seemed anymore. He had to take the warning seriously.

Ellie burst through the door with a harassed Rob behind her.

'How is he? How's Jake?'

She dropped the small case she was carrying, and Rob gratefully put down the other two huge suitcases and three bags in the hall. Matt rushed forward to greet them and pulled Ellie into his arms. He stroked her hair and kissed her cheek, telling her that Jake was going to be okay.

'I want to go and see him.'

'Hey, listen to me. He's been heavily sedated. He may not be conscious. He's had a lot of treatment on his leg, and he's exhausted. Even if he is awake, all you can do by going there today is upset him. The second he sees you, he'll want to come home, and all you'll do is disrupt his healing. You look shattered.

Let Jake rest today. You get some rest too, and then, in the morning, we can pick him up. Okay?'

'Okay, but I want to ring the vets and talk to them. See that he's okay and that he's not pining for me.'

Matt was leading her through to the lounge as he spoke. The kitchen door off the lounge was open, and Ellie caught sight of the snare on the kitchen worktop. Matt would dispose of it after he'd disarmed it, but he knew Ellie would want to see it, and he had no idea if they were going to call the police. After their accusations last time, it had to be her call. Ellie picked up the snare. The ragged teeth were still tipped with Jake's blood, and they leered at her as she ran her finger over the cold steel.

'How could she? How could she do that to him?' Ellie asked in a quiet voice.

Matt drew her to the sofa and put his arm around her. Rob tactfully asked if he could use the study and rang to cancel the rest of Ellie's engagements.

'Ellie, I'm so sorry. I'm so damned sorry this happened. If only I'd checked the garden before I let him out.'

'Listen, you. Don't you dare blame yourself for this. Don't you dare. This is her doing, that evil bitch. And when I get my hands on her, I'm going to ram that snare down her throat sideways and clamp it to her bloody intestines. I'm going to hit her over the head and stab her with a knife, then hit her over the head with a statue.' All the fight left her, and she went limp in Matt's arms. 'And then, Matty, I'm just going to ask her why.'

Rob joined them and told Ellie that everything was sorted. Cancelling at short notice wasn't going to help her career, but that was the last thing on Ellie's mind. Rob put the word out that

Miss Erikson had been taken ill, a fact born out by what had happened live on The Jules & Jerri Show.

They talked about everything that had happened. Rob was in favour of calling the police, but Ellie wouldn't hear of it. She convinced the men that even if she could make that prick of an inspector believe her, nothing could be done about it. Matt told Ellie about the photographs and the re-setting of the trap. And Ellie cried at the malice behind the action. The pictures could easily be reprinted from George's memory, but a human being hating her so much made her sad. She sifted through the confetti images of Jake. Jake photographed as a puppy, Jake with Matt, Jake with her, Jake in Scotland, all fragmented pieces of happier times breaking her heart. Eve had taken those precious memories and violated them.

'What's she going to do next?'

Matt said it, but it was what they'd all been thinking.

'What if she comes back to finish what she started with Jake?' Ellie asked. 'I don't feel safe, Matty. I don't want to be here alone.'

Matt said that while Rob stayed with her, he would go home and pack some things. He was moving in until this was finished, and he wouldn't hear any argument.

Ellie had none to give, and that broke Matt's heart. Under any other circumstances, he'd have been delighted to be moving in with her. Giving up her fierce independence without a word of protest was an indicator of just how frightened she was.

'What about Jake?'

'Jake will be all right, love. We'll be here to keep an eye on him. We'll just have to be more vigilant.'

'I've got an idea,' Rob said. 'Why don't I take Jake? Just until all this is sorted out. He'll be safe with me, and you know we'll look after him. Gail and I love him almost as much as you two do. But, I warn you, if he digs up my lawn again, I'll do for the bugger myself.'

'Would you take him, Rob?' Ellie squealed. There was no thought, no hesitation. Jake was, after all, a guard dog, insomuch as he would alert them to the presence of Eve.

Matt had seen Jake's reaction when he'd been with Eve at his house; they just hadn't picked up on his warnings. Common sense should have prevailed, and Ellie should have kept Jake at home to forewarn them of Eve's next move, but her thoughts were not for her own safety. Her priority was to keep Jake safe.

Another sign of the times thought Matt. For Ellie to be parted from Jake was an incredible wrench and a huge sacrifice to put the dog's best interests first. 'Yes, Rob, please take him. Thank you so much. I know he'll be fine with you and Gail, and you know how he loves to play in....'

Ellie had been about to say how Jake liked to play in Stanney Wood.

*Everything she sees, hears or says goes straight back.*

The sentence ran through Matt's mind, and he interrupted before Ellie could finish what she was saying. He didn't want Ellie giving any clue or indication as to where Rob and Gail lived. It was bad enough that Eve had access to his and Ellie's houses, without her stalking their friends, too.

'Well, that's all sorted out, then. Let's have another coffee, should we?'

Why had he done that? It was ridiculous. Did he think the house was bugged or something? Instinct told him they had to

214

be careful what they said. Maybe they would be better moving into his house, but he'd have a devil of a job persuading Ellie.

Better the devil, you know. The phrase drove through his mind. There were so many questions that they didn't have answers to. Their time together was limited and precious. This was a time when they should have been living each moment to the full. They shouldn't have to hide away, scared and insecure. He hated that he couldn't protect Ellie, but from now on, he would be with her around the clock to see she was safe.

While Ellie went upstairs for a soak in the bath, Matt took Rob into the garden. He told Rob in a hushed whisper about the phone call. Rob had no better ideas about who the woman might be, other than perhaps an escaped lunatic. But they decided not to tell Ellie right away. She had enough on her plate and didn't need another complication to the horrors frightening her.

Sometime later that evening, Jake woke up as the veterinary assistant went into the hospitalisation pens for the last check of the night.

'Hey, boy, you're back with us, eh? I bet you'd like a nice cool drink of water, wouldn't you?' She filled a bowl and lifted his head. Jake lapped at the cool drink, managing to dribble a lot and drink a little.

Jake's eyes don't want to open. Oh, round-and-round, everything moving. Can't shake head. Head won't work. Oh dear, head broken. This isn't kitchen, it isn't garden, it isn't 'Get off the bed Jake'. Hello lady, who's not Ellie or Matt. Lady smells like white coat and needle man, but lady smells kind, too. Lady's funny. Oh, Jake's laughing. Drink, yes, please, drink. Uh-oh, Jake made a mess. Bad dog Jake. Jake laughing again. Head won't work, head broken, round-and-round. Funny. Where's Ellie? Jake must protect Ellie. Jake growl. Uh-oh, growl broken too. Jake all broken up. So sleepy, so very sl...

The assistant lowered the big dog's head and stroked him a couple of times. He snored rhythmically and loud.

'Okay, big lad, you sleep it off. I bet you'll have quite a hang-over in the morning. You are a beautiful fella.'

Jake opened one eye and chuffed. Of course, Jake beautiful. Jake knows it. And then he snored some more.

The following day, news of Ellie's illness hit the nationals. It was only a small column in each newspaper, some with a publicity shot of her at the computer, but the word was out that Ellie was terminally ill. They had all the facts and the name of the disease killing her. Some details about the condition were twaddled out, and the fact that she might not complete the novel she was writing. Ellie felt unclean and tainted by media rape.

*TOP NOVELIST STRUCK DOWN BY KILLER DISEASE*

Even her disease didn't belong to her. She was owned by the media, the press and the public. She wouldn't be allowed the dignity of dying privately.

The phone rang as they sat down to breakfast.

'Eleanor, my darling.' Esther was sobbing hysterically, and it was difficult to make out what she was saying.

'Hello, Mother.'

'Oh, Eleanor, how could you let me find out like that? Have you any idea the shock I've suffered to read something so horrific in *The Guardian*? Please tell me it's a lie, Eleanor. Tell me it's not true. What will I do without you? How will I manage on my own? Why didn't you tell me, Eleanor? You wicked girl.'

'Yes, Mother. I'm sorry you had to find out like that. But, you know, we did tell you. You chose not to hear.'

'Oh, Eleanor, don't you dare blame me for all of this upset.'

'No, Mother, of course not. It must be a terrible shock for you.'

'Well, my darling child, there's only one thing for it. I'm going to give up all that I hold dear and move in with you. Somebody has to look after you. I'll put the house on the market this very morning.'

'No, Mother.' Ellie shrieked down the phone, making Matt spill coffee over his toast and jam.

Matt looked at Ellie, his face full of concern. It took every ounce of Ellie's tact, diplomacy and persistent determination to stop Esther from turning into a modern-day Florence Nightingale. Her feelings would never be spared no matter how tactful Ellie tried to be, and the call ended in acrimony and hurt.

'Bloody hell. Can you imagine anything worse than having my mother living with us? Shit, I'd rather invite Eve to be my nursemaid.'

Her tone was so serious, and her face so straight, that Matt couldn't help laughing and soon they were both giggling like schoolchildren and describing what life would be like living with Esther.

Jake was picked up amongst hugging and words of approval. Nothing on earth would have stopped Ellie from going with

217

Matt to pick him up and taking him to Rob and Gail's, and Matt didn't even bother to try. If it led to somebody knowing about Jake's whereabouts, then they would just have to deal with the problem when it arose.

Ellie and Matt gave in to the bullying of their friends, and, on the spur of the moment, they decided to spend a couple of days with Rob and Gail as well. Some normal conversation, fine wine and great company would do them good.

Matt went home to pack some things for them.

# Chapter Fifteen

She hid at the bottom of the garden, her face contorted with hatred. Anybody seeing her would be put in mind of a malignant pixie. She had forsaken her favoured hiding place behind what she thought of as the snare bush. It was too risky. She would have to make do with positioning at the back of the shed from now on. They were bound to be more vigilant now that the dog was dead. From here, she could be over the perimeter wall as soon as the back door opened without being seen.

Her plans were laid. Everything was set in order, ready for her—ready for them. It was time to stop playing and reclaim what was hers. Everything so far had been a practice, trial runs to prepare her for the big one. They were supposed to be confidence-building, but she'd experienced her failures along the way. Except for the dog—he had to be taken out of the picture because he posed a big problem for her. She had not, as yet, tried to kill anybody. They were wrong about that. She was indignant that they thought she had. She had more imagination than a tacky knock on the head and a stabbing. She'd planned this for a long time. She had some class and style. Did they think that bitch was the only one with any finesse? The attacks were unfortunate, but her plan was always to move and adapt as situations arose. She didn't know the bloody boyfriend was going to be there that day, and she'd only ever intended to scare the writer bitch with the knife. Well, it was going to come together. No cock-ups this time, no slips. It had to be—perfect.

She felt terrible about the dog. She liked animals. She'd never stroked one or known what it felt like to hold something soft, furry and alive in her arms, but she liked them. She knew that one day she'd like to have something of her own. If he hadn't been so loyal to that bitch, she'd have taken the dog over along with the house. That would've been nice, but he didn't like her. He was too taken in by the imposter. If only he could see that Ellie was fake, she wouldn't have had to kill him. She'd cried herself to sleep over that. She didn't want to do it, but she had to. It was regrettable, but she had no choice. The dog was expendable.

She fingered the letter in her pocket. It'd been hand-delivered to her address that morning. It worried her. What did it mean? The single sheet of paper was typed and read:

Password: Lilith

From a friend.

If Eve was sure of only one thing in this whole damned world, it was that she had no friends. Maybe they'd tracked her down and were playing a game of their own. No matter, they didn't understand that she was calling the shots. She didn't need to pay the piper. She, Eve, was the piper. When she was ready to say, 'Dance,' they would dance to her tune.

The note threw her. She'd felt safe, hidden in the anonymous bedsit. She blended and could come and go without being noticed. Somebody knew where she lived, so she could never go back there, but it didn't matter. The game was drawing to a close. She'd thrown her few pathetic belongings into a rucksack before she left. She didn't have much and didn't need the new dress she'd bought with Ellie's money to emulate her. Her plan had been to impersonate her and do some damage to her career. But all press conferences had been cancelled, what with the sad demise of poor Jakey. He was a dog, for fuck's sake, Christ, some people would milk a dead donkey. She'd burned the dress, along with other stuff, some that she had taken from the house. They were things that she felt grounded her to Ellie in a bizarre psychometric oneness. If she held an item belonging to the imposter, she thought she could home in on her and feel her terror. Eve loved the feeling of ultimate power. The bitch knew she was hunted. She was trapped in Eve's web, and she knew it. The creeping smile on the distorted face bordered insanity. Let the party proceed.

As she passed the time behind the shed, she was vigilant. She had a good view of the house and could see through most of the downstairs windows. She would know if anybody came home. That morning, everything was quiet. She would bide her time. It gave her the freedom to think this through again and make sure that her plan was foolproof. Her thoughts drifted to the password, Lilith. It had to be something to do with her impostor, the woman living the life that belonged to her. It was clever. Who was it from? The obvious answer was that it came from them, but that wasn't her dear sister's style. She wouldn't play cat and mouse. The fool would confront, like a mouse facing a tiger. It had to have come from him. She wasn't safe at all. She'd never be safe. But she was free, and that wasn't ever going to change.

Lilith, she remembered reading somewhere that Lilith was Eve's dark twin, the one who really seduced and tempted Adam, but she wasn't sure that this was correct or stated in the bible. How inappropriate that the writer saw herself as the dark twin. Surely that title belonged to Eve. Her hatred burned. That woman would take everything if she could, even her personality. As soon as the opportunity arose, she would lead their Adam character by his prissy little tie, right into her Garden of Eden.

She felt a thrill akin to sexual arousal course through her. Though this was not sexual, it was powerful. Adrenaline flowed, dancing with the blood in her veins, and she was restless. Her heart thumped to its own rock beat, and she was ready to run with the final showdown. Bring on the clowns.

# Chapter Sixteen

F lipping heck, which potions in this plethora of gunky products does Ellie need to survive? Surely to God, she doesn't
splatter all this muck on her face every morning?

Matt read some labels: toning cream, exfoliating cream,
anti-ageing cream, skin tonic. What the hell was wrong with
good old soap and water? Women were an alien breed.

He opened Ellie's largest vanity case and threw products into
it randomly. Waxing strips, eye cream, avocado facemask, St
John's wart—ugh, what's that? Ellie doesn't have warts—contra-
ceptive pills—mustn't forget those—Royal jelly—kinky, Ellie.

The internal mysteries of Ellie's bathroom cave were an education for Matt. He had lots of questions to ask her later. For
instance, what do you do with—oh, never mind.

He was so busy that at first, he didn't hear George's voice
informing him that he had a call. In his indecision of which one
to take, Matt had hung Ellie's thick towelling dressing gown and
her sexy, raw silk gown over the bathroom phone speaker. He
removed them and held them up with a frown. This would be
Ellie ringing, and he could ask her which one she wanted.

'Ellie,' he chuckled into the phone, 'never has a simple mission been so impossible, and that Apollo lot thought they had it hard. Frumpy towelling or sexy silk?'

Ellie's voice was breathless with excitement. 'Eh? Oh, never mind that now. I've got news.'

'What? Does it involve me smothering your body in one of these gunges?'

He heard her take a deep breath as though she was steadying herself to get the information across.

'We've been digging on the net while you've been gone. Revenue records, things like that. And we've had a breakthrough. We've found out where Eve used to work.'

'Ellie, that's fantastic.'

'Well, we assume it's her. We did an employment scan and came up with the name Evelyn Erikson. Sounds like her, doesn't it?'

Matt felt a cold chill go through him. Erikson? He couldn't believe the woman even used Ellie's surname. Again, everything seemed to lead back to Esther. Matt was confused.

'Ellie, I did a thorough employment scan and came up with nothing. I don't understand.'

Matt smelled a rat. His voice was guarded. With the impact of the news, he'd forgotten to ask Ellie for their agreed password.

'Ellie? What's the password?'

She laughed. 'Bit late in the day to be asking me, that isn't it? Lilith, of course.'

Matt relaxed. 'Well, come on, tell me what you've found out.'

'Right, well, it's not a lot, and of course, this woman may not be her, but until two months ago, she worked at the Valleyside

Institute and Research Facility. Rob and I are going there now. You'll follow us in your car, yes?'

'Hang on, hang on. Ellie, slow down and let's think this through. At least wait until I get back, and then we can all go together. You've waited this long. What's another half hour?'

'No time, Matty, we're leaving now. It's on the Bassenthwaite road, west of Keswick, and it's a side road apparently, that takes you down to the lakeside.'

'Ellie, just a minute. I don't like this.'

Matt was left talking to a dead connection. As much as he loved her, Ellie could be so irritating sometimes. Why the hell couldn't she have waited for him to get back to her? It was a fair old drive to Keswick, and it would make much more sense to go together. Or better yet, leave it until the next day. By the time they got there, it'd be getting dark. That was so typical of her, a bloody impulsive woman, flying off to God knows where without thinking things through.

He was still grumbling as he set off to the melodramatic strains of the Milochov Symphony. The drive into The Lakes was beautiful and calmed him, he enjoyed the challenges of the narrow and twisting road.

'Bugger,' he swore quietly, as another side road to the lake dwindled into a muddy dirt track barely big enough to get a vehicle down. Twigs were twanging onto the sides of the car, and he worried about his metallic sapphire bodywork. He'd paid extra for the finish. Twice now, he'd hit a dead end and had to reverse onto the darkening main road. It was only four-thirty, but already the night was drawing in, dusk was losing its battle to darkness, and lengthening shadows made visibility difficult. He cursed his beloved girlfriend. Why couldn't this have waited until morning? By the time he found the place, he worried that they'd be closed for the night.

Leaning forward, he ran his finger over the power sensor on his car phone. He'd have to ring her and get more precise directions. The phone was dead. The red power light didn't come on, no matter how many times he gave the voice command. He tried to connect manually with the sensor. Damn, blast and bugger it, he'd only had the car eighteen months and twice during that time, the phone had gone belly up. Leaning over to the passenger seat, he groped for his mobile in his jacket pocket. The bloody Japanese have the right idea when it comes to making cars, small attention to detail, that's what they're good at. To hell with supporting home commodities in future. Oh, for Christ's sake. His pocket was empty, and in his mind's eye, he had a clear memory of putting his phone on the coffee table as he went into Ellie's house. He couldn't remember picking it up on the way out, but he never went anywhere without it. 'Of all the stupid, empty-headed, dumb-assed things to do.' He never forgot his phone. It was an extension of his pulse and went everywhere he did. This is Ellie's fault, making him rush out of the house like that. He hoped she and Rob hadn't been as forgetful. Matt searched his pocket and tutted at the hole he found in the lining.

The fourth attempt to find the right road proved fruitful, though trade descriptions would baulk at calling it a road. Halfway down another rutted track was a small nondescript sign in discrete lettering, saying, *Valleyside Institute*. Underneath, in much larger print, were the words, *Private Property. Trespassers will be prosecuted.* Why the hell couldn't they have had this sign on the main road? Bloody country yokels, not an active brain cell between them. How's anybody supposed to find this place?

He bumped and lurched down the track and came to a pair of wrought iron gates. They were open, and a gatehouse appeared to be unmanned. Matt felt the first fluttering of apprehension. Surely a place so protective of its privacy would have locked gates and a manned gatehouse. He rounded a bend and what was once a stately country residence panned out before him. There was no sign of Rob and Ellie. Matt assumed they must be arriving in Ellie's car, Rob would've been there by now. Although the two men were good friends, there was still a healthy rivalry between them. Matt grinned, knowing they were probably touring endless dirt tracks trying to find the place.

The front façade of the structure was lost in thick, molesting ivy. It looked as though it was smothering the building and made it dark and forbidding. The original front door had been replaced by a businesslike affair, and, on looking around him, Matt noticed that the perimeter was skirted with high, electric fencing, though he couldn't hear the warning buzz indicating it was switched on. Not the friendliest of places, then.

Getting out of the car, he crunched up the gravel drive to the door. The place looked deserted. There were no lights on anywhere even though daylight was fading and visibility was murky. Typical. He knew it would be closed. And yet it seemed more than just closed. It was lifeless, as though the building had not felt human breath for some time. He leaned forward to read a brass plate on the door—and felt a blinding pain in the back of his head. For the second time in less than a week, Matt's world went black.

# Chapter Seventeen

'Where the bloody hell is he?'

Matt had been gone for over two hours, and Ellie was worried.

'He's probably gone to his own place to pick up some stuff and got side-tracked. Don't worry, he'll be soon enough,' Gail patted her friend's hand like a protective mother.

'Yeah, you're probably right. Hell, Gail, I've never been the possessive type, you know that. It's just with all this Eve stuff going on—every time we're apart, I get this feeling in my stomach. Come on, let's chop that veg for dinner and enjoy the fact that our men are out, and we've got time to gossip about them.'

They were going into the kitchen when Ellie's mobile rang. Gail motioned to her friend that she'd go and make a start, but as she watched the colour siphoning from Ellie's face, she sat down.

'What is it, Ellie? What's the matter?'

Ellie didn't hear her. Her focus was attuned to the voice on the end of the phone.

'Hey, Ellie, guess who? And I'm telling you, baby, it ain't Santa Claus. You know the password you gave to your fuckwit boyfriend? Yeah, well, somebody sent it to me. Secrets and lies Ellie, they all come out in the end. That was really handy when he asked me for it. Oh, before I go any further, I was so sorry to hear about the dog. It must've been a terrible shock finding out he was dead.'

'What do you want?' Ellie's voice was cold. She was trembling. Her hands gripped the mobile so tightly that the knuckles rose in white hillocks from her fist.

'Oh, sister.' Ellie winced as Eve drew the word out. 'Don't be so unfriendly. It's not what I want that you should be asking. It's what I've got that you want. That's the question. You do want him, I take it?'

Ellie felt sick as Eve's words sunk in, and fear's hand was ice cold and unrelenting in its cruelty.

'Have you got Matt?'

'Hey, you catch on quick. And I thought I was the sister with all the brains.'

'How do I know you've got him? How can I believe you?' Gail gave a gasp as she realised what was going on, but Ellie wasn't aware of it.

'Well, Ellie, the dumb puss fell for it again. Isn't that just like a man? They have no idea. He asked if I wanted your frumpy towelling or your sexy silk when I came for him.'

'If you've hurt him, I swear to you I'll kill you.'

'What if I only fucked him?'

Tears ran down Ellie's cheeks. Gail sat beside her and took her empty hand. Ellie squeezed down on it hard, her fingernails digging into the tender flesh of Gail's palm. But all she was aware of was the hated voice on the other end of the phone and the fact that Eve had Matt.

Eve's voice turned from tauntingly sweet to bitter and hard.

'Yeah, save the dramatics for your books, bitch. It's time to listen up, and you'd better listen good because playtime's over. I'm not in the mood to be messed about. Right, the first rule is you tell no one. Nobody, you got that? If you ring the police, they might get me, but sweetheart, they'll get me hanging on to your man's dead body. You tell nobody. Understood?'

Ellie glanced at Gail. She put her finger to her lips and motioned for her to be quiet. Then she nodded into the phone.

'Yes, I understand. What do I have to do? How much do you want?'

Eve laughed. She sounded genuinely amused. Under different circumstances, it would be a pleasant laugh, but as it was, it sent rods of iced terror tram lining down Ellie's spine. Insanity wasn't apparent in the laughter, but Ellie knew it was there.

'How much? Do you think this is about money? Ellie, I don't want your money. I'm taking so much more than that, bitch. I want your life. The one you stole from me. You get that—right? Please, you simpering idiot, tell me that at least you get that much. You stole my life, but guess what? Little sister's here to take it back, and I'll do whatever it takes. You hear me? Whatever it takes.'

Eve's voice rose to a scream. It was tinged with fury. She went quiet, and Ellie heard her taking deep breaths. Ellie recognised the effort Eve was making to get her temper under control. She had Matt, and the last thing Ellie wanted to do was antagonise her.

'Okay. Look, I hear you, no police. I understand. Just stay calm and tell me what I have to do, and I'll do it, I promise, whatever you say.'

Gail pulled on Ellie's arm to get her attention. When Ellie said she wouldn't tell the police, Gail shook her head in horror. Ellie put her hand up to stop Gail from distracting her. She had to concentrate on what Eve was saying. Matt's life depended on it.

Eve was back in control.

'Rob and his wife, I'm guessing they're out, right?'

So she didn't know Gail had taken the day off work to stay with her. Ellie thought it could work to her advantage.

'Yes, that's right.'

'Okay, you leave now. Don't even think about leaving a note to tell them where you are. Get into your car and drive up to Keswick. Listen carefully to these directions.' Eve gave Ellie directions to the research institute.

'And remember, you tell so much as one living soul and your boyfriend's soul will find itself without a body. Don't doubt for one second that I'll kill him, Ellie, I did for the mutt, and I'll do for him too. You have one hour, and then—I'll kill him anyway.'

'I want to speak to Matt. How do I even know you've got him? Put him on the line.' She didn't say please and tried to make her voice authoritative while staying calm to not antagonise Eve.

'You're in no position to make demands on me, woman. You're right. I might not have your precious boyfriend, but what if I do? Is that a chance you're willing to ignore? What then?' The phone went dead.

Ellie stared into space. Tears were flowing down her face, and she wiped them away. She had no time for crying. Either way, there'd be plenty of time for tears later. The second thought that struck her told her she might never have an opportunity to cry. In trying to save Matt's life, they might both end up dead, but she had to do as Eve told her. She had no choice.

She moved. One hour. It would be ridiculous getting from Ulverston to Keswick in an hour. The journey typically took closer to an hour and a half. She'd have to break every speed limit going, and the road as far as Windermere was treacherous. On a good day, it would be hard. All she'd need was to get stuck behind a tractor on the twisty Newby Bridge Road, and she'd had it. Surely Eve must realise that.

'Oh my God, I've only got an hour. I've got to go.'

'My God, Ellie. You aren't seriously going to go along with that psycho? You can't.'

Gail stood in Ellie's way and took hold of her arms.

'Wait, Ellie, let's talk this through. You have to go to the police. You have to let them deal with this.'

'No,' Ellie screamed at her and shook herself out of her friend's grip. 'No, Gail, you heard what she said. If we ring the police, she'll kill Matt. I don't know what the hell her plans are, but I know that I believe her on that one. It's me she wants. I'm sure that if she gets me, she'll let him go. I feel it, Gail. No police. Listen, when Rob gets in, tell him what's happened. Don't do anything at all for three hours that'll give me time to get there and, hopefully, back again. If I'm not back by then, well, I suppose by then you can do whatever you like because if I haven't come home, nothing will make any difference—I've got to go.'

She bent down and patted Jake, and then she was running for the door with her keys and phone in one hand and her purse in the other.

'I can't let you go like this.' Gail was hysterical.

Ellie looked her friend hard in the eyes and smiled.

'Gail, love, you can't stop me.'

Ellie left and roared up the road towards the first meeting with the woman who called herself her sister. She drove fast, ignoring all speeding restrictions and taking chances on the dangerous roads. It could have endangered her own life and anybody she met coming in the other direction. She made it to the institute five minutes over her allotted time. She never saw her nemesis. She came at Ellie in the dark, a charging screaming mass of fury wielding an iron bar.

# Chapter Eighteen

Ellie knew she didn't want to wake up. Please, God, just let the blackness stay. But wake up she did, despite her prayers. She did have control over whether she chose to open her eyes. Why the hell then did she opt to open the bloody things? Why not just wallow in blissful ignorance of what was going on around her?

She did open her eyes. And it did hurt. God-sodding-almighty, it hurt, and that's swearing, something that Ellie Erikson rarely did. Just lately, though, her placid vocabulary had been tested to the limits, and now she tried out all manner of delightful combinations of profanity. 'Fucking hell to twatting bastards,' was the first phrase that rose unbidden to her brain. Not bad for a novice.

For all the accusations she'd flung at her mother regarding her childhood, Ellie had led a sheltered life. Never in her twenty-seven and a half years had she ever experienced pain to equal the agony driving through her nervous system like a jackhammer now. Whether it was down to the beating she'd taken around her head or the complete alienation of her circumstances, she couldn't work out why she couldn't move. She was choking on a mouthful of blood that she couldn't spit out because of the tight gag rubbing on her broken mouth.

As she looked down, inviting the legions of hell's agony to burst torturing sun rays behind her eyes, the reason for her plight was visible. She was tied at ankle and wrist to an uncomfortable chair. Because the seat was on casters and didn't have legs, her ankles were tied together behind the central post at the back. Her wrists had been similarly tied behind her. She tested her bonds and winced as a new, fresher pain, bolted like the horses of the apocalypse through her trapped veins to the sites where the blood flow was restricted. She learned that it wasn't prudent to do that in one quick lesson.

She smelled her before she saw her. Ellie recognised her own choice of perfume. And yet, it smelled subtly different on this other woman. Hah, maybe we aren't so alike after all, she thought. Eve had no idea how to wear perfume. What was delicate and fresh on Ellie smelled cloying and overpowering on her nemesis. Maybe, when she could talk, Ellie would explain that a few drops were enough. Half a bottle only made a lady smell like a whore. But Eve had Matt, so maybe she wouldn't share her beauty tips after all.

She came towards her, and Ellie stiffened in the chair as she tried to keep as much space between herself and the crazy woman as possible.

'Oh, you're awake then? Thought you were going to sleep all night. In fact, I thought I'd killed you at one point. That would've saved me a job, wouldn't it?'

Ellie tried to speak, but the gag made it impossible. All that came from behind it was a muffled mumble, and it hurt so much

235

to try, but she had to know that Matt was all right. Now that she'd come around, the initial shock of the pain was subsiding. She still hurt all over, but at least it was a bearable hurt. She tried to look around. Matt wasn't lying unconscious—or, God forbid, worse—anywhere in the room. This could be a good or a bad thing. Dear God, please just let him be alive. Now that she was at the other woman's mercy, all fear for her own wellbeing had seeped from her. Her only concern was that Matt wasn't dead.

'Lovely place, isn't it? Mi casa es tu casa. This is where I lived for twenty-seven years while you were having your piano lessons and pony rides. This was my life, this one stinking room. Can you imagine that, Ellie? Can you? Actually, I'm not being totally honest. Sometimes they needed to pig me out, clean my sty, so to speak. You see that little door over there? They used an electrified pole, a cattle prod, to usher me through it and into another room. And you know what, Ellie? Surprise, surprise, it was identical to this one.'

Ellie winced under the bitterness of the other woman's voice. Each word was spat towards her and stung as it hit home. If she was telling the truth, it didn't bear thinking about.

Her eyes had come into focus, and she took in her surroundings. She gasped in shocked amazement as she looked eye-to-eye into her mirror image for the first time. Only it wasn't a mirror image because nothing was turned the opposite way. Eve was identical in every minute detail to Ellie, same height, five-foot-five, same slim figure, size ten, same blonde bob and grey eyes. It was no wonder Matt had been taken in by her.

She tore her gaze away from Eve, ignoring the pain crashing through her temples, and looked around the room. It was twelve-foot square, with one door to her left and another smaller one to the right. This door led into an identical room, according to Eve. Maybe Matt was in there. There was no decoration, and the room was plain white, with four walls, a ceiling and a cold tiled floor. Two small hatches were cut into the wall in front of her. When she craned her neck, she could just make out a single bed, with plain white bedding, along the back wall.

'See that bed? I once tried to hang myself with the sheets. They made me sleep without bedding for a month as punishment. Have you noticed something else, Ellie? No toilet. Can you imagine having to use a bucket your entire life? Could you live like that, Ellie? Could you be someone's pet? They used to bring me a bowl to wash in twice a day. If I had a tantrum—and you know me, that was often—and threw it around my cell, I wasn't allowed to call it that, by the way—this is my unit. I didn't get to wash for a month if I threw my wash stuff around or ate my soap to cause them grief. And that was messy, the time I ate the soap. For two days, I was shitting and puking like a syphon, and then I had to live in the filth for three more weeks and five more days. Not nice, Ellie, not nice at all. We had a birthday during that month, you and me. I watched you blowing out your ten birthday candles. Daddy said, "My big girl's hit double figures," and I puked all over my floor again.'

Ellie's eyes had grown wider as Eve talked. This couldn't be true. She shook her head at the other woman, trying to tell her that she couldn't imagine that kind of horror. But the pain doubled in intensity if she moved her head. She tried to speak, but she hadn't a clue what she was trying to say, so even if she hadn't been gagged, she wouldn't have made any sense.

Part of what the woman said turned like a snake eating its own tail in her mind. She watched me blow out my candles.

Ellie remembered her tenth birthday. It had been a fun day. Later on, Mother drank too much, and Daddy had to help her to bed, but that was later after the party finished and Ellie's friends had gone. The party was perfect, every little girl's dream, with a hired clown and Punch and Judy, everything imaginable in the way of party food, and lots of guests. Everything was just right. Ellie felt tears prick her eyes as she remembered the pride in her Daddy's eyes that day. It was a happy birthday.

As if Eve knew what Ellie was thinking, she carried on talking.

'So there you were, having your pretty parties, in your pretty frocks, with your foreign holidays and your posh house. And here I was, in this room, being fed your life along with their unpalatable food. Do you remember when Daddy used to come home on a Friday night, and you'd run to meet him? He'd open his briefcase and pull out—'

A goodie bag. Ellie thought the words simultaneously as Eve spoke them, such fond, happy memories.

'A goodie bag. There was always a chocolate-covered honey-comb bar. Do you remember, Ellie?'

Ellie nodded. She remembered. Oh, how she remembered. The physical agony she was suffering hadn't made her cry, but tears rolled down her cheeks with the pain of the bittersweet memories of her father.

'The surprise was guessing if it was mint honeycomb or or-ange. And a lollypop, there was always a lolly. Sometimes there was one of those bags of Sherbet Dib-dab, half a dozen or more good things to eat, and a comic. Do you remember those comics, Ellie? I used to sit on that bed and watch you, curled in the armchair by the fire, reading your comic and sucking your lolly.

I'd never tasted sweets, but they looked so good, my mouth used to water.'

Ellie was scared. These were her memories. How had this woman stolen them? There was no twin. No other child, just her and Mother and Daddy. They were her memories, but they were tainted and perverse spoken from another woman's mouth.

Ellie's mind was as clear as a June morning. All remnants of fugue from the beating had left her. So many thoughts and questions were circling around in her head that she was distracted from the pain crashing in waves of frothing torment. Even Matt was pushed to the back of her mind as she processed the information coming at her too fast.

'You see, Ellie, while you were living your clean little life, I was living it too, every minute of every day. I saw everything you did, heard everything you said, but I was just a two-dimensional understudy. That's what they called me—your understudy. From eight in the morning until eight at night, I was forced to sit by and see your life passing away from me. I wasn't an interactive part. I couldn't make any decisions or feel any of its texture. All I could do was watch it float by. And then, after you were turned off at eight, I had two hours before lights out to be me. But who was I? I was a non-person. I didn't exist. So for those two hours, I lived somebody else's life again. I read fiction books, reference books, biographies. All I could do for myself was fill my head with knowledge, but even that wasn't my doing. They chose what I could have when I read and what I learned. It was always them and always you, never me, Ellie. There was never a me.'

*When they turned me off,* thought Ellie. What the hell is she talking about?

239

Ellie wanted to speak. She had so many questions. At least she had an idea of why all this was happening to her. And yet, how could she see Eve in the role of the victim after torturing them? She couldn't, though, at the same time as Eve spilt droplets of her life, Ellie couldn't take any pleasure in the things she heard. She was filled with horror so unimaginable that she couldn't begin to comprehend the enormity of what Eve told her. If Eve had really been locked in this awful place for her entire life? Why? She had told her so little, and yet she had told her too much. Images of what the other woman's life was like, trapped in here, flooded her mind. Now, she was the one trapped in this room that seeped twenty-seven years of misery and yearning. Who had held Eve here? Why? And the old question that didn't bear fruit, where had Eve come from?

Ellie studied her close up. She was amazing. Ellie had been to school with two sets of identical twins, and although they were very much alike, they weren't the same. They could be told apart, especially when they were together. There was only one thing about this woman that was different from Ellie, and that was the fury in her core. The anger of her blazed in her eyes. Everything about Eve was hard. Where Ellie had soft curves, Eve had steely taut muscle. The tendons of her forearms stood out in the harsh fluorescent light. But it was the eyes that held Ellie captive as securely as the ropes binding her to the chair. Eve's eyes were exactly the same hue as Ellie's, but where Ellie's were a soft muted grey-blue, Eve's were as hard as galvanised steel, without an iota of love anywhere about them. But apart from her hard essence, Eve was Ellie. It was uncanny, horrific, the stuff nightmares are made of, and Ellie's worst nightmare incarnate. She closed her eyes to think.

'Hey, bitch, open your eyes. Don't you dare close them when I'm talking to you. You don't have that right. I'll tell you what to do, say, and even what to fucking think. I'm calling the shots now, you hear? You got me? Because you need me to survive, see? See how the tables have turned, Ellie? Miss little-oh-so-perfect Eleanor Erikson, I'm controlling your life the way you controlled mine all those years.'

Controlled her life? thought Ellie. Jesus, I didn't even know she existed.

'I've got the upper hand now, bitch, because I know everything there is to know about you, every single thing. I've watched you having sex. What do you think of that? I've watched you writhing on your bed moaning and groaning and spewing out all your pathetic I love yous. Don't like the taste of him, though. Don't swallow, do you, Ellie? I would. I'd satisfy him in ways that you can only dream of. In fact, I might just do that before I've finished with him. What do you think? Unless, of course,' She paused, watching the look of hope that had entered Ellie's eyes. She grinned. 'Unless, of course, he's already dead.'

Ellie was disgusted. She shuddered. Her most intimate, personal things were being opened up and dissected by this monster. Her home must be bugged with hidden microphones and cameras.

Again, it seemed that Eve was one step ahead of Ellie's thought patterns.

'And what about that other guy? What was his name? Oh yes, I remember now. Tony. We liked him, didn't we, Ellie? What was it he used to say?' Eve put on a stupid voice. '"Oh, Ellie, Ellie, I'm going to come, I'm going to explode, Ellie. Oh, that feels so nice. Ah." Do you remember the first time with him? On Heysham cliffs, I bet you thought he'd scare the seagulls with his yelling. I tell ya, Ellie, that was funny. I nearly wet myself watching you that day. I didn't find much to laugh at in your pathetic life, but that day was a killer. You're not really a funny girl, you know. You should have taken your role more seriously and entertained me properly. If I had to watch somebody else's life, why in the hell did it have to be yours? Pounding away at that bloody computer for eight hours a day. Where's the fun in that, Ellie?'

This was getting more bizarre. She felt ashamed, humiliated, raped. But every word that Eve said was accurate. That was word-for-word, what Tony used to say when they had sex. At first, Ellie had found it funny. She'd almost laughed herself the first time, but after two or three times, it was irritating. And after two or three weeks, it was the biggest turn off ever. The relationship hadn't lasted long.

How did she know? That day on Heysham cliffs, there were no microphones, no cameras, just Tony, herself and the ocean. None of this made any sense since the first day, but it was spiralling more into the realms of The Twilight Zone by the second.

'And, Ellie, you know that hot summer's day when you came off your bicycle? You know what I'm talking about, don't you?'

Ellie knew what was coming but didn't want to hear. It was her biggest secret and, up to recently, the worst thing that had ever happened to her.

'Yes, Ellie, that dirty old man who mopped up the blood. Took you to his allotment around the corner, didn't he, Ellie? He promised you some nice, juicy strawberries, didn't he? You were always so gullible, so bloody stupid. I saw it coming a mile off. Me, who hadn't ever seen a human being face-to-face, I knew what his game was. Didn't rape you, though, did he, Ellie? Just a touch and a feel and a big sloppy kiss or two before you screamed the place down. How did his tongue feel, Ellie, that big, slimy, old man's tongue, forcing its way into your pretty little mouth?'

Ellie felt sick. She would have put her hands over her ears to block out the sound if they weren't tied behind her back. She didn't want to hear any more. Eve knew every detail about her life. That was so private, and she had never told a soul. She couldn't find the words to tell Matt about that day in the summer of her childhood.

Afterwards, she felt so dirty, victimised, and lucky that it hadn't gone further. Ellie knew she was lucky to get away from the dirty old pervert that day. He would have gone further if she hadn't screamed at the top of her voice. She kicked him and ran, still screaming, until she reached the main road. Like many victims, she'd blamed herself. All the other gardeners had turned to look, one reached out a hand to her, but she didn't stop. And then she was silent, hoping that none of the other men tending their allotments recognised her, praying that it wouldn't get back to her parents.

'You know what I was doing, Ellie? I was sitting on my bed, yelling at him to rape you. Rape the bitch, you dirty old fucker, go on, rape her.'

Ellie felt the vomit rising in her throat. She panicked. The gag left no room for it to escape. She moaned, imploring Eve to remove it. Her eyes were wide, bulging from their sockets. She was salivating, and her stomach convulsed. She tried to keep swallowing, tried to calm her stomach, but the gorge rose, and there was nothing she could do to stop it. She was panicking, her eyelids flickered, and the world went mercifully dark.

Eve watched Ellie with interest. She saw the other woman heaving and realised she was being sick. She revelled in the thought of Ellie having to swallow her own mess. Just the way she'd had to live in hers. But it changed. Ellie's eyes disappeared into the back of her head, and her body convulsed in a fit. The chair overturned and Ellie crashed to the floor still tied to it. Eve watched the ropes cut into Ellie's wrists as the woman fitted and jerked across the room. Eve was scared. This was serious. The bitch was dying in front of her. At first, she was delighted. This was what she'd dreamed of. She'd fed on this moment—her mind had depicted it in a thousand different deaths—her entire life. Now it was happening, she was nervous.

Ellie's body was arching and convulsing in the chair. She made a noise in the back of her throat that sounded like a cow bellowing. Eve could watch her die. It was what she'd dreamed about. Conflicting emotions broiled inside her, fury, disgust, and terrible sickening fear. This had all been about making Ellie know what Eve suffered and making Ellie suffer, too, but she surprised herself in the knowledge that she didn't want to kill her. Eve realised that she didn't have it in her to kill. Up until that moment, Ellie's death had been the whole point, the grande finale.

Eve didn't want to touch the woman who was having a seizure three feet in front of her. She didn't know what to do, so she stood and watched. Her eyes widened like saucers. Eve was supposed to be in control. This was her moment, her victory. But here was Ellie taking over again. The bitch had taken back the power that for the first time ever belonged to Eve.

Ellie was still making noises, inhuman noises, disgusting gagging, choking, moaning noises. She sounded like a cow. Eve put her hands over her ears and rocked like a traumatised child. She didn't know what to do.

Get a grip, said a voice inside her head. She knew Ellie was dying, and she was standing by watching. It wouldn't take long. All she had to do was—nothing. It was horrible. Eve didn't want this. But there was no way she could run away. Her legs wouldn't work. Her brain kept her huddled there, rocking like a pendulum. She was out of control again. Like a trapped little girl.

Again.

'I don't want to kill you. I don't want to kill you,' she moaned into the sterile room. But Ellie didn't reply. 'Oh God, you can't die. You're me, and if you die, I'll die too. Help me.' Eve didn't care about Ellie, but she had an unshakeable superstition that she couldn't survive without Ellie's heartbeat. That somehow, the two were connected, and if Ellie's heart stopped, then Eve's part of the combined motor must stop too. She couldn't let Ellie die. Eve struggled to breathe. She felt as though her throat was clogged with choking vomit, just like Ellie's. Her heart was racing faster than it ever had before. She truly believed that the moment Ellie's heart stopped, hers would burn out too. To save herself, she had to keep the woman she hated alive.

Eve shuffled on her bottom across the room to Ellie. She struggled with the gag, but the more she tried to undo the tight knot, the more her hands shook and the less she could untie it. Ellie was convulsing so violently that in the space of three seconds, she had moved partway across the floor, and Eve had to shuffle to keep up with her. The leg of the chair banged into

Eve's leg, and she cried out in pain. The gag came loose and dropped to the floor. The contents of Ellie's stomach followed it, and blood, such a lot of blood, from the wound to her mouth. Ellie bounced in the vomit as she shuddered and writhed. And then, suddenly—very suddenly, she was still. Eve thought she was dead and moaned in anguish. She held her breath, waiting for her own heart to stop too.

Ellie coughed, she stirred. Eve exhaled, relief flooding through her. She set to, untying her captive. It was easier now that she was still, but the ropes at her wrists were slick with vomit and slipped through Eve's hands. She wiped them on her jeans and went back to work. Soon, Ellie was free of the restraints.

Eve pulled her onto her side and wrestled her into the recovery position. She'd read books on first aid and had seen DVDs. She swiped Ellie's mouth to remove the last of the debris clinging inside it. After putting a damp and mildewed pillow under Ellie's head and loosening her soiled clothing, Eve had done everything she could to keep them alive. She sat against the wall to wait. Her heart was pounding. Her anxiety gave way to hatred. She had the urge to kick the recumbent form for causing her so much inconvenience—the dirty bitch had made them both stink—but she controlled her anger. Deep breathing would have helped, but the smell in the small room was overpowering. Ellie had urinated while she was fitting. The lesser smell of that mingled with the strong, sour smell of the vomit.

Ellie's eyes flickered. She was coming round. She winced in pain as she tried to raise her head, but it was too much effort, so she lowered it again onto the musty pillow, grateful for the small kindness. The rest of her senses kicked in. She wrinkled her nose and groaned in disgust. Eve seemed to take it as an admission of guilt.

'Yes, you dirty cow, you've made us both stink. Happy now?'

Ellie's blood supply was making an exploratory cycle of her body to see where it could—and couldn't—go. Her nerve endings screamed in agony as the blood surged along the starved arteries. She flexed her sore wrists to help the process.

Her first attempt at speech succeeded in releasing a meaningless croak. Her second try was better.

'Matt? Where's Matt?' she managed. Her mouth tasted of vomit and blood. A tear squeezed out of her swollen eyes. She felt wretched. 'I need to know if Matt's still alive.' A little strength had returned to her voice. She was amazed at how strong she sounded.

Eve's first thought was to tell her he was dead and watch the gamut of emotions play across Ellie's face. She wanted to enjoy Ellie Erikson's suffering. But, for the second time in as many minutes, she realised there had been enough suffering. She had no idea where things went from here, probably prison as far as she was concerned, but she knew it was over.

She'd made her point and told a small part of her story. Maybe Ellie would let her tell more of it one day, maybe not. She didn't care anymore. She only knew she didn't want to cause or feel any more pain. Revenge is a dish best served cold, they say. Revenge had brought no relief. She was still angry, bitter, and hate-filled, but she realised the futility of it. She thought she might commit suicide after Ellie and Matt were gone and before the police came. Maybe she wouldn't, but at least that choice was hers now. And if she stayed, then prison would be a sentence of her own making. Eve felt she could live with all of these scenarios. She had an answer to Ellie's question.

'Yeah, he's alive. I'll take you to him when you've got cleaned up.'

Ellie saw the woman's shoulders slump in defeat. She'd watched the inner conflict battling inside Eve as she fought with herself to answer Ellie. Ellie knew as well as Eve did that it was over. She read it in her captor's eyes. She only hoped that Gail and Rob hadn't involved the police. Ellie didn't want that. She just wanted to be with Matt and be free to go home.

She felt a pang of genuine pity for Eve. She lowered her head and sobbed, crying for herself out of sheer relief and also, surprisingly, partly for the sister she never knew she had. She was too weak to think about the future, but maybe later, when things calmed down, she could find out—why.

'Please let me see Matt now,' she sobbed, 'I'll clean up later. Please, just take me to Matt.'

'No.'

Eve's voice was forceful. Ellie cringed away from her in fear. 'You stink. I'm going to get some gear to clean you up. I've found where they kept the things they used for me. Clothes and stuff.' Ellie noticed that she didn't say, 'My things.'

'I'll only be gone a few minutes. No funny stuff while I'm away. Do you promise not to try anything stupid?'

Ellie nodded. The bizarre irony of the situation didn't escape her. This woman, who had made her life a living hell for the last month, was asking her for a promise of trust. And crazier still, she gave it. Anything to keep the maniac calm.

Eve could have let Ellie go to Matt straight away. She could walk away and leave them to their own stinking mess and their own stinking lives. But she didn't.

It was important to her that Ellie went to him as unharmed as possible. Ellie had a nasty concussion and some cuts to the head and face. Her wrists and ankles were a mess from the ropes cutting into her when she'd had the seizure. Eve couldn't do anything about that, but she could make sure Ellie went back clean and intact. Eve didn't know why that was important to her, but it was.

In her clumsy way, although she hated Ellie for the life she'd stolen, Eve wanted to make some amends and show Matt and Ellie that she hadn't really hurt them. Not much. Not really. Eve tried not to think about the dog. She never wanted to hurt the dog.

That was her biggest regret.

This was more than just wanting to make Ellie respectable to clear her conscience. It was because she wanted to spend just a little while longer with Ellie before it was finished. She hated the woman. That hadn't changed. There was no miracle bad-girl-turned-good story. Eve couldn't think it through any further than her need to be with Ellie, just that.

She left the room, padlocking it after her. She secured the two ends of the thick chain she'd bought in preparation. To the left was the room containing Matt. To the right was a room that had been used for utility storage. She went into that one. It was unlocked and hadn't been used since she left the Institute. As far as she was aware, nobody had been back since that day. The building was abandoned. She'd been staking it out for weeks.

The room was organised and stocked floor-to-ceiling with pine shelving. It had everything a person needed for comfort and hygiene. A little annexe housed a washer and dryer, sink unit, and dishwasher at the end. Eve busied herself with a bowl of water and flannels. She picked out a new tablet of soap and clean clothes for both of them.

She put hers to one side. After she'd seen to Ellie, she'd come back and clean herself up. Then she'd take Ellie to see her beloved Matt for the fond reunion. It made her want to puke. She put everything on a two-tiered trolley, grabbed some towels, a couple of sheets and some cleaning spray to mop up the mess, and she went back to Ellie.

As she let herself into the cell, Eve knew Ellie could be waiting behind the door to jump her. That's what she would have done in Ellie's position, but she was a fighter, and Ellie was as much use as a fucking jellyfish. Although she was prepared for that, she knew Ellie wouldn't do it. Eve was broken, but she felt they'd made a pact—and that seemed perfectly reasonable to Eve in her warped mind. The bitch had promised to behave, each of them trusting the other to do as they said. It was demented sisterhood in practice. Eve was doing this nice thing for Ellie, and in return, her enemy would be grateful.

Besides, she had to be good to see Matt. Eve was smiling at this thought as she entered the room.

Ellie had righted the chair and was sitting on it. Her clothes were in a heap at one side of the room. She was wrapped in a sheet from the bed, another sign that she had taken Eve at her word. Ellie's trust made Eve feel something she'd never felt in her life. She felt good about herself. She felt her first pang of pride, knowing that out of all the harm she'd inflicted, she'd done something human. She was letting them go with just the injuries they'd already sustained. It felt good, but it also felt weak. Eve had felt weakness all her life. She stamped the feeling down and put the trolley beside Ellie with an air of embarrassment.

Neither woman spoke.

Ellie washed in silence. She felt no embarrassment in front of the other woman. After all, apart from the extra muscle definition Eve had, they were identical in every way. Ellie tried to sort herself out, but she was weak and dizzy. She almost fainted. Eve came from the corner of the room and took the flannel from her. She rinsed it in the bowl, soaped it and washed Ellie's hands, face and arms. Ellie was surprised that she was being incredibly gentle to not hurt her. She broke the silence for the first time since Eve came back into the room.

'Thank you.'

251

Eve didn't reply, but her cheeks reddened. After she had dried her, Eve helped Ellie with the clean clothes—jeans, t-shirt, and fleece. It was simple clothing that Ellie would have chosen herself.

Ellie wanted to ask so much, but she didn't dare question anything. Although some common ground had been found between them, Ellie didn't trust Eve as far as she would trust Cleopatra's asp. She was compliant and subservient under the other woman's manipulations. Eve was, at best, bloody dangerous and, at worst, a three times attempted murderer. She was a deranged psychopath. Ellie held her tongue in case she set Eve off on another psychotic rage. Her thoughts were only concerned with getting to Matt.

'I'm sorry about the dog.'

It came out of nowhere. From the tone of remorse in her voice, Ellie thought she was genuine. But she knew it could be a cruel trick and a lead-in for an updated level of crazy. When Eve met Ellie's gaze, her eyes were brimming with unshed tears.

'I'm so sorry about the dog.'

Ellie would never understand how Eve could hurt an innocent animal, but she knew more about Eve's circumstances. If even the bare bones of what Eve told her was true, she got that Eve wouldn't understand the love people have for their animals. It saddened her that the other woman had never felt that. Though every word that came out of her mouth could be a lie, it was genuine when she smiled. It wasn't a smile of forgiveness or understanding but of love for her dog. She was imagining Jake running in the woods.

'Jake's fine. He's got a sore leg, but other than that, he's okay.' he survived the—accident.' Ellie was going to say snare, but the word got caught in her throat.

'I never killed him?'

'No.'

'Good.' Eve gave an awkward grin. For the first time, the metal left her eyes. Ellie saw her own eyes looking back at her.

'He's a nice dog,' Eve said, as though her opinion mattered to Ellie. It didn't.

'The best.' Ellie wished she could be with Matt and Jake. She didn't want to talk about her beautiful dog with this psychotic monster. She wanted to talk about Jake with Matt. She was trying to keep her voice pleasant and steady. Anything could set the crazy bitch off again, and she had no idea how much it took to trigger Eve's violent side. She was aware that this humanity in Eve could be another cruel trap. She wanted Matt and for them to go home. To that end, she'd play any game the crazy cow wanted to. Ellie would have gone along with it if she'd pulled out the Twister mat.

Eve fastened Ellie's trainers, then she prattled on about getting rid of the things she'd used and cleaning herself up. And then she promised she would take Ellie to Matt. That they could go home. Ellie wanted to beg. She could plead with her nemesis to let her go to Matt, now, this second. Fuck the way Eve looked. Ellie didn't care—but she just nodded.

Eve was only gone five minutes. She was dressed similarly to Ellie when she came back, but thank God, not the same. The women looked at each other. An uncomfortable silence hung in the air between them.

'Right, then. Are you strong enough to walk?' She seemed concerned for Ellie's well being. What the fuck? She was off her head. This is all down to her.

'Come on. I'll take you to Matt.' Ellie thought for a second that Eve was going to apologise for everything she'd done, but she didn't. She turned and walked to the door.

'Wait,' Ellie said.

Eve turned.

Ellie couldn't believe what she was doing. Had she gone bloody nuts too? Eve was letting her out of this nightmare, and Ellie stopped her. She was going to risk upsetting Eve and having her kick off again. But she couldn't leave that room without Eve hearing the truth. She wanted to shut up but couldn't.

'Eve, I'm sorry for anything that happened to you. I can't imagine how much you've suffered. It's heinous and barbaric. But you have to know, and Christ, Eve, you have to believe that I knew nothing about it. I didn't know anything about you until the day I got that first letter from you through my door.'

'I know. I knew that all along, but it doesn't make any difference. I still hate you.'

'How can you say that? You're holding me responsible for something I knew nothing about and had no control over?' She was pushing it, but she was fucking angry. 'I would never have left you in here if I'd known about you. I would've moved heaven and earth to get you out and to see that the people who did this to you paid for what they've done. Who was it, Eve? Who held you, prisoner? Why?'

'I don't know. Sometimes I thought it was Daddy. I thought he had too much looking after you and Mother, and I was too much trouble, so he kept me here.'

Ellie's mind rebelled against this other person calling her parent's Mother and Daddy, but she held her irritation back.

'No. My father was the sweetest, kindest man on earth. He would never do that to you. Never.'

'I know that. I watched him every day until he died. And I grieved him. I miss Daddy just like you do. But I saw you taunting me, and it seemed as though you were all against me.'

Ellie was confused.

'Taunting you? Eve, how could I taunt you when I didn't know anything about you?'

'Don't you remember how you used to wish for a sister? You would sit on the balcony, and when you saw a shooting star, you always wished for a brother or sister to play with. Sometimes you'd look right at the screen when you said it. Your eyes would be flashing with laughter. I knew you were taking the piss.'

Eve's voice had risen. Ellie knew she was dancing on thin ice, and at any minute, the ground they'd made up could be shattered. This was like playing with a rattlesnake. If she snapped, Eve might not let her out. But she had to make her understand.

'Eve, that wish was genuine. If you watched my life, you must have seen how lonely I was. That tenth birthday party? Yes? You know? You said you saw it all? Well, you must have seen the way the other kids were with me.

They were only there for the food, and the party bags Mother made up. Every kid in the neighbourhood knew my parents threw the best kids' parties. They all wanted to come, but they didn't like me. They didn't want to know me, Eve. I had no friends. I know my life was nothing in comparison to the misery of yours, but I grew up lonely and unhappy. Yes, I had the pony and the holidays, but I had nobody to share them with. All I ever wanted was a sister. So you see, Eve, what happened didn't just happen to you. It happened to both of us. I don't know how you became separated from us. My mother—our mother—says she doesn't know anything about you either. What happened to you should never have happened, and I am so very, very sorry it did for both of us.'

She risked a look at Eve. The other gave nothing away, and her head was hanging. She looked like a confused child.

'Look, Eve, we can never be friends or anything, but we have things to discuss. Later, when you feel better about things, will you come and talk to me?'

Ellie put the onus of responsibility back on Eve. She needed to give her the power to choose and feel that she was making the decisions. She told Eve that she wanted to see her again without being bound and gagged to do it. Eve was the only person with any answers.

Eve nodded. Everything that could be said had been. Any more would overload both of them. Things needed to sink in and be digested on both sides. Ellie just wanted to see Matt again.

Eve went to the door without another word, and Ellie followed her. Ellie knew the interconnecting door into the second cell was locked because she'd tried it when Eve was out of the room. They went through the external doors and were in a corridor similar to a hospital. The room to the right that she'd said Matt was in was chained with a padlock. Eve unlocked the door and pushed it open.

She stood to let Ellie pass.

Matt was tied to a chair in the middle of the room, much as Ellie had been.

The difference was that his throat was cut. He'd been semi-decapitated.

Matt was dead.

# Chapter Nineteen

E llie pushed past Eve. The sob that was short of a scream wedged in her throat, unreleased. The truth was there to see. Matt was dead. But Ellie couldn't believe it. She mustn't because that would make it real. She ran to him. She didn't care what Eve was doing behind her. She didn't care about anything the crazy bitch did to her. Nothing mattered anymore.

Although tears were running freely down her face, the only sound she made was her raspy breathing. Her mind did one of those irrational flips that minds do in times of stress and trauma. Ellie was taken back to a thought she'd had hours before. There'll be plenty of time for crying later. It had been false optimism. There was going to be no time for her to cry because soon, she would be dead, too. She relished that moment. She wasn't going to play along with any more of Eve's sick games. Her act was convincing, and Ellie kicked herself for being taken in.

Over the previous few weeks, she'd spent a lot of time coming to terms with the thought of the cloaked hag of death calling for her as she was forced to face her illness. Now she was prepared to look her square in the eyes. Ellie was ready to die.

While these thoughts went through her mind, she worked on Matt's bonds. She didn't care how her body was found, if it ever was, but Matt was going to have some final dignity. Once he was free of the ropes holding him up, he slumped sideways onto Ellie. She cradled him in her arms, slumping to the floor, carried down with the weight of his body and with the density of the grief that trembled through her. As she rocked his body like a mother with a heartbroken child, she made shushing noises as she would calm a fractious toddler. Her fleece and T-shirt were saturated with his blood, and her tears fell onto his head. Her only wish was that there was something after death and that Matt would be waiting for her when she went over. She opened her mouth and screamed in the agony of her loss.

Ellie was aware of Eve muttering something and lifted her head to look at Matt's murderer for the first time. If she expected the smug gloating smile, she would have been surprised. But Ellie expected nothing and had no shock or surprise left, only a churning wad of molten hatred remained.

Eve stood a few feet to the side of the door. She was rocking too. Her eyes were open, wider than human eyes should ever be. Her lips were moving, whispering the same thing over and over again.

'Hate her, hate her, hate her.'

Ellie was getting just a little bit sick of hearing about her dear sister's hatred and had some similar thoughts of her own. Her childhood dreams for a sister had been answered, but she wished she'd never had the faith to pray for one in the first place. She couldn't believe that somebody—this second half of herself—could be so mindlessly evil.

She laid Matt's head on the floor and stroked the side of his cold cheek. Then she moved. She was up and flying across the room at Eve. Even without Ellie's wasting illness, Eve was twice her sister's strength, but Ellie was fuelled and propelled by hatred stronger than any love had ever been. Using her body weight as a battering ram, she cannoned into Eve, reeling her several feet backwards until she came up hard against the wall. In the second that her body made full contact with Eve, Ellie grabbed her sister by the front of her fleece. She had two bunched handfuls of clothing and heard a satisfying rip as she aided the momentum by pushing backwards with her arms as well as her body.

When the wall was behind them, and they couldn't travel any further, Ellie banged Eve's head against it. The initial impact knocked the wind out of Eve's body with a forceful whoosh, but Ellie gave no sign that she was aware of it. Again her head bounced off the wall as Ellie shook her by the front of her clothing. Eve's eyes were still wide and glassy. Her lips were moving in between gasps as her body ricocheted off the wall. She made no attempt to stop Ellie and didn't even try to fight back.

Ellie heard what Eve was saying. It wasn't, 'Hate her.' What she repeated in a hushed whisper on a loop was the single word, 'Creator.'

There was no reason in this woman. Ellie knew she was insane, but until now, she thought it was a rational kind of insanity if there could be such a thing. That it was insanity born of valid reason in Eve's eyes. Now, Ellie knew that the woman was just plain round-the-bloody-twist-unhinged. Ellie didn't have the physical strength to keep lifting Eve's body away from the wall to slam it back. She was fatigued, but she wasn't done. Although she couldn't keep ramming Eve physically, she could still batter her with venom and anger. Ellie screamed obscenities at Eve, still holding onto her and shaking her.

One second, Eve was limp and compliant under Ellie's grasp. The next, it was as though she was charged with power. The glazed look left her eyes, and, as though a lever had been pulled, a keen intelligence flooded into them. She tensed her body. Ellie felt the limp rag that she had been throwing around become a solid force.

'We've got to get out,' Eve screamed. She jerked and squirmed as she freed herself from Ellie's grasp. Her body was animated.

She brought her hands up and shook Ellie's fists away from her as though she were nothing more than a piece of fluff attached to Eve's sleeve. Aping Ellie's former hold, Eve grabbed Ellie by her clothing. The tables were turned, but Ellie was too far lost in her rage to back down. She screamed at Eve, beating her chest with balled fists. One of her punches flew wild and connected with Eve's mouth. She winced as Eve's tooth sliced through the stretched skin of her knuckle. But Ellie was gratified to watch her enemy's lip split wide open and spill blood in a free-flowing rush down her chin.

'You psychotic, crazy fucking cow. I believed you. I actually believed your bullshit. You make me sick. You make me feel physically sick, you murderous fucking bitch. Why? Why Matty? It's me you wanted. Well, I'm here, Eve. You've got me, and you know what, you miserable freak? There is nothing more you can do to hurt me. I know you're going to kill me, too, you bastard.

261

And you know what? You know what, sicko? I can't fucking wait. I want to die. There, that's taken the wind out of your sails, hasn't it? Pissed on your chips good-style, eh? You can kill me, Eve, but you'll be doing me a favour. You can't hurt me anymore.'

Ellie bellowed into Eve's face, splashing the other girl with acrid spittle from her earlier vomiting. 'You want me to beg? You want to hear me begging for my life? Well, you can fucking want. I'm not going to ask you for anything.'

Eve slapped her hard across the cheek with an open palm. Ellie screamed as the sting burned through her face. She brought both hands up to her cheek and stared at Eve.

Finally, she was quiet. All the fight was sapped out of her.

'We've got to get out of here,' Eve repeated. 'Listen to me, Ellie. You've got to listen to me.' Eve wiped some of the blood off her face with the back of her sleeve. Her voice held a breathless urgency.

'Listen to you? Why should I listen to a murdering bitch like you?' Ellie got no further, though she was settling in for another tirade.

'Ellie, for God's sake, I haven't got long to convince you of this, so you're going to have to believe me, and you're going to have to trust me.'

Ellie opened her mouth to begin a new rant, but she disgraced herself by shrinking away from Eve as the stronger woman raised her hand to hit Ellie again.

'Shut up, Ellie. Just shut up and listen. I don't want to hurt you, but if I have to knock you out, I will. And if I have to leave you here, I will.'

Eve's voice had risen, but she wasn't ranting. Her voice sounded urgent, desperate.

'Even if I have to kill you to get out of here, I will. Ellie, I didn't kill Matt.' Eve's eyes kept darting to the door behind them. It was still ajar.

'Oh right. Of course, you didn't bring him here and murder him. That must've been a different psychotic bastard then.'

'Goddammit, Ellie, I didn't kill him. Please believe me. He's here. The man who held me, prisoner, all those years. He's here, and he's playing with both of us. Come on, we've got to get out. Now! We haven't got a lot of time. He's probably on his way from the control room, coming for us. He's going to kill us both, Ellie.'

Eve dragged Ellie towards the open door.

Ellie wasn't about to fall for another of Eve's twisted tricks. Not this time. And there's no way she was going to leave Matt either. If Eve was going to kill her, then she'd have to do it right there.

'I'm not going anywhere.'

'Ellie, come on. We've got to move. We have to get out of here. If you don't come, then I'm going to go without you.'

Eve looked at Ellie, waiting for an answer. Ellie met her gaze with defiance. 'Bye, then.' Eve shrugged her shoulders in defeat and went to brush past Ellie.

Something snapped in Ellie. How dare this murderer just walk away from what she'd done. She wasn't going to let her go. She was going to force her to stay here in this room and face the evil she'd committed. Matty was lying dead, his blood congealing on the floor beside him, and Eve wanted to walk out like the first one to leave a party. No way.

Eve was a foot away from the door.

Ellie grabbed her and spun her around hard. Just moments before, she was exhausted from her first attack on Eve, but one look at Matt's face had recharged her. She was refuelled with hatred and anger. Eve tried to pull away. Her eyes never left the door, only inches away. She screamed at Ellie to let her go, but Ellie pulled her back with every ounce of her strength. Eve made a desperate lurch for the door, and as her hand grasped for the handle—it slammed shut.

There was a loud click as the door was locked from the outside.

Eve's eyes flew wide in terror.

'No,' she moaned. 'Oh, God, no. Please help us.' She leaned against the wall, staring at Matt's body, and she began to cry.

Ellie clapped three times. As she brought her hands together for the third time, she remembered, just days earlier, when Matt lay in a hospital bed and had made the same sarcastic gesture towards her. Her eyes brimmed with tears, and she looked at Matt. Soon, my love, soon we'll be together again. But for now, she had to deal with the snake in front of her. This was a game of wills. Ellie refused to give Eve any more sick sport.

'That was an Oscar-winning performance, Eve. Any chance of some song and dance next? It's so quiet in here.' Ellie's voice was pulled down with bitterness and grief.

'So what's next, Eve? What's happening? Are we going to sit here until you decide it's time to go into the next round? Bring it on. Okay, that suits me.'

Ellie sat beside Matt. But she didn't touch him. She knew that wherever Matt was, it was nowhere near his broken body, but being close to it gave Ellie a glimmer of comfort. She pressed her aching back into the wall. Red-hot needles of pain pulsed through her, and she needed her medication. She had her purse across her shoulder when she arrived, but there was no way she would beg Eve for anything. The pain was intense, but it was bearable. She raised her bent legs and rested a hand on each knee. Lowering her head, she closed her sore eyes to rest them, trying to blank her mind. Happy images of Jake and Matt running in the woods were too much to bear, but as much as she pushed the images away, they returned. Hot tears washed over the stinging handprint on her cheek.

'I didn't kill him,' Eve spoke, but Ellie didn't react.

'He probably won't kill us, you know. I think he'll keep us here for years and experiment on us. After just one day, you'll wish he had killed us.'

Ellie raised her head and opened her eyes. There was no emotion in her voice as she spoke.

'Eve, I already wish I was dead. There's nothing left for me now.'

Eve sat against the opposite wall to Ellie in exactly the same position. They were a mirror image of the same person. Both covered in blood, both with tear-stained eyes, both locked in their own world. Ellie's was one of grief and misery. She could only guess what was going through Eve's mind.

Eve began to cry.

'I deserve this. I know I deserve this. I never wanted it to happen. I was going to let you both go. I was going to come to your house and talk to you. It was all going to be over. Not this, never this. We're stuck here now, Ellie. You and me, sisters of hatred, we're going to be cooped up in this room for a long time. I know, you see. I know what The Creator is doing.

I thought I was so clever. When he sent me the letter with the password, I knew the net was closing in, but I never expected him to look for me here. I was going to disappear. He'd never find me. But he has. Oh, God, he has. It's just like before.'

Eve was on the verge of hysteria. Each word ended on a wail. Every syllable was tinged with terror. Ellie had to admit that she sounded convincing. She was good.

'He sees everything, you know. He's watching us now, listening to every word we say, laughing at us, playing with us. He could have been here by now. He is here, maybe only a room or two away. But he's biding his time, watching the drama unfold, and making notes. The fire only damaged the outer labs. It never touched down here. Nobody knows about this area. It's shut off. This part of the building is kept hidden. The police wouldn't even be able to find us. All they'll see is an empty, burned-out building if they come. We'll never be found. They'll only search the top place if they look for us here. Nobody knows about this area. It's isolated behind a dummy wall.'

What was she saying about fire? Ellie tried to remember about a fire burning something. It was the fertility clinic Matt had researched. Fire was often prevalent where Eve was concerned.

'So there was a fire here? Did you start it?' Ellie was being sarcastic, but Eve took her seriously.

'No, but I think he did, The Creator. I've thought about it a lot, and I think he wanted me to escape. He knew I'd look for you, seeking revenge, and this is exactly what he wanted. I thought it was my doing, but now I can see I've been led and manipulated just the way I've always been. He wanted to take the show into a wider arena. Do you know that even my clothes were chosen for me every morning? I couldn't even make that decision for myself.'

Ellie had heard enough of Eve's self-pity. She might have fallen for it before, but she was wiser now. She knew the rules better. Eve wanted to play the buddy-buddy act, to get Ellie to trust her, and then she'd pull her next psycho stunt.

'So, Eve, what's next? You must be bored sitting there. I'm not buying it, so you might as well do what you're going to do. Come on. Get up. Get your arse over here and kill me.'

Ellie felt her hysteria rising. The room felt too hot. A line of perspiration broke out on her bottom lip. She felt the walls closing in, and claustrophobia gripped her in a fist of steel, squeezing the breath from her body. She gasped in huge drafts of air, breathing hard and hyperventilating. She ran to the door. There was no handle on the inside, so she hammered on it. She couldn't breathe. The world was swimming out of focus as the panic attack gripped her.

She couldn't breathe.

She felt Eve's arms around her body, pulling her away from the door. She heard Eve sobbing, but she kept hammering on the thick, steel door.

She couldn't breathe.

'Come on, Ellie. Stop. That's not going to do any good. Come and sit down.'

They both stopped and looked up towards the ceiling. It seemed to be the starting place for a strange crackling noise that filled the cell with static. Eve's face registered horror. It was clear that she knew what this was. Ellie's features only showed confusion. Her mind was busy forming a question that she never got to ask.

The noise that brought the women to a halt was a loud static crackle. Two second's later, an automated voice echoed around the room's emptiness.

'Good evening, ladies. The date is the twenty-second of November, twenty fifty and the time is two minutes to midnight. The experiment is recommenced. I trust you are comfortable and have everything you need. I am so happy to have my two girls here together. It's good to have you both home. Good night, my Eve and my Ellie. Sleep well.'

There was another click as the connection was broken, and the room was undisturbed by uninvited noise.

The effect on Eve was shocking and horrific for Ellie to watch. As the first word of the mystery voice was spoken, she pulled herself away from Ellie. She dropped to the floor in what was a half-faint, half regression to infancy, and shuffled on her bottom to the furthest corner of the room. Pressing herself as far into the corner as she could get, she curled up and rocked. Her eyes were wide with terror. She was trembling, despite the sudden heat. Her mouth moved, and the pathetic innocent words coming out chilled Ellie like nothing ever had before.

*Miss Polly had a dolly who was sick, sick, sick.*
*She called for the doctor to come quick, quick, quick.*

There was no denying the disturbed woman's torment. At that moment, the lights went out. They were plunged into complete and utter blackness.

Eve stopped singing, 'No, not again. We're trapped. We're trapped here forever.' She was whining. Ellie heard the sobs catching in her throat as she cried.

It could still be a trick. Were two people in it together? Ellie had no idea what the fuck was happening, but she knew the sound of a tortured soul when she heard it. The sudden male voice from the silence had shocked her out of grief for Matt for a second. But as the darkness surrounded them, it came back a hundred-fold. She knew what it felt like to be tortured, and her nature took over.

'Eve, take it easy. I'm coming over, okay? Keep talking, that's it, sweetie, keep talking, and I'll find my way over to you.'

Ellie wasn't aware of speaking the endearment. All she knew was—if Eve was telling the truth— they were trapped at the hands of some monster. Somehow the roles had flipped, and she was, for now, being cast as the strong one.

She had to calm Eve and bring her out of the near-catatonic state she'd lapsed into. Ellie was wiser now, less gullible than an hour ago. Sitting in a well of your dead boyfriend's blood had that effect on you. Eve had to be coherent to tell her what the hell was going on, and the sane sister needed those answers.

Ellie felt like Alice, but all her white rabbits were murderers, and the Cheshire Cat was a psychopath.

Following the sounds of the distraught woman, Ellie made her way to Eve and cradled her head into her shoulder.

Eve neither resisted nor softened into Ellie's embrace. She was rigid, locked in her place of horror, and Ellie knew that she had to bring her out of it and fast. If this was real, Eve could sink too far into the protection of her catatonia to be reached.

'Come on, Eve. Get it together. Tell me about this man. Who is he? What does he want with us? Tell me what's going on, and we'll figure out a way to fight it.'

She kept talking to Eve, and for a long time, there was no response.

Eve felt the determination flowing from the other woman's body and into hers from somewhere far away. She wanted to go and hated Ellie for pulling her back. Against her wishes, she felt herself being tugged back from blessed oblivion. She felt Ellie's arms around her, smelled her body and discovered what it was like to be held by another human being for the first time in her life. A surge of emotions rose inside her. For those few seconds, they overrode her terror at being imprisoned in the unit. The mixture of emotions was alien to her, warmth, compassion, suffocation, confusion, comfort. The feelings swamped her, and they fought each other for supremacy. Eve wasn't strong enough to deal with them.

She pushed Ellie away.

Ellie felt Eve's sanity return. She believed what was happening and realised how little it would take for Eve to scuttle back into that world where she didn't have to deal with the present. Ellie hoped that if she left again, she'd take her into catatonia too.

The speakers crackled.

This time, Ellie knew what to expect and held her breath, waiting for the voice. She felt Eve tense beside her. If Eve's singing was chilling, this was nothing short of petrifying.

'Miss Polly had a dolly who was sick, sick, sick. She called for the doctor to come quick, quick, quick. Good night, my little dollies. I'm going now. You'll be here alone, but don't fear the dark, my darlings, for tomorrow I'll be here again bright and early.'

After the voice stopped, there was silence for a long time as they fought their own breed of monster.

Ellie's pain was worse, but it was nothing compared to the agony in her heart, and she cried. The total blackness didn't take the image of Matt away. She would never forget seeing him tied to a chair with his head almost severed from his body. But it was his eyes that haunted her the most. His staring eyes that saw nothing—and everything there was to see.

Eve groped in the dark for Ellie. When she made contact, she grabbed Ellie's arm. She had to be touching her when she said it. This time Ellie had to know the truth.

'I didn't kill him, Ellie.'

Ellie took Eve's hand. Although she didn't resist, Ellie felt it stiffen in hers.

'I know you didn't. I know that now. But you brought him to this evil. You destroyed everything we had for weeks, and for that, I hate you.'

Eve was crying again. 'I know it was all my fault, and you think that if I hadn't kidnapped him, it would never have happened. But it would have. It was always going to end like this—because that's what he wanted. But I didn't kill him. I swear I didn't.'

'I know.'

It was the truth. Ellie didn't know what was happening, but she believed Eve wasn't the monster who killed Matt.

As they sat together against the wall, Ellie tugged her mind trying to tease out anything that could help them. Her mind was trying to grasp something important that was just out of reach, something to do with Matt.

It wasn't his phone. Ellie noted that he didn't have his outside jacket on when they found him, and his phone was always in the inside left pocket. She felt a pang of longing as she thought about the times she'd nagged Matt about leaving his jacket in the car while she was trying to contact him. He might have his wallet on him, though. But what good was that? It's not as though we're in Tesco, is it? Enlightenment struck. Attached to Matt's car keys was a pocket torch. It was only tiny, but it was powerful. She told herself it was nowhere near as handy as a mobile phone, but still, it was a small strike to the little people.

'Matt's got a torch in his pocket,' she whispered. 'I'm going to get it.'

Eve grabbed her arm in sheer panic and dug her nails into Ellie's flesh.

'Don't leave me. I can't bear the thought of being alone in the dark for even a second Please don't leave me.'

Ellie winced and prised Eve's hand off her arm. 'It's okay. I'm only going over there. I'll keep talking to you all the time, okay? I'll be back in a second.'

'What if he gets you? He can, you know, he can take you whenever he wants.'

272

'Cheers. That helps.'

Eve let her go, and moving didn't seem such a good idea anymore. What if somebody was waiting for her in the blackness? Get a grip, girl. But Ellie was concerned as she heard a low continuous moan coming from Eve.

'Stick with me, Eve. Come on, baby, stay with me now. Don't you loop into some magical fantasy land and leave me in this hell on my own. We're in this together now.'

Ellie felt a stab of rapid hatred as it came back to her that Eve brought her to this. She bit down on the feeling, but it wouldn't ease. Eve might not have hurt Matt physically, but she was instrumental in getting him killed. Whoever was doing this would have done it anyway, with or without Eve. If they stood any chance of surviving this, it reasoned that they had to be allies—whether they liked it or not.

'You know, Eve, although I had no idea you existed, I always sensed you. I felt part of my life was missing, as though someone wasn't there. The feeling lessened as I got older, but I think I always knew I was only half of something bigger.'

Eve stopped moaning to listen.

'You stay with me, now,' Ellie said. 'You still there?'

'Yes,' Eve answered her in a small, frightened voice.

Ellie had reached Matt. Her groping hand found his foot. When she'd laid him on his side, his feet were lying on top of each other. The one she dislodged fell to the floor with a heavy thump. Ellie screamed and recoiled from her lover's body. It was already stiffening. His leg felt unnaturally heavy. Ellie didn't know whether she could stomach touching him to search for his keys. This was the man she loved and would have given her life for, yet she was repulsed by his dead body and couldn't bear the thought of putting her hands on him. She was crying again.

'Ellie, are you all right?'

The concern in Eve's voice repulsed Ellie as much as Matt's carcass, but it reminded her that she had to be strong to get Eve through, too. Later, their roles might be reversed again and then she'd have to rely on Eve. It was a horrible situation, but they had to help each other get through. She needed to get the torch. It might be a godsend when they didn't know what was coming at them in the dark. She put her hatred for Eve to one side, like flushing the toilet after using it.

Resolutely, she felt along Matt's body, guiding herself up against him as she felt along his leg. She had to heave him back onto his side to get her hand in his pocket. The movement forced stinking stomach gasses out of his mouth. Ellie gagged at the smell, heaving several times until she had control of her stomach. It felt like another betrayal of the man she loved. Covering her mouth, she thrust her other hand into the tight jeans pocket, searching for his keys. She had them in her hand. Thank God they hadn't been taken. As she pulled her hand out, the back of her fingers glanced across his already rigour-stiffened penis. What had given Ellie so much intimate pleasure was now a dead thing of disgust. She couldn't stop herself from wiping her hand on her pants. She'd held her breath to avoid breathing Matt's dead bodily gasses. Turning her face away from him, she let it out with a rush. She was already scudding across the floor before she had to inhale again.

The torch worked, and as it illuminated the space around them, it felt like a small victory in a great war. Ellie wanted to leave it on, but they had to conserve the battery for when they needed it. Eve was crying as well, and they huddled together, hoping the night would draw to a close soon but already dreading what horrors the new day would bring. Emotionally and physically exhausted, the women slept. Ignoring the small bed against the southern wall, they stayed upright, using the floor as a mattress and the wall for support.

So much was left unsaid, but the gentle hand of nature took control and brought them to healing sleep.

# Chapter Twenty

For an hour and a half, Gail did nothing. Her terror and indecision battled for supremacy. She should do something, but Ellie had forbidden it. So many times, she almost called 999, and she'd gone as far as asking for a call to be put through to the police. She cancelled it before the computer dialled the number. The slightest noise made her look at the door, but Rob hadn't come home.

She could ring Rob anytime, but this meeting was with the publishing house, Darley Braithwaite, one of the biggest in the country. It was an important meeting. Rob hoped to sign on the lucrative line, scoring a colossal contract for Shadine Williams, this year's hottest romance novelist. Shady wrote steamy historical romances and was a confirmed lesbian with a long-standing partner of some twenty years plus. It was unprofessional to disturb Rob with a domestic crisis to cut short their deliberations. But fuck that, she did it anyway. Five voicemails later, he still hadn't got back to her. His phone was switched off. Surely they'd have eaten and finished with the business bit. It was turned five-thirty, and they'd be at the point of congratulatory brandies.

Gail made another call to her husband. Rob had taken the car, so he wouldn't have any more than one after-lunch brandy to clinch the deal—probably. It seemed that, no matter how many signatures were put to how many pieces of paper, until a contract was sealed with alcohol, it wasn't binding. During small client meetings, Rob never exceeded his one drink limit, but with important meetings such as the Darley Braithwaite contract, he'd been known to leave the car and take a taxi home. Time was getting on. It looked as though this was the case. He should have been home by now. Oh God, Gail thought, what if we have to drive to Keswick? Her mind was made up.

Rob answered after the third ring.

'Hello, my little gilded lily with no aged tarnishing. Are you all right, sweetheart?'

'Yes, Rob, I'm fine.' Gail worked hard to keep her voice cheery.

'No darling, of course, I'm not having an affair. That thing with the maid was all lies. I was merely relieving her poison ivy rash.' Gail smiled despite the tension bubbling inside her. She could almost see Rob winking at his dinner guests. She knew from his voice that the meeting was successful, and he would tell her later that he had them eating out of his hand.

She heard Rob excuse himself.

'Are you nearly done there, love?'

'Yes, just having a drink here, and then I'll be home. Won't be long. Have you eaten?'

Gail didn't want to give anything away in her voice, but she needed him to come home quickly. By the time he drove home, it was going to be another half hour, at least. 'Rob, You aren't over the limit, are you?'

'No, love, I'm bringing the car home. Why?'

'Listen, sweetheart, just get home as soon as you can, will you?'

'What's up?'

'I can't tell you over the phone. Just come home, Rob.'

After speaking to Rob, hearing his calm voice, and knowing he was oblivious to what was happening at home, she felt no better. Far from feeling reassured that Rob would be home soon, she felt even more helpless.

When she heard his voice, she wanted him to say that he was just pulling into the driveway. Not that he was still in The Canterbury enjoying fine brandy and the taste of success.

Jake knew something was wrong. He was restless and wouldn't settle. She didn't know whether it was down to a canine sixth sense of danger or whether he was picking up on Gail's anxiety. But the dog was pacing the room. He'd lie down for a while, and then he'd be up padding to the door and back to Gail. Every few minutes, he'd whine to show he was worried, too.

Gail tried to calm him, but he wouldn't settle. She remembered reading that dogs can hear a change in the heartbeat of somebody about to have a fit or a heart attack. Not surprising, then, that he could smell her fear. She could almost smell it herself.

Rob's face worked into an expression of concern as he pressed the disconnect button on his mobile. Gail often rang to check when he'd be home. It was a woman-nurturing thing. Women needed to know precisely what time to put the pie in the oven so it'd be cooked when their menfolk arrived. It didn't matter how much the world had evolved in the last hundred years, how new-woman had emerged, or how, even newer-man had. That was the fundamental essence of a woman. She had to know when to put the pie in the oven. So it wasn't unusual for Gail to ring. What the hell had happened now?

The people he was doing business with were engrossed in a conversation about characterisation while Rob took the call.

'Excuse me, guys. I hope you don't mind, but I have to shoot. Listen, if there's anything you need to discuss, don't hesitate to call.' He gathered up the strewn papers and stuffed them into his briefcase. He shook hands with them and kissed Shady on each cheek.

Another twenty-five minutes passed by the time Rob left the country road behind. He tried to ring Gail twice, but there was no signal on his phone. Too many damned trees. Once he was on the open road, he called again and was gratified to see the blue power bar of life shining from the dashboard screen.

'Hey, sweetheart, I'm on my way. I won't be long. What's happened?'

There was no mistaking the sound of relief in Gail's voice as she spoke to him.

'Okay, Gail, come on, cut the crap. I've known you too long not to pick up when something's bothering you, darling. What's wrong?'

It would be an unwelcome bill or a minor domestic incident. Gail would brood on it until she'd had a chance to talk it through and share her worry, then she'd be fine. She was a react and act now kinda girl.

Rob heard Gail crying. And was worried sick. Gail was the happiest person he had ever known. She could be a worrier, but she wasn't given to tears over nothing. It was so rare Gail cried that Rob was overcome with a need to protect her when she did.

'What is it, Gail? Is it Ellie? For Christ's sake, tell me what's happened.'

'Oh, Rob.' The floodgates were open, and there was no holding back. She sobbed so hard that Rob couldn't understand what she was saying. 'I'm frightened our phone's bugged Rob, so I didn't want to tell you until you got home, but it's been so long now. Matt's been kidnapped, and Ellie's gone after them.'

'What? Have you rung the police?'

'No. Eve rang, demanding that Ellie meet her and Ellie's gone off on her own. She wouldn't let me call the police or you, and then you weren't picking up. Oh, Rob, I'm so scared. I've tried to do as Ellie asked, but I'm going to call the police now.'

'When? How long have they been gone?'

'She took Matt sometime this afternoon, and Ellie got the call about half four, I think.'

'For God's sake, Gail, why the hell didn't you ring me?' Rob was yelling hard down the phone. 'What the fuck are you playing at?'

'Don't yell at me. It's not my fault. You didn't pick up. Ellie wouldn't let me do anything. I know where they are, but Eve said she'd kill Matt if anyone else got involved. We believed her, Rob. I didn't know what to do for the best. And now it looks as though she's got both of them.'

Rob swore as he rounded a corner and came up behind a haulage truck. Although he could make good time if the road was clear, he was still in Hicksville, and there was no passing place for three miles.

'I'm going to ring the police, Rob. This has gone on long enough.'

'No. Don't. Ellie's right. Eve's a loose cannon waiting to go off. If the police storm in, there's no telling what she could do. Let's hold off on calling the police just for now. Where is she, at her place?'

'No, she's at some research place near Keswick. She told Ellie to meet her there alone. She only gave her one hour, and then she'd kill Matt. And now Eve's got both of them.'

After speaking to Gail, Rob rang Ellie's mobile. If Ellie was hiding out somewhere, the phone ringing might give her away. Still, he reasoned that Ellie wouldn't be stupid enough to leave her phone switched on in that situation. If the phone was off, it was a good sign. Wasn't it?

The phone rang seven times. There was a loud click as somebody turned it off. His instincts told Rob that it wasn't Ellie on the other end, and his shirt stuck to his back in patches of ice-cold sweat. Rob knew he was a man capable of murder if the need arose.

It was six forty-five when he got home. He was there long enough to change into joggers and a sweatshirt and give Gail a cuddle. Then, after confirming directions, he left.

'Please let me come with you, Rob. Don't leave me here alone.'

'Gail, I need you by the phone in case they ring. Don't call the police, baby. Promise me, on my life, that you won't call the police. I'll check the situation out when I get there. If it looks bad, I'll call them myself, okay?'

'We're way past it looking bad, Rob. Our best friends could be dead.'

After more reassurances that he'd be careful, Rob was ready. As an afterthought, he picked up Jake's lead.

'C'mon, big fella, let's go and rescue your folks, eh?' Jake cocked his head to one side inquisitively. Once he saw his lead being picked up, he didn't need asking twice.

Rob didn't know why he took Jake with him. A dog with a damaged leg was a liability, but he felt Jake had a right to be there, or perhaps Rob needed the contact of another living being and couldn't put Gail's life at risk.

It was eight twenty when he found the place. He left the car outside the large iron gate by a sign that warned trespassers off. He parked close to the hedge, secluded from the institute driveway and the road. Giving Jake a firm order to be quiet, he locked the dog in the car and set off up the winding drive on foot. He kept into the hedge, so the bushes on either side gave him some protection. The grass verge under his feet stopped him crunching up the gravel. He was more scared than he'd ever been in his life. As he rounded the last bend, the vast dark building was visible.

A car gunned to life a hundred meters in front of him, and Rob leapt into the bushes. The car's headlights never came on. When it drove down the drive, his cover would be blown. He couldn't make out any details from this distance, but he doubted the occupants were Matt and Ellie. It drove fast, moving in the darkness. When it was thirty meters away, it swerved and ploughed through the dense bushes at the side of the drive.

The car disappeared, but as it crashed through the foliage and its back end shot off into the night, Rob had a clear glimpse of the two teddies sitting on the parcel shelf.

The car somebody was hiding belonged to Ellie.

Rob strained his ears. He heard the door slam and listened, but there were no more bangs, just one person then. He didn't know if this was a good thing or a bad one.

Rob pressed into the bushes. He heard a figure crashing through the undergrowth, making no attempt to be quiet. It had to be Eve, and she must believe that Ellie hadn't been followed. That was a good thing. However, it meant that Rob never saw the person coming out of the darkness before turning to run up the drive. Rob peeped out in time to see her disappearing around the side of the house. She was bent, taking long strides and covering the ground quickly.

The dark figure disappeared, presumably into the institute, and Rob ran back down the drive. Jake whined as he opened the car door and jumped in. He wasted a precious minute calming the dog, then he drove away and left the car half a mile down the road. It was hidden from prying eyes on one of the many dirt tracks leading to the lake.

'Come on then, fella, let's go. But, Jake mate, you have got to be quiet, you understand me, man? Quiet.'

Jake cocked his head.

Of course, Jake understands quiet. Jake is a good boy clever dog. He knows when to be quiet. And he knows this is bad. This isn't walk-in-the-woods-chase-squirrels, this is something to do with Ellie and Not Ellie, and it is very bad. Jake wants to howl and find Not Ellie. He will make big bites on her leg. Jake will smell trees to see if Not Ellie has peed on them. Jake not stupid dog.

Rob set off for the institute. He had Jake's lead in his pocket but didn't fix it to his collar. Jake stopped to relieve himself once, but when Rob gave him the heel command, he didn't sniff everything and contented himself with a disgruntled whine. His injured leg didn't seem to be giving him trouble. When he moved fast, he tucked it into his stomach and limped on three legs. He kept the same pace as Rob and seemed to understand that this wasn't an evening stroll. It was as if the dog knew the urgency. Jake walked by his side, stopping occasionally to listen to the sounds of the night. He never heard anything that concerned him, and after a few seconds, they resumed their mission.

Rob was glad he'd brought the dog. He was an odd form of moral support, but he'd alert Rob to danger.

Rob got as close to the house as he dared, then hunkered down to think and decide what to do next. Somewhere in the distance, he thought he heard a mobile phone ringing, but it might have been a trick of the night.

Keeping to the shadows, he went to the back of the building. He figured ringing the doorbell and asking for Matt wouldn't be a wise decision. There was a car parked outside a small door halfway along the rear of the main house. What surprised Rob most was what couldn't be seen from the front of the place, or at least not under cover of darkness. There had been a terrible fire here, and it looked recent. The tint of devastation hung in the air. While it looked as if it happened at least weeks, if not months before, it didn't give the impression of being long burned-out.

Many of the windows were shattered, the broken glass swept and loaded into a yellow skip. At least there were plenty of places to gain entry, and Rob didn't dare tip the balance of fate by thinking about the many places to escape, too.

The car was an Audi Spartacus—flash, fast. It puzzled him. Eve had cash—lots of it. She'd stolen a considerable amount of money from Ellie, but nothing like enough to buy something as high-end as this. They didn't know Eve's background. Perhaps she had her own funds, and stealing from Ellie was for the thrill and intimidation. The sick bastard, Rob thought, not for the first time. Something else niggled at the corner of his mind. There weren't many cars like this one around, solar panelled roof, zero to ninety in 4.2 seconds. These babies were noticed. Why would Eve drive one of these when she kept a low profile? Rob assumed she was trying not to draw attention to herself. His mind was trying to focus on something about the person who hid Ellie's car in the bushes, but the rest of him was concentrating on the closest door. Telling Jake to be quiet, he sidled up to it and gripped the handle. He pressed his ear against the cold glass panel, one of the few that was still intact. Silence. He tried the handle and swore when it wouldn't yield to him.

It was locked.

Why the hell would he expect any of this to be easy? He ran along the row of windows to try another door. Body bent low, he ran at a crouch so that he couldn't be seen from the inside. The sound of a door shutting somewhere deep inside the institute complex stopped him. Altering his course, he ran to hide behind some trees at the rear of the skip. She probably wasn't coming this way, but he couldn't afford to take chances. He whistled Jake to him.

Two minutes later, the door opened, confirming his instinct to hide was a sound one. Jake could blow his cover if he barked now, and for the first time, Rob doubted his decision to bring the dog. No light shone from behind the open door. Whoever it was, they were used to the layout and comfortable travelling around the institute in the dark.

Rob assumed Eve was in this alone, but he didn't know for sure. He was taking nothing for granted. This night could be his last if he didn't keep his wits honed. The moon barely gave any light. All Rob could make out was a dark figure opening the driver's door and getting into the Audi. Jake growled low in his throat as the door opened. Rob put his hand on the dog's head to quieten him. He felt Jake's hackles rise along the length of his back. His body was taut, every muscle stretched and ready to pounce. Seconds later, the engine roared to life. Two shafts of light illuminated the night, breaking through shadows and throwing beams across the acres of grassland that was too long to be called lawns. The sudden beam of headlights startled a family of deer strolling just outside the woodland. They fled into the safety of the trees in a matter of seconds.

If Rob hid in front of the car, not behind it, which he would have if he'd got as far as the door level with the Audi, he would've been illuminated by the headlights. He trembled with the realisation of the close call. The car disappeared down the gravel drive and into the night. Perhaps Eve was returning to her lair. Maybe her work was finished. He wouldn't believe that and comforted himself with the lesser evil that Eve had gone to get something and would be back soon. Neither image filled him with delight, but this was the better of the two. He wouldn't relax his guard. He gave strong consideration to calling the police, but instinct told him he'd be putting his friend's life in further danger if the police went in mob-handed. He would call them, but first, he wanted to see if he could find anything out.

Taking advantage of the lack of moonlight but keeping his body low to the ground, Rob ran to the door with Jake trotting at his side. Listening to see that it was quiet, he tried the door handle. As expected, it had locked shut with a simple Chub lock. The retinal scanner was intact but inactive. Either the fire had blown the electricity, or the alarms and scanners had been turned off. That would explain why the electric fences he'd seen coming into the property weren't giving an electrical hum and appeared dormant. What was somebody else's misfortune was one little gold ounce of luck placed on his side of the scale. Rob could force the door, but it would alert Eve that somebody had broken in if she came back. He chose the less elegant option of struggling through one of the broken windows. Rob was forty-two, his waist measurement wasn't far away from that, and it was a long time since he'd done active service in the army. He was still an attractive man, but he was spreading, balding, ageing and not given to clamouring through small broken windows. He didn't know whether Jake would make it with his damaged leg. Only one way to find out. He picked the dog up and struggled to put him through the window.

Jake was scared and tried to scramble in Rob's arms. He didn't want to be dropped into this awful place of darkness. He stiffened his legs and anchored himself to the window frame in protest. He didn't see why Rob wanted to go for a walk here. It was horrible, nasty. Surely the beach would have been a better idea. He whined his feelings to Rob. But once he landed on the other side, he got a whiff of something familiar. It was vague, indistinct but unmistakably his beloved Ellie.

He shook his head as he smelled Not Ellie, too. That didn't please him. He whimpered, but he could smell Ellie and Matt, making him very happy. He wanted to bark a greeting to his people but remembered Rob's stern warning to be quiet. Jake was a good dog.

Rob warned Jake again to remain silent. Had he been stupid to bring the dog? Jake could blow everything if he was excited. Rob looked at Jake as he landed on the floor beside him. The dog had a right to be there. He was owed that much, and Rob trusted his instinct. He motioned for Jake to heel, and they walked down the dark corridor.

Jake's nose went to the floor, and he tracked the smell of Ellie. It was hard for him, there were so many bad smells here. The scent of fear and misery were the strongest. Jake didn't know why Ellie and Matt would want to come here. What had his humans got against the beach? Jake didn't like it and hoped they wouldn't make a habit of bringing him here for his walks.

There were rooms to either side of the corridor. Ellie could be inside any of them. Rob was going to search them all, but Jake seemed to know where he was going. Rob was happy to trust the dog's judgement. He was happy to go along with any ideas Jake had. Anything was preferable to thinking this through for himself. The only thing he was coming up with was going home, having a long bath, a huge whiskey, and calling the police.

Every half dozen doors along, the corridor met an inter-section where other corridors branched off the one they were travelling. This place was a maze. At the third junction, Jake veered off.

'Are you sure, boy?' Rob whispered.

Jake looked at him and whined.

Am I sure? Huh, why do they always think they know best? They probably know best when it comes to itchy-scratchies and cold, cold spray, but if you were talking noses, Jake is the smell king. I'm coming to get you, Ellie. Hang tight. Me and Bozo here are on our way. Whine, bad smells, bad smells. Not fun here, Ellie.

Halfway down the corridor, Jake stopped at another junction. He was indecisive and padded on a few paces, keeping to the same path. He snuffled the floor, turning his body around in circles. He whined. Even Rob could understand that. It was a whine of frustration. He waited, not wanting to confuse the dog or rush him even though he knew that Eve could appear in Freddie Krugeresque fashion at any second. Jake made up his mind and took the new path. Back on the trail, he set off with determination.

'Good lad,' Rob said.

'I know,' the look that Jake shot back implied.

He stopped at a set of double doors. They were the kind used in hospitals with the rubber section on the bottom, designed so that stretcher trolleys and wheelchairs could be pushed in. This room must have had some through-traffic of heavy equipment.

Rob listened. Everything was quiet. He pushed the door enough to let them through. Even Rob had to screw his nose up in disgust as he walked into the house of horrors. The room was some kind of lab dominated by machinery and burned out computer banks. It was enormous, the size of a warehouse or

289

the ballroom in a stately house. That's what this is, thought Rob. His eyes had grown accustomed to the half-light, and he could see that it was the old ballroom. Once filled with satin and lace, it housed smoke-damaged equipment and the caged dead bodies of so many suffocated animals.

Rats, mice, dogs, pigs, monkeys, hundreds of tortured animals were given the final blessing of death. Some of them still had wires attached to them, and Rob almost barfed when he saw the remains of a mouse with a human ear growing out of its back. Why the hell hasn't anybody cleared this room? It didn't make sense. Rob knew the things he saw in that lab were going to stay with him for a long time. It was the stuff that nightmares are made of. He didn't want to see a monkey with wide brown eyes, frozen in death, and tubes coming out of an open gash in its skull displaying its brain. He closed his eyes and tried not to see any more atrocities. Jake was impatient to get away from this horrible place. Trying not to look at what had happened to the creatures before the fire hit, Rob followed with a heavy heart. If somebody could do this to innocent animals, what could they do to Ellie and Matt? He wondered if Eve had worked here. If she did, it fit his mental blueprint of her.

Towards the end of the lab, Jake whined at a small door in an alcove. Rob pushed it, expecting it to be locked, but it swung open as he turned the handle.

'Nah, there's nothing in here, boy. This is just a storeroom.'

Jake disagreed, and while Rob looked at the jars of formaldehyde that weren't even under lock and key, he had his nose back to the ground, following the scent to the back wall. He stopped there, but only because he had to. Looking at Rob impatiently, he wagged his tail.

'What?' he said to the dog. 'You want me to open the wall? Right, it's a wall, Jake. Your nose is tripping out on you this time, mate. Come on, let's get out of here.'

Rob turned to leave, feeling stupid that he'd been happy to follow a dog whose only tracking experience to date was to sniff the lavender heads in the garden. There was no point hanging around here, though a formaldehyde cocktail with a cherry on the top and a slice of lemon seemed a damned inviting prospect. But, Rob thought, in his best mock camp, what's a fella to do when there's not a cherry to be had? At the door, Rob called Jake.

The dog gave one sharp yap but refused to move. Rob shushed him. Jake looked from the wall to Rob several times and then opened his mouth as though to bark, but no sound came out. Rob had the feeling that Jake was threatening him, that if he didn't look around for a way through the wall, he would bark the place down. Rob knew he was losing his mind. Oh Man, being blackmailed by a German shepherd? Get a grip, for Christ's sake. There must be another route to whatever lay beyond the storeroom, but in the dark, he might have a hell of a job finding it. He'd need a map of the building to know where to go. Jake whined. Rob knocked on the wall, aware that he had no idea if anybody was behind it. As he suspected, the wall was a false partition. He felt foolish entertaining the idea that there might be a secret way to move the wall, but it would do no harm to look.

'Okay, if you insist,' he whispered to the dog.

The wall was smooth, with no levers or pulleys. Rob figured that Jake was confused with the smell from the fire and dead animals. The room was stacked floor to ceiling with wooden

291

shelving, with all manner of drugs and products in a seemingly haphazard mess. Sterile suture kits were stacked next to a sack of rabbit pellets and water feeders next to IV and drip paraphernalia. It was an odd way to conduct a medical establishment. Rob hoped Ellie was behind the barrier. He felt the shelving nearest the wall while Jake whined again.

'All right. I'm doing my best here, okay? I'm new to this stuff.'

His fingers ran over something on the underside of the top shelf. He bent his head to look, and sure enough, there was a button.

'Bingo.' The wall slid back on itself, revealing a long corridor with familiar doors to each side.

Jake gave him an, about time too, look and padded through.

The scent must have been stronger. Jake flew along the corridor without stopping to relocate any lost smells.

He stopped three-quarters of the way down and knew that his Ellie was on the other side of it. He forgot to be quiet and barked his happy-bark, with his tail wagging furiously.

Ellie, it's me, Jake. I'm here. Come on, Ellie, let me in. Want to lick, Want to lick a big lot. Whine.

Jake scratched at the door, and Rob had to run to him and wrap his arms around his neck to try and keep him quiet.

Ellie woke up. Her neck was stiff, and her back burned with fire from hell. There was none of that awakening fugue, the blissful few seconds of not knowing where you are. Ellie knew exactly where she was. Eve's head had dropped into her lap. Oh well,

292

as long as one of us was comfortable, she thought. She'd been dreaming about Jake. The memory of her Jake brought a flood of tears. Ellie peered through the darkness to Matt's body, and the tears spilt down her cheeks in a torrent of misery and pain.

Jake barked a second time and scratched on the door.

'Jake? Jake? Oh, Jakie, my beautiful, beautiful, boy.'

Ellie fought to disentangle herself from a waking Eve and flew to the door. She had to grope for it in the darkness, but Jake's scratching guided her to him. Ellie hadn't thought as far as the fact that if Jake was on the other side of that door, then so was help. All she could think about was her joy that the dog was there. She was choking on her tears. They flowed so fast that she was drowning in them. Ellie doubted that she would ever stop crying.

Then she heard Rob's voice. Blessed, wonderful, Rob, thank God.

'Ellie, is that you? Are you all right?'

'Oh, Rob,' she could hardly speak because she was sobbing and trembling so much. 'Yes, Rob, I'm here, and I'm okay. Where are the police? Are they coming?' She broke down and couldn't continue.

'No, no police yet, Ellie, I didn't know what to do for the best. Hey, baby, it's okay. I'm going to get you two out of there. I take it Matt's with you? So, you've had yourselves a private party without inviting Uncle Rob, eh?'

'Rob?' There was a long pause as Ellie gathered the last of her reserves. This was the first time she had had to say it and just having the strength to spill the awful words was an effort greater than the effort of staying alive when Matt wasn't.

'Rob, Matt's dead.'

Rob sagged. He rested his forehead against the cool panel of the metal door and breathed hard. He heard the words, even through the thickness of the door, but the meaning behind them took a while to catch up. He couldn't take in the fact that Matt was dead. He had no words of comfort for Ellie. Nothing that came into his mind was big enough. Simpering words were insignificant. He was scared and too little to chip anything off the massive block of grief that her single sentence conveyed. But he knew if he listened to Ellie's heartbreak, he'd give in to his own and be useless to them all. As Ellie herself had done, Rob took all the pain he was feeling and turned it into anger.

'Ellie, I'm going to get you out of there and then I'm going to track down that evil bitch and kill her. Do you hear me, Ellie? I'm going to kill the bastard.'

Eve had shuffled up behind Ellie—to offer comfort, she assumed. Though why she thought Ellie needed her support, she had no idea. At Rob's last words, she felt Eve flinch, and although she hated the woman more than she ever believed it was possible to hate another human being, she felt a stab of pity for her, too. Eve was as trapped as Ellie, and at least Ellie had Rob. What did Eve have?

Nothing.

Rob took all his anger and turned it into physical aggression. To hell with the noise, he was beyond reason and way past stealth. He was angrier than he had ever been in his life. He wanted the bitch to come down the corridor towards him. He would

294

welcome her with clenched fists. He'd never hit a woman in his life, but, by God, he was ready to start. Rob charged the door with his shoulder. It didn't give an inch. There was no way he could break in with brute force, and he was too consumed with anger to think. He kept charging the door in temper, oblivious to the pain. He'd worry about his bruised shoulder when he'd finished worrying about their lives.

'Rob, listen, there's something else I have to tell you. Stop that and listen.'

Ellie paused, hardly daring to deliver the next shock, 'Eve's trapped in here with me.'

'What the fuck?'

'Rob, stop shouting and listen. I don't know how long we've got. I haven't got time to go into it with you now. There'll be time enough for that if we ever get out, but you have to believe me when I tell you that Eve did not kill Matt. Somebody else did, Rob, and he's pure evil. He's still out there, and he's dangerous, so for God's sake, be careful. Call the police.'

Rob scrambled for his phone and tried dialling out.

'Fuck. Fuck. There's no signal Ellie. I'll keep trying.'

Eve spoke for the first time.

'Rob, it's Eve.'

Jake growled, his hackles rising.

Rob felt every hair on his arms rise as he heard no change from Ellie's voice, and yet he knew it wasn't Ellie speaking. He was consumed with anger and hatred for this woman.

'Rob? Are you there?'

'Yeah, I'm here, and I warn you if you've hurt her, if you've harmed her in any way, I'll kill you.'

Eve stiffened against the onslaught of fury coming at her through the door, and for a split second, she was almost glad it was locked. If the dog didn't tear her apart, the man would.

'Rob. You have every right to be angry, but there's no time for anything destructive now. We have to work together to get out of here. The man—he calls himself The Creator—he'll be back. And when he comes, he won't hesitate if he needs to kill you. What he has planned for Ellie and me is anybody's guess. Every second is precious. Look, you can't break the door down. It's protected by a combi-lock, so you'll never bypass that. I've had a long time to think about getting out of here. There's a skylight. It's about fifteen feet above my head. It'll be a squeeze, but I think we'll just about fit through. We need a long rope.'

Rob's heart sank as he remembered lending a neighbour his towrope a few months earlier. As often happens with loaned items, it was never returned.

'I haven't got a rope. I'll have to look round here and see if I can find anything.'

'I've got one,' Ellie cut in. 'Rob, I've got a towrope in the boot of my car. The car's out front by the fountain. The driver's door should still be open. I left it unlocked in case I needed to leave in a hurry.'

Rob knew otherwise but didn't have time for small talk.

296

'I'm going to get it. I'll be as quick as I can, and I'll keep trying the police. Try to keep calm. You're going to need all your strength to get out of there.'

'Rob, we've got a torch, so you'll know which skylight it is,' Eve shouted. 'We'll give you five minutes and then start flashing it at two-minute intervals.'

Rob had to admit that Eve's self-control would be of benefit. Ellie was so immersed in her grief that she'd have to be treated gently.

'Make it ten,' Rob shouted, 'It'll take me that long to get to the car and back. He dumped it in the woods at the side of the drive.'

Rob heard Ellie sobbing, and it took all the strength he had to leave her with that madwoman, but he didn't have a choice.

'Come on, fella, let's go,' he said to Jake, but the dog refused to move. There was no way he would leave Ellie with Not Ellie. He could smell the danger. Jake knew this wasn't walk-in-woods-chase-squirrels, and he wasn't going anywhere. Rob saw how miserable the dog was, he felt the same, but they had to get that rope. He clipped Jake's lead onto his collar and dragged the dog against his will. Jake planted his front legs wide in front of him and made them as stiff as he could as he dug them into the ground. His backside was firmly on the floor, and no amount of coaxing would make him get up.

Rob had to drag Jake all the way through the building to the entrance, but once he pushed the dog back through the window, Jake seemed to realise that there was no point in being difficult. He went with Rob, but his ears were flat to his head, and he was depressed. Every few yards, he looked back to the horrible place where he'd left his Ellie crying. Jake couldn't understand why Rob wanted to leave her there.

Once in the open air, they set off at a sprint. Rob had no idea how many people were involved in this, but his gut told him there was only one lunatic running free that night wanting to kill them—and another one locked was in a room with Ellie. He had to move fast. Eve seemed supportive, but what if it was a trick? Despite the cool evening breeze, droplets of sweat rolled from his forehead.

The dense greenery at the side of the drive had corrected itself well, considering a ton of metal had crashed through. Rob wasted valuable minutes finding the car. He was within feet of it when he heard the phone ringing. Ellie's phone? It might be a trap. He scrambled through trees and over rocks to get to the car before the phone stopped. He wrenched the door open and flung himself across the front seats before he realised that the ringing wasn't coming from her car.

He froze. Somebody was in the bushes waiting for him. They were playing with him. He backed out of the car and stood at the side of the open door. Although it was dark, he could just make out the silhouette of a black shape a few yards from Ellie's white car in the woods. The phone was still ringing. Most people would have given up by now. It was him, this Creation bloke. It had to be.

Rob plunged through the bushes, following the sound. It led him to another car—Matt's car. The door was locked. He scrambled around in the dark until he found a rock. The sound of smashing glass was amplified in the still night as he broke the window. As he swung the door open, the mobile phone's ringing intensified. It stopped before he could get to it, but at least it meant that Matt had a signal. Matt's jacket was on the passenger seat. He picked it up and groped in the inside pocket.

The phone wasn't there, but it rang again. The shrillness of the tone made him jump. He searched all the pockets. They were empty, and yet the sound of the ringing phone was coming from Matt's jacket, and he could feel the weight of it. He thrust his hand into the inside pocket and found the hole in the lining. As he put his fingers through the hole, the phone stopped ringing.

'Shit,' he said, his voice sounding unnaturally loud in the still of the darkness. He found the phone and fumbled to ring 999. He got to the second nine and stopped. Instinct as strong as anything he'd ever felt stopped him from ringing. What was it? What was his mind trying to tell him? Ellie could be killed if he didn't call the police while playing Action-Man. He transferred the phone to his pocket. He had to remember to turn it off before getting back to the institute. He needed to check the call history, but he couldn't waste the time it would take. Every second Ellie was locked in that room was a second closer to the mad person returning.

He moved from Matt's car to Ellie's and opened the boot. The way their luck had been, he expected to either find several headless corpses in the boot or, at best, the lack of a towrope. It seemed that this time luck was on his side. He picked up the rope, slung it over his shoulder and slammed the boot shut after him. He was making his way back through the thicket when Matt's phone rang again.

His heart was thumping, and now that he had hold of it, he couldn't decide whether it was best to answer it. He pressed the button.

'Hello.'

'Oh. Thank God,' it was a woman, breathless, talking rapidly, 'I've been ringing all night. I can't live with this any longer. The guilt. It's too much, you see, too much,' she sounded drunk.

'She's not there, is she? I can't speak if Ellie's there. It all goes back to him. The Creator knows everything.'

As soon as he heard the word Creator, Rob straightened up. Until then, he thought he was talking to one more nut in a world that seemed overrun by them. Maybe he was.

'Who is this?' Rob was tense and ready for the unexpected.

'It's Maria, Matt. We talked last week. I have to speak to you. We need to meet.'

Rob came up to speed. Of course, the phone call Matt received from the mysterious woman.

'Maria, this is Rob, a friend of Ellie and Matt's,' he heard her gasp. 'No, please don't hang up. You've got to help us.' A note of hysteria had risen in his voice, 'Matt's dead. He's been murdered, but not by Eve, by somebody else. Ellie and Eve are locked in a room at a burned-out institute, and I can't get them out. For God's sake, if you know anything, please tell me.'

He could hear the shock in Maria's voice. It shook with her next words.

'They are at the Institute? You've got to get them out of there. It's his lair. Don't you understand? It's the place where he feeds. He'll be back, he'll be back.'

Maria was rambling. If he didn't keep her focused, she would be useless to him.

'Maria, what's the door code? Do you know the door code?'

Her voice lost all expression. She spoke as though she was in a trance.

'Dolly.'

'What?'

'Dolly, the code is dolly. 36559.'

Rob couldn't understand what she was saying, but then he realised she meant that the numbers corresponded to letters, as they do on a telephone. Maria was speaking in the same dull monotone.

'I've got to go now. I've already said too much. He's going to kill us all. I have to go.'

'Wait,' Rob shouted into the phone, forgetting to whisper.

'I'll be in touch.' The line went dead.

Rob's head reeled as he ran back to the locked room. He still had the rope, just in case. He left Jake locked in Ellie's car and told him to be quiet, but he heard him barking and scratching to get out as Rob went. He hated leaving him and worried he'd be in danger if somebody came back and found him. But he had no choice. If Jake came face-to-face with Eve, he'd tear her apart, and Rob would have no reason to stop him.

When he got back, he shouted through the door.

'I've got the code.'

'How?' Ellie yelled.

'I'll tell you later. Let me get this bloody number in before I forget it.'

36559. He waited for the click. Nothing happened. Maybe he'd entered it wrong.

36559. Nothing.

Grabbing Matt's phone, he opened the flashlight app and looked at the display on the door lock.

D-O-L-L-Y, 36559. The door refused to open.

'Fuck, it's not working.'

'He must have changed the combination after the fire,' Eve shouted.

Ellie was still crying. For a second, she thought they might get out of there, and they'd get Matt out to give him the dignity of a decent burial. Now she knew she was trapped. That she and Matt were never going to leave this room.

All three of them were aware of time running out. Rob knew their captor had been gone for over an hour. They had no idea where he'd gone or how long he'd be away, but somehow they all knew that he wouldn't be away for long.

'The skylight,' Eve shouted, 'I'll shine the torch.'

'I'm on it,' Rob was already tearing back along the warren of corridors. He took a few seconds to be irritated that Eve was running the show. Who the fuck died and made her the supreme ruler? And then he remembered Matt and felt a moment of deep shame. For that split second, in his haste, he had forgotten that Matt had been killed. It didn't matter who the hell called the shots. Until they were away from here and safe, they had to pull together, putting aside their personal feelings. He just hoped the bitch could be trusted.

Rob cursed the rich steak Dianne he'd eaten with delight when he was a man living everyday life in an ordinary world. He stood on a dustbin, hoping the lid would hold him as phase one of the getting-an-unfit-old-bloke onto a roof mission. He puffed and struggled as he scrambled up the wall and used the drainpipe to reach the top. Luck was with him because this part

302

of the building was an extension annexe with a low roof. The rest of the Institute was in the old house, and five -storey's tall. If fate was in the game of side-taking, she was rolling with them.

Is this a good time to remember that I'm terrified of heights? He asked himself and smirked at the irony of the situation. He stood on the roof for a second with his eyes closed, trying to imagine how a cat burglar would act at a time like this. Channelling Cat Woman, he stood straighter—tottered—despite not having anywhere to fall from this point, then bent himself over again. Straight wasn't good. He was no hero. When he'd served his time in the Great War with the Middle East, he wasn't required to climb around on rooftops, and at least with a sniper, you knew what brand of maniac you were fighting. He was just an ordinary bloke who lived life too well and should never be put in the guise of a hero. It didn't suit him. He tried to get his bearings. Everything was different outside. He worked out where the corridors branched. And, when he was semi-confident of the direction he should take, he set off at a crouch, keeping to the middle of the roof and trying not to look down. He was terrified but fuelled by adrenaline.

Ellie was sobbing her heart out. It was shattered, and she was ready to give up. She had nothing left to fight with.

'Come on, it's all right. It's only a minor hassle. We'll just go back to plan-A. As long as we've got a bit longer, we'll soon be out of here.'

'You might be, but there's no escape for me. I'm stuck here,' Ellie said.

'What do you mean? Rob's on his way. We'll be out of here and away in a quarter of an hour. Just fifteen minutes more. Hang in there and stick with it. Don't go jelly on me now. We need to stay focused until we're out of here.'

'I'm not going anywhere.'

'What? Are you crazy?'

'Eve, I'm dying. I have Tay-Sachs. It's a muscle-wasting disease. There's no way I can climb a rope and then scramble through a tiny skylight onto a bloody roof. You'll have to get out when Rob comes and call the police.'

Ellie saw the fear cross Eve's face at the mention of the police and knew she was doomed.

Eve pulled up her sleeves, and in the glow from the torchlight, she flexed muscles that would put men to shame.

'While I was locked in here, I had nothing to do. The boredom drove me insane, so I spent hours meditating and working out every day. Besides, they made me exercise—it was part of the regime. Look at me, Ellie. I'm strong enough for both of us. I'll help you up the rope.' Her face hardened, 'But don't think it's out of misguided sisterly love. No police, Ellie. We can do this. But you have to promise me. I can help you get out of here alive, Ellie, but, in return, when it's over, promise you won't go to the police, or it's every woman for herself. I know everything went wrong, but I stuck to it the last time we made a deal.'

'We've got to call them. They'll find Matt's murderer. I owe him that.

Ellie looked at Eve. She had nothing to lose, and promises to a lunatic were empty promises.

'Deal.'

The next five minutes seemed endless, but when they felt as though an hour had passed, they heard Rob's feet coming along the roof towards them. Eve flashed the torch at the ceiling.

Rob tried several times to prise the skylight window open, but it was stuck. Even if he had a crowbar, there was no way to get it open. This window had not moved in the last thirty years. It wasn't going to open in the next few minutes.

'Stand back. I'm going to break the glass.'

The twins moved to the corner of the room. They crouched low and pulled the fleeces over their heads to protect them from flying glass. Ellie was sure Rob wouldn't be able to break the window. It'd be another setback in an endless night of torture.

He raised his foot, forgetting about his fear of falling and running on pure adrenaline. He brought his heel down hard with all his strength, but his foot bounced off the glass.

The second time he took his leg higher, all he needed was more momentum. When the heel of his trainer connected with the glass, he was gratified with a tremendous crash. The window had shattered inwards, coating the room with merciless shards of broken glass.

Despite knowing it was coming, Ellie screamed, but the scream turned into a cheer halfway through.

Rob kicked the skylight, ensuring that the jagged edges were removed from the frame. It was a tight fit before, but now the hole they had to climb through was four inches smaller because of the window frame. It was only big enough for a child. Rob had doubts that they could get out.

He had to find something strong enough to fasten the rope to. He crawled around the roof, looking, but there was nothing. Panic set in. To come this far and fail was unthinkable. He had no choice but to use himself as an anchor. Rob was a big guy, six foot two and eighteen stone. The girls weighed about nine stone each. He could do it. No problem, he was twice as heavy

305

as either of them. He tied the rope around his waist, tested the knots and dropped the loose end through the skylight.

'Got it,' Eve shouted.

'I know. You nearly pulled me off the fucking roof and in there with you. Don't start climbing until I tell you.'

'Okay.'

Rob went to the edge of the roof and lay flat. He held onto it with both hands. He'd taken his driving gloves from the car and fished them out of his pockets. He hoped that he and the knots were strong enough to hold on until the girls climbed out.

'Ready? Okay, do it.'

Eve's next words made his blood run cold.

'Right, Ellie, come on, you're going to have to jump on my back. Don't hold on to my neck too tight, and for Christ's sake, don't fall off. We can do this.'

Of course, how could he have been so stupid not to realise it before? Ellie would never be able to climb the rope. How could he have been so thoughtless? This was an even bigger ordeal for Ellie than he imagined.

'Matt first,' Ellie said with determination, 'Take Matt first. I'll wait until he's out.'

'Are you crazy?' Eve screamed at her. 'Ellie, we can't take him. I won't have the strength to do this twice. We have to leave him behind.'

'I'm not leaving without Matt.'

'Ellie.' Rob tried to talk sense into her. 'I don't know if I can hold the two of you. I know I won't be able to take Eve's weight and Matt's at the same time. I'm sorry, love, but Eve's right. We have to leave him behind. Matt would understand. Now, come on. That maniac could come back at any minute, and we're all sitting ducks.'

Rob breathed a sigh of relief as he heard the oomph of Ellie jumping onto Eve's back. Thank Christ for that. He was still worried about taking the strain of both women at once. It was a weight equal to his own, and he only had the edge of the roof to hang on to.

Eve climbed, and Rob knew what it was like to be a man tortured on the rack in medieval times. With Eve gaining on the rope, Rob felt his body pulled further towards the skylight. The edge of the roof cut through the gloves and into his fingers. He hung on and gritted his teeth against the pain. His hands would have been shredded if he didn't have the driving gloves.

Eve was perspiring. The tendons of her neck stuck out like electrical cables. For the first time, she doubted they could make it. Halfway up the rope, she felt Ellie's grip loosen.

'You okay?'

'No, I think I'm going to faint. I'm dizzy. My wrist is bleeding, and I can't hold on much longer.'

'Yes, you can, and you're not going to faint. One chance, Ellie. We've only got one chance. If this fails, we might as well roll over and die.' Talking was difficult, but Eve knew she had to be strong. Ellie was losing it physically and mentally.

'Hey, remember that goofy song you used to sing when you were depressed? What was it now? I know.'

Eve found the going tough. Moving hand over hand up the rope was taking all her strength, but she had to do something to keep Ellie focused. Between ragged breaths, she sang.

'Where ever you go, I'm gonna be there. I can't sing this shit on my own.' Come on, Ellie, help me out here.

Ellie's small voice joined in.

'Whatever you do, I'm gonna be there. Pure and simple, gonna be there.'

They reached the top, and Eve grabbed the frame. That was the easy bit. Now came the real test of Eve's strength.

'Ellie, one day those old songs are going to be the death of me.'

Despite the situation, the tension, Matt's death and everything else, the women laughed together for the first time.

'Right, Ellie, you have to summon up some strength from somewhere because you're going to have to climb up me to get out. I would offer to help, but as you can see, I've got my hands full.'

The weight of Ellie's body was dragging Eve down. She could feel the combined bulk of the two of them centred on her fingertips. She was going to have to shut everything out and find somewhere quiet to retreat to in the hope of getting them through this.

'Rob, let go of the roof and help Ellie through.'

'I can't. If you lose your grip, you'll fall and pull both of us through with you.'

'Okay, but remember, if we all end up crashing back down, I sleep on the left.'

'You think this is the time for stupid jokes. What the fuck's wrong with you?'

Ellie was quiet. She was losing it again.

'Quick, Rob,' Eve yelled. 'My fingers are slipping, and I can't hold on.'

Rob let go of the rope, scrambled up the roof and grabbed Ellie by the shoulders.

'Right, come on, Ellie. Use Eve's body to walk yourself up.'

'I can't. Rob, I'm so scared, I can't move.'

'I know you are, honey, I know. We all are, but this is the only way out.'

Rob pulled hard under Ellie's arms, aware that, due to her condition, he could be doing severe damage to her.

Eve concentrated on slowing her breathing. She closed her eyes and imagined being by the sea. She had never felt the sensation of standing at the ocean but had lived it through Ellie many times. She often used this method of meditation. Her heart rate dropped from its elevated rate of a hundred and twenty through her normal rate of about sixty-four. It fell steadily until it reached its lowest rate of forty beats a minute. Her heart rate had dropped eighty beats in a little over thirty seconds. She counted the drumming from the pulse in her neck as she concentrated on the meditation. She found her quiet place where nobody could hurt her.

Ellie's head was through the window, and she could take part of her own weight by resting on her forearms. It was a hell of a struggle getting her shoulders through, but they got her top half out of the skylight with a lot of shoving between them. Ellie was exhausted—and stuck.

'Come on, Ellie. You can do this. Think about it. Your shoulders are your widest part. If you can get them through, the rest will follow.'

'I can't. I can't move.'

'Come on, love, put your arms around my neck and let me help you,' Rob said.

'I've been cursed with childbearing hips,' she whined.

Rob centred his balance by placing his feet on either side of the skylight and squatting. Ellie laced her arms around his neck, reluctant to let go of the security of the hard wood against her arms. She buried her face in Rob's neck and smelled the cool citrus smell of his expensive French aftershave. It wasn't the same brand that Matt used, but just smelling the closeness of man near her reminded her of Matt, alone and dead on the floor of the sterile cell.

Rob straightened his legs. He had the whole weight of Ellie in his arms now and felt the strain in his lower back. He concentrated on raising her through the hole, remembering to lift with his leg muscles and not his back, but he wasn't strong enough. Her slim hips were wedged in the tiny hole. He was about to relax and take a breath before trying again when Ellie shot through the hole with a plop. Rob flew backwards and rolled down the roof but regained his balance five feet from the edge. He lunged at Ellie and grabbed her to him in a fierce bear hug. Ellie sobbed into his neck—Eve was forgotten.

Eve hadn't followed Ellie out of the window, and Rob looked over the skylight. They could just leave her there. She wasn't their problem. He saw Eve hanging, and for a second, he thought she'd died in that position. He leaned in and touched her arm.

'Eve?'

She opened her eyes as if waking from a restful sleep. She grinned at Rob and put a hand out to him to help her out.

Rob wanted to take his fist and smash it into the back of Eve's head. Only the fact that she had risked her life to save Ellie stopped him, but he couldn't bring himself to touch her. He'd seen her strength—one pull, and she could have him through the skylight and falling to the ground below. He didn't trust her. He looked at her as a rabbit would a snake and turned back to Ellie, leaving Eve to get herself out.

Eve had no trouble. The two and a half minutes of transcendental meditation that she taught herself from books revived her. She wriggled through the hole as though she were indeed an invertebrate. The image of Eve as a serpent intensified. Rob shuddered and clung to Ellie in a mutual giving and taking of warmth and comfort. All Rob wanted to do was ring Gail. She would be out of her mind with worry. As soon as they were on the open road, it was the first thing he would do. The second was having one of the black-market cigarettes hidden in his glovebox.

Getting back to Ellie's car in the woods was no picnic, but they managed it. It was still dark but not pitch black. The moon had made a belated appearance and lit their way. Rob and Eve pretty much carried Ellie, and the ordeal had taken its toll. She had gone hours without her medication, and the Tay-Sachs was giving her a beating. Getting Ellie off the roof would be like a scene from a poorly scripted comedy to anybody looking on. None of the players was laughing, and Ellie was close to collapsing. Again it was Eve who saved the day. Just as she knew how to hurt Ellie so she could keep her moving.

She reminded her about Jake waiting for her in the car, a few hundred feet away. It was the push she needed, and from somewhere, Ellie pulled enough reserve of spirit to get her through.

Rob hadn't thought of that and the smile he gave Eve over Ellie's head was part thanks and part grudging respect. He had to admit that if it wasn't for the combined efforts of both of them, they wouldn't have escaped.

Jake heard them coming long before they were close. Ellie warned Rob to put Jake on his lead and keep a tight hold so he couldn't reach Eve. Although Eve didn't need any telling, she warned her to stay out of his way. As soon as he saw his mistress, he was beside himself with joy and jumped around in a bid for freedom. Then he saw the one who hurt Ellie, and he was a seething mass of confusion. The dog was half joyous and half furious and didn't know how to behave.

While Rob struggled to get Jake's lead on in the car, Eve stood beside Ellie with her hands flopping at her sides in a gesture of not knowing what to do next.

'Right, I'll be off then. I'm sorry about everything.' Now the drama was over, at least for the moment, she seemed embarrassed.

Before Ellie could say anything, she walked away.

'Where the hell do you think you're going? You aren't going anywhere.'

Eve turned. Her face had the hard stony look again.

'You agreed, no police. You gave me your word. I trusted you.'

Jake bounded out of the car with Rob struggling on the end of his lead. He ignored Eve and flew at Ellie in sheer wanton delight. She loved and crooned at the dog for a minute until he was calm, then turned to Eve. Jake growled at their enemy, warning her that if she moved one step closer to Ellie, he would have her.

'I know I did, Eve, and I meant it.' Ellie picked up the conversation as though they weren't interrupted. 'There won't be any police where you're concerned. I'll keep your name out of it. But if you think you can just walk away from this as if nothing's happened, you must be out of your mind. My boyfriend has been murdered, and you want to disappear into the night? Responsibility doesn't work like that.'

'What do you want me to do? Surely you aren't suggesting I come back with you. And I can't go back to my flat. I have to run—and you'd all better do the same. We may be out of there, but the danger isn't over. He's going to come looking for us, and when he finds us, soon after, somebody else will be finding us, too. The only difference is, by then, we'll all be dead. I'm not going to sit around and wait for that to happen. Are you?'

'So what are you going to do, Eve? Where are you going to go? Are you just going to run away like a coward leaving me to face it all on my own?'

'You've got it in one, sister. That's exactly what I'm going to do. I'm going to start walking, and as long as I live, I'm never going to stop because he'll never give up looking for us.'

'Don't you see, Eve? We have to stick together on this. You owe me, and in some ways, maybe I owe you too. You've got at least some of the answers to this mess, and together we might be able to find out the rest. I need to understand what's happening. You brought all this on us, but you also saved my life, and for that, I'm grateful. But Matt's still dead, and I want his killer found and sent away for the rest of his life. I'll keep my promise and won't call the police yet, but I want Matt's body out of there. We have to call them soon.'

Rob cut in on them.

'Excuse me, ladies, I know you've got a lot of talking to do, and God knows I've got a lot of sleeping to do, but there's a maniac trying to kill us, remember. So can we just get home, please? Then, if you want, Eve, I'll take you and drop you anywhere you want to be. Outer-bloody-Mongolia wouldn't be far enough for me, but please, let's move.'

The next problem was sorting out the travel arrangements. Jake wasn't going to let Eve in the same car as Ellie. They had three cars, and the way Rob saw it, only one driver. Although Rob assumed the car out back had been hers, Eve had never driven a car in her life. Driving was something she couldn't learn from books, so she was out. Rob said they would have to travel back in his car and keep Jake away from Eve. But every time Eve moved, the dog snarled and tried to attack her, so that wasn't going to work.

Ellie's only other solution was to take her car with Jake, leaving Rob and Eve in Rob's car. And that was assuming Ellie's car hadn't been damaged. Rob hated the idea, but Ellie convinced him that she needed some quiet time after everything. He worried about her taking ill at the wheel, but Ellie assured him that seeing Jake again and being free had returned her strength, and she'd be fine.

He had to admit that she looked better than she had. He brought up the subject of them being followed. What if they met the mad man on the twisty Lake's road? If they were in one car, they stood a chance of out-driving him, but they'd be done for in two. Ellie argued that the longer they argued, the more likely they'd meet their crazed jailer. She promised to wait at the end of the road for Rob to catch up, and then Rob's car could tail her home. It was the only solution.

Rob drove Ellie's car out of the woods for her and ensured that everything was in order with it. It had withstood the assault course well. Ellie got in and calmed Jake. Within seconds he realised he was going for a ride. Jake only loved one thing more than walk-in-wood-chase-squirrels, and that was going for a drive. So he assumed his usual position in the passenger seat and whined for Ellie to start the car.

She turned the key and heard the engine engage. There was a three-second gap with the realisation of what would happen, but the music played before she could stop it. The track she'd been listening to the day before with Matt played. Ellie loved old music, all the stuff from years back. It was a mellow album, and memories of Matt flooded the car as the music seeped through the speakers like audible velvet. She drove with tears obscuring her vision.

She made it to the road and pulled into the verge to wait for Rob. Paranoia struck her, and she felt open and vulnerable as she stopped. When the lights came around the corner, she was hit by a bolt of panic so intense that she felt her body freeze. What if it wasn't Rob? It could be the killer, and she was waiting to be picked off. The music rang through her head, and in those few seconds, she could feel Matt's presence in the car with her. In her head, she heard him telling her to calm down and that Rob would protect her. Sure enough, as the car drew close, its lights flashed, and she relaxed.

The ordeal wasn't over, but it was on hold for the time being.

# Chapter
# Twenty-one

'Y̲ou fool. You utter, utter fool. That was a mistake, a big mistake. I shouldn't have killed the boyfriend. Their fault, the dollies, they shouldn't have brought him onto the board. It was our game—ours—nobody else's. He had no right to be there. No right. No right, I tell you. Those silly dollies, they didn't think. Do they want to anger me? Anger The Creator? Do they think they can go against me and win? Do they?

'There'll be recriminations. There'll be big consequences, no less. Consequences, I say. Who'll pay the price? Not I. Not I The Creator, when the men in blue pound the doors. Rat-a-tat-tat. Not my door. The dollies will pay, my broken dolls, my girls. They'll pay. Oh, I'll make them dance on their tight strings until they can dance no more.

'They shouldn't have let him come. And now they're crying crystal tears. Judas tears, that's all they are, Judas tears. They betrayed him, such a nice young man, that Rob fella, a gentleman. Regrettable indeed. They will not bring a white king onto my board. They will not. They will not. They will not.'

The man in the crimson smoking jacket punched the wall. Though the dividing wall shook and the chandelier rattled, he felt no pain. He was too immersed in his mania. It wouldn't pain him until later when he would take to his boudoir to whimper and watch.

'Temper, temper, old man. No need for it, no need, I say. We do not display emotion, do we? Indeed we do not. Cunning is the order of the day, cunning and stealth and patience.

'Things are hotting up, Sir. What is this bond striking up between the dollies? Well, well, isn't that nice? We shall watch it now. Watch for the fireworks and explosions. 'Ello. 'Ello. 'Ello, mister policeman will say. And they'll run. My poor broken dollies. Run for their lives. Run for their freedom. Run till their hearts pound and their breath rasps. Rat-a-tat-tat. Who made Matt smile so wide? Such a big smile in his shorn throat. "Not I, Sir," say the dollies, but still, he'll chase them.

'Chase them, chase them and chase them. The men in blue will chase them. And then I, The Creator, will chase them harder, with cunning and stealth and patience. Rat-a-tat-tat. Hello.'

He threw back his head in the near darkness and laughed.

# Chapter Twenty-two

**7th March 2017—Thirty-two years earlier.**

'D o you have to go out?' He was always moaning at her. If she'd known what it would be like, she wouldn't have married him. 'Why can't you stay in, and we'll have a quiet night in front of the Television?'

Jesus, she thought. Boring, boring, boring—surely there must be more to life than this? She was only twenty-one and wanted to be out having fun. He could vegetate all he liked, but why should she? He wasn't going to pin her down to the dishwasher. He came up behind her and put his hands on her waist. God, I hate it when he paws at me like that. She wriggled away and faced him, glaring.

'I told you yesterday I'm going out, and I'm going. Why do you have to be so bloody possessive? Since you made me give up work, we sit in night after bloody night, and what do we talk about? Nothing. Not a damned thing. When was the last time you took me out? On my birthday, wasn't it? Eight months ago. We sit in every bloody night, and we've got nothing to say to each other.'

'But you've got plenty to talk about with Jenny Bailey, haven't you? Who she shagged on Tuesday night while Terry was doing the back shift, for instance. She's a tart, and you told me when we got married that you were leaving all that behind you. Can't you see that I want us to have a decent life? I'm earning good money. We can build a future, start a family and be happy. For Christ's sake, woman, I just want to make you happy.'

She'd heard it all before, same old whinging, same old song. Nothing was going to spoil tonight for her, least of all this boring old fart.

Lipstick died out a decade ago. Pigment implants were available in the backroom of any pharmacy and cost little more than the price of a new shirt. But this season, the fashion of the 1980s had made a comeback and bright red lipstick was *infashin*. She applied a third coat and wore a black lace mini-skirt with a sheer lace bat-winged blouse over a daring black bra. The neckline of her top plunged almost to her waist, and the back mimicked the front. Her torso was exposed in a V to her navel and the back to the top of her buttocks. The deep leather belt was almost as wide as her skirt, and the whole ensemble was finished with black ankle boots with lethal-looking stiletto heels.

Her blonde hair was back-combed and teased until it stuck out from her head as though she'd stuck her finger up an electric eel's backside. And though she said it herself, she looked damned good as she turned in a slow circle in front of the full-length mirror. She loved the sluttiness of the old styles, and her tiny figure showed them off.

He snorted in disgust and left the bedroom without another word, knowing that, as usual, he was beaten. She wouldn't be back until the early hours of the next morning, coming in drunken and leery. It was a familiar story.

She met Jenny in The Cry. They wouldn't have to buy too many drinks that night with a bit of luck. The place was heaving, and the crowd was in good spirits. From their working days in the local clubs, they knew a lot of faces. From The Cry, they moved around town in a crowd. The women were screeching like owls on the hunt, and the men were loud and bawdy in their beer-soaked aggression. When the pubs closed, they moved on to The Carlton nightclub. The Carlton had been around forever and was still a favourite haunt of the clubbing fraternity of Keswick.

The women wasted no time swirling onto the dancefloor in a haze of cheap perfume and glitter dust. It was still early, and the dancefloor was almost empty. They had plenty of opportunities to display themselves as they gyrated and moved their bodies to the beat of the thumping music. The women's dancing consisted of lots of stroking of their own bodies. Their hands alternated between touching themselves in a suggestive tease and raising high in the air to better display their lithe, half-naked figures. They never ceased moving, with circling waists and flicking hips, seducing every man standing around the floor.

'See that bloke over there?' Laura Jones pointed, 'I think he's following us.'

She'd noticed him too. He'd turned up in the last three pubs they went to, and Jenny Bailey had been giving him the eye, but she had no chance. She knew that this bitch right here was the prettiest of the group. If there was any having to be done, he was hers for the taking.

She was drunk and barely aware of who she was, never mind anybody else, but she'd noticed him alright. He was six foot—and some, blond and gorgeous. Any woman that pulled him tonight was a lucky girl.

He was looking at her.

She held his eyes for three seconds, a long time in flirt language. Then, with an expression of indifference, she flung her arms into the air, stroking down her left arm with her right. She stretched her torso so that it was long, bending back, moving in a slow, exaggerated, sensual wind. There was no mistaking the deal laid on the table. She was offering.

Signals sent and received, it was time to reel in the catch of the day. She left the rest of the girls dancing. Retrieving her bag from their table, she walked to the bar. She was drunk, but as a seasoned pro, she knew how to walk the walk of the clubbing scene.

He was at the edge of the dance floor. His attention was repositioned from watching all of the women to focussing on one. The tarty blonde was up for it, ripe for the taking. He was confident that she'd be leaving with him before much longer.

She passed within inches of him and flicked her hair so that as she moved past, it would graze his shoulder. Some of the hair spray had worn off with regular backcombing throughout the night. That, combined with a thin sheen of perspiration coating it from her moist neck, meant it had some movement. Half an hour earlier, it would have knocked him out.

She stood at the bar, ignoring the stares of lustful men. Her choice was made, and she had no interest in the others. She'd read the game card correctly, and he'd follow her. She ordered a double Bacardi and Coke and made a show of scrambling in her bag for her purse when a deep voice said, 'Please, let me get that for you.'

Bingo. She smiled up at him.

Bingo. He smiled back. She made it too easy. The money was in the bag.

# Chapter Twenty-three

Aron Quinn had been with the company for over two years. He was a mover, and only the best were hand-picked for the inner sanctum in this organisation. Most of the workforce did their mundane jobs and went home to their tired spouses and unbearable children.

Everybody speculated about the restricted area. The gossip was rife about what went on there. Inspectors swarmed all over the place bi-annually, and everything was strictly above board and legitimate—on the surface.

But when a staff member went beyond the restricted doors, they were never seen in the labs again. The first anybody saw of them was when they were burned off at traffic lights by the flash git in their brand new Subaru Stampede.

They didn't know that experimentation on a vast species selection of innocent animals was carried out beyond the private part of the building. They only knew about the rodents, and nobody cared about the lives of vermin.

Another thing they didn't know was that there was another—even more sacrosanct place. A restricted labyrinth had been built beyond the private area. This secret place was fitted with the latest equipment and gadgetry to set in motion the most controversial experiment ever conducted under the respectable heading of science.

Aaron Quinn never would know about this because he wouldn't live long enough to find out.

He had been noticed, though. He'd brag if he knew that Griffin, the man in command of operations, had spotted him, and he'd been picked by the big boss himself.

Very few people knew there was anybody higher than Mr Griffin.

What singled Quinn out for special treatment wasn't his drive and ambition or that he was the first to kiss-ass when the bosses were around. What set Aaron apart was his sensational good looks. That got him where he was going—nothing else.

His transport, far from stampeding, would be satin-lined for comfort and finished with brass handles.

Ron Griffin was the white coat giving the place a clean bill of respectability. Ten years on, Griffin would be found hanging from company rafters when he discovered his beloved institute wasn't squeaky-clean. He was fed information on a need-to-know basis, and his suicide came at a fortunate time for the one above him. It saved hands being dirtied by the messy business of murder again. And this man did so appreciate having spotless hands.

Aaron Quinn was a crucial player in the experiment. He'd like to have known that—but he never did.

Aaron had set himself apart from the white rats pouring over their microscopes, and viewing tiny, eviscerated pieces of other white rats. He knew he was destined for more extraordinary things. He distanced himself from the canteen gossip, choosing to spend his lunch breaks pouring over textbooks that he had little interest in. He didn't care what he had to learn to get into the restricted area. That was mere knowledge that had to go into his brain via his optical senses. Big money was earned behind the security-restricted set of double doors. Some big Bitcoin signs were waiting in there with his name on them, and he wanted in.

Two months earlier, Griffin called him into his office. He offered Aaron the laboratory assistant position in the all-powerful and super-exclusive restricted area. It wasn't the managing director's post, but it was a damn fine start.

Quinn found the work distasteful. He spent most of his day elbow deep in monkey shit, but the extra six-hundred Bitcoins a week made it worthwhile. He called it his conscience money, and new luxury pillows helped fend off the nightmares of tortured animals when they reached out to him in his sleep.

It was Friday night, for fuck's sake. He didn't want to work tonight, but old Griffin put pressure on him. The double pay was a nice incentive, but that was beside the point. There was only one Friday night every week, and everybody knew Friday night was party night.

He cleaned the pens with a frown playing against his chiselled features. Hell, even if he managed to blow this place at a rea-

sonable hour, he'd have to go straight home because he stunk
like a simian.

Griffin was in a rotten mood, too. There wasn't supposed to be
any overtime that evening. He'd planned a curry and an early
night. The memo came through that morning, demanding that
he work the back shift and keep a few people on to work with
him. One of them had to be the new bloke, Quinn. Griffin knew
better than to ask questions. His livelihood had been put on the
line when he'd enquired too closely into things from above that
he was told didn't concern him. He'd worked for the company
for five years, and he'd never seen their mysterious benefactor.
If he had a problem, he only ever liaised with the totty that was
his personal assistant. He felt he deserved more respect. But in
truth, his accelerating salary was all the respect he needed.

He had to make Quinn clean out the animals again to give
him something to do. He'd already done them earlier and wasn't
happy. Griffin wondered what the hell they wanted with the lab
boy and why hadn't they gone through him?

At seven-thirty, the top man's PA came into the labs and
demanded that Quinn go with her. She never asked for anything.
She barked orders as though she was something special. Griffin
told the lad to wash up because he had an appointment with
management.

This could only mean one thing, either he'd done well and
was about to be promoted, or he'd fucked up big-style and was
being given the boot. He weighed up the situation as he followed

the clicking heels of the lady down corridors that he'd never walked before. How could you mess up shovelling monkey shit? He was clear and could almost feel the car keys in his pocket.

He noticed that the posh bitch had a fine backside. Anybody that sashayed like that had to be approachable, didn't she?

'So darling, am I going to celebrate or commiserate after this? And where are you taking me after work?' His charm always worked on these power-hungry birds.

She stopped mid-stride and so suddenly that he cannoned into her back. Under other circumstances, he'd be happy to bump into her from behind, but he didn't think this was the time or the place.

'Steady, love,' he began but stopped with his mouth open as she wheeled around on one high heel and fixed him with an ice-cold stare.

'You will speak only when spoken to, and then only to answer direct questions. You will not ask questions. You will show the utmost respect. I will be addressed as Ma'am and the professor as Sir. Do you understand?'

She barked orders at him with such venom that, if he hadn't seen the cruel hardness in her eyes, he'd think she was playing the role of a Nazi commandant for a laugh. He figured she was taking on that role in deadly earnest.

'Yes, Ma'am,' he answered, feeling self-conscious.

She opened a door on the left-hand side of a corridor and led him into a plush anteroom. The burgundy carpeting was a wall-to-wall luxury. The office-cum-waiting room had little in it, but everything about the place screamed money. She walked to an inner door and knocked.

'Come.'

She ushered him into the room.

'Quinn, sir.'

She left, closing the door behind her. He almost sat in one of the chairs on his side of the enormous desk but realised the man was staring at him and hadn't asked him to sit down. He hovered and didn't know what to do.

Not sitting down was a good move. The big man was smiling, showing a lot of teeth, but his eyes were hard and cold as he appraised Aaron.

'Turn around.' he made a twiddling gesture with his finger.

Aaron felt ridiculous and didn't know what the hell was going on. Did this bloke want him to prance about like a fucking ballerina? Maybe he was a nonce. The bloke twirled his finger three times, so Aaron pirouetted on the spot, hoping to God that this was what was expected of him.

'Yes, you'll do. You'll do nicely.'

The powerhouse looked smug and didn't introduce himself. 'Well, sit down,' he boomed, and Aaron sat, looking like a small child in the mammoth leather seat and feeling like a prize tit.

'I've been watching you, lad.' His voice was impassive, and Aaron spent the next few seconds thinking of something worthwhile to say and wondering if that was a good or a bad thing. He didn't feel it was in his best interests to ask. If one thing could be said about Aaron Quinn, he learned fast. Catching on was his forte, and he remembered what Old Gestapo Knickers said. "You will speak only when asked direct questions."

He hadn't been asked anything, so he spent his time squirming in the big seat. His trouser leg rubbed on the edge of the chair and made a farting noise. He felt his face burning and knew he looked as red as a twatting poppy. The man-mountain didn't laugh, and under these circumstances, neither did Aaron.

'Are you trustworthy, lad?'

For a presumably intelligent fella, he asked some dumb-assed questions. He was hardly going to say, 'No, I can't be trusted an inch, sir,' was he?

'Yes, sir. I'm very trustworthy, sir, and I won't let you down, sir. You could trust me with your little girl, and I swear she'd never be safer, sir.'

'All right, economise on the bleating. I only need to ask one more thing. Are you a risk-taker, Mr Quinn? Are you prepared to drive in the fast lane?'

Aaron gave a passing thought to the Stampede with the *Quinn* registration plate that might be driving along his horizon.

'Yes, sir. I am indeed, sir. I'm right risky, I am, sir.'

He had no idea what the hell was going on or why he had to prance around like a bloody prima donna, but if this bloke was willing to pay enough, he'd dance Swan Lake in a pink tutu until the day he retired if need be. The geezer obviously had something in mind for him.

'Well, Quinn, my boy. I have a little job for you.'

He opened a drawer in his desk and pulled something out. Aaron figured that if this was a bad B-movie, it might be a gun, and he might be shot for gross misconduct with an experimental pig. But he'd only ever scratched the pigs behind the ears before they went to torture, nothing else.

The man brought out a large envelope with the showmanship of a magician. He pulled out a wad of money and spread it on the desk in front of him as though he was laying out a deck of cards.

Aaron had never seen so much cash. His eyes bugged as he tried to calculate an approximate sum. As if reading his mind, the employer stared him in the eyes.

'There's ten-thousand there, lad.'

He separated the money into two unequal amounts with a flourish and pointed to the smallest.

'That pile is approximately two grand. It's a small bonus on top of your wage, payable when you leave this office.' He pointed to the bigger stack of cash. 'And this is my gift to you for knowing how to keep your mouth shut. The job I have for you is a little continuation of your overtime tonight. You will receive this on completion of the work. Do we understand each other, Mr Quinn?'

'Yes, sir. Perfectly, sir. But what have I got to do? Is it legal?' He had spoken out of turn.

'I thought you were a risk-taker, Quinn,' he boomed, making Aaron jump.

'Oh, I am, sir. I definitely am. But I don't want anything to do with drugs, sir.' Aaron worried that if it wasn't drugs, the fat, old man wanted him for sex. He'd knock the old bastard out if he touched him.

The man threw his head back and laughed.

'Drugs, lad? Drugs? My, what a vulgar word that is. I deal with pharmaceuticals, not drugs. No, be at ease. It's nothing like that. In fact, I think you might rather enjoy what I have planned for you. I want you to pick me a nice lady, Aaron.' He used Aaron's Christian name for the first time. 'Any young lady will do—your choice. If you serve me well, boy, I may use you for a little overtime again in the future.'

The employer outlined what he wanted him to do. The phrase dirty old pervert ran through Aaron's mind like a record. He didn't like what was asked of him. He certainly wasn't happy with it. Only the thought of all that easy money motivated him to take on the job. Pocketing his two grand—approximately, he shook the man's offered hand to seal their deal. The old nonce smelled like fancy perfume and his mother's talcum powder.

Gestapo Knickers showed him along more corridors. These were richly carpeted with painted walls displaying works of art, mainly fat nudes, not his type of thing at all. He wondered if his current escort ever posed nude. That's one picture he wouldn't mind appraising with an artist's critical eye.

She took him to a suite of rooms that any five-star hotel would call the penthouse. He knew what he had to do, and he was only mildly surprised when he was told to bathe and change his clothes. She said he'd find everything he needed in the bathroom and avail himself of anything he wanted.

He didn't need to be told twice. After she left, he locked the door behind her and went into the bathroom.

He couldn't believe his eyes. Surely this was a weird dream. The bathroom was like nothing he'd ever seen, not even on one of those rich people's houses programs. There were white towelling robes and matching towels, all manner of creams and gels for men, and soft sponges to wash with.

A circular, sunken bath with voice-activated controls and a Jacuzzi dominated the room. It had solid gold taps and steps down into the tub.

The bathroom led onto a dressing room as big as his house. It had wall to wall mirrors. A rack of clothes had been left for him to choose from in the correct size. There was everything from formal three-pieces to jeans and Jaeger shirts. He chose a pair of designer jeans, a deep purple shirt, black boots, and a three-quarter-length leather coat.

A shelf at the side of the bath had a selection of aftershaves and colognes. They were top names, nothing cheap. There were three open jewellery boxes, one with a dozen gold Stella-links, the latest jewellery accessories for men. They worked as a replacement for buttons, fastening with invisible micro-grips to any garment. The second box contained a Psioden watch. He couldn't know but guessed it was the genuine article. Psioden were the leading watchmakers in the world. The last box held an elegant gold ring, nothing ostentatious or vulgar, but one that spoke with an upper-crust accent.

A gilt-edged card rested beside the jewellery.

Dear Mr Quinn, I took the liberty of picking out some trinkets and suitable clothing for you. I trust they will fit and that you find them to your liking. Please pick whatever you would like to wear for your evening out, and consider both the clothes and jewellery, a small gift for you to keep.

There was no signature.

This guy understood the finer points of bribery, and Aaron was learning the same rules fast. He looked at the packet in his hand. The voice of his conscience tried to make itself heard, but this was more than a dream come true, this was fucking paradise unlimited, and he'd be mad to pass it up. The guy gave his word that the girl would be released after he'd had his fun with her, so where was the harm? He refused to think about how the girl could be released after she'd seen both Aaron and Pervy Percival, too. 'Do not concern yourself,' he'd said. It sounded like damned fine advice.

The bath was the best he'd ever had, and he was in no hurry to get out. As the man said, the night was his own as long as he delivered the goods. He'd even chucked in an extra two hundred to fund his evening's pleasures. Far from missing his Friday night out, this was the best night he'd ever had.

'Looking damn fine,' he said to the good-looking man in the mirror, and the gold ring with the tiny diamond shimmered in the overhead light.

# Chapter Twenty-four

'**W**ould you like some ice with that?'

She smiled at him, making sure that he saw the tip of her tongue flash out to moisten her lips before she spoke.

'No, thanks, the only thing you ever want to put with Bacardi and Coke is another Bacardi and Coke.' It was a fumbled take on an old joke, and the original was snappier, but he smiled anyway.

'Would you like to sit down?' He took their glasses and went to an empty table before she had the chance to answer. He pulled out a chair and guided her into the table. Sitting opposite, he turned the charm from dripping tap to full surging flow.

'I knew I had to talk to you when I saw you on the dance floor.'

'And why might that be?' She pushed her chest out as she spoke.

The gesture wasn't wasted on him, and he wished he could have some fun with her before he had to deliver her to the boss. He'd said she was not to be tampered with, as though she was one of his official documents. The man was very clear in his instructions on that one. Aaron had never tampered with a girl in his life—but he'd shagged a fair few.

'So, gorgeous, what's your name? I could call you Princess all night, but it might get on your nerves after a while.'

'I'm Esther, pleased to meet you. And you are?'

She passed her slim hand over the table. When he kissed the back of it, she ran her hand through his until her fingertip was pressed against his lips. As was expected of him in this situation, he looked up to meet her eyes. Sure enough, she was pouting. Her body language was telling him, as plain as a wet pussy, that she was as keen to get out of the place as he was, though for vastly different reasons.

The longer he sat with her, the more likely it was that her friends would be able to give a good description of him if anything happened to her. It was all well and good Pervy Percy saying that everything was okay. Still, it wasn't him sitting at the table with her finger ramming itself halfway down his throat.

He gave the finger a little suck to play along and pleasurable though this might be in another time and place he thought he should get down to business.

'Tell me about you.' He gazed devotedly into her eyes.

'But you haven't told me your name yet.'

'Of course, how bad-mannered of me. I'm Pete Gardiner.' Percy hadn't told him to lie, but it was a precaution of his own. 'Now tell me about the lovely Esther. Esther what? It must be something exotic to follow such a beautiful name.'

This part of the job made him uncomfortable. He tried to remember all the questions he had to ask. Old Pervy wanted a shag, for Christ's sake. Aaron couldn't understand why he had to get as many personal details as possible. Hell, he called all his conquests Babe, so he didn't have to know their names. Pervy had been specific about that. Aaron had to find out about her background. His money would be docked if he didn't get all the answers. He wasn't going to lose a penny of that ten grand.

'Esther Erikson, actually. See? I'm as ordinary as they come,' she laughed.

He was a smarmy git, but who cared with a body like that? 'And you might as well know, so there's no misunderstanding, I'm married. I'm just a girl whose husband doesn't understand her.'

Esther was many things, but one thing she hadn't learned yet was the art of lying. She had no social or moral conscience, so she saw no reason to. She lived in Esther-land, a place where only her needs mattered.

She excused herself to go to the ladies. He was jumpy. He saw her friends talking to her and grinning. One was giving her a thumbs-up. He wanted to be out of there, but first, he had to get more information. He still had work to do. He took a drink of his soda water and gulped back his feeling of unease.

Sitting in what he hoped was a relaxed manner, he scanned the room for people close enough to be nosy. Everybody was too engrossed in their own challenges to bother him. He slid her glass towards him and dropped the white tablet into it. He gave it a quick twirl and put the glass back.

I don't want anything to do with drugs. He remembered what he'd said, sitting in the overstuffed seat, talking to the over-stuffed man. Well, maybe for ten grand, I don't mind so much.

When she came back, he pressed the drink into her hand. 'Come on, slowcoach, drink up, the night is young, and we have a lifetime of ground to cover.'

Esther didn't know if it was the drink or the way this man had an uncanny knack of making her talk, but within ten minutes, she had told him all there was to know about her. She was bored of him and thought about going back to her mates. This loser was all talk and no action.

She felt tingly. The room closed in, and she needed to move while she still could.

'Hey, d'ya wanna dance?' she slurred.

'I'd love to, but do you know what I'd really like? I'd like to take you out of here. What do you say?'

That was more like it. It sounded like a good idea. Esther needed fresh air to sober up, she felt unwell, and if she didn't move, she would pass out at the table.

He helped her up. The Rohypnol was taking effect quickly—too bloody quickly. If he didn't get her out, she would be unconscious and cause attention he could do without. Her friends were all away from their table. They wouldn't see them leaving. The dancefloor had filled up, which was perfect. He had to support her and half carry her across the room.

The place was spinning. The pain in her head that had only come on a minute ago dissolved into a black noise rising to a crescendo. She'd never heard pain as a noise before. Before the world collapsed on her, the last thing she was aware of was the glitter ball above her head spinning on its axis. It spun her into blessed oblivion.

Oh fuck, she'd gone. He thought about dumping her and getting the hell out of there, but that would arouse more suspicion. He scooped her into his arms. For a tiny woman, the slapper was heavy, and he had to carry her down two flights of stairs. When he got to the exit, he was gasping with exertion and fear. He looked at the doormen. 'Some women can't hold their ale, eh, fellas?'

They opened the door for him and didn't bat an eyelid. They'd seen it all before.

His car was two streets away, and he couldn't risk carrying her that far. It would be too noticeable, and besides, his heart wouldn't stand it, not to mention his screaming back. He ran as best he could with carrying her to the alley at the back of the club. Halfway along, in total darkness, was a doorway. He put her down between two dustbins as gently as he could.

His bottle had gone. He wanted to run. He needed to go like the wind, get in his car, drive and just keep driving as far away as he could get. He wanted to run, but he forced himself to walk.

He wondered what would happen if she came to in the alley. If his heart rate had been measured by speed, he would have broken the sound barrier. Worse, what if she woke up on the way back to the institute and realised that she'd had more than a shot of Bacardi? He got into his car and drove to the alley.

She was still there but felt twice as heavy as before. The woman was difficult to lift into the back of the car. She was a dead weight. He bumped her head hard on the top of the door, and it cut through her drugged state because she moaned.

She was in, and he was driving. If he'd looked at her while she was slumped in the alley, maybe a premonition of his own fate would have come to him, but he didn't. He was almost home and dry and was mentally spending the big wad of cash.

Aaron wanted to drop her off and collect his money. But he'd got away with it, and some of his cock-sure attitude was returning. He was out of town and heading along the Portinscale road, driving as fast as he dared on a Friday night, with police patrolling the place for drunk drivers.

He'd been instructed to drive to an obscured door at the back of the building. They were waiting for him, and he didn't have to knock. Before he got out of the car, two men, one of them the boss, hurtled through, pushing a gurney in front of them. She was loaded onto it and taken into the building in seconds.

He swallowed and licked his lips. He didn't know what the hell Percy was up to, but it didn't look like any sad bastard grope and fuck of an unconscious woman to him. Ten grand was a lot of silence money, and he didn't want to see any more. He just wanted to get the hell out of there and collect the rest of his money the following day as arranged.

The man in charge took the gurney and ran with it down the corridor. He didn't even acknowledge Aaron. The other man stayed to deal with Quinn.

By the time Bernie Roberts, the boss's partner, had scrubbed up and entered the operating room, the boss was already in his greens. He'd stripped and prepared the host. She was the second woman receiving treatment this evening. The other, a volunteer, was already in a sideward, sipping a cup of tea and resting for the required five hours.

Esther Erikson had been given light anaesthesia to ensure that she remained still throughout the procedure. Her legs were fastened into stirrups, and her private area was washed in iodine. The embryo was taken by the boss with reverence and distributed in the womb of Mrs Erikson. Nature would do what was required of her. He had no doubt about that. Wanting exactly two infants, he planted only two embryos, one in each woman, not three or four in each, as was usual for in vitro fertilisation. He was The Creator, and he had faith. If the great almighty God

340

was with him, he would bring each child to fruition. It would be his signal that all was well. He believed he worked with God's blessing.

And so his scheme was hatched.

# Chapter Twenty-five

A dog pissed against the wall. He sniffed his produce and satisfied himself that, yes, it was still his. He scented everything until he stopped at the bundle, intending to pee on that too, but he didn't like what he smelled. He gave a whine and trotted away from the nasty odour that followed him out of the alley. He moved on, pleased with himself.

The body slumped against the wall was partly concealed by a rolled carpet thrown out for the dustbin people to collect. The eyes were wide and glassy, still looking, in death, at the last image he saw in life. Most of the lower half of his face had been blown away. From the position he assumed, part of a large exit wound was visible at the back of his head. This was no opportunistic killing, though, because he died wearing expensive jewellery and had two thousand, one hundred and eighty-six Euros in his wallet.

The body in the summerhouse beside the river Greta slouched in a similar position to the one barely a mile away. This one had a thin line of vomit drying on her chin and a larger amount darkening her inappropriate-for-the-weather top.

Unlike the other body, this one was just coming to. She awoke as many hangover suffers do—timidly. And like many morning-after drunks, her first coherent thought was, where the hell am I?

She sat forward, elbows on knees, head in hands, and let the events of the night filter through to her. A man—there was a man. She remembered everything now, everything until leaving the club. She was drunk, happy, but not drunk enough to pass out. Though her head pounded mercilessly, she did a finger count of the number of drinks she'd had. She didn't run out of fingers, so she couldn't have been that drunk. Esther was a regular social drinker. She had a tolerance to alcohol. It didn't make sense.

She tried to stand, and her hangover receded into the background as a new pain came to the fore. She was tender, very sore between her legs. She felt bruised. Oh dear God, no. What's happened to me?

She went to the toilet left him alone with the drinks. You shouldn't do that: posters everywhere. *Never leave your drink unattended*. She felt ill, very ill. Not drunk ill, though, different. It was making sense. Oh God, I've been out all night. Jerry will go mad. He won't believe me.

A lady was walking towards the summerhouse. She stopped and looked at Esther.

Don't stop, please don't come over, carry on walking. What must I look like? The woman made up her mind and walked over to the lady in obvious distress.

'Are you all right, love? Can I help you in any way?'

Esther was the type of woman who needed looking after. She thrived on attention and sympathy focussed in her direction. She dissolved into sudden wracking sobs.

'Help me, please help me. I've been raped.'

The woman was fantastic. After introducing herself as Maria, she called a taxi to take Esther home and placated the distraught woman until it arrived. She believed Esther's story. She truly believed it. This friendly, attractive lady didn't think Esther was a common trollop who had asked for it. She said the man was despicable and agreed that she must have been drugged. Of course, she wouldn't pass out after just a very few Bacardis. Nobody would. It was always nice people that it happened to. Vulnerable people like Esther. Esther gulped back the fresh onslaught of tears and agreed. 'You're such a beautiful woman,' the lady said. 'It's such a terrible shame it should happen to someone as pretty as you.' She made Esther feel better, and soon the flood of tears dried to a mere trickle.

'I'm not really pretty,' Esther simpered, turning doe eyes with attractively wet eyelashes up to the nice lady.

'Nonsense, that's rubbish. You don't know how attractive you are. You have a figure to die for. I'm not surprised the beast picked you out of all the other women in the place. Poor you, having to pay such a dear price for just trying to keep yourself nice.'

'Terrible, terrible,' Esther agreed. She liked this woman and was disappointed when the taxi pulled up to the kerb. She'd

344

rather sit here and listen to this lady telling her she was beautiful than go home to face a furious Jerry. She doubted he'd be so sympathetic. She felt her bottom lip wobble again.

'Well, thank you so much. You've been ever so kind.'

'Silly girl, do you think I'm going to let you get into that taxi on your own? You're far too upset to be alone. I insist on coming with you to see that you get home safely.' Esther leaned on the woman's arm and said she didn't think she could walk properly. Much of her strength had returned, but Esther always played the innocent victim so well. It was a role made for her.

She slumped into the taxi. It was all too much for her— too much. 'Thank you, Mary,' she said to the nice lady.

'It's Maria, love,' she reminded her. Of course, it was. Esther looked at her, unabashed. Other people's names meant nothing to her—Mary, Maria, Martha, who cares? She made a show of struggling to remember her own address while Maria stroked her arm. Esther was genuinely worried about the reception she'd get when she got home. Jerry was going to be livid. She sobbed into a lace handkerchief. She did it with elegance, though, because Esther didn't hold with ugly crying

Maria leaned towards her and whispered soothing words. As she did, her left hand slid into Esther's handbag. She groped around until she felt what she was looking for, pulled out Esther's purse and tucked it into her own pocket.

When the taxi arrived outside Esther's house, she groped for her bag, but Maria already had money in her hand to pay the driver. She asked him to wait for her and went around to the other side of the car to help Esther out.

Jerry was already striding down the path, tight-lipped and stern. He glared at Esther before thanking the kind Samaritan for her help. Polite formalities were exchanged, and Jerry insisted on reimbursing Maria for the taxi fare, despite her protestations.

'Raped? Raped?' he shouted later when a tearful Esther asked him to call the police. 'Don't be ridiculous, woman. Why should anyone take by force something that's offered on a plate? You disgust me, you drunken whore.' That was the only time Jerry had ever lost his temper with her and lowered himself to name-calling. 'It's not the police you need, Esther. It's a sound thrashing to knock some sense into you. If you must, you go to the police, but I'll have no part in it. They'll take one look at you and laugh you out of the station. Let this be a lesson to you, woman. And I'm telling you, this is the last time that anything of this nature will happen. Do you understand me?'

His shouting was so out of character for the gentle man that Esther was genuinely ashamed of herself. Her shame would never last long, but that morning, at twenty minutes past nine by the kitchen clock, Esther Erikson took a cold look at herself. For the first time in her life, she didn't like what she saw. She pleaded with Jerry to be nice to her. She'd been through a terrible ordeal. All he'd done, after all, was sit up all night worrying about her. That couldn't be half as bad as what she'd suffered, even though she couldn't remember what it was she had suffered.

Jerry calmed. He loved his wife despite all her faults, and he hated seeing her so sorry for herself and miserable. She ordered him around, and he made her some toast with the crusts cut off just as she liked it and gave her a cuddle.

'No more, Esther.' Things are going to change, and I'm going to look after you.'

'Yes, Jerry,' she said, snuggling into his chest and falling asleep. 'Change.'

That evening, as a television drama was finishing, they had a visitor. Jerry answered the door and ushered in the lady who helped his wife that morning.

'Mary, oh how lovely to see you. Come in.' Esther had risen to take both of Maria's hands in hers.

'I just came to return this. You left it in the taxi this morning. It must have dropped out of your bag.' She held the purse out to Esther. The lady of the house, quite back to her old self, ordered Jerry to organise tea while she fussed around making their guest comfortable.

Esther was dressed in a long white mohair jumper and black trousers. She had fluffy blue mules on her feet and looked the grand housewife, a far cry from the last time Maria had seen her.

'Actually, I was glad of the excuse to come and see how you are. I was worried about you.'

The women chatted while Jerry made his excuses and left them to it. Maria said she understood why they had decided not to go to the police. 'Terrible how the poor victim is treated like a common criminal,' she said. 'Best to put the horrendous ordeal behind you and get on with your life. It's over now,' she said, patting Esther's hand.

One hour turned into two, and Esther held Maria captivated with tales of her days working as a highly-respected dancer. Maria said that she only had the position of doctor's receptionist in one of the Penrith surgeries, so she was suitably impressed.

'You are funny, Esther. It must've been so glamorous. I wish I was like you.' The words stuck in her throat. She couldn't stand the sight of Esther, let alone her voice and all that bragging and swagger. Maria had worked out within two minutes of meeting her that the woman thrived on praise and adoration. Maria was shrewd and intuitive about the best way to ingratiate herself into Esther Erikson's life. Flattery was the way to go, even though being in the vile woman's company for more than five minutes at a time was going to drive her nuts.

'Esther,' she said shyly as she stood up to leave, 'I haven't been in the area long and haven't had the chance to make many friends. I don't suppose you'd like to go into town for a coffee and some shopping tomorrow, would you?'

And so the two women became friends.

Maria was with Esther when she took the pregnancy test. She was so strong and supportive. Esther wanted a termination, but Jerry was such an obstinate pig about the whole thing. He wouldn't hear of it. Maria had cooed and simpered, but she told Esther that any baby of hers would be the prettiest child in the World. Esther liked that idea. Jerry had a lot to say, too.

'That could be my child you're carrying.' The word could hung as though suspended from the ceiling by thin chains that might snap at any moment. As much as it could be his, there was a greater chance that it might not be.

Esther was still set on termination when Maria announced that she was pregnant, too. That swayed Esther. It might be fun being pregnant together. Just think of all those cute little outfits. A few weeks later, the women hugged and laughed when they discovered that they were both due on the same date.

Of course, they didn't deliver on the same day. Little Eleanor was born whole and healthy, but tragedy struck a week later when Maria rang in tears to inform her that her baby boy had died in childbirth.

Things cooled after that. Esther was annoyed with Maria for losing her child. She felt tricked. It spoiled her plans for walking the babies in the park together. If she'd known that Maria would lose her child, Esther would have gone ahead with the termination. It really was most inconvenient. Maria still came down often, always bringing a gift for Eleanor, but Esther threw them in the bin after she'd gone in case it was something that had been bought for Maria's dead baby. Esther couldn't abide the other woman's misery around her all the time.

But Maria healed well, and the women remained friends even after Jerry and Esther moved to Morecambe. Maria drove though once or twice a month to see them. Never the other way around, Esther was far too busy to make the journey.

Maria was such a good friend, and she thought the world of Esther.

# Chapter Twenty-six

Despite trying several times, Rob had no luck getting hold of Gail on the way home. He had an up-to-the-minute micro-technology communicon with a lifetime guarantee. For Ellie's sake, as much as Gail's, he wanted to bring his wife up to speed on what had happened before they got home.

Gail ran out of the house as soon as she saw Rob coming home with Ellie. She stopped in her tracks when she saw Ellie's car following with another Ellie in the driving seat. The dark twin must have followed them. Rob had led her right back to the house. Not knowing what to do, she impulsively ran behind Rob's car, hoping to hold the enemy off. Three car doors opened simultaneously. Rob rushed towards her, but she only saw the evil person that had caused so much damage.

'Get in the house with Ellie. Ring the police,' she screamed. She was about to launch herself on Eve when the woman she thought was the evil sister flew at her with arms open and tears streaming down her face.

'Oh, Gail, Matty's dead. What the hell am I going to do?'

Realising the mistaken identity, Gail disentangled from her friend. In her rage, she didn't hear what Ellie said. She flew at the real Eve. Ellie put out a hand to stop her.

'Don't hurt her, Gail. She saved my life.'

'Saved your life? She's been trying to do you in for weeks.' On the mention of murder, Gail processed what Ellie said when she got out of the car. She stopped her rant and turned, in slow motion, a look of absolute horror on her face.

'What did you say about Matt?'

The next few minutes were filled with tears, explanations, tantrums and questions. Reliving it was as enervating as the nightmare first-hand.

'Look,' Rob said, 'as far as we know, it's safe here, but we can't take any chances. Let's get in the house, and we'll explain everything—it might not be safe in the open. Gail, you help Ellie.'

'I will not have that other woman in my house. I'll kill her first.
'

Rob couldn't believe the bravery of his usually timid wife. After all these years of marriage, there were times when she still had the power to surprise him and make him incredibly proud of her.

'If we stand here any longer, we could all be killed. Stop arguing, Gail and just get inside, darling.'

After ensuring she had the right twin, Gail guided Ellie into the house and made her comfortable on the sofa. Ellie barely had the strength left to lift her legs, so Gail lifted them for her and got a quilt to cover her to stop the violent tremors. Rob locked Jake away from Eve and gave Ellie her medication bag. He might have been wiser locking his wife up and leaving Jake to reason with Eve because all hell had erupted when he went back into the lounge. Since the day he met her, he had never seen Gail lose her temper to the point of threatened violence.

'I said get out. Fuck off out of my house, before I knock your fucking head off your shoulders, you evil bitch.' Gail was screaming like a banshee, and when her husband entered the room, she turned on him, 'Get her out of my house, Rob. I will not have her here. Get rid of her.'

Rob had to physically restrain his wife to stop her lamping the cuckoo in the nest.

Eve tried to leave twice, and Gail tried to help her twice. The second time was after she told Eve to choke on the hot chocolate that Rob had made. The room was crackling on raw emotion.

'So what have the police said?' asked Gail, in one of her few calm moments. 'I hope they don't want to talk to us tonight.'

'We haven't had the chance to call them yet, love. There are things we need to discuss first,' Rob said.

'What the hell do you mean, you haven't called them? One of the sweetest blokes who ever walked the earth is dead in that house of horrors, and you haven't bothered to call the police? What are you thinking?'

'We were thinking about getting out of there before he killed the lot of us, that's what,' Eve said.

'Shut your big fat mouth, you, before I shut it for you. Matt's dead, killed by some madman, and you'—she spat the word across the room to Eve—'brought it all about. Sod talking, I'm calling the police. The lunatic might be on his way here to finish what he started.'

Gail stomped across the room and picked up the phone.

Ellie had said very little. She broke through her fugue to speak. Everybody else was talking and yelling, but she had sat quietly, thinking about Matt and letting Rob and Eve tell it all.

'No.' She didn't bellow or shout, but the single word was said with force. With the telephone in her hand, Gail stopped dialling after the first digit, and Eve, halfway to the door again, stopped mid-stride.

'We can't ring the police.'

'What? Ellie, darling, you aren't thinking straight. You're in shock. We need the police to help us—to help Matt.'

'And tell me, Gail, what exactly are they going to do to help Matt now?' Ellie's voice dripped with sarcasm. It froze the words before they were out of her mouth. Ellie was instantly sorry. She dropped her voice, the exhaustion and stress wringing out every word she said. 'We can't go to the police because I gave Eve my solemn promise.'

'Ellie, are you nuts? Can't you see that it's because of her that Matt's dead? She was as instrumental in his death as the man who did that terrible thing to him. You owe her nothing.'

'I owe her my life. And I owe her my trust because she gave me hers.'

'Please, listen to me.' Eve moved into the centre of the room and spoke in a calm voice. 'Please, Gail, hear me out, and then, if you still want to call the police, please just give me five minutes to get away before you do.'

'Why should we give you even a second? It's more than you deserve.' Rob put his arm around Gail's shoulders and shushed her.

'I know it's more than I deserve. I've done some terrible things, I know that. But all I ask is two minutes, and then I'll go,

353

and you can do what you like. Like Ellie said, we can't help Matt now.'

'The police could get his body and give him a decent burial.' Gail didn't want to be quiet. This was her home, and needling the woman who'd brought all this about was her right.

'Yes, and you can find a way to sort that out. But we can't stay here. None of you understands the way this man works. Hell, I don't understand him. He's evil. He fed me a life of hatred for twenty-seven years. As long as we sit here, he's going to find us. It's Ellie and me that he wants. But as long as we're here under your roof, you'd better believe me when I say all four of us are sitting here waiting to die. He knows things. He knows everything, sees everything.'

'She's deranged,' Gail said with a sneer.

'I know it sounds ridiculous, but he has ways of finding information. I don't know how, bugs maybe, cameras. He's probably got this place rigged and listens to every word we say. If we want to live through this, the only way is to get away and keep moving. If you let me, I'm going tonight, and if Ellie's got any sense, she'll go somewhere safe, too. But even then, it's a waste of time. He'll find us. You might think everything's hunky-dory here, and it could be, but I promise you, it won't be for long.

'So, let's get the police in. They can take you both to safe places.' Gail purposely didn't say a safe place because she couldn't bear the thought of Ellie being in the same room as that woman any longer than she had to be.

'I agree with Gail,' Rob said. 'We need to call the police in because this is too big for us. A man has been murdered. If we don't call them, we are all accessories after the fact. And calling the police is the only way we're going to get Matt out of there.'

354

'Please, please don't call them.' Eve was crying, and Gail snorted. 'I've been locked up—with nothing I could call living—for my entire life. If you call the police, there'll be tests and evaluations. I'll be institutionalised, and I can't bear to be locked up again. What about Ellie? Think about her. Can you imagine what the media will do to her if this story ever gets out? I was fed her life day and night since I was an infant. Do you want the media prying into her life for the rest of it?' The rest of Ellie's life might be very short, if you go to the police, he'll take her and he'll lock her up and you'll never see her again. I warn you not to underestimate him.'

'How can you be so cold about her. She's your sister. Have some respect.' Gail said.

'I'm sorry. I didn't mean to imply anything, but you have to know how dangerous this is.' Ellie smiled a wan smile and waved Eve's guff away.

'She's right. I might not have long, and the last thing I want is to live in the media spotlight for the rest of my days.'

'There's something else you haven't thought of. I'm sorry, Ellie, but this man doesn't leave traces. I'd love to believe that Matt's body could be brought out of there. I'm hoping it can, mainly because I'm more than partly responsible for what happened to him. Still, I'm confident that by now, he'll have wiped every scrap of evidence out of that place, including Matt's body. If there's no body, there's no evidence or proof, and only the testimony of a sick woman and her closest friends.

Where do you think the finger of suspicion will fall? They already think Ellie tried to murder Matt once. It's on record. If you call the police, I'm going to do everything I can to get away before they come.'

'I'll go back to the institute tonight and get Matt out,' Rob said, with a voice full of bravery, which was precisely one voice full of bravery more than he felt. 'He said he wasn't coming back until tomorrow, didn't he?'

'He was lying,' Eve said, in a dull voice, 'Trust me, he'd be back. The early hours of the morning are his favourite time. They are the hours when he inflicts his most terrifying tortures. Talking, talking, talking, for hours on end sometimes. He'll be there now, and he'll be furious that we aren't.'

Ellie remembered the horrible voice on the intercom and shuddered. She nodded her head in emphatic agreement.

Nobody said anything for a long time. They all had a lot to think about.

'I say we tie her up and take our chances with the police. This is murder. We're not talking about a shoplifted packet of sweets. We can't do anything but call the police.' Gail said.

'No police.' The voice, though barely audible, was emphatic. 'She's right. We've got to get away first thing in the morning. I don't know where or for how long. I heard this monster. You and Gail didn't. Rob, I swear, he's going to stop at nothing until he has us where he wants us.'

'Ellie, you're asking us to implicate ourselves up to our necks in this mess. I'll do anything to help you. You know that, but I'm not going to get a criminal record. Rob and I could end up in prison over this.'

'There's one thing we've all overlooked,' Rob said. 'If we don't report Matt missing—someone else will. What about when he doesn't turn up for work or get in touch with his friends and family? If Ellie doesn't report it in the next day or two, they'll suspect her for sure.'

They let it sink in and tried to find a way out of the quagmire that got deeper with every new revelation.

'I'll just report him missing, then,' Ellie said. 'I'll ring the police now and say that he hasn't come home and that I'm worried about him.'

'You can't, Ellie. The police already suspect you of trying to kill him. They'll question you for hours on end. Not tonight, but eventually, when he doesn't turn up. They'll know you're lying. You couldn't tell a convincing lie if you tried, darling,' Rob said.' They'll be all over you.'

'Apart from that, there's no point ringing tonight. He's only been missing for fourteen hours,' Eve said. 'It buys us thinking time. It would be suspicious if she rang now. And she can't hang around here waiting for a suitable length of time to pass before reporting it because if we're going, we've got to go at first light.' Eve said we, and it wasn't lost on anybody in the room.

'I could stall them.' Rob was thinking aloud. 'If you take off in the morning, you'll have a few clear days before the police come sniffing around, possibly as much as a week or two. We'll think of somewhere for you to stay. When they come, I'll say you took off for a few days for a romantic break to come to terms with your illness and away from the media glare. And Eve's right, the further away you are from here, the better. I don't know what the hell we're going to do, Ellie, but at least that gives us breathing space to think things through more clearly. And, I suppose it'll be safer if you stick together. '

'Oh, no. No way, mate. I'm going on my own. I'm sorry, Ellie, but I'm fighting for my life just as much as you are, and I don't want to be hampered by a sick woman. It's hard enough having a famous bloody face without travelling as the other half of a set of identical twins. We'd stick out like King George's ears.'

'Trust me, I hate the idea of you out God knows where with Ellie. No offence, but I can't forget what you've done. I'm putting my faith in somebody who stalked her with a fucking knife. But we're not rich on options here. I have an idea. What if you travel as one person? We'll make reservations for one in a false name. Whether you like it or not, you two are in the same boat and need each other. Ellie's sick, so you can help her cope, and she can open doors with her credit and get things that an ordinary person can't. Think about it. It makes sense.'

Gail had calmed down, and all the spitting and clawing had left her. 'But when they don't come back, Ellie's going to be under suspicion for sure. They'll arrest her for Matt's murder. She'll never stand that.'

'But I could.' They turned to look at Eve. 'It makes sense. Ellie would never cope with the questions; she'd buckle in the first five minutes. But if we get our story straight, I can talk to the police and go through the interview process.' Eve had no intention of doing it. She didn't need this stinking mess and only wanted to get the hell away from there. She intended to run at the first opportunity. But at that point, she'd have said anything to stop them from calling the police.

They argued and debated the ramifications. In the end, they decided that making a run for it now and working the rest out later was the best option they had. The girls would leave together at first light.

# Chapter Twenty-seven

B y six in the morning, after a failed attempt by Eve to sneak out, the car was packed, and only one of the travellers cuddled the dog. They'd had just two and a half hours restless sleep, but the girls were ready to go. Their destination had literally been a pin-in-the-map job. If they had no advance notice of where they were going, then neither would anybody else.

They walked to the end of the street to make the arrangements in case Rob's house was bugged. The pin had stuck in Chester. Ellie had visited once on a book tour, and it seemed as good a place as any to hole up for a few days and get some rest. Every second they were outside in the cold, they felt like sitting ducks waiting to be shot.

Rob had asked C2, his humanicon, to bring up a list of hotels in the area they'd selected. Rather than using voice activation, he'd typed in the fields he needed. He took down the details and rang around for a reservation. After some discussion, it was decided that a mix of truth and fiction would be the best way ahead. They'd use Ellie's real identity, and that way, they could pull the hotel into helping them protect her.

Ellie fell under the classification of a C-list celebrity. Luckily for them, it meant that she wasn't quite dead famous, but she'd been on the panel of several afternoon game shows. More often than not, she could walk down the street without being mobbed, but just as often, she didn't go completely unnoticed. When Rob spoke to a Miss Wood on the phone, he asked to be put through to the hotel manager as a matter of urgency. When he came on the line, Rob explained that Miss Eleanor Erikson, the author, wanted to stay at their hotel. However, it was imperative that her identity must not be disclosed to any third person, be that his staff, his family, or, God forbid, the press. He said that Miss Erikson had recently had some tragic news about her health and was being mobbed by hoards of intrusive paparazzi. Rob said it wouldn't be good for the hotel if information about where she was staying leaked. His voice was deep with caution and warning. The manager didn't know just how true that statement was.

'I can assure you, Mr—' he forgot Rob's name. 'I can assure you, sir, that Miss Erikson's privacy will be respected and followed per instruction to the letter. Here at The Castle Mount, we pride ourselves on running a discrete hotel. And I will personally undertake to make sure that Miss Erikson is made as comfortable as possible.'

He went on to elaborate that in his ten years at The Castle Mount, they'd never had anybody famous, not even anybody a little bit famous, so this was a feather in his cap.

'Good man,' Rob said. 'No fuss, though. Remember, Miss Erikson is sensitive about her illness and needs undisturbed rest.'

Ellie was accustomed to staying at the most extravagant hotels in recent years. Only places with a five-star rating and a world-renowned chef of volatile temperament were booked for her. The trouble with celebrity—even C-list fame—is that you have a particular façade to live up to. Ellie kept her homelife modest because she had to live the glitz until it oppressed her when she was away with work. She didn't have a room in hotels. She had a suite, usually at the top of the bloody building with panoramic views. The suites were a pain in the arse to get to, and she hated it.

She christened the hotel The Old Ruins and didn't need to worry about the insincerity of opulence. There was none. The place had seen better days. But although it was picked at random and not for its situation, it was secluded in its own grounds and seemed little inhabited. This was no Estrelle Residence in Berlin or Caesar's Palace in Vegas, but it would be home while they took stock.

Eve knew what she was thinking. She had a disconcerting knack of knowing what was happening in Ellie's mind. 'It's not quite what you're used to, eh, sis?' Her voice was laden with bitterness

362

and sarcasm. The hostility, recently lacking, was back again, with knobs on. 'Never mind, I'm sure you can slum it like a mortal for a few days.'

Ellie shot her a withering look.

They gave each other the once over for any flaws in their appearance, and then, while Ellie lay low in her seat with a magazine pressed up to her face, Eve took their single suitcase and walked into the hotel.

She had to go in first because, not knowing how long they'd be on the road, they had to pack as much into one case as they could. The other aim was not to draw attention. If she was recognised, a celebrity with a truck-load of baggage would be the most natural thing in the world, but they were travelling as Mrs Janet Brown, Mrs Epitome of Ordinary.

The short lady with mousy brown hair and large spectacles signed the guest register and was given directions to her room. She took the stairs and hardly struggled with the heavy suitcase.

Forty minutes later, Janet Brown walked into the hotel and past reception. Elaine Wood looked up from her computer.

'Hello. I never saw you go out,' she said it in an accusatory tone. It was her job to be aware of all the comings and goings in this hotel. And she didn't like people going about their business without her knowing about it.

'I just went to the car for my glasses case,' Janet said, holding the case aloft as though it was an exhibit for the defence. Wood smiled as the guest went up the stairs, first floor, fifth on the right, no lift—thank God for a decent cell phone signal. She liked putting guests into types. This one was married, frump. Nobody wore glasses these days. Laser treatment took five minutes and lasted years. I bet she loves cooking from scratch as well, she thought.

Ellie made it up the first flight of stairs and out of sight before the ache in her legs crippled her. She launched herself on the bed as soon as she got in the room, and within seconds she had an array of medication spread around her. She was pale. The last few weeks had taken their toll on her.

Eve felt a massive pang of guilt.

'Can I get you anything?' Eve asked. 'A cup of coffee?' Ellie nodded and smiled. Eve still got a buzz out of boiling a kettle and making coffee. She was like a child with a tea-set and measured a spoonful of instant coffee into each cup with care, while other people would spoon it in with practised lack of thought. This was the first time Eve had ever made coffee for anybody else, and she wanted to get it right.

'Not poisoned, is it?' Ellie asked as Eve put the steaming mug on her bedside table. Eve looked hurt, and Ellie was sorry. It seemed her dark sibling had yet to develop a sense of humour.

'How do you feel?' Eve had genuine concern in her voice.

'Safer.'

This was the first time Eve had ever stayed in a hotel. When she entered the room, she'd sat politely on an old armchair, waiting for Ellie to come in. Now she was like a big kid. She bounced on the bed, making Ellie's head rock. She opened and closed cupboards, turned the TV on and off, and crammed one of the complimentary chocolate mints into her mouth.

'Can we call room service?' she asked excitedly, around a mouthful of chocolate.

'No. Low profile, remember?'

'Aw, that'd be fun. Wonder what the bathroom's like?'

Ellie was still smiling at Eve's enthusiasm when Eve backed out of the bathroom as though a venomous snake coiled towards her, poised and ready to strike.

She had a card in her hand, and the look of horror on her face made Ellie's stomach contract in a tight knot.

'We have to leave,' Eve said in a monotone.

The cloying sweetness of fresh flowers permeated the bedroom with opening the bathroom door. Ellie pushed past her and stopped in the doorway. The bath, the shelves, even the toilet seat and every spare inch of floor space was strewn with bouquets of exotic flowers. There were lilies and orchids, lotus blossoms, and artificially dyed blooms of such magnitude and beauty that any woman would be enraptured to receive such a token of love. Ellie gagged on the perfume and thought she was going to be sick. She wheeled from the bathroom and slammed the door behind her.

Eve handed her the florist's card. Apart from the shop logo, it was similar to the one Eve sent weeks earlier. The words printed in a neat hand read,

To my darling Janet. Better the devil, you know. Love always, Matthew xxx

'Oh my God, is this you?'

'No, of course not. Ellie, no.'

The bastard. How dare he sicken Matt's memory? How dare he?' Ellie was furious. 'We have to think, Eve. How did he find us? Have you called anyone?'

'No. I haven't. Stop accusing me. This is nothing to do with me.'

'No. Not like you have a track record or anything. In that case, it has to be the hotel manager. He must have shouted my arrival from the bloody rooftops. I'm going down to have it out with him, and I'll ring the florists to find out how the flowers were ordered. My guess is by telephone.'

Eve was throwing Ellie's medications back into the medication bag in a blind panic. 'No, Ellie, he's on his way to get us. I know he is. Come on, we have to move. We've got to get out of here, now.'

'But—' Eve cut her off.

'No time, Ellie. Come on, move. I was right last time, wasn't I? Now please, this time will you just trust me? I know him better than you. I know how he works and the way he likes to play. Come on, move it.'

They ran down the stairs five seconds later and didn't care about being seen.

When Janet Brown came into sight, Elaine Wood smiled for a split second. 'Oh, are you coming to ask about the beautiful flowers?' The smile died on her face, and was replaced by shock and confusion, when not one but two Janet Browns ran straight through reception and out of the front door. The last one had their luggage in her hand. 'Hey, you—both of you—you can't leave. You haven't paid.'

'Hey,' she shouted, battling with the lock on the half door to get out from behind the desk. But the two Janet Browns were climbing into their car. They flew down the drive, oblivious of the 20mph speed limit. The hapless receptionist didn't even have time to get their registration number.

'Where to?' Ellie asked at the end of the drive.

'Just drive,' Eve said. 'Left here.'

'Then where?'

'Hell, I don't know, do I? There's a motorway sign there. It's four miles ahead. Hit the motorway, and then we'll have time to think.'

'North or south?'

'Shit, Ellie, whatever you think best.'

'South, then. London maybe, lots of people and somewhere to hide. And places where you don't need bookings. We can walk in off the street.'

'Good plan.'

Neither of them spoke for the next four miles. It seemed to allow their thoughts to pass from their cluttered minds into the car. The congested A-roads gave way to the open plan of the motorway.

'On the other hand,' Eve said, as though there was no lapse in conversation, 'Scotland might be a good idea. You know, one of those remote islands in the Hebrides or something.'

'Eh?'

'Well, we could rent a cottage by the sea. He'd never find us there.'

'Eve, honey, you must have fallen asleep in your cell before those movies finished—the ones showing idyllic bliss on a remote island. They always, but always, turn bad. The bliss part comes just before the mother of all storms. It cuts off the electricity and stops the ferry from getting through. But the bad storm comes just as the wielding axe murderer lands on the island. I'll leave you to work the rest out for yourself.'

'Oh, yeah. I told you London was a good plan.'

Neither of them wanted to bring up the subject of their common enemy, but he might as well have been sitting between them in the car, as though he was leaning forward from the back and pushing his face between the seats.

'How did he find us so quickly?' asked Eve, in a small voice. 'Even if the hotel manager told all his staff, who then told every single person in a ten-mile radius, it still had to get back to him. How could that be?'

368

'Loyalty is one of the buzz words of the hotel,' the manager told police. They questioned him about the disappearance of Miss Erikson and her partner Mr Matthew High, days later. Though he never met her, Eleanor Erikson briefly stayed as an honoured guest in his hotel. He felt somehow responsible for her disappearance. The greasy little man rambled on in a self-important way. He said he felt an affinity with her and thought it his duty to protect her from the scheming sewer rats that called themselves the press. He shut Woodsy up about the other Miss Erikson. Fancy her travelling with a body double. It was just like the movies.

They drove for miles, fuming about the betrayal of the hotel manager. Or at least Ellie did. Eve had her own thoughts that were a damned sight closer to the gearstick than hotel management.

'Ellie?' She had to pick her words carefully. She knew she was on dangerous ground and needed to display a tact that she'd never had the opportunity to learn. 'Ellie, how well do you know Rob and Gail?'

'Very well, why?' Ellie negotiated traffic cones at another set of road works. It took a couple of seconds for the accusation behind Eve's question to sink in, but when it did, she almost slammed on her brakes in the outside lane of the motorway. It was only the car behind, flashing his lights, that made her catch up with the flow of traffic. She didn't say anything until she had come through the last cone and onto the three-lane open road.

'No way. Forget it, Eve. Rob and Gail are my closest friends. No, I won't even contemplate the thought that they'd betray me. What motive would they have?'

'I don't know, Ellie, but The Creator knew where we were. Somebody must have told him. I don't see how it could be the manager. And that Gail was adamant about calling the police.'

'The police are a far cry from ringing a crazed murderer for a cup of tea and a slice of cake. They are my best friends. They would never betray me. If it wasn't the manager, the only other explanation is that he must have tailed us to Rob's. He could have ordered the flowers to be sent ahead from his car. I'm sure we aren't being followed now. I've been watching the traffic behind us and the cars overtaking. Nothing is with us for at least ten cars back that was behind when we set off.'

If they had company, there'd be an opportunity to do some quick turning and lose them when they hit London. 'I know how he operates. He's not scared of authority—or who else he hurts. What if he rams us off the road before we get there?'

'I'm going to have to stop and rest up, Eve. I can't drive much further.' They were still two hours from the centre of London when Ellie took ill.

'No, we've got to keep moving. A moving target is harder to hit. I don't feel safe out here, Ellie. As soon as we get to a hotel, we can rest, I promise. Come on, let's sing, put the radio on.'

Ellie pulled a face and turned on the radio. They sang along for a few minutes, but Ellie felt her eyes growing heavy. She shook violently, and sweat poured from her forehead, stinging her eyes. The music was too loud, and the bass rammed into her head like a jackhammer. She leaned over and switched it off. 'I've got to pull over.'

'Keep moving.' Eve shouted in the stillness of the car. There was no mistaking the tone of threat in her voice. 'I'm trying to save our lives. Please, Ellie, keep moving.'

'Save our lives? You're going to kill not only us but anyone who's fool enough to be near us when I crash this thing.' Ellie was already pulling over towards the hard shoulder. She was retching before the car stopped and just managed to open the door and lurch the top half of her body out of the car in time. She vomited several times while Eve covered her face in disgust. When Ellie was done and fell against the support of the seat, her lips had a deep blue tinge, her breathing was harsh and ragged, and her face was as pale as a hospital sheet. She hadn't had a proper night's sleep since the day her life had changed. The build-up to the climax of the last few days was too much for her. It would have been enough for anybody who wasn't suffering a terminal illness. She had used the last reserves of her strength.

'Okay, you've made your point—gross. As soon as you can, we'll make our way to the services. I saw the sign a while ago, and it's only a few miles ahead. You can have one hour there, okay? I'll keep watch, and then we have to move again, but you need to get your shit together. Can you make it that far?'

Ellie nodded. 'Deal,' she murmured. 'Girl, you're all heart.'

They made London by late afternoon. It had been one hell of a day, and Ellie was exhausted. At Eve's insistence, they drove around London for an hour to make damned sure they were alone. She refused to let Ellie call Rob and said to humour her for a few days.

They found a small run-down hotel on Gower Street with parking to the rear. It was ideal because it was centrally situated and in a mixed-race area where people minded their own business and didn't make eye contact. The Longland Hotel had vacancies without needing a reservation. Although the process of getting in as one person was more difficult, they were soon in the room. Eve went into the bathroom to see that it was as it should be. If it wasn't for the different coloured bed-spreads, it could be a replay of their earlier experience. As before, Ellie sank onto the bed and reached for her medications.

Ellie was too tired to have coffee this time, and as the first sounds of the steaming kettle filled the room, she drifted into blessed sleep.

# Chapter
# Twenty-eight

E ve was stirring her coffee, and Ellie uttering her first soft
snore when the telephone rang. Ellie's eyes opened wide
on the first ring. She was instantly alert, and a look of trepidation
passed between them. Eve picked up the phone on the second
ring; they'd been in their room for less than ten minutes.

'Hello?'

'Ello ees this Mrs Chalker?' It was the Spanish lady operating
the reception desk when Eve had signed in. They dared to
breathe a sigh of relief.

'Yes,' Eve replied cautiously, answering to the new name they
used this time.

'I 'ave the message for you. The man said ee is Mr Matthew,
and ee says ee busy an as not the time to be put through right
now. But ee be with you very, very soon. Important I say very,
very soon, fank you.'

Eve stared at the phone in horror.

She ran around the room, packing Ellie's drugs and picking up her purse for the second time in five hours. This time she stuffed Ellie's things into her own rucksack, and she slung it on her back.

'Come on, pass me your suitcase. We've got to go. He's found us.'

In a state of panic, Eve relayed the wording of the phone conversation. 'I know what he's doing. He's keeping us moving. His plan is to not let us rest or sleep. He's experimenting and wants to see what happens when you can't carry on any longer. He's pushing us to the limit and knows you can't keep it up and will crack. It's psychological warfare. But I'm telling you, Ellie, you have to carry on, or you die.'

'No way,' Ellie was sitting on the edge of the bed. 'I can't run again, and I'm not going to. It's a pity I didn't bring my best designer cocktail dresses. We could have dressed up and gone out in style. Because I'm telling you, Eve, if he wants me tonight, he's going to have to come right in this room and get me because I'm not running like a frightened rabbit again. Where the hell's it going to end? And how has he found us so quickly?'

Eve turned on Ellie. The same thought had occurred to her. 'You stupid, stupid bitch,' she spat at her, fury contorting her face into a mask of rage. 'You rang him, didn't you? You rang Rob when I signed us in. I told you it was him. He's the only link from us to The Creator. Do you believe me now? I can't believe you did that, Ellie. You promised me you wouldn't.'

'I didn't, Eve. I swear I didn't. And I'm telling you now, Rob would no more betray me than betray his own mother. You are so wrong this time.'

'Don't lie to me. Ellie. You must have rung him. It's the only explanation. He, Gail, or both of them, are in on this, and you're too bloody prissy and trusting to see it. Hell, for all we know, Rob might actually be The Creator—after all, The Creator had left the building when Rob came to rescue us.'

'Now you've lost the plot. Don't be so bloody ridiculous. I've only known Rob for eight years, and yet you say The Creator has been holding you for as long as you can remember, so how do you explain that?'

'I don't know, Ellie. I really don't know, but somehow he knows where we are all the time, and the only common denominator between him and us is Rob. So you tell me how he fits into the equation. Okay, maybe he isn't The Creator, but he sodding well knows who is.'

'Rubbish. If it hadn't been for Rob, we'd still be in that awful institute. He risked his life to save you, you ungrateful cow.'

'Did he? Apart from climbing up on the roof, what risk did he take?'

'God, Eve, The Creator could have come back at any time and caught Rob, then he'd have either been killed or ended up in there with us.'

'In your tidy little mind, where everything has a neat little compartment, that's just the way it is, isn't it? You take what you're told as the truth. Will you look at the facts? If you stop thinking about Rob as your friend for just one second and look at the hard facts, you can only come to one conclusion, and that's the same one that I've landed on.'

'No, there must be another explanation. We just have to think it through.'

Ellie managed to stop Eve from leaving and got her to listen, Ellie maintained that she wasn't going anywhere and refused to move. They drank coffee while the hunter came to take them. They went round in circles, both tired and irritable, and neither one getting anywhere with the other. For an hour, they tossed things around, and Ellie tried to persuade Eve that she hadn't contacted Rob.

'Ellie, you can sit here, be a target and think through whatever the hell you like, but as of right now, I'm outta here.' Eve turned to go, and Ellie stood to stop her. Eve was just in time to catch Ellie as she fell to the ground. She'd fainted and didn't answer when Eve called her. Eve had seen first-aid films. They were fed to her in the cell as part of her education, but watching a video and working on an unconscious woman were poles apart. Eve struggled to get Ellie into the recovery position and see that her airway was free and open. She loosened the top two buttons of her shirt. Ellie came to gradually and sat up, confused. Eve was waiting on the bed, staring at her.

'I was going to leave while you were out, but it seemed cowardly,' she said. 'And anyway, you were breathing funny, so I thought I'd better wait to see that you pulled through. If you hadn't, you wouldn't need your purse and extra clothes, so, just to let you know, I would have taken them.'

'Oh, thanks, Eve, you'd make a wonderful nurse. So compassionate.' Ellie poked herself to see if she'd broken anything in her fall.

'You're okay. I caught you. Gave me a nasty crack on the elbow, though, if you want to check my bones out.'

Ellie grinned and held out a hand for Eve to help her up.

'You're right, you know, Ellie. You're sick, and you can't keep running. Why can't you see what's in front of you? It was a dumb idea, and that was down to that Rob bloke as well.'

'Oh, for Christ's sake, don't start all that again.'

'Okay, I won't. I'm done, anyway. You should stay here and call in the police now or something. I'm going to go for it and get out of here. I stand more chance of getting away on my own, and you'll be better off taking your chances with the law. Hell, if they lock you up in a loony bin for Rob's murder, at least you'll be safe from The Creator. But I can't keep carrying you. You've got a terminal illness, and you're going to die anyway. I'm not a nurse, and I'm fighting for my life, too.'

Ellie looked at Eve, shocked at her bluntness.

'I'm sorry, but you are. I've only just been born, in a way. So I can't let you hold me back. I'm going to be long gone. Having to look after you, we stand no chance, but we might make ourselves safe on our own—well, I might.'

'How can you be so selfish?'

'How can you? Sorry, Ellie, but this is where we part company. Maybe one day, another time, another place, and all that.'

'Are you finished? I think that's a damned selfish attitude, but if you want to go, you'll go. There's nothing I can do to stop you. I'm sure as hell not going to lower myself to begging. But if you go alone, now, you're going to run until he tracks you down and kills you like vermin. If we stick together, we might run, but only until we find out how he's getting to us and get some answers. I know I'm holding you back, I can't help that, but I can help us think. Together, we have to be stronger and harder to take out than alone as two single units. I know there's no love lost between us. We're together through circumstance, not choice, but you have saved my life more than once, and I'd like to think that I was instrumental in saving yours. We've supported each other through this so far. Let's not lose our heads and make rash decisions now.'

'Nice speech, sis, but not worth getting myself killed for. Sorry, doll, you're on your own. Every second I stay here is a second that he's gained on me. I hope you get away from this. I hope we both do. But I've made up my mind. Sorry.'

This time, Eve made it through the door and didn't bother looking back. Ellie heard her footsteps pounding down the hall. In a fit of sheer panic, she knew she couldn't be alone and scared. She followed Eve. Some of her strength returned with the rush of fear. She ran down the hall and took the stairs two at a time, catching up with Eve at the front door.

'Leave me alone, Ellie. You can't stop me. Go back to the room and call the police.'

Ellie looked around the foyer to see if anyone heard what Eve said, but they were alone.

Eve pushed the heavy door open. They'd only walked down the first two steps when the silence of the night was filled with the scream of a persistent car alarm.

Ellie looked at Eve. They instinctively knew that it had to be Ellie's car, though, in the middle of London, it could have been any vehicle in the area. Without a word, they ran to the car park. This was it. He was here.

The passenger side door of Ellie's car was wide open, but the car park was deserted.

Ellie screamed and fell to her knees on the gravel as she picked up the rag left on the seat. She was the first to recognise it for what it was—the blood-sodden T-shirt Matt was wearing when he was murdered.

# Chapter Twenty-nine

E llie wanted to hold the shirt up to her face and inhale the sweet scent of Matty, but even that primal instinct was denied her. The blood had soaked through, fusing back and front together and souring before it dried. Over the last twenty-four hours, the shirt had starched as the blood dried to become stiff and brittle. A hundred thousand of these T-shirts must have been printed, but Ellie knew this one was Matty's shirt—with Matty's blood. She felt him on it. Not the smell of him, because that was foisty and metallic with the sheer amount of blood, but the essence of him.

She was on the point of losing it. She felt the burning tears filling her up and rising to explode from her, pushed from behind by a force of anger more fierce than any emotion she had ever felt. She locked into her grief and didn't care about anything else. Without Matty, what was the point of running?

Eve saw Ellie knocked backwards by the discovery of the shirt. She watched her disappear in front of her eyes. Ellie was still there, a look of sheer horror on her face, but her spirit was in a warped wonderland of the macabre. Eve could have run and been away in seconds. Ellie wouldn't even have noticed, but she couldn't leave her to the mercy of The Creator. She was kneeling in the open, maybe feet from where he crouched in a bush, and she had no intention of fighting for her life.

Eve grabbed the shirt from Ellie's hands and threw it into the shrubbery, where it wouldn't be discovered. She thought the distraught woman was going to follow it, scrambling and snuffling in the undergrowth like a retriever until she came back out with the shirt.

'We've no time for this, Ellie. Later, honey, later. Come on, we've got to move.' On hearing Eve's voice, Ellie snapped out of her trance. She pushed down on the urge to weep forever. That would keep, but the anger burning inside her was a thing of substance longing for an outlet. She shot Eve a look, grateful for pulling her back from the brink and for not leaving her when she had the chance.

They were in this together again. Eve helped Ellie up.

'I'm okay,' she said, in a gritty snarl. The alarm was blaring. It was amazing that nobody had come to see what the noise was. Still, there was nothing at all unusual about a car alarm blasting in central London at seven o'clock in the evening. Back in the real world, Ellie went to immobilise the car and get the hell out of there.

'No.' Eve screamed at the top of her voice, 'Don't touch the car. You don't know what he's done to it. I think it's bugged, and that's how he found us. But he could have planted anything.

Run, he's watching us and could grab us any second. Come on, we'll have to go on foot.'

Eve pulled Ellie by the hand and dragged her out of the car park. 'What are we going to do?' Ellie grunted as her feet pounded the rough concrete. Adrenaline, fear and outright panic had given her a new boost of fuel, but she knew she'd pay for it later.

'I don't know. Let's just wing it for now. If we're still alive and free in ten minutes or so, we might be able to come up with some sort of plan. But for now, you just keep doing what you're doing because you're doing okay.'

The side street they were on opened into Tottenham Court Road. A large gaudily-painted tour bus taking visitors round the London sights was lumbering towards them.

'The bus,' yelled Ellie. 'Get on the bus.'

'It won't stop for us. There's no designated stopping place.'

'Yes, it bloody well will,' Ellie ran into the middle of the road and waved her arms.

'Ellie,' Eve screamed.

'Hey,' Ellie grinned, never taking her eye off the bus, 'I'm dying, remember? I've got nothing to lose.'

The bus screeched to a shuddering halt. Far from the scenario of the movies, where the heroine's breath gets crushed by the mega-tonne vehicle and her nose leaves snot on the windscreen, this bus stopped with plenty of room. But the driver didn't look pleased. He opened his door and fired a torrent of angry words at the wild-looking woman.

The second the door opened, Ellie pulled Eve onto the bus, giving the driver no opportunity to refuse them access. After making his displeasure noted, he agreed to let them ride, but not before he told them how low in his esteem crazy tourists rated. Ellie turned on her sweetest smile and blatantly gave the driver the eye. It cost them eighty-five Euros each as Ellie had to pay for the entire excursion even though there was less than an hour to run.

They grabbed an empty double seat towards the front and flopped into it. Ellie had the window seat and scanned as much of the street as possible to see if they were followed. It didn't look as though they were; certainly, nobody had got on the bus behind them. Eve was staring at her, open-mouthed.

'What?'

'You flirted with him! I can't believe you just flirted with him to get us on the bus. Miss Erikson, pure as the driven snow, just used her body to get her own way.'

Ellie grinned. 'Well, it worked, didn't it?'

'Hussy.'

They discussed in low voices what they should do next. They'd ditch the bus somewhere with lots of people. It was a green line get-on-get-off tour bus, where you could lose one bus and grab another at any of the city attractions. They didn't know if they were being followed and had to lose anybody on their tail before they stopped for the night. This time they'd find somewhere safe. After twenty minutes of discussion and argument, it was decided that they'd spend the first hour melting into the city, then they'd find somewhere to hire a car. No phone calls, no advance bookings, no chance of anybody getting a lead on them, just two more aliens in a city that didn't care.

They looked at the route map posted on the bus and tried to come to some sort of agreement when Ellie made a decision. 'Next stop.'

'Leicester Square. That's near Soho, isn't it? We can lose ourselves there.'

'No, I've got a better idea.'

The bus slowed, and Eve left her seat, but Ellie pulled her back. 'Wait, we'll jump off at the last minute in case he's watching for us to leave. It'll give him less time to prepare.'

The driver was shutting the doors when Eve jumped up from her seat and cried, 'Wait, please. We're getting off here.' They got off the bus, leaving the irritated driver shaking his head and scowling at them.

They ran along the street to the walkway leading to Leicester Square proper without looking behind them. Along the bottom side of the gardens, opposite the Odeon cinema, a line of street entertainers had attracted a large crowd. The girls pushed into the centre of a mob, watching an athletic fire-eater. People looked at the bad-mannered identical twins, and they smiled their apologies. They heard one lady comment to her partner that she reckoned the twins were part of the act. 'Fire eating would be a doddle compared to this lark,' Ellie whispered.

They watched for newcomers joining the crowd, anybody walking around with an air of looking for someone, or anybody who looked suspicious. They seemed to be in the clear but were taking no chances. After ten minutes, Ellie told Eve to keep close and follow her.

They only moved a hundred yards into the Odeon. It was as good a place as any to watch for company. They bought tickets but went straight into the ladies'. Anybody following them would go into the cinema, assuming they went in there. Or, if unsure which film they were seeing, they'd hang around the foyer.

Ellie needed to sit. The restroom was pleasant and had seating. It beat, resting her bum on a cold toilet seat, but at that point, she would have been grateful to rest anywhere. Eve peeped out of the door three times before the foyer was empty, apart from the lady operating the ticket sales and the people in the retail franchises. She went up to the lady and spoke to her quietly.

'Excuse me, please, my sister has an illness and passed out in the ladies. She needs to get home, and there are so many people out the front. She's fine now, but I was wondering if there's a back door we could leave by?'

The lady was very helpful and showed the girls through the staff door. She remarked several times about how pale Ellie looked, and they had a job stopping her from calling an ambulance. Their escape was perfect. There wasn't a soul in sight until they rounded the corner into another bustling street. They could have gone back to Leicester square and caught a bus from there, but it was too risky, covering old ground.

Ellie was exhausted.

It wasn't a long walk to Trafalgar, but it seemed to take forever. She chanted a mantra on a loop to help her keep pace with Eve until she drove her mad. 'A moving target is a hard target to hit. I am a desert lizard, moving to stay alive. Move to live, move to live. I am a moving target.'

Eve said she felt vulnerable walking at half speed with Ellie but never once said an unkind word or cut in on her concentration. Twice, when she stumbled, Eve put a hand under Ellie's arm and gave it a squeeze. When Ellie had to stop at the bottom of the Tube escalator, Eve said, 'You did great. Well done. You've got guts.'

'Maybe I'm not as ready to die as I thought.' Her eyes were dull, her face horribly pale, and the pain was written in a delicate scroll of lines across her forehead. They made four Tube changes. Twice just changing lines and twice leaving the station and walking to the next. Ellie had her destination in mind but didn't dare speak it, even to Eve, in case their abuser was the person behind them in the carriage.

They arrived at Euston station. In the terminal upstairs, they went to the car hire kiosk and rented a small run-around hatchback that was discrete and inconspicuous. They were on edge until they were free of the city and cruising along the M1 at a steady eighty miles an hour. The traffic was light, and after less than an hour's driving, Eve suggested they come off the motorway and head for the Pagoda roundabout. This was for no other reason than she liked the name.

They left the M1 behind and were driving along the darkly atmospheric A-roads. They'd stop at the first hotel or B&B they came to. There wasn't another car in sight when they found the perfect place. The roadside sign said that the Palisades Motel was just five hundred yards on the left.

Pulling into the car park, they were delighted to see their journey's end. The motel had rows of chalet-style accommodation, perfectly anonymous, all with en-suite, kettles and telephone. Perfect. The main office was brightly lit with neon signage and harsh fluorescent lighting. Eve signed them in under a new name, Amanda Stephens, and she was out of the office with a key in hand in less than three minutes.

Several of the chalets had lights glowing behind drawn curtains, but other than that, and the bored youth behind reception, the place appeared to be deserted. They had a clear view for hundreds of yards of the only road in and out, and there wasn't a vehicle in sight.

Dispensing with the cloak and dagger stuff, they walked together the short distance from the car to their chalet. Theirs was number forty-three, and they counted off the numbers as they walked along the well-tended path.

Eve put the key in the door. Before it had even finished opening, the phone rang. They tried to convince themselves that it was just the lad at reception ringing to tell Eve that she'd left her purse, or to wish her a good night and sweet dreams, or to ask for a date, but they knew who it was.

They knew the routine.

Ellie picked up the phone but didn't speak. She could hear him breathing, waiting for her to say something first, revelling in their terror and exhaustion. She counted off the seconds in her head. She only got to seven, but it seemed like so many more. An eternity ticked away in a mere seven seconds. She wasn't going to give the bastard the satisfaction of hearing her speak first. They had been given a random chalet, in a random motel—How?

'The date is twenty-third of November, twenty-forty-seven. The time is eleven thirty-six. How are my dollies tonight? Are we enjoying our little game? I have some news, my children. It won't be long now. I tire of our toying. Shall we up the ante? How much are you prepared to stake on your lives?'

'Fuck off, you bastard.' Ellie spat the words and slammed the phone into its cradle.

She looked at Eve. They'd been so careful. How had he found them? Eve wasn't madly stuffing things back in bags. They hadn't had time to take anything out. She wasn't heading for the door, ushering Ellie into headlong flight. She realised that there was nowhere to go. Here, in the *Palisades Motel*, was as good a place to die as any and better than some. They hadn't known where they were going themselves, hadn't planned, hadn't told, hadn't even got through the door.

But he knew.

He would always know. There was no safe place on this earth.

They were going to die.

'He's a demon,' Ellie said. 'Possibly the Devil himself.'

'Huh, tell me something I don't know. Don't forget, I've lived with this freak all my life.'

'No, I don't mean that. Don't you see, Eve, this is something unnatural. He's tracking us with supernatural means. Telepathy, evil spirit guides, witchcraft, or something. How can we fight the devil? Better the devil you know, Eve. You said it yourself. Did you know all along what he is?'

'No, Ellie, no. I swear. That was just something to freak you out.'

'Well, Evie girl, let me tell you, I'm freaked. I'm freaked to little pink freaksicles, and if there is a God out there, I hope to hell it's not his night off because I've got a feeling that before we see sunlight, we're going to need him rooting for our side.'

Neither woman had moved since the telephone call. They sat on the side of the twin beds, facing each other. Their faces had identical expressions, and the only difference between the two women was the sick condition of Ellie. Their eyes said they were done for but not necessarily beaten. Knowing that there was nowhere to run had taken the panic out of the situation, though none of the fear.

They took the mattresses off the beds and piled them up with all the furniture against the door. He didn't need to knock when he wanted to come and probably wouldn't be waiting for an invitation. But he could still come through the window. Hell, he might even be able to float in through the walls.

Eve made tea. Eve liked making tea.

'What now?' Ellie asked.

'We might as well sleep. It's about the only constructive option left to us.'

Ellie said she was too scared to sleep, but she took a handful of medication and went out like a light two minutes later. Eve sat up to wait for their night caller, but she, too, was soon banished to a world of troubled sleep.

# Chapter Thirty

E llie awoke with surprise. That is, she was surprised to
wake up at all. She came to with none of the usual hang-
ing-fugue. She awoke with her eyes tight shut, didn't want to
open them and didn't know what she'd see. For a while, she
didn't dare look. She fully expected Eve to be lying on her mattress with her throat cut open. Or maybe she'd be hanging from
a rope above her head. The chair would be gone from against
the door. It had such a pretty cushion. Despite the apathy of the
pimply receptionist, the management wanted people to enjoy
their stay here.

It was a comfortable place to be, but Ellie felt far from peaceful. She felt fear like she'd never known. Eve could be dead,
either hanging or horribly slashed, the demon sitting on the
pretty chair, watching her. He'd be biding his time and enjoying
the anticipation of the final round of the game. He might be
decaying and inhuman, with red eyes, or yellow eyes, or no
bloody eyes at all. Ellie tightened the grip on her closed eyes
but risked a silent sniff at the air. She couldn't smell decay or
the pieces of rotting flesh falling from his long-dead body. She

couldn't smell the sharp metallic tinge of Eve's blood like she smelled on Matt, and that was a smell she'd never forget.

'Well, it's about time you woke up. I've been sitting here for hours waiting for you.'

It was Eve's voice. But it must be a trick. It was Eve's voice, but it came from his rotting mouth.

'Oi, come on, stop pretending you're asleep. I know you're awake. I guess we live to see another day, eh? Or at least some of it.' No demon could be as gobby as Eve. She risked checking out her roommate.

The girls got up, and each kept watch while the other showered. Their belongings were depleted since they only had what Eve had stuffed into her backpack before Ellie fainted. Ellie was more grateful than she could express. The first thing Eve put in the pack's side pocket when they escaped was Ellie's medication. While Ellie dressed and let her morning cocktail of drugs take effect, Eve nipped to the motel shop to buy hot croissants and sandwiches. Neither of them had eaten for two days, and they were starving. Now that they knew The Creator was super-human, an air of inevitability settled over them. It didn't matter where they went or what they did when he was ready, and at his convenience, he'd come for them and zap them dead with killer rays from his eyes or something equally horrific. When there's nowhere to run, you just have to wait for the bad to come. With the acceptance came an eerie calm. They had survived the night because he let them, and now they would live by the minute until he came. How do you fight supernature? They didn't know what The Creator was, but they were pretty sure he wasn't an ordinary human.

They munched on cheese and pickle sandwiches for lunch, and Ellie sat cross-legged on the bed and opened her Travtech-pad. They couldn't be caught by Technology now. He already knew where they were. She had fourteen e-mails, but only four were of interest. Three were from Rob asking where the hell they were.

Ellie felt sorry that she hadn't been in touch. Had she really doubted him for a second? She'd convinced herself that she stayed incommunicado to prove to Eve that she was wrong about Rob and Gail? She'd ring him to bring him up to speed on their happenings.

The other mail was from Victor Khazanza. She remembered asking him for information on TSD. It seemed funny that she was finding out about an illness that should cause her death. Now, if her body was ever found, she would forever bear the title of *Murder Victim*.

Victor said that since the headlines about her illness were confirmed, he'd been researching Tay-Sachs at every opportunity. His letter was full of well-meaning sympathy and some reproach for not coming to him sooner. He said he'd be away at an unavoidable conference in the States from the twenty-third to the twenty-eighth but wanted to meet up with her after that to discuss his findings.

It was an appointment Ellie doubted she'd make, let alone keep. She wrote a brief note back, thanking him for his concern, apologising for her deceit, and saying they'd arrange something when he was back.

As she was closing the Travtech, a new message came in from Rob. They'd agreed to only communicate by e-mail until it was safe to go home.

Ellie, ring me. Urgent. I have news.

Ellie read the message to Eve, 'What do you reckon it could be?'

'Your book's made number one in the charts?'

Ellie threw a pillow at her. The seconds it took to connect to Rob's phone seemed like an age. It was switched off. They weren't at home when she rang there, either, so Ellie called the office to see if he was in a meeting at work. He hadn't been seen all day, and she was alarmed. Lately, any news they had was bad. Ellie left a message to call on her mobile as soon as he got in. She left similar messages on his home phone and personal and business mobiles. They'd know soon enough if anything was wrong either with a call or by an ominous silence. Neither of them said what they were thinking, but they knew what the other was mulling over. What if The Creator had done something to Rob and Gail first?

Ellie pondered the stupid bloody name. The Creator, it had narcissist written all over it. Who did this guy think he was—God, the devil? Rested, fed and showered, she felt physically better than she had for days. It was as though the disease had taken a backseat for a while. Death didn't need to come at her from all angles, just the one would do. She sat in front of the vanity mirror and rubbed moisturiser into her skin. She had dark circles under her eyes and felt as though she'd aged ten years in two days.

She was brushing her hair. It was both girls' practice to give their hair one-hundred brushstrokes morning and night. Esther taught Ellie to do it when she was a little girl. The same ritual had been forced on Eve in the institute because she was ordered to emulate Ellie in every way. They both carried it on in adult life as a matter of habit.

Eve was slouching on the bed, watching Ellie brush her hair.

She sat bolt upright, and Ellie alerted to the change in her attitude, turned.

'Don't move,' Eve yelled. 'Don't move a muscle.'

'What? What is it?' Ellie was terrified. She looked at Eve through the reflection in the mirror and then, ignoring her instructions, turned to face her.

Eve was kneeling on the bed. Her mouth gaped, and she was white with shock. Ellie tried to speak, but Eve put a hand up to silence her. She looked wildly around the room. Her expression wasn't one of fright or panic—just shock. She seemed to be thinking something through.

'That's it,' she screamed. 'That's how he's tracking us. Oh my God, Ellie, it's horrible. I've been so bloody stupid. It's you. No—probably both of us. He's seeing us through our eyes and hearing us through our own ears. Ellie, somehow—I don't know how—but somehow, we are fucking transmitters.'

'What do you mean? I don't understand.'

'Neither do I, but somehow he's living through us just the way I lived through you for all those years. That's how he got the films of you. Listen, when you were brushing your hair in the mirror just now, I realised what's been staring me in the face all the time. The only time I ever saw you was in a mirror.'

Ellie looked blank, trying to take in the new information.

'I didn't see a film of you, Ellie. I saw a film of what you were seeing. I was looking through your eyes. I should have realised before now. There were no camera angles. The scene didn't come from corners of the room or behind potted plants. They were coming from you. That's how he knew where we were every time. He's watching us right this second and listening to every word we say. There's nothing we can do to stop him short of gouging our eyes out and perforating our eardrums.'

'How? What does it mean? Is he inside us? Some malignant possession?'

'I don't know, Ellie, but my guess is, it's scientific, not supernatural.'

'Well, that's good, I suppose. No deadly eye rays.'

'Eh?'

'It doesn't matter. So does this make our position better or worse?'

'I don't know,' Eve said. 'I suppose that depends on how he's seeing what we see.'

'Well, let's assume it's not supernatural. For him to do that, he'd have to have cameras, wouldn't he?' She went on without waiting for an answer. 'We must have tiny cameras and radio transmitters in our heads. Bloody hell, Eve, can you hear what we're saying? It sounds incredible. Are you sure? Maybe you're mistaken.'

'No mistake, Ellie.' Knowing he was listening to every word, Eve told Ellie more about her life in the institute. They had talked about it a lot since escaping. Every new detail made Ellie's heart tear for the suffering Eve had been through.

Eve never had toys. That was her existence for as long as she could remember. She lived Ellie's life and learned academically through the books chosen for her and the information projected on the walls. She ate, learned, washed, and slept in the breaks between Ellie's life.

Apart from images on the screen, she had never seen a human being. She was shown films of her early life. In those days, her food hatch was a workstation. Gloved hands came through the wall to attend the tiny baby deprived of all human contact but the most basic essentials. She was fed, bathed and changed to a strict time schedule. She was never picked up when she cried, never comforted when she was upset.

When she was two years old, she heard the voice for the first time. It would issue commands until she understood them through trial and error. She learned to walk via starvation. If she wanted food, she had to get to it. She was ordered to clean herself. If she didn't, she was refused food until she did. She didn't speak until she was five, and that first word was Ellie.

The little girl hadn't been fed for two days. She didn't understand what the voice wanted.

'Say, Ellie. Ellie.'

But like a lab rat, she learned that if she didn't do as she was told, she wouldn't be fed. The voice was two people, a man and a lady. She preferred the lady, even though she never talked to her and only ever issued orders. For all those years, the impersonal voice only issued mono-phrase commands. Eve was raised without stimulation other than the voice, and the recordings played to her. She was raised clinically and without love. She never had a cold or a virus. She never had happiness but knew there was more to life than what she got because the real Eve was called Ellie and lived a full life. As she grew older, Eve knew her life wasn't normal. She toileted in a bucket for twenty-seven years and bathed from a bowl.

On her ninth birthday, she watched Ellie's birthday party, just as she'd watched every party Ellie had. When it was over, Eve was given a present. The only present she ever had in her life. It was a gift from Ellie, the voice said. It wasn't wrapped in fancy paper like her presents and was passed through the food hatch without ceremony.

It was a doll. The voice said it was to be called Polly. It was a two-foot rag doll with a porcelain face. Eve knew what mockery was. She already hated Ellie for her comfortable life and focussed all her rage on the doll. She tore the blue glass eyes from the doll in a fury. At least Polly wouldn't have to watch Ellie having fun. Eve hated Ellie and hated the doll as a symbol of Ellie. She'd punish the doll, but Polly didn't seem to mind and smiled her smug smile.

Polly was her only friend.

Ellie was crying when Eve got up to make another coffee. She was crying for Eve, and she was crying for herself.

'Here, let me do that.'

'No, I want to do it. I like it.' Eve hugged the Nescafe sachet against her chest as if this small thing could be taken away from her, too.

They were drinking their coffee and talking when Ellie's mobile rang. They exchanged a look, and Ellie picked up the phone without giving The Creator the courtesy of hearing her voice. It was a small defiance against him.

'Ellie? Are you all right?' It was Rob's voice, tight with concern. They brought him up to date—but it was garbled because he had something to tell them.

'Listen, Ellie, in the panic the other day, I forgot to tell you about the phone call from a strange woman.' He told Ellie about the woman who used to work at the institute and the call to Matt telling him not to speak in front of Ellie because it all went back to The Creator.

Rob's voice rose in excitement when he told them that she'd been in touch again, this time through the local paper. She'd wanted to meet the previous day, but they'd already missed the appointment when Rob saw the classified ad.

Eve. Thursday, twenty-third November. Ten am. Macdonald's Portland Walk. Don't tell you-know-who, Birthday surprise. Come alone.

They were devastated to have missed the appointment. This woman had answers and seemed keen to help them. But Rob reasoned that she'd made contact once and would again. He explained that she'd rung Matt's mobile when they were at the institute, so Rob kept it close to him. Ellie felt a stab of jealousy. She wanted to be the one keeping Matt's phone close to her heart.

He assured the girls that another meeting would be arranged. He'd place an ad in the same paper when they hung up, and it might draw the woman back to them.

The advert could be another element of The Creator's game—a trap. They knew by placing a counter-ad, they might be setting the perfect snare to catch themselves.

Ellie had been quiet for a few seconds. 'Don't you see what this means, Eve? You must be in the clear. It's just me with the head implants.'

'Yes, it looks that way, but for the moment, we can't take anything for granted. We don't know anything. Until we find this woman, it's all supposition.'

Ellie told Rob their theories about the cameras in their heads. They talked for ages before coming up with a plan.

It would be dangerous, but Eve explained to Rob that he was as much on death row as they were. He knew too much, and, what's more, The Creator was aware of every single thing that Rob knew, including their current conversation.

'He's going to kill you and Gail, too, Rob. He won't let you live. He doesn't like loose ends.'

Rob didn't want to do it. It was lunacy. Ellie and Eve didn't want him to do it either, but it was the only chance they had to fight. At least it was something they could do to save themselves. The Creator was either listening to them making plans, or he would have it on tape to listen to later. Rob and Ellie would write down everything they knew about him, the institute and Matt's death. As a small insurance policy, they'd send the information, in a sealed envelope, to their solicitors with instruction that it was only to be opened if they hadn't made contact with the solicitor's office by Tuesday the twenty-eighth of November.

It wasn't much, and none of them thought it would make much difference to a man as evil as their enemy. But at least it was positive, aggressive action.

The following night Rob would go back to the institute. He'd try to find and destroy all the transmission and recording equipment enabling The Creator to track them.

For the first time in his life, Rob understood what Deadman walking meant.

# Chapter Thirty-one

S o tired. So weary. So bored. My toys have become dull. Even my little boy dolly is tedious. Chase, chase, chase. The hunt was fun for a while, but now I want action.

The sick bitch is dying anyway. That wasn't meant to happen. She wasn't told to get sick. She's supposed to be perfect. I have no place in my game for broken dolls. Sick dollies are ugly dollies. I will not tolerate ugly dollies. Nasty, ugly dollies. Hearing her diagnosis, we had to bring about an end game by releasing the strong one. Where will it lead?

It's no fun hunting something that will die soon anyway, not enough emotion. She played well for a time. I was optimistic about bringing her into the game, allowing the other one her escape, setting the fire, bringing my pretty toys together.

My dollies should give me more sport. Snivelling, weak dollies. They should be Amazonian toys, my Amazon girls. I won't have weak, sick, broken dollies. My girl let me down, getting ill. That wasn't part of the deal. I let her be special. I made her special, and this is the way she repays me.

I roll a six, Ellie dolly. You die.

The other one is healthy but no fun for the game if she's alone. I need to make me some more dollies. Strong, pretty, new dollies. Next Generation warheads. Perfect dollies.

I roll a six, Eve dolly. You die— You bore me. But not yet, I have plans for you first.

And my boy dolly had better shape up, or I'll be rolling my dice for him.

From Adam's rib began Eve. From Eve's rib beget lovely new dollies

# Chapter Thirty-two

R ob was on his own. He doubted that he would get out of this nightmare place alive. He left Jake at home rather than risk his already endangered life any more than it need be. Now he realised how much courage and moral support the dog gave him last time. Tonight, he felt like a little boy finding his way to the bathroom in the dark.

Every second inside that dark place of death and misery, he waited for the spade falling over his head, or the chloroform rag pressed onto his nose and mouth.

He didn't know where to look for the freak's operations room. In cinemas, the projectionist always has his room at the top of the building. Would that follow in this case? He listened for the slightest sound and made his way along corridors and up every flight of stairs. It was as good a place as any to start.

He wrote his name and the date in giant letters with an indelible black marker pen on every corridor wall and in each room he entered. If the letter was opened and the solicitor read the contents, it would send the police here. If that envelope was opened, Rob was either already dead or in a heap of serious trouble.

The fire and smoke damage were less severe at the top of the building. He felt encouraged to find rows of fancy offices. This all looked hopeful. He searched them in order, going through drawers and filing cabinets, and he wondered what was hidden in the locked ones. Everything seemed meticulous and above board. He was no expert at deciphering the scientific documents he found, but there was no mention of their experimentation concerning caged and tortured little girls—or murder.

Rob was confident that if The Creator was coming for him, he was already in the monster's web. He'd be flexing his mandibles and waiting for his prey to come to him.

Rob jotted down the names of people who cropped up in the files. He stuffed a few pieces of paper that looked interesting in his pockets, they might yield clues later, but nothing seemed very hopeful. He felt safer using his torch up here, though anybody arriving from the drive would see it shining in the upper windows, and it'd give him away. It was a risk worth taking.

After an hour of searching, he was no closer to finding the control room. It was only guesswork that brought him to the institute. The recording equipment could be at The Creator's home.

The institute was a warren of connecting and inter-connecting rooms and corridors. It was the perfect place to hide or to be pursued. He'd covered the top storey of the building. He worked his way down the building, room by room, cupboard by cupboard. He had a feeling that, like the inner cells where Eve had been kept, the control room might be well hidden.

Logic told him that if it wasn't at the top of the building, the best place to look was close to the cell. But he didn't want to waste time doubling back if he was wrong. Mostly, he wouldn't admit to himself that he was scared of going through the secret storeroom into what lay beyond. Matt could still be there, even though Eve said he wouldn't be—but the thought terrified him.

His search wasn't fruitful, and he came to the storeroom. On the corridor wall outside and in the storage space itself, he wrote clear directions for the police to find the release catch for the false wall. He was sweating. He could've been picked off any time over the last few days. He felt more vulnerable in this part of the building. The respectable façade outside this hidden part provided some protection because of its clean image—they wouldn't want another body soiling the place with DNA. Like Alice with the Eat-Me jar, he was walking into a land of otherworldliness.

As the wall closed behind him, Rob felt doomed. He hefted the eight-pound sledgehammer he'd brought to his front and held it like a shield, pretending to be ready for anything coming at him.

There were many rooms in this part of the building. Some were locked, with eye scanning or combi-lock units protecting them from intrusion. Any of them could be the control room.

When he got to the cell doors, one stood open. It was the other one. Not the one he'd rescued the girls from. He looked in, expecting The Creator to be waiting for him, with the Mad Hatter and the Dormouse. Alice would offer tea, and the Cheshire cat would grin menacingly.

The room was empty. Only the overpowering smell of stale vomit gave away the secret of its recent occupation. He pressed on the interconnecting door between the cells. Its lack of height added to the impression of his Alice in Wonderland analogy. The same comparison had occurred to Ellie, and the memory of their conversation made Rob feel sick.

The door flew open, and he jumped because he expected it to be locked. Dear God, please don't let Matt be there with his throat slashed.

The room was empty.

This tiny cell was where Eve lived for twenty-seven years until the fire gave her an unexpected means of escape. The Creator had returned to his lair. Matt's body was gone, and Ellie would be heartbroken. He was in Eve's prison. He felt a pang of pity for the poor little girl turned troubled woman. It was no wonder she felt the way she did about Ellie.

Matt was gone—removed like garbage. There would be no marked resting place for him. If there was ever a funeral, it would only be a service. Rob's heart was breaking for him and for Ellie. He felt guilty that he'd suggested leaving Matt's body in this awful place when Ellie got out. She'd never forgive him for it.

He shuddered. It may have been a scared man's fancy, but he felt malevolent eyes watching him. He turned and ran the way he'd come. There was nothing to see here.

With every step, he expected the door to slam shut in front of him, the way it had with the girls. Back in the corridor, he felt a moment of relief, but he still had to do what he came for and get out.

He found the room where Eve's clothes and toiletries were kept. As he went, he left huge notes on the wall.

The cell where Eve was kept, prisoner.

Storeroom containing Eve's things.

He worked methodically along the corridor, checking the rooms on either side and every door he came to. He tapped on walls to see if they had secret rooms behind them. The third from the last door on the right was ajar—an invitation? A trap? Anything of importance would be in one of the locked rooms—unless he was meant to find it.

Rob pushed the door open without going in and hefted his hammer.

Bingo.

There was nobody in the room, but this was what he was looking for. It was open, waiting—for him? Why was The Creator letting him do this?

The office was big and airy. Twin whirrings were audible as he crossed the threshold. The walls were coved with close to a hundred CCTV screens. They were all switched on, though without sound, and showed every angle of the institute and its grounds.

Several high-end leather computer chairs lined the central workstation. Three CCTV monitors stood in a row on desks, and one was switched on, powered by a portable generator.

The screen replayed a scene from a few minutes earlier. As Rob watched—transfixed. He saw a door opening into the second cell. A small scream preceded the hand coming through the door, followed by Rob, terrified. The recording showed him standing in the centre of the cell.

Rob took the hammer to all three monitors and equipment. Venting his rage, he smashed them until they were tiny shards of glass and plastic. A loud bang invaded the stillness of the room as the monitors blew. The noise echoed through the silent building. Rob gave no thought to being cut down where he stood. He had a job to do. The note left in the middle of the desk enraged him to ferocity. He took all his terror and frustration out on the projector and recording equipment, paying particular attention to the black box on the floor. At the heart of the operations, the processor transposed what Eve saw into film, viewed by the sick monster hounding her.

He smashed the lead crystal glass and the open, but loosely corked, bottle of champagne, left beside the taunting note. He only stopped when his arms couldn't manage another swing of the hammer. Exhausted by his exertions, he flung himself into the middle padded chair—the one he sensed belonged to the backside of the creator. He was wheezing and breathing heavily. But despite that, he felt good for the minor victory.

Before thrusting it into his coat pocket, he reread the note and wondered if it was genuine. It could be a dire error by the creator, should the police ever have him as a suspect and need a handwriting sample. Maybe the great man genuinely couldn't be here tonight. Rob felt he was pretty adept at all this fighting for your life and living by your wits stuff.

So sorry not to make our little rendezvous, my dear chap. Have a drink on me. You've earned it. I would love to be with you tonight, but never fear, we will make up for lost time very soon, but first I have a meeting arranged with the girls. They are expecting me, and I'd so hate to disappoint.

He didn't sit for more than a few seconds. This could still turn nasty, and he wasn't letting his guard down. He turned for the door and jumped back with a yell.

Somebody was sitting in a chair by the door, watching him.

Not a person at all—a doll. A horrible rag-doll, but she wasn't watching him after all because some sicko had taken out her eyes. The empty sockets mocked him as he ran for his life. He didn't stop running until he was scrabbling with the handle of his car door.

As he drove away, he couldn't help thinking that it had been too easy. Getting back through the secret door was simple. It wasn't locked. In fact, on the inside, there was a plainly visible handle.

Why? Why had the creator let him walk away?

Rob swung his car into the grass verge two miles down the road. He opened the door and vomited acid bile onto the grass—he imagined the creator laughing at his weakness.

The girls were delighted by Rob's victory. They whooped and hollered, high-fived and jumped on the beds like a pair of kids. They even hugged as though it was natural. It was a ten-point score to the little people.

They were alive, and the fact that the enemy let them score didn't matter. The gold, silver and bronze medals in this game were melted into a cast of life, and this time, they had come up tops. He couldn't monitor them any longer. They could run, and they could hide.

Ellie's mobile rang with a withheld number. She answered it, knowing who it was before she pressed the button.

'Hello, my dollies, quite a party you're having there. Am I invited? I shouldn't wonder that you'll have a new bed to pay for with all this frivolity. I trust you'll be in later when I call to see you?'

Ellie hung up without saying a word. She didn't gratify the bastard with a response. It was too cruel. The room felt cold. All the joy dissipated with the change in mood.

'It didn't work. We were bloody stupid to think he'd only have one set of monitoring equipment. Rob said it was too easy. He's watching us now. Listening. He says he's coming for us.' Ellie sat beside Eve and grabbed her hand. 'We'll get through this.'

'Will we?'

'No, not a chance, but it's something to say, maybe even something to cling on to. The thing is, I know that anytime now, you're going to strike out on your own. You haven't got a head-implant telling him every time you take a crap. You might be able to get away. And there's nothing I can do to stop you.' Ellie's eyes filled with tears.

'We don't know that, though, do we? We're just going by the message in the paper. I could be as bugged and buggered as you are.'

'Don't you want to cut loose and see?'

'What's the point? I've got nowhere to go, and he'd find me eventually. He's not going to set me free. I've got no money. What can I do? I wouldn't stand a chance on my own any more than I do here.'

'I've got money. I could give you what you need to get away. You could use my passport to leave the country. I'm dying, Eve. We could swap identities, and you could take over my life. Has-been writers fade from the public eye very quickly. You could keep moving for a while, and if you don't have an implant, he'd never find you. I can set you up, not for life, but long enough for you to build a life.'

'Why would you do that after everything I've done to you?'

Ellie sat for a few seconds, and it didn't look as though she was going to answer. When she had collected her thoughts, Ellie said. 'Because we've been through so much in the last few days. Because I don't want the bastard to win with a full hand. Because I care about you. And, most of all, because you're my sister.'

Eve was crying. Nobody had ever said they cared about her before, and Ellie could see that she didn't know how to cope with her emotions.

'Well, I don't care about you, so don't go getting any stupid ideas about us having a big happy reunion. We're in this because we're in this, not because we like each other. As soon as this is sorted, I'm off.'

Ellie smiled.

'And what the hell do you think you're grinning at?' Eve wiped her hand across her nose, leaving a trail of watery snot up her forearm.

'You do care, Eve. I know you do because if you didn't, the second you found out you might not have an implant, you'd have been off. Or, if not then, when we saw the shirt in the car, or now when I've offered to set you up. You're not staying with me because you have to. You're staying with me because I'm all you've got, and because we need each other, and because we're desperate—and because we do care.'

'Oh fuck off.' Eve stomped off to the bathroom.

They holed up at the motel for another two days, waiting for his arrival and the hammer to fall.

He never came.

Everything was quiet, and they rested, talked, and rested some more. Ellie was weak. The trauma had taken more out of her than she was prepared to admit. The creator didn't come, and they couldn't understand why. Eve said Ellie was a selfish bitch for getting sick with a stupid disease just when they could become friends. Ellie laughed. Sometimes Eve was like a stroppy little girl learning to cope with her emotions.

Fully aware that their foe was listening to every word, Ellie used the telephone to set up meetings with her consultant and Victor Khazanza. Two weeks earlier, the thought of two appointments in one day would have been too much for her to cope with, but now it was like a gentle walk in the park.

There was no point in them staying there any longer. When the creator chose to pick them off, he would have no trouble doing it. Ellie wanted to get Jake and go home, and despite Eve's protestations, she said she was going too. Eve would have to keep her head down and behave herself. Old Jackson never missed a thing, and his curtain twitched so often it was afflicted with a permanent tic.

'There's something we have to do first, though,' Ellie said. 'We have to go and see my mother. It's time we got some answers, and I need to go to the police about Matt.'

'Going to your mother will put her in danger?'

'No more than she already is, and no more than the butcher I go to on a Friday or the old lady I talk to in the park. It looks as though I've had this implant, or whatever it is, all my life. He knows where everybody lives. Unless we find some way to stop him, everybody in my life is in danger.'

Esther's face was a picture when she saw the girls. She prodded Eve to see if she was real. Then she spent the next half-hour crying because Jerry must have had an affair with another woman to produce this person who looked just like Ellie.

Ellie had trouble getting her to concentrate. Even when she told her about the institute and Matt's death, though she left certain parts out, all Esther could focus on was the fact that Jerry had been unfaithful to her. Their mother could only perform for one trauma at a time, and this was the performance of a lifetime. This situation focussed the conversation on her and cast her in the role of the pitiful victim. One that Eleanor's mother had always played to the hilt.

'Mum, that's impossible,' Ellie said. 'Look at us. We're the same in every way. Half sisters could never be as identical as Eve, and I are. We came from the same womb, Mother. We must have done. Please tell us the truth. Either Eve's your daughter, or I'm am not. It's one or the other.'

Esther was having none of it. 'Oh, how could he do this to me? I thought your father was devoted to me. How could he hurt me so?' Soon the only word that Ellie heard was, 'Me, me, me.' She didn't have time for it and was annoyed.

'Mother, this isn't about you. Surprising as it may seem, it's about us, Eve and I.'

Esther kept looking at Eve and shaking her head in disbelief. 'Why did you have to come here and scare me like this? I don't understand. Are you a ghost girl? Ellie, I'm scared. She's scaring me. Make her go away, Eleanor.'

'I'm sorry, Mrs Erikson,' Eve said. I don't hold a grudge against you; it's too late for that. I—we—just want to know the truth. I need to find out where I came from and how I ended up at the institute.

'I am telling the truth. I am. I am. Oh, why won't you believe me, you wicked girl?'

Ellie noticed that every time the institute was mentioned, Esther shuddered.

'What do you know about the institute, Mother?' Ellie asked, trying a different tack to stave off the next wave of Esther's self-pity.

'Nothing, nothing at all. I don't know anything about any woman's institute.'

'But you lived in Keswick before I was born, right?'

'Yes, right up until I was seven months pregnant. I remember because my back was hurting so much, and my ankles were swollen.'

Ellie looked at Eve. 'Well, that puts her in the right place at the right time. Daddy too, if that has any relevance.'

'Oh, don't you talk about me as though I'm some sort of criminal. I wasn't in any place. I was pregnant.' Esther was crying with indignation, but her tears were waning. She went back to her favourite line of conversation.

'I bet it was that Maria, the dirty slut. She was never away from here at the time. She was pregnant, too, and her with no husband. I bet it was all your Father's doing, the dirty dog.'

'Mother, for God's sake. Daddy didn't do it.'

Eve put a hand on Ellie's arm and stopped her from saying any more.

'Go on, Mrs Erikson. Who was Maria?'

'Just some woman who took me home when, well, when I wasn't very well. Maria brought me home in a taxi. We were friends. But we fell out when she dropped Eleanor on her head. I didn't see her after that, but if I could get hold of her now, I'd have a few words to say to her.'

'What happened, Mum? You must tell us.'

413

'I can't. It's too horrible.' Esther saw the tables turning to bring her into full focus again. She buried her head in her hands and covered her face. Her shoulders heaved as she warbled out huge sobs. 'Oh, Ellie, don't make me tell you, dear. Don't. I've protected you from it for so long. Oh well,' she continued brightly, 'it was like this.' Ellie and Eve exchanged glances over Esther's head, Ellie rolled her eyes, and Eve pulled a face.

Once Esther told her version of events, there was no stopping her.

'One evening, Ellie, your father left me alone in a nightclub. Another man had been looking at me. He shouldn't have left me like that, Ellie. He shouldn't have left me alone in that awful place. I was so young and so beautiful. I was an innocent, Ellie, an innocent.' Ellie patted her mother's arm and risked a glance at the virtually naked portrait of her innocent mother on the wall.

'Of course, you were, Mum. I know that.'

'Well, dear, it was awful. The man, you see, came and sat down beside me. I tried asking him to go away. "Oh, please," I said. "Please leave me alone. My husband will be back for me soon." But he wouldn't listen, the brute. Anyway, Ellie, you'll never believe what happened to me.'

The girls had to wait until the next flood of tears had passed before they found out. 'He took me outside and raped me, Ellie. I tried to be brave. I tried to fight him off, but he was too strong for me, and I couldn't get him away. His awful breath was in my face, and his weight on top of me almost crushed me. He smelled of beer and nasty male sweat, Ellie—and he raped me.'

Eve busied herself making tea while Ellie mopped up a soggy Esther.

414

'Oh, no, dear. No, that's no good at all. We have the lovely china cups, the ones with matching saucers. Tea always tastes better in Doulton, I always say.'

'I haven't been to Dalton,' Eve said conversationally. 'And it's only a couple of miles down the road from Barrow. Ellie smiled, hoping that despite Eve, and her mother, they could arrive at some valuable answers. She bluntly brought the conversation back to the night Esther was raped.

'Where did he rape you, Mum? '

'Really, Eleanor. In my lady garden, of course, dear. Do you have to be so personal?'

'No, mother, where did it happen?'

'In Keswick.'

'Whereabouts in Keswick did he rape you, Mother?' Ellie couldn't hide the impatience from her voice.

'Well, I don't know. Somewhere.'

'So you claim you were raped, but you don't know where. Did you go to the hospital?'

'I was raped, Eleanor. I don't claim anything. I was raped.'

'Sorry, Mother, you were raped. Did you go to the hospital?'

'No dear, you see, I met Maria the next morning, and she took me home.'

'The next morning? Where were you all night?'

'I don't know. I don't remember.'

Ellie lowered and softened her voice.

'Mother, if you were raped, you must remember where you were and what happened.'

'Well, I don't because he drugged me. It must have been something he put in my drink. I don't remember anything after I came back from the toilet.'

'But what about his breath and the weight of his body?'

'Well, that's how I imagine he felt.'

'Oh, Mother,' Ellie said, exasperated.

'And then, you see, Maria came along, and she was nice and kind and said that I wasn't a tart. She said it always happens to the nicest girls. Nice girls like me. She took me home, and then we became friends, and she was pregnant, too, see? She even had the same due date and everything.'

Ellie and Eve looked at each other again. They might be on to something here. If this was right, it couldn't be a coincidence. If Ellie could just cut through the fantasy and get to the facts, they might have a clue to work on.

'So this Maria, she had a little girl too, did she?'

'Oh no, dear, she had a boy. But he didn't live. He was born dead. It was such a shame. You see, we talked about how nice it would be if we both had girls. She even persuaded me to name you Eleanor, dear. I wasn't keen at first, but when she said she was calling her little girl Evelyn, they matched, you see.' Esther's voice trailed off as she realised what she was saying. Her voice was small, incredulous and frightened.

'She was going to call her little girl, Evelyn.'

This confirmed it was tangible stuff. Maria was the key to the mystery. They had to find this Maria and fast.

'But she spoiled all our lovely plans because she had a boy, you see, and he died. I didn't see her for a few months after that. The grief she said, but then after you were born she popped up again—and that's when she dropped you and we didn't see her anymore.'

Esther was still talking in a pathetic baby voice, and the girls had to concentrate to catch up. 'We were friends for a little while, and then, when she dropped you on your head, we fell out. You had a little mark just above your left eye. It's gone now, but oh, it did give me a fright at the time.' Both girls came to attention.

'What do you mean she dropped me on my head, Mother?'

'Well, she didn't admit she'd dropped you, of course. She said you fell off the sofa and banged yourself on the corner of the unit. Said she took you to hospital, too, but they had no record of it. We had to take you back when the wound went septic, but the hospital said they had nothing written down about you being in before. We decided then, your dad and I, that she wasn't to be trusted. We've never seen her since.'

'How can we contact this woman, Mother? Do you have an address or phone number for her?'

'No, silly. I told you she was no use to me after that, so we didn't bother with her again. And I can see why now. I can't believe your father did that to me.'

Esther talked for another half hour, but there was nothing that might be helpful. It was time to go home, and Ellie couldn't wait to get back to the place where she'd last been truly happy. Her house held all her fondest memories of Matt.

The homecoming greetings were ecstatic. Jake jumped, frolicked and talked to Ellie before Rob could get a look in to welcome her. It was twenty minutes of chaos, coffee making and keeping Jake away from Eve, while Ellie stamped herself back into her home before they could sit and talk.

The alarm hadn't gone up about Matt's disappearance yet, but they knew his absence couldn't go unreported for much longer. Rob had been scanning the paper for replies to their advert, but nothing had come through so far.

They were discussing the woman and her messages to Matt and Rob. Eve had an idea. It was crazy, but what if?

'Rob, did the woman tell you her name?'

'No. I'm pretty sure she didn't.'

'Think back over the conversation and what Matt told you about her,' Rob furrowed his brow and repeated as much as he could remember about the conversation. He had been wired, scared, and in a state of wild panic. It was difficult to remember what was said. He jumped up, was animated and waved his hands in front of him. His mind had delivered the goods.

'Maria. She said her name was Maria.'

This was fantastic news. They felt as though they were getting somewhere.

Ellie had her medical appointments, and a call to Victor was arranged for the next day. She was in a bad way. With her homecoming came the torrent of grief that she'd held back since Matt's death.

She cried all night, and it had taken its toll on her health. Rob had a plan. He glanced at Ellie awkwardly and looked thankful that she was the one who suggested she leave the room while he discussed it with Eve.

Not even happy with that, Rob insisted that they went into the garden, in case the house was bugged as well. If their conversation went to their tormentor, then at least they would know for sure that Eve had a transmitter, too.

They were aware that they'd opened her to danger by discussing Maria. The fact that she'd been able to call probably meant she was in hiding. Presumably, as yet, the creator hadn't found her. They had to get to her before he did, for all their sakes.

It was decided Rob would pick up Eve the next day. He didn't trust his home or office—or Eve for that matter. But, he arranged the use of a friend's house and computer. They were taking a risk on Eve not being tagged. Rob was loath to bring another innocent person into the web of horror that had befallen them, but they had no choice. He arranged a chauffeur-driven car for Ellie. The man would be armed and was hired from a security firm that Rob sometimes used. While Ellie was as safe as she ever would be, he'd be with Eve. They were spending the day going through births, deaths and marriages to find any Maria who had lost a male child around about the time of Ellie's birth. It wasn't much, but it was something.

After a bath, with Jake sitting beside the door to alert them of incoming danger, Ellie came downstairs looking better.

She stood in the kitchen archway watching as Eve and Rob worked in harmony on a giant omelette. Eve had seen it done through Ellie's eyes, but this was her first-ever attempt at cracking eggs. The results were hilarious, and Eve and Rob laughed, unaware of Ellie watching them.

'You know, Eve,' Rob said, 'I don't want to, but I can't stop myself from liking you a bit. The real Eve is warm and friendly, and she's funny, just like Ellie. But honey, don't take this the wrong way, and I don't blame you for anything that's happened. I understand why you did what you did, but I can't help rueing the day you came into our lives. I want to say I'm glad I met you, but if you had never escaped from that place, Matt would still be here.' Rob's words were cut short as Ellie came into the kitchen. She kissed Rob's cheek and squeezed Eve's arm. Eve blushed and pulled away from the arm Ellie draped around her shoulder.

'You still don't see it, do you, Rob?' Ellie said, but her words weren't unkind. 'What happened was always going to happen. I've got the tag. I've been monitored my whole life. He could have reeled me in any time he liked. And with or without Eve being here, with or without the illness, I believe that one day he'd have come for me.'

The debate continued as they cooked then moved to the table to eat. Eve finished a mouthful of omelette and looked at them with a puzzled expression.

'There's something I never understood before. When the institute caught fire, I should have burned in my cell. And yet, that day, for the first time ever, my door opened, and I just walked out. It was the middle of the night, and it puzzled me that somebody had unlocked the door. Until now, it didn't seem strange that there were no people. No fire alarms went off, no emergency services came, there was nothing. Just the smell of smoke, the sound of windows exploding far away, and an easy escape route.'

'What are you saying, Eve?' Rob asked.

'I'm not sure, but with everything that's happened. What if it was the creator that let me out to play his game? He must have known that I'd come here looking for you. It wouldn't take a genius to work out that I'd have revenge in mind.'

It was a sobering thought, and they munched on omelette and mulled over the ramifications of what Eve put forward. It made a lot of warped sense.

Rob finished his coffee before going home at eleven-thirty. As he was leaving, sharp rap at the front door made them jump. Whoever this caller was, they were in a hurry to be acknowledged. They didn't know who their visitor was, but one thing was sure, it wasn't the milkman calling for his money. The person, or people, expecting an answer knocked harder. Jake's hackles rose, and he was barking at the door.

Eight seconds is a long time when somebody is banging on the door as though the hounds of hell are on their tail. Ellie stood up. She went to the study to get a door scan of the visitors, but Rob put out his hand to stop her.

'I'll go,' he sounded more assured than he probably felt.

'Can I help you?' they heard him say. There was the sound of a scuffle. A woman appeared in the lounge. She was middle-aged, slightly overweight, with long greying hair that hung in greasy tendrils across her face. She wore black joggers and a sweater that was washed out and shapeless. She looked at the girls huddled on the sofa and nodded. They smelled the alcohol on her breath from five feet away.

'Please forgive the intrusion, Miss Erikson. I am Maria.'

She seemed confident that the mention of her name was her right of passage. Speaking that word meant she wouldn't be thrown out on her ear.

'How did you find us?' Eve asked.

'Miss Erikson is a local celebrity; I've known where she lives for some time but was fearful of causing distress. When you didn't answer my advert in the paper, I thought I was too late. I knew this was no time for manners and, please forgive the intrusion, but here I am. I got this letter today, and I had to warn you.'

She handed them a crumpled piece of paper from her tatty handbag. It was a single line of print made up of letters cut from a newspaper.

Found you. I'm coming, ready or not.

'I'm so sorry to come here like this, but he's on his way, and when he catches up with me, he's going to kill me. Whatever happens now—my life is over. There's nothing left for me, and I know I don't deserve it, but given a choice, I'd like the dignity of ending my part in this evil in my own way. I have no right to ask anything of you, but please, don't make me take this to my grave. Hear what I have to say.'

Rob made coffee, and after pleasantries were passed, they sat around to hear Maria's story. There was little preamble. Maria came to get things off her chest and asked that she say it her way.

'Please, time is short. He could come for us at any second. He watches us even now. Ellie, this will be a shock, but I have to warn you. He can see and hear everything you do because you have a tiny transmitter in your head. It's harmless and can't hurt you. You've had it nearly all your life, but it allows him to see your every move.'

Ellie said they'd worked that much out. Maria hardly drew breath before she was talking again.

'I have been a wicked, foolish woman. I know I can't atone for what I've done, but I must tell you how sorry I am before my life is finished. Let me start at the beginning. My life is over. He'll get me now. I'll tell you everything I know, and maybe you can use it against him. I'm ready to die one way or the other. But it might not be too late to save you, and if I do nothing else before I die, I'll know I've made some atonement for the ill I've done.

'I was seventeen when I met him. Young, fresh out of school and with a head full of ideas. I wanted to be somebody. I aimed higher than that downbeat town full of yokels offered me. I was an idealistic fool.'

422

'Who is he, Maria? Please tell us the creator's name.' Eve leaned forward to the edge of the sofa.

'I don't know his name. Even after all these years, I know so little about him. I only know him as Genesis. That's what he liked to be called. He's a private man. He kills anybody who asks questions. You learn to do as you're told and say nothing fast. I know it sounds ludicrous, but if anybody can believe that, it's the three of you. But please, let me tell it from the beginning. It's better that way. Questions will be answered in order as they come along, and it'll make more sense. Our time is limited, and I've spent long hours thinking about what I would say to you. Please, if I don't say this now, I never will.'

Her eyes moved from Ellie to Eve to Rob.

They were all dying to pepper Maria with a million questions, but she had answers.

'I got my first job at the institute. I was only a runner, setting up equipment and cleaning up after the laboratory assistants. But you see I had this,' she pointed to her face. 'Oh, not as it is now. In those days, I was pretty and slim too. I thought I was something when I was taken out of the labs on the boss's order. I met Genesis in his private office. He liked me. I was a foolish girl, this was my chance to shine, and I took it. He fired his PA. He did that whenever he got sick of someone. People knew to take the generous severance and not make a fuss. I was given her position. I was hopeless. I couldn't make a decent cup of tea, never mind write shorthand and type. But I had other uses. I was eager to learn, and there was the sex.' She shuffled in her seat and gave an apologetic smile.

'I knew how I got the job, but I wanted to learn to do it properly and not just have a title and no work to go with it. Genesis and I were lovers, but I worked my way to competency. I was the brunt of office jokes. There was bitchiness and catcalling, but who could blame the typing pool? They worked hard for their living, and a mop-it-up girl over-ranked them all. I ruled the company and was a hard taskmistress. I soon had them toeing the line. Genesis saw my potential and gave me more responsibility. He'd pulled me out of the ranks to kneel between his legs, but I was worthy of my hire.'

Rob opened his mouth, shut it again and contented himself with, 'Wow.'

'For some time, I was his whore and his legitimate PA. He primed me for the business, and I groomed myself to go all the way. I was hungry for the money, yes, but my real craving was for the power I received working for Genesis. It wasn't long before he brought me into the inner sanctum. I'd served my time and learned about the barely legal experimentation and horrifying work in genetics. It was an immoral practice that no government would ever give its public name to. Though government money funded the projects behind the curtain. They knew the score. Anybody who left the inner sanctum, for whatever reason, was never seen again. However, bodies were discovered floating in the lakes or in cars filled with exhaust fumes.'

They were so engrossed in Maria's narrative that they hadn't once tried to butt in with questions. She took a drink of coffee, moistened her lips and continued.

'Genesis dressed me; he dined me and showed me off. He gave me responsibility and power. I made pay-offs, I smiled at politicians over dinner. I even slept with people he wanted sweetening. The money was unlimited, and I had no problem being a whore for it. I learned my trade and knew it well. After

I'd served my time in the sanctum and proved my loyalty as a valuable servant to Genesis, he told me his plan. He had an idea for the ultimate experiment. It was vile, heinous, but his eyes danced with the flames of a million naked fires, and I was caught up in his mania.'

'Jesus.' Rob was the epitome of the mono-exclamation.

Maria smiled at him, glanced nervously and the girls and went on.

'There would be two babies, raised from birth. One to be brought up in a typical family unit. The child would be loved, nurtured, and given everything to make the idiom of the average child. The other baby would be raised in isolation, schooled, given only the reading material picked for her, and fed, the other girl's life daily.

'It was wrong, evil, but the social implications of such an experiment were immense. Sure, he spoke about his plans with mania, but with such surety too. He convinced me the experiment was a valid one for the good of humanity. We would answer the age-old question once and for all, what sculpts a human being, nature or nurture? The human race could learn about social integration from the experiment. I agreed to go along with it. However, later, it was too late when I wanted to pull out. When the maniac dream became a nightmare reality, I begged him to let you go, Eve. I said I'd take you and bring you up like a normal child. I promised to never utter a word about what happened, but he was immovable. He had his girls, his dollies, and nothing could stop him. You've got to believe me. I didn't want this. I begged him to let us go, just you and me, Eve. I tried to make it right for you. But he was addicted to the power. He wouldn't free us. I tried my best to make your time in there as easy as possible. It was horrible—horrible.

'But I'm moving forward too fast. We made our babies, Genesis and me. We'd been lovers for five years, but he wouldn't let me conceive in the usual way. He was insistent it was done via in Vitro fertilisation.

The experiment had to be clinical from the first stage to the last. My eggs were harvested. Now, all we needed was a donor. A lad was taken from the labs, hired to find a woman, drug her and bring her to the institute. That woman was your mother, Ellie.

'He implanted the eggs—my eggs—one in her, and one returned to me, and then, after several hours with our feet raised in stirrups, Esther Erikson was dumped. She was unconscious and left in the summerhouse by the river just after dawn. The Good Samaritan walking past when she woke up, confused and disorientated, was no coincidence. I was planted for her waking, and it was the most natural thing in the world to befriend her.'

'You are my mother?' Eve said in horror. Maria nodded in reply and tried to continue with her story.

'I—'

'Wait, wait a minute. Stop,' Ellie shouted. 'Are you saying both eggs were yours? You're my natural mother, too?'

'Technically, yes.'

'So that means that him, Genesis, the creator, is our father?' Ellie knew the answer and didn't wait for Maria's reply.

'Oh, my God, what the hell are we born of?' She was too shocked to care about the implied insult that included Genesis and Maria.

426

Maria picked imaginary lint from her joggers and gave them a second to let the revelation sink in. Then she continued as though there was no interruption.

'My task was to befriend Esther. We discovered our pregnancies together. It formed a bond between us. I told Esther mine was a boy who died at birth, but while both of you came from my eggs, Eve, you're the daughter of my womb. Our babies were born, two little girls—just as forecast.'

Eve didn't respond. She sat with her arms locked around her legs, rocking as though she was in a trance. Only the focus of her eyes gave away the fact that she was listening to glean answers from this crazy woman's confession. Maria continued in a monotone, her eyes locked in the past, and her mind tangled around evil.

'I visited you often, Ellie. When you were eight months old, I was babysitting you. I took you for an operation to have a tiny implant put into your brain, just behind your eye. The implant is a monitoring device that records sound and vision. The minute camera was inserted with a large reed dispensing needle. It was nothing more than a simple injection, like microchipping a dog, but it left a scar that didn't go down well with your folks. My job with you was done, and I had no need to see you again. Your mother threw a tantrum when I gave you back with a tiny cut on your forehead, and I used the argument to sever ties between us.

'I'm sorry, Ellie. Please don't take offence, but we were disappointed with the random choice of surrogate. Esther wasn't the caregiver we hoped, but even so, you were brought up well, and it sufficed for the good of the experiment. If not, we'd have taken you from her and put you with a second surrogate family.'

Ellie couldn't believe that this monster, with all the maternal instinct of a cement block, had the cheek to criticise Esther's parenting skills. She wanted to defend her mother, but no words came. She was dumbfounded, but Maria continued talking.

'Genesis was obsessed, and although, to the world, he was competent and still ran his institute as before, he was an invisible figurehead. He had total control, but only the top institute management saw his face or knew his Genesis identity. His cruelty and torture of Eve became increasingly elaborate and advanced. When the girls were born, Genesis gave himself the creator title.'

'He used to wake me in the night and not let me sleep,' Eve said in a small voice. 'Sometimes, he wouldn't let me sleep for days on end until I fell unconscious to the floor.'

'Yes, Eve, that was a human stamina exercise. As you know, Ellie and Rob, if you've ever stayed awake all night, missing one night of sleep isn't fatal. People will be irritable the next day, either slowing down or wired because of adrenaline. If they miss two nights' sleep, it gets worse. Concentration is difficult, and attention span falls. Mistakes increase. After three days, the subject will hallucinate, and clear thinking is impossible. With continued wakefulness, they lose their grasp on reality. Your record, Eve, was a hundred and forty-six hours. That's six days and nights without any sleep at all.'

Maria sounded proud of Eve. Most mothers were proud of their child's first steps or first picture. Maria bragged that her daughter was tortured for a hundred and forty-six hours and survived to suffer another twenty years of the same.

'How do you explain the times he starved me or left me without water for days on end and when I had no light? I used to bite and scratch myself out of sheer frustration. I craved my screen and the images of Ellie's life, but all I had was my cell and the darkness that seemed to go on forever.'

'It was the same thing, Eve—stamina. You did fifteen days without food or light and only a few sips of water a day.'

Maria bragged about the statistics. Eve was stony-eyed and rocking on the sofa, and Ellie sobbed quietly. Rob was shaking, his fists tightly clenched in his lap.

He stood up. He'd reached the point where he couldn't listen to another word. 'You monster, you vile, evil, monster. Get out. Get out of here and don't ever come back.'

Ellie stood up and grabbed Rob. 'No, Rob, we need to know how to find him. Maria's our only lead to this man. We have to keep her with us. He'll kill her if she leaves here now.'

'Good, I hope he does. Now get out.'

'I'm so sorry for what I did. I'd do anything to turn back time and make different choices. I promise I'll do everything I can to put this right. But if it wasn't me, he'd have found someone else to run his obsessive experiment with him. He went away on business and left me in charge. Please believe me, I always did what I could for you, Eve, but I was monitored as much as you were. At least I managed to set you free when I set fire to the institute.'

'So it was you?' Eve said.

Maria scribbled down a number on a piece of paper. 'Here, look, here's a number where you can reach me. If I can do anything to help you, please ring at any time. If there's no answer, you'll know it's too late for me. I'd do anything to help, but all I can really do is say how sorry I am.'

'Get out,' Rob said.

Ellie was about to speak. Rob screamed the last order, and Jake stood up, barking. Maria was the next to stand. Jake growled low in his throat and moved closer to Ellie.

'It's all right. I'm leaving. I'm sorry, Ellie, Eve, but there's nothing more to say. I could tell you more about the operations and life in that place, but you can get that from Eve. I don't know anything that can help you find him. I don't know any more than you do. Except that this is far from over. He'll stop at nothing to reclaim you both.'

She went to the door, and Ellie saw her out, begging her to stay.

'If you can't reach me on that number, then draw your own conclusions. Goodbye, Ellie, and take good care.'

Maria moved forwards to embrace her, but the younger woman stepped out of reach. She could forgive Maria for being another pawn in the creator's crazy games, but she didn't want to touch her. Maria left the house and shambled down the path.

They talked late into the night. Eve was withdrawn and quiet. Rob seethed with white-hot anger, and no amount of Ellie trying to persuade him that Maria was just another victim of the creator did any good.

Ellie had a dream that she hadn't had since she was a small girl.

She was alone with a strange lady, and her mummy and daddy were a long way away.

'Don't struggle, child. It'll be over soon,' said a cold woman's voice. The lady pushed a massive needle into Ellie's head.

She woke, terrified, and understood the origins of her child-hood monsters.

# Chapter
# Thirty-three

E llie was troubled by the drama of the night before. That morning, they rang their respective solicitors to ask that the sealed envelopes be held over for a further week without being opened. That they could make the telephone call seemed a small victory in a bitter war.

The meeting with Mr Fielding, the consultant, wasn't productive. Recent events had taken a significant toll on Ellie. Though Fielding didn't know the cause, he was surprised that her platelets showed marked deterioration of her condition. He wrote prescriptions, strengthened some of her medications, and changed others to ensure the time she had left would be comfortable. Tests were performed and recorded, bullshit about positive attitudes was spouted, and the meeting ended on a firm handshake.

The damning result of the consultation was there was nothing more medicine could do for Ellie. The disease was advanced, markedly more so than her previous tests had shown. Ellie left the office knowing that it wouldn't be long before she saw her Matty again.

Her next meeting was a happier one. Victor Khazanza was a big soppy form of sympathy. He fussed and fretted, and Ellie had never seen this side of the hard businessman. He had always been kindness itself, but he'd never shown his softer side.

At first, Ellie felt awkward, but Victor was concerned, and she relaxed into his presence as she always had.

He asked about Matt's well-being, and Ellie hated lying to him when she said he was away for a few days with business. Victor served excellent coffee, and they sank into the large leather sofas in his Lakeland offices.

Victor had never talked about his past. She knew he'd been successful in the Czech Republic and made his millions in computing from nothing.

He told her he'd had been a doctor but changed the direction of his career when he discovered his love for technology.

Ellie told Victor about her consultation with Fielding. He was dismayed to hear her platelet count was so low, and the disease had taken a rapid and savage toll on her.

By the time she finished her tale, Ellie was sobbing. The last few weeks had been too much for her, and she longed to tell Victor chapter and verse about everything.

He put a strong arm around her shoulders and gave her his silk handkerchief. He'd researched the disease, but there was nothing new that she hadn't heard and read a hundred times before. She'd made herself an authority on the condition in recent weeks.

'If only things were different,' Victor murmured into her hair, but his words trailed off. Picking up on a grain of hope in his tone, Ellie lifted her head and sniffed in an unladylike fashion.

'If only what was different?'

'Nothing, my dear. I'm sorry, I was thinking aloud. There's a new treatment that's shown some encouraging results, but it's no good for you, and I don't want to give you false hope.'

'What treatment. What is it?' Ellie shrieked. 'I'll try anything.'

'Shush, Ellie, no, I'm sorry, I shouldn't have brought it up. It doesn't apply to you. In certain cases of paediatric Tay-Sachs, where there are siblings with close DNA, some cells from the healthy child can be donated to the sufferer. The healthy cells reproduce and overtake the diseased ones. It's been successful in other countries, but you're an only child, so you wouldn't be eligible for the treatment. You need a sibling donor with a close DNA match.'

Ellie's heart was pounding like a runaway horse. 'What about my Mother? Couldn't we ask her to be a donor?' Ellie almost laughed at the thought of asking her mother to donate her precious life cells, but she was sounding Victor out and didn't want to give anything away.

'No, I'm afraid that's no good. This procedure only works with sibling DNA.'

She had no choice; it was time to face the situation.

'Actually, Victor, I have an identical twin sister.' Ellie smiled and shuffled in her seat.

'You have what? Wow, Ellie, that's fantastic. You can't get any closer match than an identical twin. Wonderful. Why have you never mentioned this before?'

433

'She's very private and has no desire to be seen as an extension of my career.'

'I wish you'd told me this sooner. I might be able to help you, after all, and don't worry about funding. I want you to go private. I'll get you the best doctors, and I'll pay. Even if it's a slim chance, we need to see if this has got legs. From what you've just told me, there's no time to lose and everything to gain.'

Within minutes Victor was a whirlwind of activity. His phone was close to meltdown under the intensity that he used it. He rang a private surgeon and arranged a clinic and theatre time and everything else needed to give the eleventh-hour long-shot a try.

'But Victor, I can't do this now. Things are happening, other stuff, it's impossible.'

'Ellie, you have no choice. If we leave it any longer, you'll be too weak to undergo the treatment. The stronger you are at the time of transplant, the more likely it will succeed. You've already lost precious days. I've booked you in for nine o'clock this evening. Everything else can wait, and every second gained is a second closer to beating this. We'll get you in tonight and at least have the preliminary tests done. That's the beauty of going private.'

He held both of her hands in his and stared into her eyes. 'I know you're frightened, Ellie, but we can beat this. You have just given us the means to cure you. You'll have to hurry; it's a long drive to London. I've arranged transport for you and your sister.' His voice trailed off as he forgot Eve's name.

Ellie felt bamboozled. This was happening too fast. She needed time to think it through. Victor was so good for arranging it. But, he had no idea the danger he was putting himself in. It was

434

somebody else that Ellie was drawing into the net. He'd left her no choice but to tell him everything. She wasn't prepared to risk his life to save hers.

She opened the conversation slowly. The words were cumbersome and difficult to enunciate because she knew that with every one she was pulling Victor deeper into the web of destruction that the creator spun. Once she began, the feeling of release was incredible. Victor was a powerful man with contacts who could help her. Before she finished her story, he was on the phone again, arranging around-the-clock security for them.

For the first time, she felt a glimmer of hope. If anybody knew what to do to go up against this man, it was Victor. She had a fighting chance with him on her side. The words tumbled out so fast that she forgot to breathe and had to stop to inhale.

Victor listened to what she had to say. Occasionally he'd interrupt with a relevant question, but for the most part, he just left Ellie to tell it in her own words. When she got to the part about Matt's death, her voice broke. Victor covered her hand to comfort her and fortify her with his strength.

'So you see,' she ended with a sob. 'You're in danger now, too. I'm so sorry, Victor. He could be listening to everything we say.'

'Well, then he already knows that I've got the balls and the bucks to stand up to him, doesn't he? Don't you worry about me.'

Victor patted the back of her hand as a Grandfather would placate a troubled child.

'I've got some of the best security in the world and can soon bring in extra men. Let's see what this creator dickhead makes of that. I wish you'd come to me sooner. I know a lot of people, including every big-wig software designer, scientist, doctor and groundbreaker going. This guy knows his onions, and I know every mover in the field. From what you've said, I can blow this man out of hiding. We'll find him. I give you my word, I can sort this for you. If you'd come to me immediately, we could have flushed him out by now. The safest place for you and Eve right now is in my friend's private clinic in London, where my security team can keep an eye on you both and see that you don't get into any more mischief.'

She smiled; he said it as though they'd been caught parking without a ticket.

'I'm going to find this man, Ellie, and it's going to take all the efforts of my top muscle to stop me from killing him with my bare hands when I do. I'm going to get him for you and hand him to the proper authorities, where he'll be put away for the rest of his life. Believe me, honey, this guy's not so damned big and clever, and I've got his card marked. I have some ideas of where to start looking and who to talk to.'

Victor was a powerful and influential businessman with the right contacts. With Victor going into battle alongside them and knowing how to fight the creator, Ellie felt more confident that things might come right. For the first time in weeks, she felt calm and safe.

She was terrified at the thought of the procedure. What if Eve wouldn't offer her DNA? And even if she did, it could go horribly wrong. As Eve was only the donor, Victor explained that the danger was limited to the standard risk of anybody undergoing anaesthesia. Other than that, it was perfectly safe.

However, he wasn't as happy about Ellie's health. She was weakened. She assured him that if she could come through the last few days alive and fighting, then no operation was going to get the better of her.

Victor insisted that as soon as the girls were fit enough to be moved, their post-operative care would be transferred to Victor's London home. He said he had rooms that could be turned into a comfortable recovery suite. While they were at the clinic, there would be people posted around the building and two security outside their rooms at all times.

'Victor, I couldn't hear of it. It's bad enough disrupting your time without taking over your home as well. We'll be fine going into the general hospital to recover.'

'I rattle around in that townhouse like a nit on a drum. I would barely know you're there, but I can make sure you're safe. I'd like to see this creator fellow break through my security. Call it a trap to lure him into our domain, if you like. Let's flush the bastard out and bring him to us where we can roll out the big guns. He'd be brought down in seconds. And there's a challenge for you, old chap.' He loomed close, peered into Ellie's eyes, and finished by sticking out his tongue and waving two fingers in front of her face. They both laughed.

'Ellie, I've tossed you along on my enthusiasm, haven't I? Before we go any further with this, I need to point out that what I'm planning is highly unethical. I am no longer a practitioner. I can do this procedure blindfolded, with one hand tied behind my back. It's child's play, but you must understand that I am playing God because you mean so much to me. I've kept my hand in over the years with a few simple procedures and operations in my partner's private clinic, but I need you to understand that I was struck off the medical register a long time ago. So

I'm afraid going into a local hospital for postoperative care was never going to be an option.'

'I'm trusting you with my life. Thank you, Victor.'

To lighten the sombre mood, he said he wouldn't trust her care to the town's hospital anyway.

'Pack of philistines,' he said. 'Might as well entrust you to a troop of trained orangutans. After the Methicillin-Resistant-Staphyloccocus-Aureus epidemic, in the latter half of the second decade, I'd be loath to send a pet worm in there for treatment.'

Victor referred to the superbug epidemic that wiped out half of the British population in two thousand and twenty-eight.

'Victor, you're funny. Why don't you call it MRSA? It's simpler, don't you think?'

'Eleanor,' Victor puffed himself out to immense proportions and stuck his ample nose in the air. 'Any name that damned big should be enunciated with a rounded vowel and a tone of reverence.'

Ellie rang Eve and Rob to tell them the fabulous news.

She didn't mention the operation straight away, only that Victor had offered protection and vowed to beat the creator and put him away for the rest of his life. It was just the boost they needed. For the first time since they'd escaped the institute, they felt that they had an ally with the power to go up against the enemy.

Rob and Eve had a useless day and a fruitless search. They came up with nothing, despite pouring over old records and information for five hours. Rob had tried ringing Maria on the number she'd left. They got the dull ring of a disconnected line. He rang the service provider to find that the number hadn't been operational for months and was registered to a Mr John Smith. Maria didn't trust them as much as she'd made out. While Ellie was with Victor, Rob and Eve reverted to their original plan to find out everything they could about Maria. After a full day's work, that proved to be nothing.

Ellie said she was on her way home and would meet them there in thirty minutes.

Her face was tense when she let herself into the house. She had beaten the others home and put the kettle on, busying herself making sandwiches and coffee for their return. They were only a few minutes behind her and burst through the door full of excited chatter and questions. Ellie did her best to answer them all, but her voice was flat and listless. The operation was the elephant in the room, and she dreaded asking Eve to help her. If she said no, Ellie's chance of survival would be shattered.

'Come on, Elle,' Rob said. 'Something's bothering you. What is it?'

For the second time, Ellie didn't know what to say. But once she started talking, the words fought over each other to get out and be heard.

'So, I suppose what I'm asking is, will you do it, Eve?'

'Don't be bloody ridiculous. Of course, I will.'

The other girl didn't hesitate, and everybody was hugging and shouting and fussing over each other. Jake leapt, frolicked and even let Eve stroke him though he gave her the benefit of the whites of his eyes.

His mistress was pleased by this turn of events. Jake thought they were all jumping and laughing because he was in the room with them, so he jumped and laughed too. It was fun again, and although he didn't trust the Not Ellie, nothing was going to spoil this moment. Only ice cream could make it more perfect.

The girls said their goodbyes to Rob and Jake. There had been a lot of goodbyes. Jake wanted to play and jump some more. He didn't want Ellie to go away again, especially when she was off with Not Ellie. He lowered his ears and whined. The only good thing about the goodbye was that he got to stay with Gail, and Gail loved him almost as much as Ellie did—and she gave him more digestive biscuits. So Jake was a good sport about it.

The drive to London took forever. Both girls were excited and frightened, but Ellie knew that anything that could be done for them would be.

When they got to the Harley Street clinic, they were shown to their room and given gowns to change into. The urgency was palpable, but the doctor was nice and said they were to have the best care on Harley Street.

The next four hours passed in a blur of blood tests and examinations. If the DNA was a close enough match, they'd be going into theatre early the following day.

Victor arrived a few hours later. He'd cancelled his late afternoon appointments to clear his diary and be with them. He sat on each of their beds and put them at ease. The other man, the doctor answered their questions and gave as much information about the procedure as they needed to know.

It was Victor who came back four hours later with the results of the tests. The smile on his face told them that the girls were a perfect match and the operation could go ahead.

His smile lit up the room, and they could tell there was something else going on.

'I have more good news for you.'

'What?' They said and smiled at the perfect voice match.

'I made some calls, did some digging—and we've found the guy at the top of the dodgy operation in Keswick. We're pretty sure it's the same bloke.'

The girls screamed.

'The police are on their way to pick him up for questioning now.'

Ellie tried to stop Victor from talking.

'It's okay, don't worry about the thing in your head. He's going nowhere. If they aren't already in, they have the house surrounded. And while you're asleep tomorrow, we're going to get that thing out of you, Ellie.'

Neither of them slept well that night. Eve's sleep was fitful and tormented by disturbing dreams. Ellie knew being here was too close to institutionalisation for Eve to lie in comfort.

Ellie dozed a couple of times but stared at the blackness for most of the night, knowing that this night might be the last one she ever experienced. But it wasn't the first time she'd stared death in the eye only to meet the dawn breathing that week.

Morning arrived, and they were as ready as they ever would be.

They were wheeled down to the preparation room together and held hands lying on adjoining gurneys. Eve had never faced anaesthesia and was terrified, convinced that once that needle went into her arm, she would never wake up.

As the anaesthetist prepared the mix of drugs to knock them into instant slumber, he introduced himself as Bernard Roberts. He explained that it was his clinic and he would be assisting Mr Khazanza with the procedure. They felt the cold fluid flowing through the cannula, and the world went black seconds later.

Eve was only given light anaesthesia. That, coupled with her healthy metabolism, meant she came around faster than Ellie.

When she woke up, she was back in the pretty twin-bed room allocated to them. The first time she came round, everything was blurry. She drank tea brought by Ellie's friend with the huge hands. Her fingers shook, and she spilt some on the pristine sheet pulled up to her chin. She asked the man not to fuss, but he insisted on bringing a fresh sheet and faffing around getting it perfect. Such a deep voice. Sleep, she thought, must go back to sleep. She was so tired and just wanted to be allowed to go back to darkness—nothing else mattered except the need to sleep. Around a mouthful of what must have been feathers and duck-down, she asked after Ellie. But she was asleep before the man, whose name she couldn't remember, finished speaking.

The next time she woke up might have been five minutes or an hour later, she had no idea, but she was more alert this time.

Ellie. I must find out if Ellie made it through the operation.

She turned her head, expecting it to hurt, but there was no pain, just a peculiar heaviness filling her head with stuffing.

Ellie was in the other bed, her face white against the white pillow. Eve figured she must be all right to be back in the room.

She watched her, counting off the seconds in her head.

Ellie wasn't breathing.

Eve flung the blanket back, her heart pounding in terror and her eyes filling with tears. Later, when she had time to analyse the situation, Eve would know it was at that precise second she knew she loved Ellie. Though Ellie knew it much earlier. Without stopping to think about her own condition, Eve jumped out of bed and landed in a heap on the floor. Her legs didn't belong to her, and the jelly legs she had on loan didn't seem to have any bones in them.

Grabbing the bed for support, she stood up with more respect for the borrowed legs. Once upright, she began to shake, and her legs which formerly consisted of gelatine and water had set in a mould of lead. She had been fed the footage of the first moon-walk, and this was her one small step for woman. She thanked God for the chair between the two beds and sank into it. The world was spinning, and it took several seconds of deep breathing to make it stop. Her body was trembling, and all she could think about was Ellie lying dead beside her.

She leaned over Ellie's bed and took her hand. It was cold, horribly, unnaturally cold. But Ellie's eyelashes fluttered, giving the only indication that she was still alive.

Eve sobbed with relief. Her sister's breathing was so shallow that it didn't raise even the smallest mound in the smooth sheet. Eve pulled Ellie's blanket up from the bottom of the bed to keep her warm.

Eve was cold, too, and it was another great effort to pull the blanket off her own bed to cover herself. And that's how Mr Roberts found them when he looked in a few minutes later.

'All right?' he asked with a smile. He assured Eve that Ellie had come through the operation well. Early indications showed that everything had been an enormous success. Eve thought it was strange that no nurses were fussing around. She had expected pretty nurses in stiff white uniforms, but this was an illegal operation, so maybe they had been given the day off.

It seemed unlikely, but Eve reasoned that she knew little about hospital procedure. That's something she could find out when they were both recovered, and Ellie had her new long life to look forward to. Ellie was going to grow into an old woman, after all.

They could watch all the hospital dramas together, and Ellie would tell her how unrealistic they are.

Ellie didn't wake for some time.

'Hey you,' Eve said. 'Welcome back.'

Ellie managed one word, 'Matty,' before drifting off to sleep again.

Sometime later, Eve was given another cup of tea. Roberts hovered over Ellie, feeding a syringe of medication into her cannula. Eve had a raging thirst that she hadn't noticed until he came in with the tea. She drank like a camel.

Ten minutes later, she felt odd. Her limbs were heavy, and then refused to move at all. Tiredness, unlike any other, came over her, and she couldn't resist it. She heard noises in her head, muted voices but couldn't make out what they were saying.

She knew she'd been drugged.

A woman's voice, so there were nurses. It couldn't be familiar; she didn't know any nurses.

And then she was gone.

# Chapter Thirty-four

The next time Eve woke, she heard a man's voice. He was presumably in a chair across the other side of the room. His voice was soothing, lulling Eve back to sleep, but although the words were coming at her down a long tunnel, she knew them well. They were disturbing words. Wrong words. They had no right being here.

The man was singing.

*'Miss Polly had a dolly who was sick, sick, sick. So she phoned for the doctor to be quick, quick, quick.*

*The doctor came with his bag and hat,*

*And knocked at the door with a rat-a-tat-tat.*

*He looked at the dolly and shook his head.*

*And said, "Miss Polly, put her straight to bed." He wrote a pad for a pill, pill, pill.*

*I'll be back in the morning with my bill, bill, bill.'*

Ellie. Must see Ellie, Eve thought, turning her head to the left, but Ellie's bed was gone. 'No,' she murmured, trying to fight the lethargy sending her back into the world of oblivion. If she went there, she felt sure that she'd never come back. She turned her head to the right, and there was Ellie's bed.

See, silly, she's still here, just on the right this time. Everything was so confusing, and her mind refused to work.

Ellie was holding something in the crook of her arm nearest to Eve. It took a minute for Eve to work out what it was. Empty eye sockets were staring at her. 'No,' Eve said again.

Ellie was holding Eve's doll. Polly's empty eyes seemed to mock her. She gave in to the sleep that rat-a-tat-tatted her brain, gratefully, blissfully, desperately.

The next time Eve woke was the last time. She knew she wasn't at the Harley street clinic anymore.

Was this Victor's house? She remembered his name now. The window was in a different place, but what a window it was.

The outside wall of the room was almost all window. It was a huge stained-glass arch depicting the Madonna and Child. It must have cost a fortune. These days even cathedrals have double glazing. The late afternoon sunlight cast prisms of light across the room and Eve was transfixed with the pretty effect. She could hear lots of street sounds and figured they were still in the city of London. There was heavy traffic and people shouting to each other and clip-clopping as they walked along the street outside.

She had the feeling of height. She felt that she was several floors above street level. The bustle outside reminded Eve of Christmas. She'd never had—or tasted one, but she thought about a Christmas with her sister. Anything to distract her fuzz-bombed mind from what was going on. Christmas was an excellent place to be. This place right here was the worst imaginable—so she chose not to imagine it—if everything would just stay exactly as it was. If nobody moved or said anything—or did anything, it would be alright, and they could stay in this second forever.

She'd never had a Christmas before. They were pleasant thoughts. She wondered what gift she would buy Ellie, and for some reason, a doll came to mind, a pretty porcelain doll.

And her nightmare was back, she'd asked it not to intrude on Christmas, but here it was. And she screamed, fearing that she was back at the institute, alone.

Victor rushed to her side. He assured her that she'd had a horrible dream and patted the back of her hand like a concerned uncle.

She looked at Ellie, the bed was still on the right, but there was no eyeless doll bringing death into the pretty recovery room.

Ellie had lost the drip that made her look poorly while aiding her recovery. She was doing just fine. Ellie was stirring, and Victor went to attend to her.

He stayed for a while, talking in his deep, soothing voice. Ellie's friend was such a nice man. He convinced her that everything was all right. There'd be strawberries in summer and hot chocolate on the cold winter nights. He said that both her anaesthesia-induced nightmare and her waking terror were finally over for good. He told her Ellie would make a full recovery and live until ripe old age—like the strawberries, Eve thought.

He winked at her and whispered that he had a big surprise for them when Ellie was conscious and sitting up.

'Why did you drug me when we were brought here from the clinic?' she asked Victor.

'You weren't drugged, my dear. True, you slept throughout the transfer. It must have been the after-effects of the anaesthesia. What a fanciful thing to say.'

Before he left the room, he helped Eve out of bed, at her insistence, to sit with Ellie. She wanted to be beside her sister when Ellie woke up so she wouldn't be frightened. Victor wouldn't leave until he was sure that both women were warm and comfortable.

Ellie woke as Eve had done, fitfully, coming to several times before the fugue of the anaesthetic evaporated into proper wakefulness. They had snippets of conversation, and Ellie felt drunk and giggled as Eve told her they were dressed in matching nighties. She said that they had twin towelling dressing gowns and slippers too. 'Like two peas in a plonk,' Ellie said and giggled herself back to sleep.

Victor had left juice and tea-making facilities in the room, and Eve shakily set about making a brew for them. She had her back to Ellie and didn't realise that she'd woken up again.

'You're obsessed with making tea,' Ellie said in a voice that sounded weak. If ever a voice could sound weak and thirsty at the same time, then Ellie's certainly did.

'Lovely. Just what the doctor ordered,' Ellie said, as Eve handed her a cup of not-too-full tea. She helped hold the cup for the first few sips to not spill it as Eve had.

Eve told Ellie that Victor had been in and said the operation was a huge success. She was expected to make a full recovery and live to average old age. Ellie was ecstatic but cried, and Eve said she didn't think she could ever be so happy for another human being. She'd only ever had self, and all she'd known was preservation. Eve wanted Ellie to sleep, but they were far too excited. They talked about the creator, but he wasn't a threat since Victor had taken control. The police had the monster in custody, and it was his turn to live the prison life.

'There's just one thing that's been playing on my mind a bit,' Ellie said.

'What's that?' Eve grinned.

'When I told Victor I had a twin sister, he never asked how that had come about. Doesn't that seem strange to you?'

'But you said you told him everything.'

'Yes, I did, but that was later. When I first told him about you, he didn't bat an eyelid. It was as if,' Ellie stumbled on her words. 'Almost as if....'

'Almost as if I already knew?' Victor breezed into the room with a grotesque smile on his face. They looked at the gift he'd brought them.

And at that moment—they knew.

# Chapter Thirty-five

V ictor held the eyeless doll out to the girls.

'So my dollies are awake, and my, don't you just look the picture of health. Look who I've brought to see you.' He threw the doll to Eve, and she recoiled from it as though it was a cobra spitting venom. It landed on Ellie's bed. She was weak but found the strength to throw the doll from her. It landed on the floor with a thump.

For a few seconds, neither of them said anything. The shock was too immense. Victor didn't speak, either. He stood with his arms spread wide, an enormous smile on his face, and insanity in his eyes.

Ellie was the first to break the silence. 'Victor, it can't be you. You're my friend.'

'I know.' Chuckling, he said, 'Delicious, isn't it? It's worked out beautifully. You came to me like a child to a paedophile with sweeties. You really are too trusting, you know, Eleanor, you silly goose. You made it far too easy for us, darling. We do so like a tougher game. I'm disappointed in you.'

'It's been you all along? You've been trying to kill us all this time?'

'Don't be ridiculous. Of course, I wasn't trying to kill you. If I'd wanted that, you'd already be dead, my dear.'

Ellie knew what was in front of her, but her mind couldn't come to terms with it. Victor was one of her oldest and dearest friends.

'However, you're correct about my genius. Of course, it was me, poppet. Why do you think I set you up and backed you when you wanted to author? Surely you don't believe that your writing's that good. You've been so gullible right from the beginning. You never once asked why I came to you with my stupid story about you winning our talent scouting competition. Even if there'd been one, you never entered it—you idiot. With an ego that size, you're Daddy's little girl, all right. Now Eve—my lovely, lovely Eve—she's my spitfire doll. They say an apple never falls far from the tree, don't they? But Ellie, my darling, you play a tiresomely easy game. You always have.'

'You're my father?' Ellie choked on the words. The fusion of Genesis and Victor was complete in her head.

'Good God, no,' the smile left his face, and his voice rose in anger. 'I am nobody's father. I didn't merely conceive you. Any insipid man could do that. I created you. Don't you see how unique you are? You are my creation. Now please, dollies, don't anger me. Not today of all days. Today is special because we're together for the first time. I went to such a lot of trouble getting the use of the clinic again. That stupid little man thought I'd thrown all that money at him to set up out of the goodness of my heart—severance pay, we called it. But, nothing comes free in this life, my darlings. I'm hurt that he couldn't get us out of his clinic fast enough. Now, let's just enjoy our time together, shall we? Did Eve tell you I have a big surprise for you both, Ellie?'

He laughed.

His baritone vocal chords and immense frame were high-pitched and out of sync. It was the laugh of a megalomaniac high on victory.

Eve had moved closer to Ellie's bed, and they had their arms around each other and stared at victor with wide, frightened eyes.

'Oh, come now, come. Humour me just a little. You want to know what your surprise is, don't you? Of course, you do.'

His eyes danced with merriment as he stared at his captives.

'Seeing as you've been such well-behaved dollies, I'm going to tell you. Ellie, by the end of the week,' he clapped his hands together in glee, 'You'll be dead.'

'And do you know whose going to kill you? Oh no, not I, my dear. No, not I.' He pointed his finger at Eve in accusation. 'She is.'

Eve spoke for the first time. 'I'll never do it, never. You're going to kill us anyway, so we won't play your fucked up mind games. Do you think it will be a good sport to make me kill Ellie? Well, I'm not going to. So stick that up your arse and smoke it till the sun don't shine.'

'Such sisterly love. Such devotion, but never say never, my precious little freak because you already have killed her.'

He threw his head back and laughed his insane laugh. This time he laughed so hard that tears rolled down his cheeks. He grabbed his stomach and bent over.

Eve moved towards him while he was distracted, but Ellie put a hand out to stop her.

452

'No, Eve, he's too strong. What do you mean by that, Victor? That she's already killed me.'

He straightened, and his laughter died as quickly as it came. He spat his next words in a fury, and the girls shrank against the end of the bed in terror. 'Don't call me that. Don't you dare call me that. I am The Creator. The creator, do you hear?' With each of the last four words, he had taken a step towards them, his face red with temper.

They nodded to pacify him. He was out of breath from his outburst and took a few seconds to regain composure. When he spoke, his voice was calm and soothing, the voice of a benevolent doctor talking to his patient.

'You see, Ellie, when I explained this morning's procedure to you, I only told a half-truth. Eve's DNA will indeed kill off all the diseased cells. But I didn't tell you that it will also kill all the healthy ones. You are dying at the rate of a million cells a minute, and your dear, lovely sister is the one who killed you.'

Eve dropped her head into her hands and cried. 'I'm sorry, Ellie, I'm so damned sorry.'

'Shush,' Ellie comforted her. 'You didn't do this. He did. Listen to me,' she pulled Eve's head up to look at her. 'When I'm gone, don't you ever regret what you did. I was dying anyway. All you did was learn how to love. I love you too, Eve, and don't you dare ever feel sorry for that.'

Victor clapped his hands. 'Very touching, girls. I'll remember this poignant moment forever, but you've made one big mistake, Ellie. You said, "When you're gone," assuming that Eve will be around. She won't be, dear. Don't worry. You aren't the only one about to die, but Eve has a vital job to do first. Let me tell you the best bit.'

'This won't work, you know,' Eve said. 'You've left too many loose ends this time. Rob knows where we are. He'll come looking for us.'

'Details, my dear. Small, irrelevant details that are going to be dealt with. But as I said, let me tell you the best bit.'

Victor lost control and screamed at the girls. They needed time to think, and the longer he ranted, the more chance they had of finding a way out of this. Ellie squeezed Eve's hand in a silent warning not to rile him.

'Don't interrupt me again, dollies. This is the moment I've been waiting for, for such a long time. You see, I haven't told you why Eve's cells will kill you, Ellie. When I said that Eve was a close match, I lied. She was a perfect match, as I had known all along. Perfect, can you see what I'm saying? No? Well, let me spell it out for you. You can't return function cells into the brain of the original host. It's an impossible procedure, one I made up. It can't be done. Now, do you see? It's obvious you don't. You really are a pair of dim dollies, aren't you?'

He paced up and down, letting what he said sink in. He had a new role. He was the college professor, imparting knowledge onto dullard students. He tapped his bottom lip as he paced until he was ready to continue his lecture.

'Think of your mother, Eve. Who is your mother?' Eve stared at him, too horrified and scared to open her mouth.

'Answer me, Eve. Who is your mother?' Ellie answered for her, trying to placate him and keep his temper at bay.

'Maria,' she said in a small but clear voice.

'Wrong.' He lurched towards the end of Ellie's bed, loomed forward, and plonked his hands on either side of her feet. Ellie winced, and both girls cowered away from him.

454

'Daughter, murderer. Murderer, daughter. One and the same. You are Eve's mother, Ellie. You are. You were never twins at all.'

'But that's lunacy. You're mad. It doesn't make sense.'

'Ah, but it does, my dear Ellie. You see, you were my first ovum, but you were just like any other in vitro embryo. But here's where my genius comes in, from Ellie begat Eve. Eve is my true first woman. She was born of you, Ellie, not a twin at all, but a clone.

Before they could absorb what he said, he was talking again.

'And Eve, my wonderful first-ever clone, do you really think you had it so hard? You didn't, you know, because it was an experiment of five parts. Two of the later ones didn't fare well and died very quickly. But first, there was Ellie.' He raised one finger. 'She was to be brought up with a charmed life, or if not charmed, then certainly in the stratosphere of normal. You, my dear Eve, were the middle ranker.' He raised a second finger. 'You were brought up and fed an existence of your alpha clone's life. But then there was Erika. My darling, beautiful baby girl Erica. We made her later, from Eve.' He said it matter-of-factly, as though he was talking about making a rice pudding. He raised a third finger and waggled it excitedly at the girls. 'My poor baby-clone, Erika. She led a similar life to you, Eve. She lived in an identical cell not a hundred yards from yours. But she lived void of all stimulation. Her room was soundproofed. Otherwise, you would have heard her screaming like an animal in the night.'

Both the girls gasped and felt sad for the other little girl who suffered at the hands of this monster.

'She never walked or talked, and she enjoyed playing in her own filth. Erika never heard another human voice nor saw anything other than the white walls of her cell.

We couldn't let her loose on the world, so she had the blessed release of being burned to death when we set the fire. It was a spectacular execution.'

'How could you do that? What kind of man are you?' Ellie asked, horrified. They couldn't take in the enormity of what he was telling them about themselves, never mind come to terms with the fact that there was another one just like them—the third sister.

'I'm a genius, my dear, that's how. Oh, I wanted to show my beautiful girls to the world. But it isn't yet ready to deal with a man such as I. The west is still backward and retarded. But, you see, we've grown tired of you now. If you hadn't been sick, Ellie, the game might have gone on longer, but you're no fun anymore. That really is too bad. Our possibilities have run dry, and it's time to part company with you both. But first, you have to know the very best bit of all.

'We're going to make a brand new batch of dollies tonight. You came from Ellie, Eve, so they will come from you. The room is ready for us. Are you excited, my very special dolly?'

'What new dollies? What are you talking about?' Eve asked. 'You keep saying we? Who's we?' Nothing seemed unrealistic, and if he said that he'd come from Mars on a camel, it wouldn't have been out of place in this conversation.

'Eve, Eve, Eve, don't be even more stupid than you've already shown yourself to be. You're going to be the donor for our new clones.'

Victor opened his mouth to say more, but his words were drowned by a crackle of static.

'The date is twenty-ninth November, twenty forty-six. The time is twenty fifty-one.'

The voice was distorted, as the voices always had been, by a voice distortion programme.

'It's good to see you again so soon, my frightened little rabbits. Don't look so puzzled. Have you forgotten me already?'

The voice became babyish and mocking.

'Oh, I'm so sorry. Please forgive me before I die. I love you so much.' The cruel laugh piped into the room was more sinister from the distortion.

It didn't take long for them to realise that the female voice belonged to Maria, but the tone was different from the last time they'd heard her. This Maria had a voice as hard as a bucket of iron and assured as a queen. Eve recognised it as the female voice she had heard all those years in the cell. It was a voice devoid of inflection or accent. This was a woman incapable of human emotions.

It was Victor's reaction that was most surprising. His eyes shone bright, and his face was one part fear to two parts rapt attention and wheedling subservience. The hard man of moments before turned from smug bully to a smarmy little boy in the space of a second.

'Did I do well, Mother? Did I?'

In any other circumstance, this bizarre turnabout would have been hilarious, but in this time and place, it made the scenario more sinister and depraved.

Ellie couldn't believe this snivelling maniac was Victor, her friend, and a man that had taken on a father-figure role after she lost her dad. He'd attended book awards with her and even did the eulogy at her father's funeral.

'Mummy is proud of you, my little boy. I couldn't ask for a better little boy. What a good boy you are. You have served me

457

well. Now take my other dolly to the cell and let the re-cloning commence.'

Eve eyed the door. At exactly the right moment, Ellie squeezed her hand once and then let go of it so that when Eve moved, Ellie wouldn't hamper her for even a split second. This was the only chance they would get, and they knew there was no time for goodbyes.

Despite his bulk, Victor was surprisingly quick on his feet. He was like lightning, and while the good life had turned most of his muscle to fat, he was no stranger to the boxing ring. Neither of them expected the speed or brutality of the man. They expected him to try and block Eve's way, and she was ready to side-swerve him to escape. But they never saw the massive fist cut through the air. His fist crashed into Eve's face with a sickening crush of breaking bone. Her head whiplashed back, and a spurt of blood splattered the wall nearest her head. She was out cold when she hit the floor.

'Silly girl,' Victor said calmly. 'I'll have to get the decorators in again.'

Ellie was sickened by the unnecessary violence of the bene-factor she had always called her friend. This man-mountain had cuddled her while she'd cried and seemed the gentlest man on earth.

She turned her face to the blank wall. She didn't care what was going to happen to her anymore.

Victor walked to the wall Ellie was facing and removed a moulding square. He pressed a couple of buttons. Before her eyes, the wall came to life. Ellie wanted to turn away, but she couldn't.

This, the greatest horror of all, was morbidly fascinating. The screen showed a little girl, maybe nine or ten years old, sitting on a bed clutching an eyeless doll to her chest. She was rocking and murmuring to herself. The words weren't clear enough to be heard, but the tone of the child's voice was menacing. The little girl also watched a projection on a similar wall. This one depicted another female child enjoying a day at the circus with her parents.

Ellie wasn't even aware that she was crying.

'Now then, my dearest Eleanor,' Victor said. 'I trust you will not be bored with the in-house entertainment. I may be gone for some while. I know you're weak, dear, but I'm sure you'll understand my precaution of locking the door on my way out. We wouldn't want you getting any silly ideas now, would we? We'll be in the cellar should you need us, dear, but don't call. Nobody can hear you. It's a pity you were so dull, Ellie. It's been a long and special relationship. I'll be sorry to see you go.'

His words were sickly sweet. She wanted to shoot back at him with something venomous and nasty, but the fight had been forced out of her. She never moved a muscle as she heard Victor pick Eve up off the floor and carry her out of the room.

Ellie knew she'd never see the woman she'd come to love again, and that, on top of the loss of Matty, caused her heart to break. She heard the locking mechanism click and felt nothing.

Eleanor Erikson accepted her death and was ready to shake it by the hand. The only thing she wanted now was that somehow Eve would survive this nightmare. They'd agreed that if Eve survived after Ellie's death, she would walk into the life that was all set up for her.

Ellie smiled at the tragic little girl on the screen, and a plan formed in her mind. She closed her eyes to pray for the strength to see it through.

# Chapter Thirty-six

R ob had been trying to get hold of Victor all morning. The girls were scheduled for the operation at eight o'clock, and it was after twelve. He trusted Victor to keep the girls safe. But he wasn't answering the number Ellie left him. Something was wrong. Rob wondered if Victor's security wasn't as secure as he thought. God forbid the creator had broken through their defences.

Rob couldn't concentrate on work. He cancelled meetings for the rest of the day and drove to London to find out what was happening.

When he got out of the taxi at Victor Khazanza's townhouse, it was six o'clock. He'd left his car on the outskirts of town. It was easier to travel the city via the good old London cab. Khazanza was a celebrity, and when he'd explained the situation, it hadn't been difficult to track down his London address through his agent contracts.

The house was an impressive five-storey limestone on a busy Knightsbridge street. Its focal point was the enormous stained glass window on the upper floor. Rob knocked for five minutes but didn't get a reply.

No lights burned anywhere in the front of the house, and only a strange flickering glow came from the stained window. He tried shouting, but his voice was lost in traffic noise. He needed time to think and somewhere quiet to call Victor again. He hadn't thought through what would happen if he got to London and there was nobody home. The girls should be there by now, lying in bed, drinking hot sweet tea and recovering after their ordeal. Maybe something had gone wrong, and they were still at the clinic. Whatever was happening, Rob felt it wasn't good.

There was a small coffee shop across the street. The waitresses were clearing tables, and there didn't seem to be many people still sitting. It looked as though they were ready to close. Rob decided to try and get a coffee while he thought his predicament through.

The girl behind the counter eyed him balefully as he walked in the door. She sighed in defeat and asked what he'd like in a bored monotone.

Rob ordered coffee and sat at the furthest table from the smattering of other customers. He had a good view of the house from here and would see if anybody came home while he was in the cafe. He thumbed in Victor's number. He'd rung it so many times that he knew it by heart. Even in the café, the noise from the street was a disturbance. Rob had to turn his body away from the window and cover his ear with one hand.

It didn't stop him hearing the scream of car brakes, though—or—seconds later—the far worse screaming of terrified people.

He turned in his seat to see people running towards something white, lying in a heap on the pavement. A rainbow of small pieces of the shattered stained glass window littered in a cascade from the top floor onto the street. The last rays of the setting sun caused prisms of colour to light the muted scene.

Rob glanced up and saw the jagged remains of the broken Madonna in the desecrated window frame. A deep crowd formed, obscuring the bundle from view.

Rob was in motion. His knees caught under the table as he stood, sending the carpentry, and its contents, flying. The vinegar bottle bounced three times. By the third bounce, Rob was out of the café and running down the street with his jacket flying behind him. He pushed through the throng, manners forgotten. He knew what lay on the cold pavement of a Knightsbridge street, but he had to see it for himself to believe.

He didn't know one person could leave such a big pool of blood. It was glutinous and flowing in a thick stream from the pavement into the gutter. Somebody was screaming, a woman, a large woman on the other side of the street.

Little pieces of the broken glass partially covered the twin like a pretty blanket. She was lying on her back, but he could still see the mess that used to be the back of her head. Her eyes were wide and staring. The overweight woman couldn't see the carnage he could, but she wouldn't stop screaming. Damn her. He wanted to punch her in the face.

He didn't know which one it was.

'Who are you?' he said aloud. 'Dear God, which one are you? Don't let it be Ellie. Oh God, please don't let it be Ellie.'

She was clutching a doll, a doll with no eyes. It was the same toy that had mocked him at the institute. Sirens were rounding the corner. Ambulance? Police? There would be both. Lots of police? What Rob needed more than anything in the world was a truckload of SAS teams in full riot gear. But the one patrol car was a start.

Rob had a story to tell, and somehow he had to convince the two officers that the creator had gained access to Victor's house and the other twin was still in there. A thought occurred to him that was so obvious, yet none of them had considered it for a second. What if Victor was behind this from the start? If Victor was the creator, Victor Khazanza was a megalomaniac murderer. Either way, it would be easier to get the cops' attention if he screamed the theory from the rooftops than trying to convince them of nameless other people being at fault. If he was wrong, he'd sincerely apologise to Victor later. But there was that niggling hunch implanted in his mind, and despite Victor being Ellie's oldest friend, it wouldn't go away. If one of the girls had been thrown from a top-floor window to her death, what must the other one be going through? What Rob needed most was manpower— manpower with big fucking guns.

# Chapter Thirty-seven

S he came around without that moment of blessed amnesia when you wake up. Instantly, she was aware of a mouthful of blood and a head full of agony. She tried to put her hand to her head, but she was shackled, hands and feet, to a table.

She looked down and saw her feet were fastened with leather bands into stirrups, but this was no operating table. Ropes and pulleys were attached to the ceiling above the central contraption she was bound to. She was in some sort of dungeon.

The walls were hung with strange apparatus. One thing looked like a medieval rack used for stretching people. Clamps, chains and whips hung around the room. There were suits of leather and chain clothing. Boots with impossibly high heels stood beside leather pants with a giant phallus attached to the front. Rubber headgear and strange masks, with tubes coming off them, grinned beside paddles and bizarre sex aids.

It didn't even seem out of place that this was where she'd be abused under the false guise of medicine. Nothing surprised her anymore.

Victor was waiting for her to regain consciousness. He wanted to do the procedure with her wide awake and aware of what was happening. He explained what he was doing and was back in character as the pleasant professor conducting a lecture.

'We are so excited about our new batch of super-dollies. You are fortunate to be chosen to enter this first phase of stage three with us. You should be honoured and humbled to be following in the footsteps of Mother Genesis. She has done you many great services. She bore you and gave you life. It's fitting that you're here because she gave birth to you in this very room. Up there.'

He pointed to eight enormous meat hooks suspended on chains and springs from the ceiling. Their purpose was obvious: they were designed to hold a person supported in mid-air.

'Can you imagine the exquisite pain she endured while having you? And she never uttered a word nor screamed out in agony. Her moans were of sheer ecstasy. She still bears the scars from the hooks, and sometimes, when I've been very good, she lets me open them with razor blades, and I lick her wounds of creation in reverence. Do you understand what an honour that is?'

Victor smiled a lunatic grimace, and she turned her face away in disgust.

'You could never tolerate the pain that the great woman did, so we'll use more conventional means for you. Mere bonds to hold you fast will suffice unless, of course, you're a naughty girl, and then we'll see if you have the stamina of your surrogate mother.'

The threat was enough to still her from struggling against her binds. Victor and Maria were a warped and intertwined mix of scientist and sexual deviant.

'We have already harvested the DNA. In fact, we have enough of your DNA to make a thousand babies, but today, you are going to have the supreme honour of being impregnated with five babies that are both mother and fatherless. These babies are pure—you. We took cells, you see, while you were at the institute, froze them and have nurtured them for this moment. We watched them day and night, and at the exact moment when the stem cells were about to turn into function cells, we separated them. For every stem cell, we had two. Then they would replicate individually until they metamorphosed into function cells. With basic nurturing, they'd multiply and divide in the normal way to produce the embryo. This fusion process is greatly simplified, so you can understand it. However, you must see the momentous piece of history you are making? For the second time, you are being cloned. Five new people who are not merely like you but are, in fact, simply, you.'

She was horrified and tried to turn her face away, but he forced her to look at him with a painful grip that made her cry out.

'By the way, dear, feel free to scream all you like. It shouldn't hurt too much. We are, of course, making a film for posterity, so you can make it as dramatic as you wish. It all adds to the drama. This room is soundproof, so we are private and will be undisturbed. Apart from the aesthetic, there was no point in gagging you—and besides, I'm so looking forward to hearing you beg, so give it your best shot.'

He brought a trolley of instruments to the table and put on gloves and gown. He was the mad scientist in this role and thrived in his terrifying chamber of horrors. Even Mary Shelley would be impressed.

Eve closed her eyes and prayed in earnest that she would die soon.

The door flew open, and Maria came in.

'Mistress,' Victor gushed in delight. 'It's Mother Genesis. Give praise for Mother Genesis, dear.'

This was Maria, all right, but she looked very different. Her greying hair had been dyed raven black. Her eyes glinted cold and hard. There was no weakness or mercy in them, just an ice-mania that would brook no pleading.

She wore high heels and a beautifully cut grey business suit. She wore false padding for her role as scared and downtrodden Maria. Now she was forty pounds lighter. She wore nothing under the man's suit, tailored to her measurements and perfectly hung. Her nipples were visible under the lapels, and her waist was trim. Her legs were long, and her attitude powerful. This was a far cry from the low-grade woman, driven to drink, of the night before.

After twenty-seven years, Eve was face to face with the actual creator, the force behind the nightmare. Maria was the true face of evil that brought the madness about.

Victor Khazanza was the knowledge and the money, but he was nothing. He was a stupid man who did as he was told. Maria Kilcher was the real force and the greater madness. It was her dream. They were her dollies, and it was her evil that the twin, bound to the table, was part of.

'Let the cloning begin,' Maria announced from a mouth painted with perfectly applied crimson lipstick. 'Commence phase three.'

The Police and ambulance arrived simultaneously. Rob pushed through more people to get to the marked police car, and in his distress, he ran into the road before the car stopped. He planted his hands on the bonnet and ran backwards as the car finished its parking. He was shouting at the officers inside to hurry up. Rob knew he was behaving like a madman. They might not believe him, but could they take the risk that he was a delusional idiot? What if there was another girl up there, at this moment fighting for her life, in the home of a crazed psychopath? They couldn't refuse to act and be held to account later. He had to make them understand.

'Thank God you're here,' he yelled before they were out of the car. 'We've got to get in there. Please hurry, for God's sake, hurry. There's another one, another girl, her twin. Please, get in the house and stop him before he kills her, too. He calls himself the creator. He's insane. It's a crazy game to him.' Rob was sobbing. The policeman nearest him put his hand on Rob's shoulder to calm him. The other joined the paramedics with the dead woman.

'Take it easy, sir. You aren't making any sense. Let's just start at the beginning and see what's going on, eh? Now, do you know the lady who has fallen?' The policeman led Rob through the crowd to get a good look at the body. It looked like a lover's tiff or a bloody messy suicide even to Rob.

'She hasn't fallen, officer. She's been murdered. Victor Khazanza has murdered her.' Rob felt guilty that he might yet be condemning an innocent man, but his instinct made him think it was true. Khazanza was a household name. This could be the most significant thing the young officer had ever dealt with.

'That's a serious accusation, sir. Before we bandy things like that about, I think we'd better get some facts.' Rob interrupted him mid-lecture.

'There's no time for facts. If we don't get up there and stop him, right now, Khazanza is going to kill her twin sister. It may already be too late. It's the doll you see, the doll. As soon as I saw it, I knew it was him. Please officer, please do something, and for the love of God, do it now.'

Officer Gaskell hadn't a clue what this nutter was on about. He'd heard about people accusing celebrities of all kinds of stuff—it was a thing. And the next thing you knew, the superstar went out and got a bullet in his head. Look at John Lennon. It happened to him. Gaskell didn't like it at all.

'Please, sir, I need you to sit in the car for a few minutes, and I'll radio my superior to come and talk to you?'

'No, I will not sit in the bloody car. You're not listening to me. There's another girl, identical to this one, up in that room. If that crazy bastard hasn't already killed her, he's going to. Are you prepared to take the responsibility of another girl's death, officer?' What if there was another girl up there about to drop from the window, like a dying swan? What then? Gaskell felt out of his depth and needed backup to deal with this.

'Listen, sir, let me put it another way. I'm not asking you. I'm telling you to just sit in the car while I get some help here, and then we can do something. If you don't comply with my request, quietly, I'm going to have to arrest you, and you'll be taken to the station. So the best way of helping this other woman is to do as you're told.'

Rob had little choice but to get in the back of the car. At least the twerp was calling in more police.

Gaskell walked around his car and thumbed the phonacom. 'Ma'am, I think you'd better get down here. We've got one woman dead and some nutcase saying there's another one in the house about to be murdered. Get this though, Ma'am, he says Victor Khazanza is the murderer. It looks like suicide to me, Ma'am, but I don't like the look of this fella. Requesting back up.'

The ambulance was taking the body away. Rob ran from the police car to be with her. He kissed the back of her hand. In his heart of hearts, he thought it was Ellie, but he couldn't be sure. His goodbye was brief. He knew that whichever twin it was, she'd want him to do everything he could to save the other.

With every ounce of willpower, he wished that he was wrong, and it was Eve lying broken in the back of an ambulance and not Ellie. He took his last ever look at the body.

He still didn't know.

Five minutes later, another six officers arrived. A woman in street clothes talked to the PCs before coming over to Rob.

Seven precious minutes had passed while Rob sat, useless and impotent, in the back of the car. The other officers stood around the van doing nothing.

'Hello, sir, I'm Chief Inspector Woodburn. My officer tells me you think there's a hostage situation in the house. Now, can you tell me your name, please?'

Rob couldn't believe she was wasting time taking his details.

'Listen, love, I don't think anything. I know he's holding her hostage. She's probably already dead. Please, please, just get in and stop the bastard, or let me in, and I'll do it for you.' Rob was sobbing.

'You aren't helping the situation, sir. We can only do our job efficiently with calm people. Officers are trying to gain entry now. I know this is very distressing for you, but there's a way of doing these things. I understand that it must seem longwinded to you, but you have to understand that I can't send my men in until we have a clear picture of what's going on. At the moment, nobody is answering the door, and we have to proceed legally and cautiously. My officers are highly trained and know what they're doing. Now, you say there are two women? Twins, I think you said.'

Rob took a deep breath. He realised he was only holding things up by getting annoyed and shouting. For the second time, though this time more calmly, he told his story. Briefly, he explained about Eve and the institute and Matt's death. He explained that the woman was either already dead or in grave danger at the hands of the entrepreneur Mr Victor Khazanza.

Nine minutes.

Tears coursed down his face, more through sheer frustration that nothing was being done than grief over the dead woman. That emotion would take over later.

'And you never reported this murder?'

'No.'

And so it went on. Fifteen minutes had elapsed since Rob had been forced into the back of the police car. Finally, CI Woodburn had enough information to take action. She left Rob in the car and assembled her officers. Rob had sat doing nothing long enough and went over to the van.

When the police had been briefed and given their orders, Chief Inspector Woodburn tried to stop Rob from going in. Rob argued that they'd need him. He knew what was happening. CI Woodburn said that if this bloke was speaking even ten per cent truth, they were walking into the biggest case of their career. She didn't want to go in blind. She agreed to let him go with them but ordered him to stay in the background.

They stormed what appeared to be an empty building. One officer was sent to guard each entrance in case anybody made a run for it. Two more were dispatched to search the house from the ground floor up, and CI Woodburn, Rob and another officer made for the top floor bedroom with the broken window.

Following their training to the letter, the search officers systematically scoured every room of the house. Each officer had their handgun drawn, and they wore bullet-proof clothing and face shields. CI Woodburn had donned trousers, a Teflon vest and had a riot shield.

She threw a vest to Rob before they pounded up the stairs, ordering him to put it on. The two original officers were left outside to clear the street and get traffic flowing again. Rob was impatient. He wanted to get to the room where the woman had fallen. Although they moved up each flight quickly, their approach was cautious, and Rob was getting fed up with their damned training procedures. He nearly got himself thrown out of the house and was barked at to stay back and do as he was told, or he was out.

They got to the top floor room, and the officer behind Woodburn kicked the locked door open.

The room was empty.

Two unmade beds stood together. The right-hand bed had a drip frame standing next to it. By the side of the bed, and written on the wall in blood, was the single word, Dungeon. But it was the remains of the window that drew Rob's gaze. The jagged shards of glass cast dappled shadows onto the wall, leading his eye to even worse horror.

A projector was playing onto the same wall. A little girl rocked on a bed and watched an identical girl playing from another recording.

It seemed that the unlikely rambles of this man were true. Woodburn ordered more Scenes of Crime teams to be on standby outside the house to collate the evidence for a conviction. Rob couldn't tear his eyes away from the tragic scene paying out on the wall.

'Jesus Christ,' said Woodburn, watching the disturbed little girl staring at the screen and talking to the hideous doll with no eyes.

'She gouged the eyes out herself so that Polly—that's the doll—wouldn't have to watch Ellie's life too,' said Rob. He needed to tell this woman so much to make her understand, yet he was talking about a fucking doll.

'Oh dear God, where is she? Where's Ellie? Please let her be alive.'

'So you think it's Miss Eve Erikson who came through the window? You couldn't be sure which one it was before.'

'Still not sure,' Rob said. 'I'm just hoping, that's all, just hoping. Isn't that unforgivable, Inspector, wanting one woman's life to be saved, even at the slaying of another?' Rob shook his head and wanted to move somewhere, do something, find Khazanza, but he just stood looking at the young Eve on the screen. His heart broke for her.

Woodburn's phonacom crackled to life. 'Woodburn,' she barked into it, exchanging a look with Rob.

'Think you'd better come and see this, Ma'am,' the officer said. 'Now,' he shouted more urgently.

'Oh Christ, no, this is it. She's dead, isn't she?' Rob said. Woodburn didn't answer him; she was already out of the door and running along the corridor to the stairs.

'What we got, Josh?' she asked the officer at the bottom of the stairs.

'I couldn't begin to tell you, Ma'am,' he said. 'You've got to see this for yourself.' He led them into a room next door to the lounge.

'This is similar to the operations room at the institute,' Rob said, scanning the equipment. He was about to tell them more, but the words never left his lips as he saw the unbelievable nightmare being recorded from another place.

A camera relayed the action in the dungeon room and played it live on the plasma screen. Victor and Maria were beside the leather contraption that the woman was strapped to. The officers piled into the control room and gathered around the screen.

'She's alive,' Rob sobbed, bursting into tears again. 'Thank you, God, she's alive, and I swear it's the truth, at this moment, I don't care which of them it is. I'm just so glad that she's not dead, too.' He sank into a chair. 'Please stop him before he kills her. You've got to get in there.' He put his head in his hands, crying bitterly.

While Rob was talking, the policemen behind Woodburn saw what was on the screen.

'Fucking hell, look at the size of the dick in those rubber pants. This is fucking mental.'

Woodburn glared at the officer. She indicated Rob with her head and warned the officer to conduct himself properly. 'Carney, watch your filthy mouth, or you'll find yourself on report,' she barked at him.

He hung his head and blushed. 'Sorry, Ma'am, I just got carried away. I've never seen anything like this. Sorry, sir.' Rob didn't even look up.

While the police summed up the situation in the dungeon, Rob pulled himself together.

'Who's the other woman?' asked one of the police.

Rob dragged his eyes from the twin tied to the bed and noticed her. 'My God, he's got Maria, too. She looks different, but that's her. That's the woman I was telling you about who worked with him and helped him with the experiment. He's been threatening to kill her. She's been on the run. He's got her, too.'

The surviving twin's voice cut into the room, pleading for her life. 'Please, let us go. You've done all you can do to us. This crazy scheme is madness. You'll never get away with it. Can't you see that? Just let us go.'

Woodburn saw a microphone on the workstation. She flung her head around to the officers. 'How the hell do you work this thing? Get it working for me and get on the com for the negotiator.' One officer turned on the mic and explained how to use it while the other called to ask for the hostage negotiator. Woodburn was about to speak into the microphone when Rob grabbed it from her.

'Please, let me, I know this guy, I know what makes him tick.'

Woodburn still had her hand on the mic, and they tussled with it. 'Listen, I didn't even want you in here. I'm in charge of this investigation. We're trained to deal with this kind of situation, so please, just let us get on with our job, sir.' I warned you at the beginning to stay back.

Rob put his other hand over the top of the mic to stop her from taking it. 'This might be your case, but I know this man. I can rattle him. He'll talk to me. He'll want to gloat. Think about it, if he doesn't know you're here, I can buy some time. While I get him talking and keep his filthy hands off her, you can have the negotiator here and find a way to stop the murdering bastard.' Woodburn hesitated and wasted precious seconds.

'Okay, but don't rile him. One wrong word, and we could be dealing with two dead bodies, not one. Our negotiator is a highly trained psychologist, and he'll be here any minute. Just keep him talking until then. And if I say cut, you stop immediately. Understand? Remember, she's relying on you.'

'You think I don't know that?'

Woodburn was about to relinquish the mic to Rob when the officer called Carney interrupted. 'Ma'am, if they get panicked, they might escape before we can get to them.'

'Good point. Right, you and Todd, round up Watson and Jones. Find the door to that place. We'll stand by here. Do not. Repeat. Do not enter until I give the word. Understood?'

'Ma'am,' the two men said.

While Woodburn and Rob listened to what was happening in the dungeon without doing anything about it, Carney and Dave Todd searched for the entrance. They found the other two men, and the two pairs separated to search the house in finer detail. More back up, and the negotiator arrived.

Paul Shannon was given directions to the control room, and the rest of the squad joined the search. They decided to go back to the lounge and search drawers and cupboards for any clues. They'd scoured the cellar, but it turned out to be predictable storage rooms and an impressive wine cellar.

More than five minutes had passed, and they were no nearer to finding the dungeon entrance. They concluded that maybe it wasn't part of this house, and the recording was delivered from somewhere else. They had to get an address for that dungeon and fast. They ransacked the lounge and came up with nothing.

Mike Watson leaned on the wall to catch his breath and almost landed in a heap on the floor. The wall hadn't disappeared exactly. It just wasn't there anymore.

'Mike, what the hell?'

Like the images of the little girl projected on the wall upstairs, this was a clever projection. There was a film running showing the continuation of a wall. It was high tech stuff. They were in a short corridor with a metal door at the end. If ever the projector malfunctioned, all visitors would see was the corridor. The rest of the time, the door was hidden by the film of a piece of wall covering it. It was the perfect camouflage for the dungeon entrance.

'This is a bloody circus funhouse,' one new policeman said.

'Man, you don't know the half of it,' Carney hadn't had the chance to prepare them for what lay behind the metal door.

They called it in to Woodburn. 'Ma'am, we've found the dungeon, but it's behind a locked metal door. It's going to be tough to get in. We need somebody to get us through a solid wall of steel.'

'Okay, stand down. I'm on it.' Woodburn arranged for the force locksmith, it was going to take him another quarter of an hour to get there, and that's before he got them in the room. It was time they couldn't afford to lose, but they had no choice. Rob was at the end of his tether and wanted action. He couldn't understand all the waiting around. One office suggested he knock on the door to be let in. Policeman or not, Rob bunched his fist to smack him in the mouth before the officer pulled his neck in and shut up. The wait was interminable, but it wasn't wasted. The assembled officers used the time to prepare for raiding the room. Watson, the most senior officer downstairs, talked them through their positions and what would happen when they got in.

Everybody had a part to play, and, as it was down to minute timing, every man needed to know where he should be. The recording gave them valuable information about the layout of the room and the situation inside that they wouldn't have had. Watson told them forewarned was forearmed.

Upstairs, Shannon, the negotiator, listened to Rob's idea of making first contact. He agreed that it would buy them time while the locksmith worked, and he would step in if the situation put the surviving twin in greater danger.

When the locksmith arrived, he examined the door. Cutting through the thick metal was out of the question because the noise would alert the captors. After taking note of the security pad, he told Watson there was an easy way of getting into the room, but it would cause a whole new problem. The pad was fitted with a safety device. If the electrical current was disturbed for any reason, for instance, a power cut, the door would unlock. All they had to do was flip the trip switch in the fuse box.

It would give them an advantage in that they'd be bursting in while the occupants reeled from being thrown into darkness. However, the officers would also be in the dark until the light supply was reactivated. They would still have the upper hand, though, because they held the element of surprise.

Shannon spoke to Rob, projecting a professional, calm demeanour that he hoped would rub off. 'Be careful, and tread slowly. Think about what you're going to say before you say it, measure every word. Listen to what I tell you, and if I ask you to say something, you say it immediately. That's the deal, understand?'

Rob nodded as he took the microphone. He had three breaths to compose himself. All that had happened during the frantic preparations to storm the dungeon was Victor preening and posturing while he presented instruments on a trolley and rearranged the height and position of the table. Poor Maria was assisting.

The girl pleaded for her life before she fell silent and limp on the table. Rob didn't like it. The silence in the dungeon was similar to that in a church just before a funeral. It looked as though Victor was bigging himself up to do something important.

Rob kept his voice as level as possible.

'The date is twenty-ninth November, twenty-fifty-eight. The time is nineteen-ten. The game's up, Khazanza, and you're busted. There's no escape now, man, so do the sensible thing and let the women go.'

When the unexpected voice broke into the reverent pre-ceremony in the dungeon, Victor was so shocked that he dropped a tray of surgical instruments on the floor. The stainless steel scalpels and specula clattered to the ground and the echoes reverberated around the room.

Victor stared at the camera mounted on the far wall, his face contorted into an expression of surprise and shock.

The woman tied to the bed screamed. And, after a moment of registered surprise, Maria flung back her head and laughed.

'The Game's up?' questioned Victor, recovering his composure. 'My dear sir, you are very much mistaken. Phase three of the game has just begun. Do you think any punitive efforts to stop me could affect us in any way? You think we're going to stop now, just because the almighty literary agent says so? Sit down, take a ringside seat and watch history being made for the third time. But of course, you don't know, do you? These women, these marvellous, wonderful women, are not merely twins. They are history. Here is the first human being to ever be successfully cloned. And right here, this very night, it's going to

481

be done for the third time. We are about to make a new batch of clones using our donor. I'm sorry you won't be able to watch her die tonight because we are using her as both host and succubus and will have to keep her for the gestation period. But never mind, she can watch your death instead.'

He was about to go on, but Maria held up her hand and, speaking for the first time, she rocked Rob's perception again.

'Shut up, little man and know your place. This is not your moment. It's mine. Mine, you understand? How dare you flaunt my law of obedience because you have an audience? You know the rules; you speak when you are spoken to. Do I make myself clear?'

Although she was well out of Victor's range, she raised her hand as though to beat him. Victor hung his head in supplication and was silent.

Rob was so shocked that his backside dropped unbidden into the chair behind him.

'So,' Maria said, facing the camera. 'You're here. You're a little early—bad manners on your part, sir, but no problem, we were expecting you.'

She raised her hands and gave Rob a round of applause. 'Very clever of you, Mr Price. In fact, more intelligent than we gave you credit for. But all you've done is saved us the trouble of coming to get you. It does spoil the surprise for you, though. It's going to be quite a scandal. You see, we have several pieces of DNA evidence that ties you neatly to the murder of Mr Matthew High. A blood-soaked shirt, for instance. But that's not all, my new plaything, because we have items that will look so pretty at the back of your closet or under the stairs in your home. They belong to Miss Ellie and Miss Eve, and they'll guide the police to the conclusion that you've killed them and then, wracked with guilt and mania, killed yourself too.

Rob opened his mouth to speak, but Shannon covered the top of the mic with his hand and indicated to Rob to let them keep talking. It was recording and was all the evidence they'd need for a conviction.

Rob wasn't happy. He wanted to blast them and demand they let the surviving twin go but realised his testosterone and male pride were taking control of his common sense. While Maria was ranting, it gave them both the confession and the time they needed to get in the room. Speaking now could only damage the good Maria was doing on her own. And she was far from finished.

'We'll be holding this one for a few months. She has a vital job to do for us, so her body won't be discovered for some time—but the evidence against you will be damning price. And here's where it gets fun. We're in here. You're out there. You could bring the police. But we know you're too smart to do that because there's your mousy little wife. Gail, isn't it to consider? We have a backup plan ready to set in motion if you give us any trouble. We can set her up for the multiple murders instead. Consumed with jealousy over your affair with the Miss Erikssons. Revenge of the woman scorned. Worm turning, and all that. An old story, but a good one. And so easy to execute—almost as easy as the other one will be to put out of her misery.'

There was a long pause, and Maria tilted her head to listen to the intercom. Shannon waved Rob to speak but warned him to go cautiously.

'You'll never get away with it,' Rob said. 'You've been a bit too clever for your own good this time.' Rob still couldn't believe that the scared-shitless, drink-sodden, Maria, was in this mess up to her neck with Victor Khazanza. What the hell was their story? It was getting crazier by the second—and still, he clung to the hope that it was Ellie alive on the table. He'd mourn Eve's death, the kid had balls. But it'd be nothing compared to the pain he'd feel if the crumpled body outside the building had been Ellie.

'And why wouldn't we get away with it, Mr Price? We have up to now. Almost thirty years and we haven't been caught yet, so why should things change just because the great Robert Price has walked into our home? Oh wait, let me guess. You aren't stupid enough to think you've come to rescue them, are you?'

They had all the evidence they needed. And the perpetrators had been kind enough to record it for them. It was time for action. They had to get the three people out of the dungeon, preferably alive and unharmed.

Woodburn liaised with the men downstairs, commanded them into position and told them to be ready to go on her command.

Rob was reluctant to hand over the mike to Shannon.

'You hang in there, sweetheart,' he said to the twin, 'We're going to get you out.'

Woodburn nodded to Shannon to continue the negotiation. Shannon thumbed the mic.

'This is the police. We have the building surrounded. There is no escape. We would like you to move away from the table and walk out of the room, with your hands raised where we can see them.'

Victor and Maria weren't expecting any other company and, for the second time in a few minutes, shock painted their faces as perfectly as Maria's lipstick. The girl on the table was the first to speak.

'Help me.'

Neither Victor nor Maria was armed. Victor held a scalpel before him, but it was a half-hearted gesture. Like all bullies, he was cut down to size when outnumbered.

At first, Maria screamed and spat and shouted obscenities at Shannon. Then she tried to reason with him, flirted coyly, and told him he could be in on the biggest breakthrough in medical history.

She implied that killing Ellie with Eve's cells couldn't be considered murder because she was dying anyway. She sneered when she bragged. 'Ellie will be dead within the week. Haven't we done the poor cripple a favour? We've spared her months of undue suffering.'

Ignoring the incessant rant, Shannon told them, 'Lay your instruments down, hold your hands up and step away from the table.'

'This way,' Maria continued, 'Eleanor will drift into a painless and peaceful sleep when the time comes.' She had the gall to call it euthanasia.

'I can assure you Miss Erickson's death was neither peaceful nor painless. She threw herself out of the top story window almost an hour ago. She blew your cover by heroically trying to save her—' he didn't know what the correct colloquial for a pair of clones was, '—sister,' he finished lamely. 'A selfless way to scupper your plans, wouldn't you say?'

The girl felt her heart twist in pain. Maybe they were bluffing, a ruse, some plan they had for rescuing her. Since Rob admitted he didn't know which twin she was, her mind had been working. She could use this to her advantage.

Her first attempt at laughter caught in her throat and sounded more like a cough. She wanted to break down and sob for her sister, but her instinct for self-preservation had to come first. Her second attempt was more successful. Victor was shaking, and even Maria's calm composure was ruffled by the advent of the police.

'What are you laughing at?' she spat at the hostage. 'Nothing changes, nothing, do you hear me? They're out there, but we have you. I'd call that a tight stalemate. Before they can open the door, we'd have split your pretty little throat wide open.'

'Give me the knife, and I'll do it myself,' she said in a firm voice and with a serene smile on her face. 'You see, you talk about how clever you are and pat yourself so heartily on the back, but you haven't got the brains to know when you've been outwitted.'

She had to be careful to make them believe her. She had to underplay her hand.

'What are you talking about?' Maria was outraged. This little slut wasn't going to make a fool of her in front of others. Why wasn't she cowering? What the hell was she smiling at? Maria brought her hand up and slapped her across her face. Her lip split. She was already sore from her earlier beating from Victor and thought she would pass out, and she was still nauseous from the aesthetic. She had to think fast and have her wits about

486

her. The blow knocked her head back into the leather of the table. Ignoring the threatening blackness, she lifted it again, still smiling.

In the control room, Rob mouthed obscenities and turned his face away. He couldn't bear to see her being hurt.

'Come on,' Victor said. He'd been silent. 'We've got to use the girl as a shield to get out of here.'

'You go if you like,' Maria answered. 'You were always gutless. I'm not giving up now. Go on, go, but she stays with me.'

'Well, I agree with you, you know. It's about time we got to know each other. Let's see what you're really made of, Mother. Get rid of him, and let's play the game for real. One to one, just you and me. My sister has had you all to herself up till now, but I think I can outwit you because I'm the one with the brains. In fact, I've already won, if you didn't know it. Come on, let the procedure commence, as you are so fond of saying.'

The negotiator was repeating that they should leave the room with their hands raised above their heads. Victor was watching the altercation between the women. Maria and the hostage had locked eyes, and neither one was giving way in the battle of wills. Shannon was ignored, and his constant monotone was the only background noise to the melodrama in the room.

'If you've got something to say, I suggest you say it,' Maria said. She blinked once but didn't look away.

The other's eyes were stinging from the beating. She couldn't hold out and knew that valuable ground would be lost if she looked away first. This was psychological warfare, and she had to convince Maria that she was still strong in spirit.

'Oh no, Maria, spoil your moment of glory? I couldn't do that. No, please, carry on. I'm coming around to your way of thinking.

Give me your freaky babies. I want lots of them. I want lots of crazy dolls for us all to play with together. You can be the mother, and I'll be the big sister.'

'You're crazy,' Maria said.

'That's rich coming from you.' She felt stronger by the second. She had Maria jumpy and doubting herself. It would be easier to convince her now. She pretended to tire and wilted into the table, breathing heavily. She'd sat with her sister enough. As long as she didn't overdo it, she could pull it off. She let her left ankle spasm, just a little bit, and gritted her teeth as though trying to stop it. 'Come on, woman. What are you waiting for? Make me pregnant with my clones.'

Maria looked closely at her. Atta girl, you just keep doubting.

'Who are you?' Maria asked.

'I'm your worst fucking nightmare, you crazy bitch, but you know who I am. I'm Evelyn Erikson, the clone, the freak, the nonentity that you made me.'

'Liar. You're Eleanor, aren't you?' Without waiting for an answer, she turned on Victor. 'You useless idiot, you brought the wrong girl. How could you let them switch on you? Fool. You're nothing without me, you moron. You couldn't even kill the boyfriend. I had to come out in the middle of the night because you were too damned gutless. Victor Khazanza, the great I am. That's a laugh. Victor Khazanza, the lily-livered idiot, is nearer the truth.'

Victor was moaning and looked half his former size. . 'It's gone wrong. It's gone horribly wrong. Everything is crumbling around our heads, police swarming all over the house, the experiment blown sky-high. We're finished.'

Maria calmed after her outburst at Victor. She'd been glaring at the hostage.

'Yes, we're finished, but Victor, we can go down in history. Let's go out with a bang. I can't be locked away. I can't be locked up, Victor. You know I can't. You know what it's been about for me. Let's kill her now, right in front of their eyes. There's nothing they can do to stop us, Victor. By the time they get through a foot of solid steel, she'll be dead, and we'll be the most famous serial killers in the world. Let's' do it. Let's go out in style. You and me, Victor, just like it's always been.'

'Don't do anything rash,' Shannon cut in. 'We can make a deal. We can compromise. I promise you faithfully that this isn't as bad as you think. We can negotiate a nice placement. That's what I'm here for.'

'Shut up, little man,' Maria screamed before turning to Victor. 'When they come in firing, if they take us out, it'll be a bonus. They can't hurt us if we've already decided to die. Let's do it. Let's do it now. No more talking. We kill her, and then we kill each other in the last glorious act of ultimate power. Do it, my darling, kill her. They'll be writing books and making films about us for years, Victor.

'Victor, listen to me, Shannon said, 'I promise you, no harm will come to you, just put the knife down.'

'Do it, Victor, slit her now. You've got the knife in your hand. Show me that you've got the balls to be worthy of me, at last.'

Everything had gone mad in the control room. Rob was screaming at Woodburn to get in there and stop it before he killed the twin.

Victor's hand rose. He looked scared and confused. His hand shook as he put the scalpel to the hostage's throat.

'Do it, Victor,' Maria screamed.

'No,' Rob yelled from the control room.

'Wait,' Shannon said. 'Let's talk this through before you do anything stupid. We can cut a deal. You'll get a few easy years in a cosy psychiatric facility, and you can be out again, feeling better, with new lives to lead and new identities. This doesn't have to be the way. It doesn't have to end like this.'

Woodburn was twitchy. She wanted to send the men in, but it could sign their death warrant if she did. Woodburn hated hesitation, but all she could do was hesitate and hover. Her hand was half raised, ready to flag them in. Every second was crucial. But all she could do was wait.

'Do it, you useless piece of shit. I command you to do it. Haven't I always given the orders? Haven't I always beaten you if you don't do exactly as I say? That's the way you like it, don't you, Victor? Me in charge. Me telling you what to do. Listen to my voice. Not them. Cut them out, my clever boy doll. You're mine. My special boy. Listen to me. You know it's the only way. They can't lock me up. You can't let them lock me up, Victor. Focus on my voice. That's it, that's it, Victor. Yes, good boy. Good boy, Victor. I'm very proud of you. Now cut her. Cut her.' Maria was screeching with blood lust.

Victor had the scalpel pressed into the woman's throat. A small cut opened under the point of the blade. He had madness in his eyes, and he was about to slice her throat wide open. He wanted Mother Genesis to be proud of him. He wanted her to beat him because she was happy with him. But he didn't want to die—not that. He was Victor Khazanza. He wasn't ready to die. He was sophisticated. He was somebody. This was ugly, and above all else, he so hated anything ugly.

'Don't do it, Victor,' Shannon said soothingly. 'We can sort this. You and I, together, we can find a way through it. Just put the knife down and walk out of the room. I give you my word. You will not be harmed. My men are ready to just walk you away, nice and calm. Nice and gentle. They'll take you somewhere warm and give you a good meal. You'd like that, wouldn't you? You'll be treated like a gentleman Victor.' The mogul had crumpled into himself and seemed to have regressed into a childlike figure that couldn't think for himself.

'Yeah? They'll treat me nice?'

'Of course, Victor, it doesn't have to end badly.'

Victor Khazanza wasn't ready to die. The last vestige of his sanity cracked in his endeavour to save himself.

He went wild.

491

He ran around the table and plunged into Maria, who tried to block his way. He used his bulk to force her hard into the wall. He had the scalpel up to her face and dug it into her flesh. Maria's cheek peeled away from the bone like an orange.

'Yes, Victor. Do it, my child. Do it for me, do it to me. Let's die. You and me together, Victor. Let's die together, now.'

She glanced up and pulled down hard on one of the meat hooks with a smooth movement.

Both perpetrators were far enough away from the woman tied to the table.

'Go. Go. Go,' shouted Woodburn, bringing her arm down hard to emphasise the order.

Jennings, at the fuse box, cut the electricity. The house was plunged into darkness, and six uniformed police officers in protective gear stormed the room.

Maria thrust hard on the meat hook and drove it into Victor's stomach. She felt it cut through fat and muscle and, as the lights came back on, she pulled upwards with all her strength.

His intestines fell out of the jagged hole in his stomach. He was eviscerated. He stared in horror at his insides and shook his head, confused. Victor looked for salvation in Maria's eyes.

There was gunfire. Victor's dying body jerked as rounds of ammunition peppered him.

'I am the creator,' he wheezed with the last of his breath.

Maria was fighting with the weight of his body. He swung like a stuck pig on the hook and knocked into her. She was drenched in his blood and stomach contents. The smell of his intestinal gas and waste products filled the room, and a policeman bent over to vomit into the corner.

# Also By Katherine Black

A Question of Sanity
Leverage
Pedigree Crush with a Twisted Gene
Nowhere Boulevard
Lizards Leap
Murmurations of Silence Book One: Travesty

Made in United States
Orlando, FL
07 April 2024

45539684R00278